Guilty by Default

Renée Morgan-Hampton

Foreword

I have known Ms. Morgan-Hampton for the better part of four years. What a storyteller! Her grasp of plotting and dialogue and "places no other writer would dare to go" grabs one by the nethers and never lets go! That being said, there is also the Ms. Morgan-Hampton of the Pasadena community; she is a tireless promoter of equal rights for minority women and a great Defender of the Faith in terms of the city's beautification and historical preservation including landmark districts. Renée is not only a great writer but a great humanitarian.

When I met her over twenty years ago, she characterized herself as 'a girl who would like to write one day.' Well, Ms. Morgan-Hampton, you have achieved that goal and more. I look forward to your next adventure, Tainted Fabric…the plot and story of which I will not give away, but rather allow Renée to regale her readership directly.

We must continue to watch Ms. Renée Morgan Hampton with literary acuity. Hers is a unique talent and it will no doubt continue to excel. As a guy who has written a little himself, I thoroughly enjoyed this novel you are about to journey into…you will not come away disappointed…though the story and the ending may haunt your dreams for years to come.

So, dear readers, begin the adventure now! Prepare yourself for a trek into thrills, horror, love, sex and redemption.

George P. Saunders
June 13, 2018

Dedication

After a long twelve years of life's challenges, battles and wins, this book took every breath I had to see it to completion. And I said, "…see it…" The act of not being able to see and losing my vision became a reality, and I won that battle to see again and to live in the present. I won that battle because of my Mom. My Mom is my rock. I dedicate this book to my mother, who taught me perseverance, strength, dedication, humanity, love and being a lady. Her motto is "Always finish what you start, no matter what. Live in the moment."

Cheers to you Mom! Thank you for your undying love and encouragement.

Love you forever Mommie,

Renée

Acknowledgments

Geoffrey Moyer, M.D.
Consultant
Los Angeles, California

Michael Zimbert, Esq.
Attorney at Law
18401 Burbank Blvd., Suite 123
Tarzana, California 91356
24 Hour Line
Michael Zimbert has been a Criminal Defense Attorney
for over 35 years.
zimbertcriminaldefense.com

Robyn Harrod, MSW, LCSW
Los Angeles, California
robynharrod.com

Patrick Benefeld, Private Investigator
4821 Lankershim Blvd., Suite F-180
North Hollywood, California 91601
clandestineinvestigations.com

Special Letter to the Editor

Dear George,

When I started on this very special journey, you were there encouraging me to write this story—a story that was believable to some and others who might find it not believable at all. I remember you telling me that if you did not write this story, *you* would. I have to say that my life of late has been a roller-coaster ride of topsy-turvy events, exacerbated by health and death. However, here I am…still alive and well.

Your astute editing abilities and keen sense of my subject matter, allowed you to play up my thoughts and enhance the very essence of my characters; these are characters with whom I've lived with for many years and have now finally brought to life. You let my characters breathe by making each of them unique to the reader. I thank you, my friend, for your thoughtfulness, intelligence and perseverance in editing this realistic, modern-day mystery suspense thriller – a book that will make you think twice when you meet people in your everyday life.

We live in a society that is proactive regarding various causes and issues, which has created a movement affecting every human being. Your editing style epitomizes that movement.

YOU ARE MY MUSE!

Comme cela devrait être.

Concert d'eloges!

Sincerely,

Renée

People like to say that the conflict is between good and evil.
The real conflict is between truth and lies. – Don Miguel Ruiz

Chapter One

Friday, September 5, 2008 – 6:30 a.m.

In the early morning hours the Alcott Construction crew pounded three to four inch nails into plywood planks, and drilled holes into metal beams supporting a new wing of the Calvin House Preparatory School, while bulldozers kicked up huge dust clouds on the campus. Built in 1865, after the Civil War came to a bloody close, the all-boys boarding school was nestled on twenty acres of lush green lawn in the foothills overlooking the cities of La Cañada Flintridge, Glendale and Pasadena, California.

The screeching and grinding noises of brakes were heard for blocks around by local residents as big rigs pulled in and out of the school driveway. Other construction workers, wearing orange vests typically seen on such sites, watered down the dirt in the active zone.

As a bulldozer shoveled dirt to one side, making space for a flat surface, the lift operator noticed the bare feet and hands of a human protruding from the pile of earth. He immediately stopped the bulldozer and yelled to his co-workers for help.

"Hey, I need some help over here," he hollered frantically as he disembarked the vehicle.

"Dude, what's going on?" yelled one of the other nearby workers, as he ran over to see what the frantic operator was hollering about.

"That's what's going on!" the operator replied, pointing at the earth and the resurrected human remains. "I think I just dug up a body. Look at that! The feet are sticking out!"

"What do you mean you dug up a body?" another worker asked as he lumbered over to the others. The workers immediately grabbed shovels and began digging. Within minutes the body of a young boy was dug out from the dirt. They turned over the naked corpse. The boy's pale white skin also cast a concomitant and ghastly bluish hue and a large, red-and-brown birthmark caught the eye on his right leg. A slight breeze blew his dark brown, bristle-like hair, adding to the overall grizzly appearance of the boy's stark and pathetic corpse.

Many of the workers had children of their own and were finding it difficult to take in such a gruesome sight. Titters of horror and disgust floated through the air. As more workers gathered around the boy's body, discussion over the situation ensued.

"Wow! I've got two boys of my own at home," said the lift operator. It was more a silent acknowledgement of mortality versus any general announcement. He looked profoundly horrified, an alien to despair up to this point, it seemed, and a stranger to true loss.

"This is deep, man. I can't even imagine something like this happening to my two girls!" exclaimed one of the younger workers on the site. His look belied the horror of his innocence to such terrible things as what was being experienced by one and all.

"Yeah. It makes me sick to my stomach. How could this happen? Who would do something like this?" yet another worker declared in commingled disgust and horror.

"A lot of evil people out there," said the foreman of the crew, Varner Davis, as he pulled his cell phone from the phone holder connected to his jeans. He hit a few numbers and waited. Someone on the other end picked up.

"Yeah, this is Davis. I've got a cluster-fuck of a sitch out here. We just dug up a body. Better get someone's ass out here in authority. I'm calling 911," he said, though he could feel the bile rising in his throat as he stared at the dead boy.

He then glanced around at his crew, who stood still, mesmerized by the presence of the dead boy.

"Okay, gang," he called out. "Take a knee for half an hour until someone from the office gets out here and has a gander."

The workers wandered off, a collective morose mood hanging in the air like smoke from a fire long burned out.

Christ, Davis thought. Helluva way to start the day.

He took one more glance at the dead boy and whispered "God

bless you, son. Rest in peace."

He then turned away and yarked up his breakfast.

***

Forbes Madden, the Headmaster for Calvin House for the past eight years, was the first to get to the site. Forbes was a slightly overweight man in his mid-forties and walked with a pronounced shuffle that was more fitting for a man twice his age. Upon hearing the news about what was discovered at the site, he ran as fast as he could through the playground, and just barely made it over the boxwood hedges in his run-down loafers. Forbes was not accustomed to running or indulging in any form of physical activity whatsoever, so when he reached the construction zone, he was fairly panting. Davis pointed to the dead boy and for a long moment, Forbes could only stare in bleak horror. Then, he knelt down slowly and placed his hands on the boy's face. Forbes then picked up the boy and held him close in his arms, cradling the corpse as if it were a newborn. His eyes began to tear as he looked to the foreman.

"It's one of our sophomore students, Jaime Herrera." he said quietly, as the workers regarded him with a kind of distant reverence.

"We were moving dirt when we saw the body," the foreman explained. "Poor kid," he added as an afterthought.

Forbes, grief-stricken, lowered his head to regard the boy's face. "Who would do something like this? How could this happen at my school?" He asked to no one in particular and to deaf heaven that, as always, was silent to such tragic queries of sorrow.

Forbes pulled his cellphone from his pants pocket and dialed 911. The foreman didn't bother to mention that he had already called the authorities but rather let the grief-stricken Forbes make his call.

Within minutes, two sheriff helicopters hovered over the site. Two black-and-white squad cars arrived shortly thereafter, followed by a parade of black vans and SUVs. Other EMT vehicles followed close at hand. It was turning into a crime scene right and proper.

Bright flashes of light radiated from the cameras from Crime Scene Investigators. Everyone wore blue latex gloves as the body of the boy was photographed from all angles. Various pieces of evidence was collected, tagged and catalogued, then placed into plastic bags for later forensic analysis.

Detectives Tracey Sanders and Zack Grimes emerged from their black 2008 GMC Yukon Denali as another officer secured the area with yellow ticker-tape. Tracey and Zack approached the boy's corpse, as criminologist, Randy Yew and crime scene investigator, Aline Lazar, combed the damp earth surrounding the area where the boy had been extracted.

Tracey turned to Randy. "Who's the new lady?" he nodded toward Aline.

"Aline Lazar. Two years out, graduate of Northeastern University, with a Masters in criminology."

"Guess the young ones are moving in on your territory."

"Not really. They still need us old guys."

Tracey took a deep breath and turned to Randy.

"How old?" Tracey asked.

"I'd put him at fourteen, fifteen."

"TOD?" Tracey asked.

"Time of death was roughly between nine o'clock and midnight, yesterday evening."

"Any distinctive marks on the body?"

"Other than a birthmark on his right leg, not even a pimple."

"How about signs of trauma or drugs?"

"Well, it's early still. But on first blush, none. No drugs on site and we'll know more from toxicology after the autopsy," replied Aline.

"Possible suicide?" Zack mused.

"Not sure. Nothing is present to indicate that so far. Besides, suicides don't usually go and bury themselves, right?"

Tracey chuckled humorlessly. "Good one."

A few minutes later, County Coroner and Medical Examiner, Dr. Cole Peduska, arrived. Dr. Peduska approached the body donning gloves and began her requisite inspection. Peduska was a tall, strikingly beautiful red head; her layered wavy hair draped over her back that set off her fair skin and freckles. She gave a nod to Tracey and Zack then wasted no time in her examination of the dead boy.

Twenty minutes later she glanced up at the two detectives. "Looks like he's been dead for about ten hours. The current temperature outside is 68 degrees. It appears as though the body has decayed faster than usual."

Tracey put his hand to his nose, as Zack followed suit. The smell from decomposition was stifling and no matter how many corpses you might be exposed to, one never grew accustomed to the horrific stench of death.

Peduska brushed the dirt off the boy's legs and feet, seemingly immune to the odor, sniffing the air briefly as if she was sampling Chanel No. 5. "You see these scrapes on his heels and ankles? Someone dragged his body for part of the way before arriving at the construction site. Some of the dirt is moist and other parts are dry, thus the body was dragged through different areas and through different soil types before arriving here. Whoever killed him, put him here last night when the soil was damp…my best guess on TOD would be approximately ten to midnight. Moisture frequently causes accelerated deterioration. "If I may speculate a little bit. People in fires that actually breathe in flames get forms of cyanomethemoglobin. High levels of cyanomethemoglobin ties up the blood. There are certain medications that cause cyanomethemoglobin. But they're not relevant in this case."

Tracey sighed. "So, the body was brought to the site around midnight, been dead approximately ten hours. Now to figure out where he was dragged from which will hopefully give us more information as to how he was killed and why," Randy said after Dr. Peduska returned her attention to the body.

"Do you smell that? That odor seems familiar to me," Tracey stated as he looked around the crime scene.

"Yeah, I do smell it. Smells funny…kind of like nuts." Randy replied.

Dr. Peduska, oblivious to their conversation, pronounced Jaime Herrera dead and the boy was loaded into the coroner's van pro forma.

Tracey looked to Zack. "Looks like we have some work ahead of us."

Zack nodded. "No shit."

***

8:45a.m.

News of Jaime Herrera's death spread like wildfire across the Calvin House campus. The boys busily texted friends and family; concerned parents jammed the school's phone line. Those who reached the school's administrative secretary were directed to the Calvin House website for up-to-the-minute information concerning their children.

As Dr. Peduska's van pulled away, Forbes approached Tracey and Zack. He had been standing back observing the interactions between the doctor and the detectives and tried to collect himself prior to introducing himself. He extended his hand in greeting to Tracey.

"Hello, I'm Forbes Madden, Headmaster of Calvin House."

Tracey sized up the man in an instant. Middle aged, disheveled in dress, nervous by nature.

"Detective Tracey Sanders, Homicide Division. This is Detective Zack Grimes. First names are fine." Tracey stated. "It's nice to meet you, sir."

"I can't believe this. This is—never in the history of this school has something like this occurred," Forbes stammered. Tracey noticed the man fidgeted with his hands, as if they were errant appendages with minds of their own, uncertain as to what to do next.

"There's a first time for everything," Zack replied. "No one ever thinks it will happen to them or that it will happen in L.A."

"Mr. Madden, we need to ask you some questions," Tracey said, clearing his throat. "Is there some place we can talk?"

"Sure. Follow me; we can talk in my office." Forbes turned and led the way back to the school's entrance.

Tracey and Zack followed Forbes through the main entrance. As they walked through the halls, Tracey and Zack absorbed the surroundings.

Zack glanced to Tracey. "Looks haunted."

Tracey chuckled humorlessly. "If it wasn't before, it is now."

Gallows humor, Tracey thought. But not entirely inappropriate.

Chapter Two

Friday – 9:00 a.m.

It had already been a difficult year for Forbes Madden. Construction of the school's new wing had been fraught with problems, and the country's troubled economy was presenting new challenges. Headmaster of the Calvin House Preparatory School for eight years, he relished his scholarly life and took his job seriously. Forty years old, six feet tall, with brown, slightly graying hair, he purchased his classic wardrobe from discount shops in downtown L.A.'s garment district. Occasionally he visited Barney's in Beverly Hills for new ties, but he was frugal and loathed spending money unnecessarily. His chief indulgences were eating healthy meals and working out every day.

Forbes guided Tracey and Zack down the wide halls of the school, lost in thought. Forbes glanced around the halls—halls he had walked these many years a hundred times. The floors were worn from the many decades of students walking from class to class; the cement floors were cracked and attenuated, left unresolved. The walls were adorned with paintings of scholars and past presidents of the United States. Old pictures of the school from the 1920's, framed in bronze rested on an antique credenza against the opposite wall.

"Quite a cast of characters," remarked Zack.

They finally arrived to Forbes' office where diplomas and other certificates of accomplishment were either framed or rested on side-tables and the office's one and only bureau. The office was old, evidenced by the odor of the room, but it had an undeniably historic charm. Four schoolhouse pendant lights hung from each corner of the high, cherry wood-paneled ceiling, casting light on a beautiful Venetian tapestry adorning one wall. A large cherry wood desk was positioned in the back of the office where Forbes directed Tracey and Zack. Forbes shuffled to his chair behind his desk.

"Have a seat, gentlemen," Forbes said, indicating two black leather, gold-studded wingback chairs facing the desk. "Can I get you anything? Coffee or water or maybe a *Pepsi*?"

"No, thank you, we're good." Zack said as Forbes took a seat in a black velvet chair. "Why don't you tell us what you know happened here?"

Before Forbes could answer Zack's question, Tracey interjected with "What is the boy's name?"

"Jaime Herrera. He was a student in his sophomore year," Forbes stated dejectedly.

"Has anyone contacted his parents? "Tracey asked.

"No, one of the officers said he would be going to their house to notify them. I didn't think letting them know over the phone was appropriate."

"Good point. We will need them to identify the body at the county coroner's office but I am sure the officer will let them know that."

"How old was Jaime?" Zack asked.

"He was fifteen, the eldest of eight children. He received a grant to attend Calvin House."

"A grant?" Tracey repeated.

Forbes nodded. "Most of our students come from wealthy families that have ties to exclusive clubs including the Jonathan Club, the Athenaeum at California Institute of Technology, the Valley Hunt Club, and the California Club. Most of them obtain paid internships and go on to Ivy League colleges. But not all of our students are that connected or privileged. And some can't even afford the tuition here. Additionally, Calvin House has strict rules and regulations. For example, students can be expelled if they fail the same class two consecutive times."

"That seems kinda harsh," Zack said.

"We aim to instill high standards and discipline. Honestly, we care and want to help the boys in the community as much as we can. Typically, private schools of this caliber would not be likely to tolerate failing two years in a row. However, we want to give the students an opportunity to succeed. We try to encourage students to excel academically but Calvin House does not allow consistent infraction of general rules, disobedience and disrespect towards staff members or other students."

"Sounds like a fairly strict environment," Tracey observed.

Forbes nodded in agreement. "Calvin House is known for their many rules and regulations. Some of the others include zero tolerance for dubious moral character, irregular attendance, distribution of harmful or obscene literature, habitual late payments by parents, irregular attendance, damage to school property, and leaving school grounds without written permission from the Headmaster or the Dean of Men. For some parents and students, the rules and regulations can be a turn-off, thus requiring the search for a different school."

"Wow! A lot of rules! 'Dubious moral character.' Fancy. All you *really* had to say was questionable," remarked Zack.

"Zack please!" Tracey exclaimed.

"Sorry," Zack said, shrugging defensively.

Tracey returned his attention to Forbes.

"So, is there a reason why you are telling us about these expectations? Was Jaime guilty of breaking these rules or did he ever disobey a staff member?" Tracey queried.

"No. Never!" exclaimed Forbes as he looked away from the detectives and out the window, his mind momentarily a million miles away.

"Well, was he disrespectful toward you or others? Was he known to have a temper? Was he the type of person who would curse at you or other staff members?" Tracey pressed to get a better idea of what the victim's character was like.

"No…well, not necessarily. For the most part, he was a pretty good kid," Forbes replied.

"For the most part? What about the lesser part?" Tracey asked.

When Forbes lowered his head and didn't answer the question, Tracey pressed Forbes on more fundamental issues.

"So, can you tell me a bit about a day in the life of a student at Calvin House? How do the days start, what is expected of the boys?"

"Every morning, the boys are required to strip the sheets from their beds, place the dirty sheets into white sacks with white rope draw strings and place the sack in the linen room. Each boy takes a shower every morning and is required to leave the water running for the next boy in line just outside the shower. They attend their scheduled classes and other events during the day. Before retiring to bed, their shoes are placed by their bed the night before, awaiting a good polish."

He took a moment and stared out the window.

"When we saw Jaime's body at the construction site, he was lying in the dirt naked. We didn't see any sign of any clothes around. As we were walking to your office I noticed most of the boys dressed in similar clothes. Are the boys expected to wear certain clothes? Is there a mandatory uniform for the students?" Tracey questioned.

Forbes swallowed, cleared his throat and then stated, "I still can't believe this has happened! It just makes me sick to my stomach that someone out there did this to him." He paused trying to regain his composure before saying, "Yes, we do have a required uniform regimen, except for special events. As you may have noticed, the boys are required to wear a school-approved blazer bearing the Calvin House monogram. Black trousers with a conventional cut and a bottom flare of nineteen inches for pants, along with black socks, a Calvin House cardigan and a tie. Additionally, each boy is required to own two pairs of black lace-up shoes."

"Do the boys have cellphones?" Zack asked.

"Yes. They are required to carry their cell phones at all times. In addition to the cell phone, a USB drive is provided to them on the first day of school, containing an introduction and instructional video about Calvin House."

"Do you know if Jaime normally had his cellphone with him?" Tracey asked.

The look on Forbes' face was one of surprise as he answered the question. "Yes, he always had his phone with him. Did anyone find his phone near his body?"

"That's a good question. No, we found no phone. This is something we are going to have to look more into now that we know he actually possessed a phone," Tracey stated, looking at Zack. "Zack, make a note of the cellphone so we don't forget to check more into the whereabouts and the most recent calls made. Forbes, can you provide us with his cell phone number?"

"Sure. I have the roster here on my desk," he said, grabbing a piece of paper from a folder before looking at Zack and saying "555-0104."

Zack scribbled down the number along with some more notes in his notepad while Tracey continued on with his questions.

"When does school start its academic year?"

"Our year runs from August through June," Forbes said.

Zack picked up the year book on the table between him and Tracey and flipped through the pages, nearly all of which contained football team photos. "Huh, interesting yearbook. I don't suppose you could tell us a bit about the school?"

"Absolutely. Calvin House is a preparatory school for young men of different racial, ethnic and socio-economic backgrounds. Diversity plays a role in the greater Los Angeles community. Calvin House is committed to developing and educating the person as a whole through a rigorous and thriving educational system. Calvin House is dedicated to challenging its student body to become inspiring, responsible, intellectually secure and conscientious leaders with a compassion for service to others throughout the world."

"Well, that's quite a commercial pitch," Zack whistled softly to no one.

"The school follows the six journeys that are illustrated in *The Graduate Life Journey Journal*: The first is the Journey of Growth; the second is the Journey of Intellect; the third is the Journey of Faith; the fourth is the Journey of Love and Acceptance; the fifth is the Journey of Justice; and the sixth is the Journey of Leadership. These journeys are taken very seriously by all the boys at the school and are reiterated through the courses and activities on a daily basis."

Tracey nodded in admiration. "Impressive. Sounds like the school has high expectations for its boys. What does tuition cost per semester here?"

"It's not cheap.$16,000-$22,000 a year."

Tracey whistled at that. "So those attending know the expense and usually do well in class and want to excel I assume?"

Forbes merely nodded.

"Can you tell us what kind of home life Jaime had?" inquired Tracey.

"The Herreras live in Eagle Rock. Jaime's father works two construction jobs and his mother is a cosmetics clerk at Macy's in Pasadena. She's a very nurturing woman. She emigrated here from Mexico—very proud of her U.S. citizenship. They don't have much time for home training but they're good people."

"What do you mean by 'home training'?" Tracey asked.

"Teaching social graces or etiquette to their children." Forbes paused. "As I said before, Jaime wasn't exactly an angel."

"What exactly do you mean by that, Mr. Madden?" Zack queried.

"He had a mouth on him. Let's just leave it at that," Forbes waved his hand dismissively.

"How were his grades?" Tracey asked.

"Scholastically, he is…I mean was brilliant." Forbes rubbed his hands through his oily hair, lightly dusted with dandruff. "I just can't believe it. I'm numb." He glanced over at a manila file and a black, leather-bound book on the side of his desk. His eyes drifted, as if he had momentarily abandoned the conversation. This was not lost on Tracey.

"Mr. Madden. Mr. Madden, are you with us?" Tracey asked.

"Sorry. Yes, I am here," Forbes said. "Just still in shock."

Forbes knew that he needed to keep his composure while the investigators were in his office. Doing so was quite difficult as he continued to think about tragic recent events.

"I'm just…distracted," Forbes side. "I just can't believe that Jaime is dead."

"We understand, Mr. Madden. Just a few more questions and we will be on our way," Tracey said gently. "Did Jaime have any enemies? Did any of the boys dislike him?"

"Not that I know of. He's a pretty good kid most of the time, aside from occasional verbal outbursts that were inappropriate and as I already mentioned. There were times where he would rub me the wrong way but I just learned it was his nature."

"Most of the time?" Tracey pressed.

"Well…" Forbes faltered.

"What is it you are not telling us? Was there something that happened or something that he did that you don't want to talk about?"

Forbes took a deep breath and leaned forward, looking at both officers, his gaze steady.

"Well…we…sort of had a fight yesterday evening."

"What kind of fight?" Tracey asked.

"It was a scuffle, not a fight," Forbes exclaimed.

"Okay…okay," Zack said. "So, can you tell us about this scuffle?"

"Was it a verbal argument or was it a physical fight? Did you hit him?" Tracey asked.

Forbes cleared his throat and polished off his lukewarm coffee in a stained white mug on his desk. "I wanted to, but I refrained from doing so."

"What do you mean you wanted to? Is that a prerequisite of being a Headmaster to a school? Wanting to discipline the boys on occasion by way of physical example?" Zack asked.

Tracey gave him a look and then said "Sounds like there is a bit more to this story. The more we know about what happened prior to Jaime's death, the quicker this case will get solved. So if you could tell us what the fight was about that would certainly be appreciated?"

"It's a long story," Forbes replied through a cough.

"We've got time," replied Zack.

"Yesterday afternoon, I entered my office to complete some paperwork," Forbes explained. "In the eight years I have been the headmaster at the school, I have always maintained an open door policy. So it isn't unusual for a student to come knocking on my door. Well, Jaime knocked on my door shortly after I arrived here. Almost immediately, he made some threatening comments. When I called him on this, he turned and ran down the hall."

"Could you be more specific in terms of the language he used when he blew up at you?" Tracey probed.

"He said, *'You're not a real man! You're a fuckin' freak!'*"

Forbes took a moment then continued through gritted teeth.

"I was fuming. I phoned the Dean of Men immediately."

"Who is the Dean of Men?"

"Brolin Chapman. He's a Calvin man. He earned a Ph.D at Harvard. A brilliant writer and a good person," Forbes replied.

"Please continue," said Tracey.

"I called Brolin and he met me at Jaime's room. Brolin grabbed Jaime by the collar, led him out of his room and took him back to my office. While Brolin supervised Jaime, I phoned his parents and apprised them of his unusual and inappropriate behavior."

"Had Jaime behaved that egregiously in the past?" questioned Tracey.

"No." Forbes replied, tipping his coffee cup back and forth. He knew the questions were going to just keep coming and he was really ready to have some time to himself to digest what all had happened.

"Did you do or say anything to him that would have provoked him?" Zack asked while scribbling down notes on his pad.

"No."

"What time did you call his parents?"

"5:45p.m. After that Jaime was allowed to leave because dinner is every evening at six o'clock and it was time for dinner."

"Then what?"

"After dinner, I asked Brolin to go back to Jaime's room with me to speak with him again about the incident. The school rules would require discipline for such a behavior and I wanted to see if there would be some other option. However, the entire time we were in his room, his voice was raised while he cursed at us. His demeanor was different than normal. Something wasn't right. I was concerned for all of us, especially the other boys. I'm responsible for everyone at the school." Forbes paused then went on. "By chance, I glanced at the laptop on his desk. The website that was up on his computer was a social media site of some kind. There was a picture of a man, but I couldn't make it out."

Forbes stopped talking and just looked down at his desk.

"Please continue," Tracey said.

"Due to his unusual behavior, Brolin and I escorted Jaime back to my office and I contacted his parents yet again. After gaining his parent's consent, I called our school psychiatrist. He evaluated Jaime in my office."

"What is the psychiatrist' name?" Zack asked, pen poised.

"Dr. William Jayson."

"Did the Herreras show up for the evaluation?" Tracey asked.

"No. They just gave their approval over the phone," Forbes said.

"It's not uncustomary to get parental approval on certain matters telephonically."

"That's interesting. I would have thought as parents they might have wanted to be present or you might require a signature of sorts for an evaluation to be conducted?" Tracey said. "Does Jaime have a roommate?"

"Yes, he does. His name is Chase Buckman," Forbes replied.

"Where was he when you had the altercation with Jaime?"

"He was gone. He left yesterday, Thursday, for an out-of-town trip with his parents."

"Really? And where were they headed?" Tracey asked.

"Carmel, California. His dad was scheduled as the keynote speaker at the California State Bar Annual Conference," Forbes said.

"So he's a lawyer."

"Yes, Chase's parents are both lawyers. Boston Buckman is a partner at the law firm of Murphy & Arbuckle, LLP, in downtown L.A. Pamela Buckman is General Counsel for Abercrombie and Fitch. There is an article in the *Business* section of the *Los Angeles Times*. He's running for Congress."

"Is he now? Does he make contributions to Calvin House?" Tracey asked.

"Yes. He's a major benefactor to Calvin House. He has been for years."

"Really? Interesting. So do you know what time they picked up Chase?" Zack said.

"I don't recall the time," Forbes admitted.

"You don't recall the time that he left the school property? Didn't you say earlier that one of the rules was there had to be written permission to leave the school property from either yourself or the Dean of Men?" Tracey countered.

"Yes, that is one of the rules."

"Does that mean that Chase had written permission to leave the school property?" Tracey said.

"Yes, he did."

"So there is no confusion. Can we see a copy of the permission slip?" Tracey asked.

"Sure." He reached for the phone. "Balian! Can you bring me a copy of the permission slip for Chase Buckman, please."

"We'll need the telephone numbers of Chase Buckman's and Jaime Herrera's parents," Tracey said.

"Of course," Forbes said agreeably.

"We'll also need to speak with Brolin Chapman at some point."

Forbes picked up the phone and dialed Brolin.

"Hey Brolin! Could you come to my office please? There are two detectives here looking into the situation with Jaime Herrera. They would like to speak with you."

"Sure, I'll be right there."

Balian literally arrived within minutes.

She knocked gingerly on the door, then entered and handed Forbes the permission release.

Forbes in turn handed the paper to Tracey. Tracey scanned the document briefly.

Forbes unclasped his hands which had been resting on the desk, and again glanced over at the manila file on top of the black leather-bound book.

Balian again knocked on the door. She opened the door and stood there with a confused look on her face.

"Um…sorry to interrupt. I wanted to let you know that the news crews are arriving, the press is phoning non-stop and the web sites are chalked with all sorts of misinformation and rumors. They would like a statement from you."

"Thank you, Balian. Everything will be okay. I'll take care of it," Forbes said reassuringly.

"Mr. Madden? The phone numbers, please?" Tracey pressed.

Forbes turned to Balian. "Balian, would you provide the detectives the contact information for the Herreras and the Buckmans."

"Certainly," Balian said, then returned five minutes later. "Are you ready for the numbers, detectives?"

Zack nodded with pen and paper in hand posed to write.

"The Buckman number is 555-0196 and Herrera is 555-0188."

"Thanks," Zack said as he jotted down the numbers.

Brolin Chapman entered the room. Brolin had dark hair and pale white skin. He was slender, borderline anemic. When he spoke, his Norwegian dialect was easily detected; there were no "C, W, Q, Z and ch" letters in his sentences. Brolin had been living in the United States for over ten years and was the second Dean of Men at Calvin

House; holding the position for the past five years. He took his position seriously and knew every student at the school better than anyone.

"Brolin, these are the investigating detectives in Jaime's death. They have a few questions for you about him."

Zack stood up and gestured to Brolin. "Hello, Mr. Chapman. Please, have a seat."

"Can you tell us when the last time it was that you saw Jaime on Thursday?" Tracey questioned.

"I witnessed the evaluation done by Dr. Jayson. Jaime would not look Dr. Jayson directly in the eye during the entire evaluation. He continued to look down at the floor, never lifting his head as if he was ashamed of himself. He responded to all of the questions, but out of clear anxiety, his right leg twitched continuously during the entire evaluation. It was a very sad meeting. I thought he was sick at first but couldn't tell one way or the other. Shortly after the evaluation, I escorted Jaime back to his room and told him to behave himself."

"And that was just after dinner?" Zack said.

"Yes. If I had to say a time I would guess just before 7p.m."

"What was his attitude like at that time?" Tracey asked.

"He seemed irritated but fine. If you're asking me if he was angry, I couldn't tell ya. Jaime wasn't very easy to read."

"Is there any other information you would like to share with us regarding the situation at present?" Tracey asked.

"No, I am just as shocked as everyone else and would like to know how this happened and who is to blame."

"Thank you for your time. Don't go too far, we may have further questions as the investigation continues," Tracey said.

***

Friday – 10:30a.m.

As Tracey and Zack walked back to the construction site, Zack dialed Jaime's cell phone number. It went straight to voicemail. It was either turned off, dead, or in use.

"So what do you think?" Zack glanced at Tracey.

Tracey shook his head. "Don't know yet. Sounds like a soap opera so far."

"This fight between the boy and Madden," Zack said. "That's rather incriminating against our good Headmaster."

"Yes, on first blush, it puts Mr. Madden on the person of interest list," Tracey said.

"He must know that," Zack replied.

"I'm more interested in this Buckman kid," Tracey said. "Him being off site—I'd place my bets on that kid versus the headmaster."

"Still," Zack sighed. "We've been doing this long enough—you never know."

"True Zack," Tracey said. "But we need more intel."

"Agreed," Zack said. "Wait and see."

"It's what we do best," Tracey grinned.

Chapter Three

Saturday, September 9, 2008 – 7:00 a.m.

Zack sipped coffee and picked fruit from his plate with a white plastic fork—and drooled over a box of Krispy Kreme donuts sitting on the precinct kitchen counter.

"Thinking about everything you lost with Weight Watchers?" Tracey teased.

Zack nodded. "Thirty pounds." He backed away from the donuts and texted his wife instead. After a lengthy separation, Eve, his wife, had recently returned home.

"I have some news. Eve came back home," Zack said.

"Eve! You're kidding."

"No. I'm not. She said she had to leave to clear her head. That she realized she'd made a huge mistake by leaving."

"To say the least. She probably got dumped by somebody else so what else was she going to do but come running back to you. Did you take her back?"

"What do you think?"

"I don't know why I even asked that question. I know you."

"Yup! I love her. She's the only woman that—"

"Gets you all worked up and knows how to push your buttons. How long is she going to stay this time?" Tracey asked.

"Damn it, Tracey! I don't do that to you! You and Harianne aren't perfect."

Tracey picked up the photo facing him of Harianne DeCanter on his desk. She was truly his soul mate, notwithstanding his love for his deceased wife. As a combo of white and black himself, Tracey felt a kinship to Harianne that was sublimely profound; his own father had emigrated from Nigeria and his mother, likewise, came from England. Harianne, a mixed raced brunette with long slightly curly hair, had been raised by her nanny, Austria Fairden, after her parents were killed in a plane crash. Harianne became a brilliant criminal lawyer. With over twenty years of practicing law, she had enjoyed a stellar career of getting any and all criminals out of trouble. Not a single death penalty did she incur and she was particularly proud of this achievement. She knew what to say, how to say it and when to say it to the jury. Tracey always teased her that she could evoke sympathy from a king Cobra.

"No, we're not perfect, but we're damn near! Harianne and I have been living together for a good while and now we're remodeling our home. I love everything about that woman! She's my heart." Tracey realized he was gushing but he didn't care.

"No, relationship is perfect; you know that and so do I. Forget it. I don't want to talk about it anymore. She's back and I'm happy. That's what matters," Zack said.

"'Nuf said, I'll quit. So, how about the press conference last night? How'd I do?" Tracey probed, as the smile on his face slowly spread from ear to ear.

"Yeah, I saw your performance. You were great!" Zack conceded.

"Wasn't I, though! I think I like this lieutenant thing," Tracey chortled.

"Ya think?" Zack came back without losing a beat.

"I admit, I'm basking in the glory of the moment. I do love it. But…it is still hard knowing there are all those killers on the street. I want those people locked up."

"Well, that's why you have the luxury of doing press conferences and still going after the bad people. That's the real deal! Some of us aren't that lucky," Zack sounded mildly self-pitying.

Tracey motioned his partner into his craftsman style office modestly situated with camel color fabric walls adorned with Robert Louis Tiffany lamps and décor. He waited for Zack to enter then closed the door. He sat at his mahogany desk with brown leather accessories atop, trimmed in gold, while Zack took up a chair on the opposite side.

"What's up?"

"Let's try to give Jaime's phone another try before we stop by to speak with Mr. and Mrs. Herrera."

Zack grabbed his notebook, found the page with the phone number and handed it to Tracey. He put his phone on speaker phone and dialed the number. This time, it rang three times before going to voicemail.

"What the hell? Yesterday it went straight to voicemail as well. Figured it was either off or dead. Now it's ringing." Tracey shot off an email to the forensics investigators asking them to check on the phone.

"Okay, let's go see Mr. and Mrs. Herrera."

***

Saturday – 8:15 a.m.

Tracey and Zack left the precinct and headed toward Eagle Rock, just off the 134 freeway near Glendale. As they drove they engaged in conversation about their discussion with Forbes the day before.

"Wasn't it interesting that Forbes Madden was a bit petulant?" Zack asked.

"Yeah, that whole thing has me scratching my head. There is something more to that story. It seems that Forbes and Jaime didn't get along very well. We will have to keep digging and see what we come up with."

They arrived at the Herrera house and observed a number of vehicles parked in front of the place, making it difficult to find a parking spot. After a few minutes, they watched someone leave the house and go to their car so Zack was able to park just in front of the quaint red Pueblo-style bungalow, masterfully known for its flat roof with wood stained windows. The home was situated a few yards from the street, exhibiting a rustic landscape with drought-tolerant plants which mirrored a desert scene. A row of cactus with a small reticular fence, lined the red tile walkway to the Spanish front door, resembling an Aztec motif.

As the detectives walked up to the house, they could hear crying coming from within. They approached the front door, which was slightly ajar. Tracey knocked softly. No one came to the door. Tracey and Zack then pushed the door open and the two men made their way inside. They found the Herreras in the living room, locked in a sorrowful embrace, both weeping uncontrollably.

Yolanda Herrera was a petite Latina, with short, curly brown hair that complemented her olive skin tone. The tears from her eyes washed the smears of mascara from her face, creating a blank canvas of inconsolable anguish.

Zack walked slowly toward Yolanda, moved the wingback chair in front of her, and placed his hand on hers in an attempt to absorb her pain and sorrow. Zack looked over at Jose Herrera, who was unable to lift his head to regard the detectives. He was sobbing uncontrollably, nearly choking on his own saliva, as the tears continued unabated.

"Mr. and Mrs. Herrera, I'm Detective Zack Grimes."

Zack stepped to the side. "We are terribly sorry for your loss. We have been put in charge of the investigation and would like to ask the two of you a few questions. I'm sorry to do this to you now, but it's important if we wish to find your son's killer."

She continued to sniffle but found her voice. "Okay."

"Do either of you know if there was anyone at the school who Jaime didn't get along with or did your son ever mention to you that he wasn't liked at school?" Tracey said.

"No, not that I know of." Yolanda looked to Jose to see if he agreed or had anything further to add and then finished answering the question. "As far as I know he got along with most everyone. Well, he never mentioned anything to us anyway," Yolanda conceded, wiping her nose with a handkerchief.

Tracey approached Jose who was a small man dressed in dark jeans, and a blue shirt with a white t-shirt underneath, which accented his short dark spiked hair. He looked at Jose's grief-stricken face, soaked by tears, and placed his hand on the man's shoulder.

"Mr. Herrera, I'm so sorry for your loss. I'm Detective Tracey Sanders. I can relate to some degree to your pain and suffering because I suffered a loss years ago, My wife was killed. She was a police officer and she was on a stakeout that went bad. She was shot to death. For myself, the pain has never gone away but I continue to believe and know that the person I lost is watching over me."

Jose nodded at Tracey's admission, a look of sympathy creeping into his pain-filled expression.

"I have been crying constantly since we were told what happened. I just can't stop. I can't believe my Jaime is gone. He's gone forever," he choked then continued crying, nearly hyperventilating.

Tracey didn't know if he was in any condition to answer some of the questions they had, but he made an attempt anyway.

"Mr. Herrera, do you think you could answer a couple questions and then maybe we can talk again at a later time?" Tracey asked.

"Sure. I know accidents can happen on construction sites, but I never thought my son would be a part of something like this. My son was a victim of irresponsibility. Someone made a big mistake," Jose found some anger in his belly with this last statement.

"Why are you referring to accidents at construction sites, Mr. Herrera? You do realize that we are fairly certain that it was not an accident at that site where your son was found, right?" Tracey said as gently as he could, knowing that this news may very well put Jose over the edge.

Jose regarded Tracey without expression then looked to Zack trying desperately to wipe the tears away that were streaming from his eyes. He stood up in front of Tracey and said, "What are you trying to say, Detective? Are you telling me it was not a construction accident that killed my son?"

"Yes, Mr. Herrera that is exactly what I am saying," Tracey replied softly. "We believe your son was murdered."

The tears came at an even faster pace than they had previously and Jose nearly collapsed where he stood. Luckily, the chair he was sitting in was right behind him and he was able to catch himself. With the shocking news he was just given, Tracey and Zack were not sure he would be able to answer even one question they wanted to ask.

"Mr. Herrera, I am so sorry to be the one to break that news to you. If you don't mind, can you tell us how long Jaime had been attending Calvin House?" Tracey pressed.

Jose took a deep breath, fighting for solvency of emotional control.

"He received a grant to attend the school. We would have never been able to afford it otherwise. He has been going there for the past two years," Jose said, now numb from sobbing.

"Do any of your other children go to Calvin House or hope to?"

"We would have liked to send some of his brothers or sisters to the school but it just hasn't worked out. And now this…how will we ever move on?" Jose broke down crying again while Tracey did his best to console him.

"Mr. Herrera, I know this is difficult and you are still in shock. Just a few more questions and we will be on our way," Tracey said.

By this time, Yolanda and Jose were again locked in an agonized embrace, oblivious to everything save their own grief.

"Do either of you know if your son ever experimented with drugs or had any over the counter medicines in his possession? Or if he was acquainted with anyone else who may have been involved with drugs of some kind?" Zack said.

Jose and Yolanda looked to one another before Jose finally said, "I don't think so. I never saw him with drugs nor did he ever talk about drugs or friends taking drugs. I have seen him take something like *Nyquil* for a cold in the past. But as his parents, we would probably be the last to know. You know—kids and all, keeping stuff from their folks. Kinda natural at that age, right?"

"It seems parents most times are the last to know about their kids involvement with drugs but we always have to ask." Zack commented then continued with another question, "I know I asked you, Mrs. Herrera, previously if there was anyone Jaime didn't get along with. Overall, how was Jaime mentally? This will come as a difficult question but we must ask…Did Jaime ever express being unhappy or/depressed, or speak to you about suicide or attempt suicide in the past?"

Jose sat up straight in his chair and looked at Tracey, then back to Zack. As he began talking, his voice was raspy as he stated, "I can accept this as being an accident. But suicide? No, I am certain suicide was never in his thoughts."

"When we spoke to the Headmaster, he mentioned that all of the students are given cell phones and GPS trackers when they start at the school. Do either of you know where we might be able to find his? Did he keep his cell phone and GPS Tracker in a backpack or in some other safe place?"

Jose took a moment to ponder the question in earnest. He shook his head and took a deep breath.

"Not that I know of, Detectives. He was always a quiet kid and didn't share things with us that he didn't think were things we needed to worry about. He was always good about calling us once a week to check in on the family and tell us how school was going," Yolanda explained as she grabbed yet another tissue from the box of tissues sitting on her lap. The tears just kept draining from her eyes as the sobs escaped her lungs.

Tracey moved closer to Yolanda and placed his arm around her, giving her a sympathetic hug. "Mrs. Herrera, you said he would call you weekly. So, can you tell us when the last time was that you spoke to your son?"

Yolanda continued to dab her eyes and nodded. "Wednesday evening. He called to tell me about a test he took and was talking about coming home for the weekend. That is the last time I would ever get to hear his precious voice. Thank goodness I ended the call telling him how much I loved him and how proud of him I was." Yolanda buried her head in her husband's chest making it clear that she wasn't up for any further questioning.

Tracey and Zack expressed their condolences once again to the grieving parents and then let themselves out of the house negotiating their way through the friends and family who had gathered at the house. The two of them had heavy hearts as they got into the cruiser to head back to the station. The drive back was spent in silence as the two of them tried to imagine losing a child in a situation like the one they were in the middle of investigating.

"Well, that sucked," Zack said at last.

"Correct," Tracey agreed.

"This kid Jaime seems pretty clean so far, aside from some questionable behavior attested to by Forbes," Zack said.

"It's early, pal," Tracey sighed. "We're just beginning this rodeo."

Zack nodded in agreement. "Got that right, Cochise."

***

Saturday – 3:00 p.m. – Back at the Precinct

Tracey and Zack returned to the precinct somewhat discouraged with the information gathered thus far in the investigation. While Tracey headed towards his office, Zack made a beeline for the kitchen to search for something to nosh on. His search for grub was successful so he made his way to Tracey's office munching with great gusto on a RyKrisp cracker with cream cheese and green olives.

When he got to the door of the office he could tell there was something bothering Tracey. "Hey man, what's wrong? Looks like you know something I don't and I have only been gone long enough to rummage through the kitchen for a snack," he said trying to make light of the situation.

Tracey nodded his head and said, "Yeah, Randy Yew left me a message while we were out. I just called him back and he is on his way up here."

Zack took a bite of his cracker and, with his mouth half full, asked, "Did he say what he found?"

"No, he wanted to tell us in person." Tracey glanced at his watch. "Hell, I need to call Harianne."

"Call her, he probably won't be right up."

"No, I better wait until after we talk to him. He sounded like he had something significant that he wanted to tell us," Tracey said as he spotted Randy walking down the hall toward his office. "Here he comes anyway so looks like the call will have to wait."

Tracey had known Randy for years. Randy was a simple man. He was single and extremely dedicated to his job. He lived in a one bedroom apartment in Venice Beach. The furnishings of his apartment consisted of an old blanket, a sheet, a pillow, and a sleeping bag. These were the kind of cases he lived for because it gave him a purpose, something to do. Jaime Herrera's death would occupy his every waking moment until its conclusion.

Zack and Tracey watched as Randy strolled into Tracey's office. He was wearing blue jeans and a beige shirt with sweat stains under his arms, evidence of a late, stressful night at the precinct. He pulled a brown oak chair close to the desk as Tracey and Zack tried to decipher the look on his face. It didn't take either of them long to realize that Randy was greatly concerned about what he had found germane to the case they were investigating.

"Well, don't keep us hanging! What did you find? What can you tell us?" Zack snapped as he licked the cream cheese off of one of his fingers.

"Ok...ok. First of all, there were no obvious signs of trauma to Jaime Herrera's body or anything that would suggest a hemorrhage," he said. "His color seemed strange though."

"How's that?" Tracey asked with raised eyebrows.

"His color was kind of a bluish gray. It was an odd color, like what I have seen in people that have pulmonary disease."

"So he died of some kind of lung disorder?" Zack asked.

Randy looked at Zack trying to take in the question and decide on how best to answer it. "Well, I suppose he could have. But I don't think so. There was nothing indicating as such. Additionally, there were no marks on his neck to indicate that his oxygen was depleted from strangulation or anything like that." Randy paused then looked at Tracey this time and said, "I think he may have been cyanotic."

Tracey poured a cup of hot coffee from the thermal carafe on the sideboard table against the wall.

"Ok, there must be a reason that you are saying something about being cyanotic. That isn't something that just any investigator would come up with. What else did you find?" Tracey asked, sipping his coffee.

"You're right. There is more." Randy continued. "As expected, a search warrant was issued for Jaime's room. Because he is dead and his roommate is out of town, there are still some unanswered questions. However, we found an apple juice box sitting on one of the night stands. Within the night stand was also a notebook with Jaime's name on it so we are gathering that side of the room is Jaime's. We will have to confirm that when his roommate returns."

"Okay, so you found an apple juice box. What's the big deal about that?" Zack asked grumpily.

"Well...we collected it as evidence due to the odd odor emanating from the container. Apple juice is acidic and when we ran tests on it, it was positive for traces of cyanide," Randy explained.

Zack and Tracey looked at each other, clearly puzzled.

"And just where do you suppose the cyanide came from?" Zack asked.

"I don't know. That's what I am still trying to figure out. Maybe a lab class or science project. I'm going to get the toxicologist to confirm this," Randy said, clearly mystified.

"Interesting. You mentioned it was collected as evidence partly because of the odor. Does cyanide have a distinct smell?" Tracey asked.

"Dr. Peduska could shed more light on this. But, yeah, actually it does. It smells like bitter almonds from what I have been told. Why do you ask?" Randy looked at Tracey waiting patiently for an answer.

"Just curious. Did you find anything else?"

"One other thing, Aline found a gold necklace and the clasp appears to be broken. Maybe a pendant or locket hung from the necklace. It was on the floor near Jaime's bed."

"Wonder who the necklace belongs to? Anything else?" Zack questioned taking in all of the details that were known so far from the investigation of the crime scene and the victim's room.

"That's it for now. I'll let you know when the reports are finalized."

Randy got up from his chair, turned toward the door and left without another word. Zack and Tracey sat in silence trying to comprehend the concept of Jaime being cyanotic. So, did that mean that he was murdered with cyanide or that he committed suicide? The information presented by Randy created even more unanswered questions.

Zack glanced over to Tracey, who nodded. "Yeah. Cyanide."

"The plot thickens," Zack agreed.

"I know one thing about that chemical. At least the kid didn't suffer," Tracey said.

"I don't think that's gonna give the Herreras much comfort," Zack said.

"No, but it may lead us to the killer," Tracey said.

Chapter Four

Saturday – 6:00 p.m.

Tracey threw his keys and cellphone on the table in the foyer and yelled into the void.

"Harianne, I'm home. Are you here?"

Harianne's response was immediate. "Yep, I'm in the kitchen with Austria. We're fixing dinner."

"Hi, baby," he said as he kissed her gently upon the lips, entering the kitchen.

"Hi! How's your case coming along?" Harianne asked as she sliced tomatoes and threw them into the salad bowl atop the romaine lettuce. Harianne was always interested in the work that Tracey was involved in. Anytime Tracey was on a case, she always wanted to know more about what was going on than he was legally able to tell her about. It was frustrating for her at times but part of what she had learned to live with when it came to their relationship and his career.

"Don't ask," Tracey shook his head.

Harianne gave Tracey a look of disappointment, but continued to prepare the salad she was working on. He reached for a tomato in the salad bowl on the counter.

"How was your day?" Tracey asked as he sat on the stool on the opposite side of the black granite top island from where Harianne was preparing dinner.

"Well, I got another domestic violence case today. Apparently the wife killed her husband in self-defense when he pointed a gun at her."

"Honey! That's great. Who is she?" Tracey snatched another tomato from the bowl to munch on and headed toward the bar to get a drink.

"She's in her thirties, wealthy, but was unhappy with her husband. She says it was not uncommon for him to manipulate and beat her on a regular basis. She's one of the wives who was scheduled to be on the reality show *The Real Housewives Of Beverly Hills*. Apparently, pointing a gun at her was the icing on the cake. She feared for her life so she killed him with a pistol she'd gotten a permit for without him knowing."

Tracey poured a glass of red wine and looked up at Harianne.

"Apparently, she was having her usual cocktail that evening in the living room. He walked in, angry as usual, and bellowed out 'You're a fuckin' bitch. You're not to say anything in this house. Shut up!' He went for his leather strap very much like a whip, walked over to her where she was sitting and raised it towards her face and under her chin. She just sat there quietly, saying nothing. Breathing hard he turned his back, walked to the bar and poured a bourbon. Then he fumbled with some items on the shelf behind the bar."

Harianne had Tracey's attention. "No shit? Then what?"

"She knew he was coming back to beat on her as he had done most every night. While his back was turned, she reached inside…"

"Don't tell me she shot him in the back?" The look on Tracey's face said it all. The suspense was killing him; he could barely sit still listening to the story.

"No. Will you let me finish the story?"

"Yeah. Go ahead. Sorry," Tracey said anxiously.

"She reached inside her purse, pulled out a jewelry box, removed the pearl handle revolver and placed it by her side, just under her dress. His temper got worse as he drank. He placed his drink on the table, turned around with a pistol in his hand and headed towards her. She fired two shots straight into his chest and he fell to the floor, dead on before he hit the ground. She got up from the sofa to see if he was dead then dialed 911."

"Wow! Sounds like an interesting case." Tracey said as he sipped his wine. "Sounds like she was a damn good shooter and wasn't about to take another beating from that SOB."

Tracey sipped his wine. "Should be a slam dunk case. Definitely self-defense."

"Not so fast," she said as she walked towards the refrigerator, stopped and placed her hand on the handle.

"The prosecution is going for premeditated first degree murder. Because she had the gun nearby and was prepared for his return, which is considered premeditation in their opinion. I'm with you on the self-defense because he beat her every night and he did have a gun."

"Babe, that's a tough sell. It's self-defense. No doubts about it," Tracey said reassuringly.

Harianne turned towards Tracey and sighed. "It depends. Prosecution said she shot him before he pointed the gun at her. I'm waiting for ballistics."

"A yeah! Ballistics would be good. But you know everything will be okay. She has the best criminal defense attorney in Los Angeles County," Tracey said grinning.

"What about my private detective work?" Harianne said, blushing at Tracey's last comment.

Tracey had always admired Harianne for her hard-work and dedication to her cases. She could sometimes be a bit on the nosey side but she was always able to glean a bit of extra information for her clients by doing her own private investigative work on the side. Solving the crimes in the cases while nosing around was her specialty...and something she took very seriously.

Tracey hesitated and paused. "Hum! Hum! Well I guess so. I'm the private detective."

Harianne finished slicing the tomatoes and pushed the salad bowl to the side.

"What does that mean? When I met you and Zack in the alley that night you didn't even know me. If it hadn't been for my best friend's gruesome murder and my hunt for her killer, we would have never met."

"That's true. It's cases like these that bring Jasmine to the front of my thoughts. She was like a sister and my best friend. I really had no family after I lost my parents, except for Jasmine and Austria. She was the best private detective in L.A. County and she taught me the ropes. It's too bad she was murdered and didn't get to see my performance as a criminal lawyer. I feel sad right now just thinking about her. She meant the world to me," she said, wiping tears from her eyes.

"You're right, baby. My bad. I know how much you miss her," replied Tracey, shaking his head.

After Harianne's old law firm, which handled mostly civil litigation, closed due to the recession, Harianne chose to return to the criminal law practice against her wishes although she had a great win with the Sosushi family case. Matthew Daytona changed all that when he was accused of murder and, as it turned out, the person murdered was his ex-girlfriend and Harianne's real mother, the deceased MacKenzie McShay, aka Gretchen Duet. Harianne went through some tough times after that case but things gradually improved.

"I miss her terribly. Having lost my real mother and my best friend, my criminal practice grew and became very prosperous because of Jasmine. She helped me win a number of cases because of her dedication to private investigation. As well as her willingness to teach me all she knew," Harianne said, heavy with emotion.

Tracey moved closer to Harianne and pulled her towards him, hugging her tightly. Then he pulled back just a little and kissed her forehead. "Remember, baby, she's always watching over you. She is an angel helping to guide you with all of your current and future cases."

Harianne grilled the chicken while Austria cooked the rice. Harianne lifted the chicken with a pair of tongs and placed it on a white platter near the stove.

"Smells great!" Tracey exclaimed.

Since living in the house, Tracey and Harianne wanted to make some changes. In the last three weeks, their dream was coming true. They had hired Christophe Dubois as the general contractor to add a sunroom on to the house. To make that happen, a wall had to be removed making it such that the project was no small undertaking. Since they were already doing some work, they decided to upgrade their bathroom as well. By the time they were ready to sign Christophe's contract, they decided to remodel the entire house from top to bottom. The thought of a remodel was exhausting to Harianne, yet she couldn't wait for the project to be completed.

"How is the contractor doing?" Tracey asked.

"All right, but I think he needs a foreman to oversee the addition. He comes and goes all the time," Harianne replied.

"Honey. That's the nature of a general contractor's M.O."

"Whatever! It's not good to leave them unattended; they take more breaks than they do work. It is hard for me to watch when I know I am paying so much for the addition. I have to talk to Christophe about one of the sinks. I noticed it was leaking. I really would like to have a *Rohl* farmhouse sink. I know we're kind of on a budget, but that sink would make all the difference and besides, it would look fabulous in here."

"Oh really, I didn't know that. You're a little con artist, Harianne. You know I love you and you know what 'yes buttons' to push. Don't worry about it; I'll give him a call tomorrow and let him know and maybe even talk to him about the extra breaks the men are taking. Soon we will have to move to Austria's cottage while the renovation is going on so maybe you won't be as bothered by all the breaks they are taking since you won't be so close to them all the time."

Austria dished up the plates and served Harianne and Tracey. Then she put on her jacket, preparing to leave the house.

"Sorry I can't join you both for supper. I have to get to my Yarn Sisters," Austria apologized. "We have a contest in two weeks."

"How are things with the knitting club, Austria?" inquired Tracey.

"Good. I am enjoying it. I signed up on 'Meet Up.com' and it's local, right here in L.A., just down the street on Santa Monica Blvd. Right now we have ten women but we're trying to get more women involved. We practice on one common item like a sweater or hat for a month. Then we comment on each other's knitting techniques and see if each other's knitting item has problems or we might comment on how good it is. If we all do well on a certain common item, then we choose it and then enter it for the local contest in hopes of winning. I will let you know the outcome. I also played with the thought of taking up an upholstery class, but I think I'd be rushed and cram my calendar."

"This is true, Austria. I don't know how you do all those things," Harianne remarked.

"Interesting. How do you like your new cottage in the back?" Tracey said.

"I love it!" Austria beamed with delight. "Especially the circular window seat in the kitchen that overlooks the English rose garden in the back. It reminds me of my childhood house in Surrey in the South East part of England. Makes the cottage feel just like home."

"Good. I can't tell you how glad I am to hear that. It is nice to have you so close," Harianne said.

"I wouldn't want to be anywhere else, except right here with the both of you. I've got to dash. I don't want to be late for class, "Austria said as she opened the door to leave.

"Yeah. It's okay. Get going." Tracey stood up, smiling at Austria.

Harianne stood next to Tracey, "Bye Austria. Love you. See you later."

Austria left closing the front door behind her.

Harianne walked into the kitchen with Tracey following and poured herself a glass of wine. Tracey leaned on the kitchen island.

"Well what should we do tonight: watch a movie and eat popcorn, snuggle or just work?" he quipped.

"I know Austria is a grown woman, but I worry about her. She's like my mom."

"Hey, listen, babe. You've got to stop worrying about her. She's fine and has her health."

"Movie and some snuggling sounds like just the thing for me. Let's eat up, clean the kitchen and settle in for the night. What do ya' say?"

"Sounds good. I'll make my famous Parmesan and olive oil popcorn," Tracey said excitedly as he sat down at the table to finish the chicken Harianne had prepared.

For now, thoughts of work, cases and an impending murder investigation took the back burner to deliberate recreational time.

It was a brief respite that would not last in the coming days.

***

Sunday – 5:30 a.m.

As day barely broke, the first order of business for Tracey and Zack was to ring the on-call judge to get a court order for two search warrants—warrants required for the DNA and forensic evidence gathering at the school in Jaime Herrera's room. The judge had been a bit persnickety in terms of specifics, i.e., did the detectives plan on swabbing all the students or strictly to obtaining additional data from Jaime's room. Tracey assured the judge that there would be no Buccal smears from the general student population—merely accumulating any additional evidentiary data from the crime room venue. While Zack seemed impatient, Tracey was appreciative of the judge's concern as he was making sure nothing bit them on the ass later in the courtroom vis a vis questionable investigatory practices. After some deliberation, the Judge seemed well assured, and following obtaining the search warrants from the judge, the detectives returned to Calvin House.

They arrived at Calvin House at half past six o'clock and walked to Forbes Madden's office. Upon arrival, they noticed that Forbes' secretary was not at her cluttered desk yet so they made their way back to Forbes' inner sanctum. Tracey and Zack stood in front of his door waiting patiently for Forbes to notice them. They were trying not to be rude, as they could see that he and Brolin were having an intensely private conversation about something in his office. They finally gained Forbes' attention, as well as Brolin's.

"Good morning, gentleman," Forbes said as he stood up from his chair. Forbes' eyes were red and he looked as though he hadn't slept in days. He was dressed in black pants, a white shirt only half tucked in with the shirt sleeves rolled up half way to his elbows. "You met Brolin the other day in my office."

When Forbes noticed the detectives initially, Brolin turned around to see who he was talking to. Brolin stood tall in a black suit and a crisp off-white shirt. His expression belied a piercing intelligence.

"Good morning, detectives," replied Forbes, shaking Tracey's hand and then Zack's. "What can we do for you this early Sunday morning?"

"We'd like to take a look at Jaime's room. However, before we check it out, we'd like to ask Brolin a few more questions if we can?"

"Sure. I'd be happy to help," Brolin smiled amicably.

"Great, thanks. Forbes, would you mind if we talk to him alone for a minute?"

For a second, Forbes looked like he had been gut-shot. As head of the school, he was not asked to absent himself from meetings involving his staff. But he recovered quickly and smiled, nodding equitably.

"Oh, of course not. I'll be just outside my office when you need me." Forbes left his own office and shut the door behind him.

Tracey turned his attention to Brolin. "So, Brolin, can you tell us what your relationship was like with Jaime? Did you get along with him?"

"Yes. That's a no brainer. We got along great. I always availed myself to him when he seemed to need any kind of assistance," he said easily.

"Did he respect you as the Dean of Men?" Tracey asked.

"I believe so. He never did anything to make me think otherwise."

"Did he ever lash out at you? Forbes mentioned he had a propensity for this kind of verbal inappropriateness on occasion."

"No. I know Forbes had such issues with the boy, but not me. We would talk about sports and just general things. No animosity at all," Brolin said in a calm voice.

"We understand that you were a witness to the argument that happened between Jaime and Forbes. Were you surprised by his lashing out at Forbes?"

Brolin paused and glanced over at the door where Forbes had just exited. "Yes. Frankly, I was shocked. I couldn't believe it."

"Did anything happen earlier in the day? Anything that you know of that would have increased the tension between the two of them?" Zack chimed in.

"Nothing happened that I am aware of. As far as I know, it was just another ordinary day. I don't know what set him off," Brolin admitted.

"Okay. Thanks. Once again, we appreciate you taking the time to answer our questions." Tracey turned towards the door, opened it and the three of them walked out to find Forbes. "Would you be able to take us to Jaime's room? We received a search warrant this morning to look around a bit more."

"Of course, follow me. I'll take you there," Forbes said as he walked over to his office and closed the door. Forbes turned to Brolin and said, "Brolin, we'll finish our conversation later."

"I hope so," Brolin said coldly, and this tension between the two men was not lost on Tracey or Zack for a moment.

Brolin moved off as Forbes turned to the two men. "A small family issue," Forbes said, as if this explained everything. "You know how these things go between colleagues," he said through a chuckle.

"Yep. Shit goes down on occasion," Tracey said through a smile.

But Tracey was far from put at ease by Forbes' increasingly odd behavior.

Chapter Five

Tracey and Zack followed Forbes down the clinker brick walkway towards the large brick dormitory behind the school. Secluded under flourishing oak trees, it resembled an ancient Gothic structure, much like the buildings on the East Coast, blanketed with moss.

"Just so you know, I must be present during your walk-through of the room. Those are the school ground rules…I can't let you search a student's room without myself being present," Forbes said as he turned to look at Tracey half way to Jaime's room.

"We completely understand. We would rather have you there as we look at the room anyway," replied Tracey.

"So, you said earlier that you have been the Headmaster at the school for eight years. How did you end up with the job?" Zack asked, trying to ease the tension as they walked down the hall.

"This school is my life. My brother and I inherited the place when our father passed away. Prior to his death, I worked in various other positions at the school, always paying as much attention as possible to what was going on with procedure and the business side as well as the education side of things. My father and I talked about the future of the school and that it would be passed down to my brother and me."

Tracey walked behind Zack, listening to his voice mail, hearing bits and pieces of their conversation.

"Inherited? Really," Zack said through a whistle. "Nice."

"My grandfather left the school to my dad. My brother has never really been interested in education, nor this facility. As kids, we were required to help with different things around the property including cleaning, maintenance and upkeep as well as other odds and ends. That was enough for my brother to abdicate any future interest in assisting running this school. Thus, all responsibility for its upkeep and continuation fell to me."

"A great legacy. Pretty neat to have the property and business be in the family for so many years," Zack smiled warmly.

"Well, it has its moments," replied Forbes as he walked towards the dorms. "The responsibility is quite daunting."

Tracey pushed the red phone sign to end his message retrieval, put the cell phone in his pocket, and caught up to Forbes and Zack.

When they finally arrived at Room 6A, Zack knocked on the door. They knew that no one should be in the room because Chase was still gone with his family, but the knocking was part of warrant protocol. They waited a few minutes before Forbes unlocked the door with a master key.

Forbes opened the door slowly stating his name upon entry. "Forbes Madden. Anyone in here?"

As expected, no reply was forthcoming. Tracey and Zack entered the dark room where the drapes had been closed by the occupants prior to leaving. Clothes were scattered about the room, newspapers covered the floor and Red Bull cans cluttered the table by one of the beds. A videogame, Unchartered 3-Drake's Deception, was set next to the Sony PlayStation on one of the desks.

Tracey walked over to the videogame and picked it up to take a closer look. He held it up to Zack and said, "Have you ever heard of this game before? It looks brutal."

Zack walked over and looked at it and said, "Nope, that's a new one for me."

Forbes chimed in, "I am pretty sure that desk is Chase's."

Zack and Tracey continued combing through the room. They looked at each of the two desks pilfering through the drawers, notebooks, and other items on and around the desks. Tracey took a closer look in and around the nightstands while Zack examined the room's only closet. The closet was clearly split in half for each of the two roommates. As Zack perused the interior, he came across a case of apple juice that was pushed to the back on one side of the closet.

"Tracey, look at this," he said as he slid the full case of apple juice from the back of the closet. "Wonder if this is the same brand as the open juice box they tested previously."

"We better bag it and take it with us just in case," Zack suggested.

"Yeah, this is probably what Randy was talking about, but the boxes are not open. We really have no way of knowing if this entire box was tainted," Zack mentioned as he was putting the case of juice in a bag to be processed.

"Mr. Madden, do you know if there is cyanide on the premises that may be used for experiments in the science classes?" Tracey asked.

"Yes. It is used quite frequently for chemistry classes and science projects, but it is locked up. You have to have access to the key to the chemical cabinet."

"Who has access to that key?" Zack asked from the other side of the hall.

"Just the science and chemistry teachers, no one else. Oh, and myself, of course."

"And Jaime got along well with those teachers?" Tracey said.

"Well, as far as I know. They didn't ever contact me with any concerns about Jaime and I never heard anything from any of the students. You know how students talk. If there were problems, I would have heard something," Forbes said with clear conviction.

"Do you know of any other students that were close to Jaime?" inquired Tracey.

"Yeah, he had a study partner, Wyatt Nance. They spent quite a bit of time together."

"What's his background?" Tracey asked.

"Wyatt is the son of Dr. Charles and Mrs. Kelli Nance. Mrs. Nance, Executive Director of SIDS Foundation of Los Angeles founded by her to promote awareness out of the loss of her little sister that devastated her parents. Charles Nance, his father, is the owner of a medical laboratory with two offices, one each in Southern and Central California."

"Where's his room?" Tracey asked as he gestured to Zack to be sure that he was taking notes on this new development.

"On the seventh floor, the next floor above this one."

"Do you know if Wyatt is around this morning so we could talk with him?" Tracey asked as they were exiting the dorm room.

"He should be, I can lead the way," Forbes said as he locked the door, turned and started walking toward the stairs at the end of the hallway.

Forbes, Tracey, and Zack climbed the stairs to the next floor. Zack noticed the brown plaque with gold lettering, "Elite Scholars."

"What was the name of that last floor?" Zack asked.

"Political Scholars; it's on a blue plaque with silver lettering," Forbes said.

They knocked on the door of Wyatt Nance's room. Standing at six feet two inches tall, Wyatt was the shooting guard on the winning Calvin House basketball team. He had a GPA of 4.5, an impressive straight A student and got along with most everyone.

"Yeah! Who is it?" a voice rang out from the other side of the door.

"It's Mr. Madden, Wyatt. I have detectives Tracey Sanders and Zack Grimes with me. They'd like to ask you some questions."

"About what?" Wyatt called out.

"We're investigating the death of Jaime Herrera," Forbes continued.

"I don't know anything. I was studying," Wyatt said defensively.

"It will only take a few minutes. Can you open the door so we can talk please?"

Wyatt, a brown-eyed kid with blond hair combed off to the side, opened the door and the detectives stepped inside. The room was the complete opposite of Chase Buckman's. The bed was made and everything was in its place. Fruit, cheese, vegetables and a green salad adorned a plate next to an open MacBook on a mahogany secretary desk—a family heirloom, Zack surmised. The rest of the furniture looked like it came from Ikea.

"How can I help?" Wyatt asked through a broad smile.

"We understand that you were Jaime's study partner," Tracey said.

"Yes. We usually studied three times a week together."

"Did you get along with him?" Zack asked.

"I did. Spending time together three times a week would be hard to do with someone you didn't get along with, don't you think?"

Tracey and Zack looked at each other, then Tracey continued with the next question. "Do you get along with Mr. Madden?"

Wyatt looked uneasily to Forbes. Forbes offered a gentle smile. "It's okay, Wyatt. Just tell these gentlemen what you know. No need to prevaricate. Tell them everything," he said reassuringly.

Wyatt nodded and looked to Tracey.

"Yes. Mr. Madden is a nice man," Wyatt said, glancing at Forbes with a smile.

"Did Jaime get along with Mr. Madden?"

Wyatt dropped his head and shot a glance to Forbes. "Not really."

"Why is that?" Zack asked.

"All three of them were always going at it, but separately."

"What do you mean by 'all three of them?'"

"Chase, he liked to play practical annoying jokes on Mr. Madden, while Jaime yelled and started arguments with him."

"What type of annoying jokes?" Zack and Tracey asked simultaneously.

"Chase would take Mr. Madden's shoes out of his closet in his office and Mr. Madden would have to wear his tennis shoes with his suits until Chase returned them. Mr. Madden now has another pair of shoes, but he doesn't keep them together."

"How do you know that?"

"He told us in class one day after it happened so many times. Mr. Madden was clearly annoyed with the pranks."

"I was at that," Forbes nodded, scratching his head.

"What about Jaime? Did he get along with Mr. Madden? You haven't really said much about their relationship," Tracey said.

Wyatt again hesitated.

"Go on, Wyatt," Forbes said. "It's okay."

Wyatt sighed and frowned.

"Actually, Jaime and Mr. Madden had a fight on Thursday morning in one of the empty classrooms. The door was locked, but all of us could see through the glass window on the door and hear them from the hallway. Everyone was staring. It was hard to go to class. Loud and…"

"Volatile?" Tracey suggested.

Wyatt didn't agree or disagree but instead went on with the story. "Jaime called Mr. Madden a child molester and spit on him. Mr. Madden has always treated us nicely and with respect. I respect Mr. Madden. But Jaime and him were at odds," Wyatt said.

"Go on," Zack urged.

Wyatt looked to Forbes. "Mr. Madden, are you sure—?"

"Tell them everything, Wyatt," Forbes urged.

Wyatt again sighed the sigh of the eternally damned. "Mr. Madden was so enraged he grabbed a chair and threw it across the room, cracking it into pieces."

The detectives tried not to look surprised by hearing about the chair being thrown. "Did it hit Jaime?" Tracey asked.

"No."

Wyatt looked away for a moment. He sensed he had said too much; Mr. Madden was his friend and he didn't want to get him in trouble. He developed an uneasy feeling in his stomach. The air felt suddenly heavy in the room.

Tracey could sense that Wyatt was starting to feel uncomfortable with what he had already said so he decided he had better end the questioning for the time being. "That's enough for now. Thanks, Wyatt," Tracey said. "We'll be in touch."

As Tracey and Zack headed towards the door with Forbes, they passed the adjacent bathroom and Tracey noticed a black bag on the counter with a syringe and pharmaceutical vial beside it. Tracey took two steps backward; making sure what he saw was real.

"Hey, Wyatt, one more question for you!" Tracey yelled out.

Wyatt walked towards Tracey. "Yes sir? Whatcha need?"

"What's up with the syringe and the vial?" Tracey asked as he motioned toward the bathroom where the bag was sitting.

"I'm a diabetic," Wyatt said easily.

"Oh."

"Anything else?" Wyatt asked through a good-natured chuckle.

"Nope, that will do it. Thanks again for your time."

"Hope I was of some help," Wyatt said.

"You were," Tracey said reassuringly.

Chapter Six

Tracey closed the door behind him where they met back up with Forbes. He proceeded down the stairs with Forbes and Zack following closely behind.

"Mr. Madden, I don't think you have been completely forthcoming with us." Tracey said as he stopped abruptly in the stairwell.

Forbes nearly ran into Tracey because he wasn't expecting him to stop so quickly.

"So, did you have a fight in the evening with Jaime or was it in the morning? Or was it both? Do you have your times confused or did Wyatt?" Tracey pressed.

"I uh…well…um…" Forbes stammered.

"Forbes, we can't do our jobs if you don't do yours. And right now, your job is to tell us the truth so that we can determine what happened to one of your students. And it sounds like the student in question is one in which you didn't get along so well with."

Forbes sat down on the stairs with his head in the palms of his hands as they rested on his knees. "Okay, Jaime and I fought twice on Thursday; once in the morning as Wyatt stated and once in the evening. And, yes, I did throw a chair during the morning argument. Jaime's behavior was off. I was frustrated but I know it doesn't make what I did right. I should have told you about the first argument but I…well, I didn't want you to think less of me."

"Thinking less of you isn't the issue, sir. Lying or omitting critical information to investigators certainly doesn't help your situation. And after talking to Wyatt, it sounds like you're not liked by those two boys!"

"I know. It's really bad. At least it's just two."

"So far," Zack offered.

"Are there any other students that you know of who do not care for you, sir?" Tracey said.

Forbes looked at the two detectives as he stood up and shifted his feet uncomfortably. "No, there are no others that I know of that may not like me. However, there is one other student who you may want to talk to. He is friends with Wyatt so he might know something we don't."

"Who might that be and where can we find him?" Tracey asked.

"Wendall Dobbs is his name and his room is just four doors down from Chase's room. I will take you there," Forbes said as he turned and headed down the hall.

Tracey's gut told him that Forbes had nothing to do with Jaime's murder, but the fact that the headmaster had chosen to edit his story with the dead boy and the altercation that had transpired did not rest well with him. He would reserve judgment for the time being but he unofficially designated Forbes Madden as a person of interest in the current investigation.

***

Sunday – 12:00 p.m. – Noon

They arrived at Wendall Dobbs' room, knocked once and stood waiting for a response. No answer was forthcoming. They knocked again.

Wendall cracked the door open. "Hey!"

"Hi Wendall! This is Detective Sanders and Detective Grimes. They'd like to speak with you," Forbes said.

"About what?"

"Jaime Herrera," Tracey replied.

Wendall opened the door and motioned them into his room. He had his iPod on and earphones attached.

"Can you stop the iPod?" said Zack.

"Oh, yeah, sure. Sorry, I always have this thing playing so just used to talking to people with the buds in my ears," Wendall explained as he turned off his iPod, took out his earphones and set the contraption on his desk.

"What was your relationship like with Jaime?" Tracey got right into it.

"I didn't like him at all. In fact, I hated him. He was a jerk," Wendall stated as his face reddened.

"Wow, why was that?" Zack asked.

Wendall walked over to the window and looked out on the school grounds.

"He wanted attention all of the time. Smart guy, but too needy," he grumbled.

"Needy? How so?" Tracey pressed.

"He constantly went to the Dean of Men. If we said anything to him, he would make more of it, take things too personally. Make it into something that it wasn't, blow things out of proportion."

"I see," Tracey said softly.

"I didn't get a scholarship like Jaime and I had to work hard to get here. My parents aren't wealthy, nor are they poor. I come from a family of scholars: my mother is a professor at UCLA and my father is a professor at Cal Tech in Pasadena. If I screw up, my parents will totally thrash me."

"We understand. So…" Tracey paused before going on to ask, "when was the last time you saw Jaime?"

"At dinner, on Thursday evening, in the dining hall."

Zack noticed the three computer monitors on a nearby desk.

"Why do you have three monitors?" Zack asked.

"Homework, research and the other one is for *Skype*."

"That's pretty cool. I suppose that is how you stay in touch with your family and friends who aren't nearby, right?" remarked Zack.

"Yeah, I think it is pretty cool. And yes, I Skype my family and friends on a regular basis."

"Mr. Madden said that you are friends with Wyatt Nance? Is that right?" Tracey asked as he wandered around the room.

"Yes, Wyatt and I like to exchange ideas and theories about chemistry assignments. I think Jaime may have been a bit jealous of my relationship with Wyatt. It wasn't unusual for us to exclude him because of his attitude. Wyatt and I are tech monsters, something that Jaime never was. He didn't always get what we were talking about so it was easier to not involve him sometimes."

"But Wyatt and Jaime were study partners from what Wyatt said. Could it be that you were the jealous one?"

"Make it what you want it to be," Wendall said as he looked pointedly at Tracey. "I already said that I didn't like Jaime so I'm not hiding anything from anyone."

"So, Wendall, how did Jaime act that evening at dinner?" Zack asked.

"I suppose he seemed fine. I didn't sit with him at dinner. Like I just said, I didn't like him. He wasn't my friend. He was nothing to me. Just another classmate."

"Thanks, Wendall. I think that is all we have at this time. If we come up with any other questions, we will come find you," Tracey said.

Wendall walked over to his desk, grabbed his iPod and shoved his earphones back into his ears while the detectives walked out of the room.

***

After talking with Forbes in front of the school, Tracey and Zack returned to their car, got in and Zack turned towards Tracey, clearly confused.

"Tracey, are you thinking what I'm thinking?"

"Zack, we don't know if Madden killed Jaime or not. He could have. But you've got to prove it. Right now we have to be patient."

"Wait it out."

"Bingo," Tracey said. "We wait for mistakes to be made."

***

Sunday — 1:30 p.m.

Forbes returned to his office and settled into his worn leather chair that belonged to his grandfather, Brinks Madden. He stared at the black leather-bound book on top of his desk, deep in thought.

Recently he'd found the tome, which turned out to be a diary, tucked away on one of the bookshelves at the school. After he found it, he opened it briefly and then closed it and placed it on his desk. Since then, it had been nothing but a distraction; so much so that at times he was unable to focus on what the detectives had been asking him. Finally, he grabbed the book and opened it to the first page. His grandmother, Lauren Madden, had written an extensive diary about her life, her family and Calvin House.

Tucked inside was a lengthy newspaper article, its edges slightly torn, dated September, 1941"Prominent and Elite Headmaster Found Guilty of Murder" plastered on the front page of the *Los Angeles Times*. The article read: Headmaster Brinks Madden, in a crime of passion, killed a Calvin House student, Thomas Peyton, son of Clay and Talia Peyton, with an axe on the campus of Calvin House Preparatory School.

Forbes involuntarily shuddered as he read the bi-line. At length, he opened the diary and began to read.

September 18, 1941 — Today was a brisk autumn day. A home-cooked aroma permeated the kitchen as I pulled a black tin roasting pan filled with pot roast, braised carrots, potatoes and celery from the oven. It is one of my favorite recipes. Brinks has offered numerous times to hire a cook. I would take him up on the offer except for the fact that I really love to cook. It's a skill I carry that makes me proud. One that I learned from my mother and grandmother and would like to continue to perfect. Preparing all the family favorites once a week is by far my favorite part of cooking.

Frank arrived home at the usual time and was anxious to complete his homework—cursive handwriting and math—so he could listen to his favorite shows. Every day at 3:00 p.m., Frank listened to "Dick Tracey" and "The Aldrich Family" on the Zenith radio while waiting for his father to arrive home…today was no different.

Brinks arrived home at his usual time today but he seemed to be preoccupied. He went straight to his study without saying a word and slammed the door.

Forbes closed the diary in total shock after reading the headline of the newspaper article. He knew there was more to the story than he had suspected, but he couldn't bear to read anymore of the diary and certainly not the article. At least, not now, not today.

He set the diary to the side and went to work on some of the paperwork that had been piling up on his desk since the body had been found on Friday.

There would be opportunity to again peruse the diary.

After this investigation.

After the horror was over.

***

Sunday – 5:00 p.m.

Tracey and Zack left the precinct and headed home for some quiet time which was desperately needed by both men. Zack arrived home around 5:30 p.m. and was greeted at the front door of his condo by his wife, Eve. He pulled her toward him and kissed her passionately.

Eve Grimes was the epitome of classy. Blessed with olive tone skin, light brown hair, and a slightly freckled visage, she was medium height and athletic. Eve was a triplet, had grown up in Vermont and was the daughter of a machine operator and homemaker. She had a Masters in Deaf and Hard of Hearing from New York University. Her siblings, Brianna and Bella, remained on the East Coast after their parents had died. They owned a ballet school together on New York's Upper East Side.

Zack and Eve had been together for over ten years. She had never lived on her own and married Zack just after he was hired by the L.A. County Sheriff. When he got transferred to the homicide department, their world fell apart. The constant absences in the middle of the night for a murder case never settled well with Eve. She wanted the stability that existed before Zack had been transferred to the Homicide Department. The new position that Zack held was hard for Eve to get used to and their relationship had suffered over the course of time.

As the months passed, Eve decided that she wanted to try living on her own and she left Zack. Zack was devastated with her decision but understood that she needed to do what was best for her. After several months of being separated, Eve realized that Zack was the strong one who had always protected her and told her the truth.

Homicide investigation was Zack's passion and the position gave him an opportunity to work with a great partner, Tracey Sanders. Eve leaving gave her a chance to think and realize that Zack was the best thing that ever happened to her.

"What's gotten into you?" Eve smirked with delight as Zack continued smothering her with kisses.

"I'm just happy that you're back. I know I'm working a lot again, but it's my job. I don't want to—"

"Zack! Calm down. I'm not going anywhere. I love you. We had our troubles, but it's all good now. I'm not leaving again. Promise."

He hugged her, then pulled back and locked his eyes with hers.

"When you left, I knew I had to change, not just for myself, but for you. I kind of had an idea what I had done."

"Zack. I ran because I was looking for something different. I didn't know what I wanted."

"Are you sure this is what you want? I can't go through what I went through before when you left."

"Zack, I am not going anywhere. I promise. So let's go forward from here."

This was exactly what Zack had wanted to hear.

Maybe his anxiety that his wife would leave again was without foundation.

He figured only time would tell.

"Come on," he whispered in her ear. "Let's fool around."

"You got it, mister," Eve giggled and kissed him passionately.

***

Sunday – 6:00 p.m.

The room was dark except for a medium-sized Victorian lamp that cast a yellow glow from a corner next to a large brown sectional sofa. Silence was pervasive through the entire room. The boy awakened groggily, moving his head back and forth, lolling in a circular motion. Moaning, he noticed that his hands were tied to a cement pillar; the fabric-covered chair he sat in felt wet and cold. He looked down and saw that his clothes were torn and completely shredded around his groin. The room reeked of a horrible smell. Retching, the vomit reached the roof of his mouth quickly, pouring onto the wood floor and all over his clothes. He wanted to scream, but realized immediately from somewhere deep inside his assaulted psyche, that no one would hear him. Deaf heaven would not respond with either compassion or explanation. He was a prisoner, by whom and for what reason, there was no immediate answer forthcoming.

Where was he, he asked himself in a sudden sense of despair and panic? What's going on? Why? Why?

The horror of the moment remained extant and inexplicable.

And the boy knew suddenly in his heart that he would soon be dead.

***

Sunday – 7:00 p.m.

Tracey's cellphone rang as he finished drying dishes. He walked quickly to the foyer and swiped the screen on his phone, revealing the caller. Tracey frowned as he recognized Forbes Madden's number.

"Detective Sanders?"

Tracey could tell by the sound of Forbes' voice that something had happened. He sounded panicked.

"Mr. Madden. What's going on?"

"All the boys were at dinner in the dining hall tonight, except for one," Forbes stated frantically.

"Who was missing?"

"Wendall Dobbs."

"Why do you consider this significant, Mr. Madden?"

"Well, given his conversation with you, I find it disconcerting that he's disappeared," Forbes replied.

"He's not really a person of interest for us, Mr. Madden," Tracey said evenly. "This sounds more like an in-house problem better addressed under your jurisdiction."

"I don't know," Forbes said dubiously. "I have a bad feeling."

"I'd take comfort if you could come down here immediately, Detective," Forbes said emphatically.

Tracey glanced at his watch and sighed.

"Alright. Give me an hour."

"Good enough. I'll see you soon."

Tracey disconnected and stared out the window. In truth, he had his suspicions about Wendall's involvement with Jaime's death, but there wasn't even anything remotely tied to the boy merely on a circumstantial basis.

Still, it couldn't hurt to oblige Forbes Madden with a little visit.

Chapter Seven

Wendall Dobbs was fifteen years old and had been attending Calvin House for the past two years. His parents, Mr. and Mrs. Ellison Dobbs, were well off, but not wealthy, keeping themselves deeply involved in Wendall's life and goals, unlike Chase Buckman's parents who seemed little interested in what their son was doing on any given basis. Wendall had been a good student and wasn't known to leave the campus without prior approval. When Tracey got the call from Forbes that the boy had gone missing, all he could think about was what Wendall had said to them earlier that day about how much he hated Jaime.

After hanging up with Forbes, Tracey called Zack and told him the latest development and asked him to come pick him up from his house so they could go back to Calvin House.

"What are you thinking?" Zack asked over the phone.

"Nothing ominous. I'm heading over there simply out of curiosity," Tracey replied.

"You think he bolted because he's involved in this mess?" Zack asked.

"That's what I hope to discern," Tracey replied.

Zack signed and cleared his throat. "Okay. Let's do this."

***

Sunday – 8:00 p.m.

Tracey and Zack arrived at Calvin House exactly one hour after

Forbes had called Tracey. They pulled their black Chrysler sedan into the circular drive and were greeted by Brolin and Forbes, who both looked exhausted. As evidenced by their weary appearance, the murder of Jaime Herrera and now the disappearance of Wendall Dobbs had taken a toll on the two of them, both physically and emotionally.

"Good evening, gentleman," Tracey said. "Sounds like we have a missing boy on our hands. Do either of you recall when you last saw Wendall?"

"I can't say for sure when I saw him last," Forbes said, rubbing his hands together. "It wasn't uncommon for him to be outside underneath the pergola at a table, near the playground studying."

"Come to think of it, I believe I saw him there earlier," Brolin said before taking out some papers from his jacket. "I pulled all of the attendance records for today and it appears as though he attended all of his activities throughout the day." He handed the papers to Forbes.

"May I see the records?" Tracey said to Forbes.

"Here they are," Forbes said as he handed the records to Tracey. "Because today is Sunday, they don't have regular classes but we have activities for the students. There is a sign-in sheet for each activity. We didn't notice that he was missing until dinner time."

"Did any of the students see him leave the campus grounds earlier or see him talking to anyone unusual?" Zack asked.

"No. After we noticed that he was not at dinner, we talked to everyone. None of the boys know his whereabouts," Brolin said.

"Ok. If the two of you don't mind, we'll take a look around. It would be best if you both wait in Forbes' office. After we've searched the grounds, we'll meet you there directly."

Forbes and Brolin turned and entered the main building. Tracey and Zack walked along a path that traversed the entire campus. It was completely dark except for the porch lights outside each building. No footprints, tire marks or bicycle tracks could be detected by the two officers. Aside from a few persistent and vocal crickets chirping from the trees, the grounds were eerily silent.

Both men glanced over at the construction site and saw the light on by the door to the trailer used by the workers. They walked up to the steps and knocked on the door. When no one came to the door, they looked inside the trailer with their flashlight. They didn't see or hear anything unusual and continued on with their search.

After several hours of looking around the campus, Tracey and Zack returned to Forbes' office. Tracey sighed deeply before speaking.

"Well, we searched the entire back area behind the construction site, and the site itself, along with the entire grounds. No sign of the boy whatsoever. I'd say he's officially MIA," Tracey said.

"Not a single trace of him? No shoe prints? No clothing?"

"Nothing," Zack confirmed. "He's gone like a fart in the wind."

"Are there any other places you think he might have gone?" Tracey asked.

"None that I can think of. It's odd. I have never had any problems with Wendall. He's a good kid. He goes to all of his classes and he never misses dinner. This isn't like him," remarked Forbes.

Brolin nodded in agreement "Not at all like him. The kid is a model student."

Tracey glanced at Zack, who shrugged. Then he resumed his queries with Forbes.

"Have you contacted his parents yet?" Tracey asked.

"No, I was hoping I wouldn't have to and that you would find him," Forbes admitted. "With a murderer still out there, I'm concerned."

Tracey nodded. "We'll send an officer to their house to give the parents the news that their son is missing. We'll keep working and put everyone we have available on this to help locate your boy."

Forbes lowered his head in disappointment. "Alright. Please, let us know what else we can do on our side. I can't believe this is happening."

"Don't be too panicked yet, Headmaster," Tracey said reassuringly. "He could just be playing hooky for a bit. Boys have been known to do this now and again."

Forbes wasn't placated. "Not Wendall. This kid doesn't do that kind of thing. Something is terribly wrong."

***

Sunday – 11:30 p.m.

Forbes continued working late into the night as his mind wandered from Jaime to Wendall, trying to figure out what was going on in his life…and at the school. Who could have killed Jaime? Where had Wendall disappeared to? The thoughts just kept swirling through his mind, a maelstrom of imagined horrors cascading from synapse to synapse. As he was finishing up the paperwork for the day, he looked down at his cell phone realizing that he had missed a text message. When he opened it up, it was from Jaime Herrera, several days back.

"You're a selfish bastard! You owe me."

Forbes winced. The missive was just another painful reminder of the agony and pain caused by Jaime a few days earlier. Sitting quietly, he thought about how he wished his last moments spent with Jaime had been different and how he hoped that Wendall would be found safe and unharmed.

The last thing this school needs is another dead boy, Forbes thought dismally.

***

Monday – 8:00 a.m.

After leaving Calvin House around midnight the night before, Tracey and Zack were pretty slow getting around on Monday morning. They wanted to try to catch Chase before he went to his first class so they arrived at the school well before the First Period bell. As usual, they found Forbes in his office behind his desk looking as if he didn't have enough energy to even stand.

The news of a second student missing was spreading like wildfire and Forbes was not handling it well.

"Good morning once again. Looks like this is going to be a daily ritual," Forbes said dully.

"Apparently so," Tracey agreed. "We were hoping we could speak with Chase before his first class. Is he back from his family trip yet?"

"Yes, he got back yesterday evening. I can take you to his room," Forbes said as he stood up from his desk.

"Has there been any sign of Wendall? Has anyone spotted him off campus?" Zack asked hopefully as they walked across the campus.

"Nothing. We have no idea where he has gone. Obviously if you are asking, you haven't found him either," Forbes said.

"Sorry, we haven't. We're still looking though," Tracey replied.

They arrived at Chase's room and knocked on the door. There was a long silence as the three of them stood in the hallway waiting for a response. They could hear a chair slide across the floor on the other side of the door. Zack let out an exasperated sigh, cleared his throat, turned around and observed his surroundings.

Finally the door opened. Chase stood inside the room looking out, first at Forbes, then to Tracey and Zack. "Hey Mr. Madden, what's going on?" Chase inquired as he leaned on the door.

Tracey pulled his badge from his lapel inside his jacket. "Detectives Tracey Sanders and Zack Grimes."

"What do you want?" Chase asked with a bit of an attitude.

"We'd like to ask you a few questions."

The game they looked at the day before was playing on the Sony PlayStation. Chase cleared newspapers with his feet and tossed shirts on a nearby chair.

"We'll stand," Zack said.

"OK," Chase smiled broadly.

"That's a brutal game you're playing there. Do you play it often?"

"Yeah! So what! What are you going to do? Arrest me?" Chase questioned showing a bit more of an attitude toward Tracey than what was appropriate.

"We'd like to ask you some questions about Jaime Herrera," Tracey said. "Can you turn off your computer game?"

"Yeah. Sorry about that," Chase said as he turned the volume down on his computer but left the game running.

"How long were you and Jaime roommates?"

"Couple of years."

"Were the two of you good friends or close as schoolmates?"

"Not exactly. We were just roommates; not that close."

"Why was that?"

"We come from different backgrounds, and had different classes. If we had finals, we were both here studying, but Jaime and I basically just slept here. We spent very little time together," Chase said, a slight edge creeping into his voice.

"So you were passing ships in the night, nothing more?" Zack fished.

"Kind of. I mean he was a cool, nice guy. I liked him, we got along well."

"Was he the quiet sort?"

"With me, he was. In class, he was raw."

"Raw?"

"You know. He was cool, in the know. He talked back to all the teachers and picked fights."

Zack glimpsed a stack of masks on Chase's desk. He picked up a wolf mask and placed it over his face. He began laughing.

"Hey! Take it off!" Chase exclaimed walking over to Zack taking the mask and placing it back on the desk.

"All right, dude…sorry." Zack exclaimed throwing his hands up after Chase took the mask. "What's up with the masks?"

"I wear them when I'm off campus. It's my hobby—a collection. They are mysterious. I like mystery."

"Let's get back to our conversation," Tracey interjected. "Did Jaime have any enemies?"

"No. Just Mr. Madden."

"Mr. Madden?"

Tracey looked at Forbes with a surprised expression. He then resumed his conversation with Chase.

"They hated each other. Are we done yet?" Chase said.

"No, we aren't done yet! What do you mean they hated each other? What gave you that impression?" Tracey pushed.

"They just argued a lot out of the classroom. I must admit, it seems most of it was started by Jaime, not Mr. Madden."

"We were here yesterday looking at things in your room. We found a case of apple juice in the closet. Was that yours or Jaime's?"

"That's Jaime's. He loved to drink apple juice."

"Do you have any idea where Jaime usually got his supply of apple juice?"

"No idea. I just know that he was always drinking the stuff when he was around. Now, are we done yet?"

"One last question. Which bed is yours?" Tracey asked, irritation creeping into his voice. This kid was distinctly annoying and a part of

Tracey wanted to take him over his knee and provide a sound thrashing.

"This one," Chase said pointing at the bed and Zack made a note in his notepad.

"Yep, that is all for now. We may need to take another look around the room or ask you questions later. Thanks for your time," Tracey said.

Tracey, Zack and Forbes left Chase's room and stood in the hallway. Forbes scratched his head and sighed as he sensed a battery of questions coming his way.

Tracey paused, looked at Zack and then asked Forbes a point blank question.

"Is that true what Chase just told us? Did you and Jaime really hate each other?"

"I don't think using the word hate is appropriate. We try to teach not to hate people but I'm afraid the two of us definitely had our disagreements. I told you earlier about our fights so I am not trying to hide anything. I didn't want to make a bigger deal out of it than it was."

"I can see why. So why don't you tell us a bit more about your relationship with Jaime?" Tracey said as he stood in the middle of the hallway staring at Forbes waiting for an answer.

"Most kids hate people in authority. He was like most kids; he just didn't like being told what to do. That was it."

"You do realize this puts your position in this case at a rather precarious point," Tracey said.

"I'm aware of that," Forbes said. "Except, I didn't kill the boy."

"I'm not implying that you did," Tracey said. "I'm just saying that at the moment, you're a viable suspect in the murder of Jaime Herrera."

Forbes bit his lip. "I wasn't going to mention this but now I guess I have no choice," he said. "Jaime and Chase were seen having a pretty serious argument in the schoolyard last week."

"How serious?" Tracey asked.

"Chase threatened to kill him," Forbes said softly.

Tracey glanced at Zack, then back to Forbes. "And you thought this was unimportant?"

"Kids threaten each other all the time," Forbes said dismissively.

"True. But when one ends up dead after such a threat, it kinda takes on a different meaning," Zack said derisively.

Forbes sighed and nodded.

***

Tracey and Zack exited Forbes's office and shook their heads simultaneously.

"The kid whose dead was threatened by the roommate," Zack said. "Pretty open and shut case, right there."

"Maybe," Tracey said. "But I remember fighting with a roommate in college and I got so nuts one night, I threatened to kill the guy."

"Why?"

"He was screwing a girl I was seeing," Tracey said.

"Good reason," Zack quipped.

"We're going to pay a visit to the Buckman residence," he declared abruptly.

"The roommate's parents?" Zack asked, mildly surprised.

"You got it!" Tracey said.

***

They traveled the 2 Freeway North to the 210 East and exited at Gould Avenue approximately 15 minutes later. Upon seeing the Buckman estate, both detectives nodded in mutual appreciation of the grounds.

"Wow! Look at this palatial estate!" Zack remarked as they pulled up to the Buckman's place of residence. It was a black and gray colonial style two-story home, with black granite planters, a pool, tennis courts, complete with horses and a stable. It was more than evident the Buckmans had more money than they knew what to do with.

"Do I see three Ferraris in that large garage over there?" Tracey exclaimed as he gawked at the garage located off to the side of the main house.

"Yep, I believe you do. You're not imagining anything; either that or I am, too. I want to drive those babies!"

Chase had grown up in a lavish palatial estate in La Canada

Flintridge, with a staff of servants to cater to his every need. Chase left home to attend Calvin House and when the recession hit, the Buckmans cut back and reduced their household staff. It was no longer necessary since Chase was older, to have so many attendants. Mr. Boston Buckman, a partner in the law firm of Murphy & Arbuckle was ostentatious and a workaholic, known to his partners as "King Rainmaker." After becoming a Congressman he received no compensation for legal services. Mr. Buckman seemed charming and the perfect husband, but was known to many as a womanizer in the legal arena. The illustrious Mrs. Pamela Buckman was engaged in a multitude of discrimination lawsuits. Neither of them had time to raise Chase properly, instead, he was left to fend for himself in terms of everyday living. Chase knew right from wrong, but immensely enjoyed antagonizing people to gain attention. He didn't need much grooming when it came to attire protocol and general etiquette. Extremely intelligent, Chase suffered from huge emotional outbursts, tantrums, really, and playing practical jokes.

Tracey pulled into the flagstone circular driveway of the colonial mini-mansion and walked to the front door. Zack rang the doorbell, while Tracey stood there looking straight ahead. The door opened and they were greeted by a woman who was the spitting image of Audrey Hepburn.

"Mrs. Buckman, I presume?" Tracey asked as she looked past them at their vehicle.

"Yes, that's me, how can I help you?"

"We're Detectives Tracey Sanders and Zack Grimes." Tracey stated as he showed Mrs. Buckman his badge before putting it back in his back pocket.

Mrs. Buckman was a woman with long even cut brunette hair standing 5'6" tall. She was conservatively dressed in a white blouse neatly tucked into her black slim pants wearing a pair of glaring black and white patent loafers.

She looked at them inquisitively as she said, "Okay," she said hesitantly. "What's going on? Does this have anything to do with Calvin House? My husband and I just walked in the door."

"Yes," remarked Tracey. "I'm afraid it does."

"May we come in? We have a few questions we need to ask," Tracey asked.

"Yes, of course. Please come in. What's this all about anyway?" Mrs. Buckman asked as she led them into the living room and motioned for them to have a seat. "Can I get you anything? Would you like some coffee, tea, or some water?"

"No, thank you," Tracey and Zack replied simultaneously.

"So what did you say the reason is for this visit?" she asked as she took a seat in one of the chairs across from the detectives.

"Actually, we haven't yet answered that question of the day ourselves. We are here to discuss Jaime Herrera. Did you know him?"

"Yes, of course I did. He has been Chase's roommate since school started. What happened?"

"We don't know exactly, except that Jaime Herrera is dead. We need to ask you a few questions, if possible," replied Zack.

"We're exhausted from our trip and traumatized by all of this; can we do this some other time?" the woman pleaded.

"Ma'am, everyone is traumatized and we understand it has been a long weekend for you however, we still need to speak with you about the situation."

Pamela sat looking at Tracey waiting for him to ask her what he wanted to ask. She fumbled with the arm of the chair she was sitting in, clearly somewhat nervous about their presence.

"Can you tell us when you left for your trip?" inquired Tracey.

She cleared her throat before speaking. "We left Thursday around 3:30 p.m.; maybe 4:00 p.m." replied Pamela.

As Zack penciled down some notes in his notebook, Pamela continued looking at the detectives intensely. She let out a sigh before making a statement.

"Look, Detective Sanders, Chase was not even at the school last weekend! He was with us. We took him on a weekend trip to Carmel. My husband was a keynote speaker at a conference. With my husband and I both being lawyers, it makes it hard for us to get away as a family. We took the conference as an opportunity to get away from here and spend some time together."

"We're aware of the trip." Tracey said and then continued. "Did Chase and Jaime get along? The reason I ask is that both boys were seen recently arguing in the schoolyard."

"They got along so-so, I guess, but they weren't exactly close. I know Chase said on occasion that the roommate was pretty sloppy.

Chase is pretty meticulous with his hygiene and lifestyle. He gets that from his dad. Me, I'm more loosey-goosey."

She paused, then added: "The headmaster..." she paused again, momentarily lost in thought.

"Forbes Madden?" Zack prompted.

"Yes. The Headmaster doesn't particularly care for Chase or Jaime. Although they are both smart, they like pestering him."

"Pestering?" Tracey echoed back.

"Playing jokes—at least Chase likes to do that. Jaime was different."

"What do you mean Jaime was different? And what kind of jokes did they play on Mr. Madden?"

"Detective Sanders! Again, must we do this now? It's been a long weekend, I'm in shock over the news and I haven't even spoken to Chase since I dropped him off at the school last night," Mrs. Buckman clearly wanted to bolt from this inquisition.

"Yes, we do have to do this now. We can't do it later. Your son and Jaime shared a room. Jaime was found dead the morning after you all left on a trip and I need some answers. Your son and the deceased were in an argument, witnessed by more than a few kids, wherein your son threatened to kill his roommate. This line of questioning is rather important, so bear with us, please." Tracey gave Pamela minute and then repeated his question, "Mrs. Buckman, can you please explain to me what you meant by Jaime was different when it came to pestering Mr. Madden? What did the jokes consist of?"

"Jaime was mean-spirited. He was a provoker and always angry."

Just as Tracey finished re-asking the question, a tall man standing 6'3" with slightly grayed hair walked into the living room wearing beige pants and a black *Izod* shirt. Boston Buckman had been just down the hall in his office finishing up a phone call for work but overheard the detectives when they first arrived and introduced themselves to his wife.

"Good afternoon Detectives! I'm Chase's father, Boston Buckman."

Simultaneously Tracey and Zack responded, "Hello, sir."

"We'd like to ask you a few questions, if you don't mind?" Tracey said.

"Sure, how can I help you? I overheard this has to do with the death of Jaime Herrera?"

"Yes, actually it does. Did you know Jaime Herrera well?" Zack offered.

"As well as could be expected. We rarely saw him when we picked up Chase. Seems he was always busy with other activities or not around when we were there," Buckman responded dryly.

"Did you see Jaime when you picked up Chase on Thursday?"

"Nope. As usual, he wasn't there."

"When was the last time you saw Jaime?" Zack asked without looking away from his notebook.

"One week ago, maybe. Could have been longer than that. I can't really say for sure. Gentleman, I'm afraid I have an appointment that I need to get to so we are going to have to be done with the questioning for now. If you have further questions later in your investigation, please call me or my wife at our office. Until then, we'd appreciate it if you could be on your way so we are not late for our prior commitment," said Mr. Buckman, escorting them to the front door.

Zack shrugged his shoulders and looked at Mr. Buckman. "Sir, we're not done yet. We'd like to ask you a few more questions."

"I'm sorry but I have an appointment and my wife and I just got home from a road trip and we're exhausted. We both have to prepare for work tomorrow."

Zack and Tracey made their way to the front door disgusted with the way that Mr. Buckman cut off their questioning and resolved to look more into the possible connection between the Buckman family and Jaime's death.

They left the residence and drove in silence until Tracey broke it.

"Wow! That was intense!" remarked Tracey.

"Yeah, man. Weird."

"He's a lawyer and has a habit of being a bastard. I'm surprised he cut us off so quickly and didn't want to answer our questions. Hopefully our investigation won't come back to them being involved but, I am starting to wonder!"

"I'm having doubts, too," Zack agreed. "Something stinks."

"Amen to that," Tracey nodded.

***

Tuesday – 8:00 a.m.

As Tuesday rolled around, a caravan of news vans and paparazzi lined the street outside the main gate of Calvin House. Flash flurries from cameras blinded Tracey and Zack as they emerged from their sedan and entered the administration building. They heard their own hard footsteps echo as they approached Forbes' office. Hearing them, Forbes lifted his head from the paperwork on his desk, removed his black-rimmed glasses and stared down the long hallway, taking in the view of the approaching detectives.

"Detectives."

"Mr. Madden."

"I gather you noticed the media camped out in front of the school?" inquired Forbes.

"Yeah, we noticed. It looks like the media is pretty focused on Calvin House. With Wendall Dobbs being the second student in a week gone missing, I suppose they think that it is a bit newsworthy," Tracey said as he strolled into Forbes' office and took a seat.

Forbes sat back in his chair and clasped his hands.

"What's this about this time?"

"DNA test pursuant to a court order," Tracey explained.

"For which student, if I may ask?"

"Chase Buckman."

"So you actually think he had something to do with this?"

"The apple juice that was found on the nightstand between the beds in his bedroom tested positive for cyanide. The lab was able to collect DNA off of the juice box so we need to see if it matches that of Chase," replied Zack.

"And there was the fight between the two boys last week," Tracey added as an obvious analog.

"Before you can do anything, I need to contact Mr. and Mrs. Buckman since Chase is a minor."

"We've already called them. They're on their way here. We'll drive Chase to the lab with his parents following us," Tracey stated, noting that Forbes was visibly agitated. The latter rubbed his fingers through his hair, as beads of sweat dotted his forehead. He was clearly in total shock by this latest revelation.

"He's a good kid and just likes to play practical jokes. Can't you wait until—"

"We're not arresting Chase. We just need to get a DNA sample for now," Tracey said.

Forbes nodded and sighed. "Okay. I'll get him for you. I think he's in the study hall."

"Not so fast," Tracey said. "We'll need another individual's DNA as well."

"Seriously? And whose DNA do you need aside from Chase?" Forbes asked with a bit of edge to his voice.

"Yours, sir," Tracey said softly.

"Me? You're kidding, right?" Forbes said, standing.

"No. We're not," Tracey said. "I told you that your position in this case is sketchy at best."

Forbes glanced over at his grandmother's leather-bound book lying on his desk. His face turned red, and the perspiration on his forehead was now palpably noticeable.

"Mr. Madden, are you all right?" Zack asked.

"No, I'm not all right. I'm in shock. I just can't believe you think—"

"It's routine, Mr. Madden," Tracey said casually. "Don't be unduly alarmed."

"Routine, huh? What the hell is routine about having the Headmaster from a school submit to a DNA test for a murder?"

"Forbes, don't make this more difficult than it has to be," Tracey said. "From talking to the few students thus far, it is pretty clear to the two of us that there was no love lost between you and Jaime Herrera. Now, you can either cause a scene and make more out of this than necessary or you can do what needs to be done to determine who had a part in Jaime Herrera's death."

Forbes frowned, then picked up his phone and dialed Brolin's number. He was sitting behind his desk not making eye contact with the detectives. "Brolin, can you bring Chase Buckman to my office immediately?"

"Sure. What's going on?" Brolin asked.

"You don't want to know," Forbes said wearily.

"Well, no, I kinda do want to know," Brolin replied petulantly.

"Just bring him to me," Forbes angrily stated. Then a bit less harshly said, "Thanks, Brolin."

Within five minutes, both Chase and Brolin arrived to the office.

"What's this about?" Brolin inquired.

"We need Chase and Mr. Madden to come with us," Zack explained.

"Where?" Chase asked confused as to why he was being required to go anywhere with the detectives.

"Mortimer Lab. We're going to need to get a Buccal DNA Collection from each of you," Tracey explained.

"Buccal. What is that?" Chase asked suspiciously.

"It's a way to obtain cell information from your cheek," Brolin said. "That's the simple version, anyway. It's a kinda smear test, won't hurt at all."

"Brolin," Forbes stated as he stood from his desk preparing to leave, "please keep an eye on things until I return."

"Sure," Brolin said, clearly confused.

"I'm not going anywhere with you assholes!" Chase cried.

He leaped toward the door but Brolin grabbed him and held him tight. Tears rolling down his cheeks, Chase fell to his knees. Brolin helped him back up to his feet as The Buckmans entered the office. Boston gave the detectives a look of disgust as he walked over to his son.

"Son, I know you didn't do this but it sounds like they need you to go to the lab to make that more clear. Now, I suggest you walk to the sedan and do as the detectives ask to make it easier on you and them."

Chase looked at his father with tears in his eyes. Brolin escorted him to the detective's sedan parked in the circular drive entrance. Forbes followed behind them.

Boston and Pamela got in their vehicle, as Tracey followed them with a weary gaze.

Somehow he had the feeling things were going to get ugly fast around here in the next few days.

Unfortunately, Tracey would be proven correct on his hunch.

***

At Mortimer Lab, Forbes and Chase completed database collection cards and waited patiently until they were called into an examination room.

Chase stared at Forbes with disdain. "This is your fault. I shouldn't even be here. I'm innocent. You're just—"

Chase's mother reached over and touched his arm "Chase, calm down. This will be over soon." Chase leaned over with his elbows on his legs and put his head in his hands as his mother rubbed his back.

"I don't believe that, mom," Chase said dismally. "Jaime is dead and they're gonna try to pin his murder on me."

"No, they won't, dear," Pamela said softly.

"Just watch," Chase said. "You'll see."

***

Tuesday – 8:00 p.m.

Tracey was tired. Longing for a hot shower and the sweet caress of his fiancé, he phoned Harianne.

"Hey, baby. How are you?"

"Are you on your way home?" Harianne inquired.

"Not yet. I am waiting for DNA results. Hoping they will be done soon so I can come home."

"Whose DNA? I take it that means you have some sort of a lead on your investigation?"

"Forbes Madden and Chase Buckman. Hoping it will lead to something."

"Do you think they killed Jaime?"

"I think they had motive but I could be wrong," Tracey admitted. "I'm more concerned and moved by the fact that Jaime and this Buckman kid were actually in a fight."

"Yeah, that is kinda ominous. Oh, by the way, I was thinking today and I realized something that I should probably tell you later."

"What is it? Why can't you just tell me now?" Tracey pressed.

"Forbes Madden," Harianne paused, "I know him," she stated hesitantly.

"You're kidding. How do you know Forbes?"

"No, I'm not kidding. I met him at an event I attended a year or so ago."

"Wow, small world. Well…so, is there anybody else that you know at the school?" Tracey said.

Harianne laughed. "No, baby. Don't worry I haven't been nosing around on your case. Just happens to be that I know one of the main players you are dealing with."

Tracey was glad that he could get a laugh out of Harianne and it helped to relieve a bit of his stress as well. "I was only joking anyway. Better get off the phone for now. I'll call when I'm in the car."

Across the hall, Zack was craving a snack, but restrained himself from going near the kitchen. Instead, he phoned Eve. After hanging up with his wife, he stretched out on the black suede sofa in his office; he fell asleep within minutes.

But his nap was far from restful.

The image of the dead boy Jaime Herrera haunted his one and only dream.

***

Tuesday – 11:00 p.m.

Tracey walked over to Zack's office and knocked on the office door.

"Zack! Wake-up! The lab results are in!" Tracey said, his voice raised. He then turned around and headed back to his office.

Zack, startled by Tracey's knocking, roused himself to an upright position. He quickly realized where he was, snapped out of his sleep and jumped up and ran across the hall to Tracey's office, where they listened intently to the pathologist.

"The DNA of Chase Buckman and Forbes Madden appear to have a high number of matches."

"What do you mean by matches? Can you explain as simply as possible."

"The overall homologies are very close to Chase Buckman's. The probability of having another individual with this molecular profile and/or genotype is one in literally billions. Is that good enough for you?"

Tracey raised his eyebrows. "No kidding? Please, continue."

"There are very high conserved similar sequences in the genotypes of Forbes Madden and Chase Buckman. Some laboratories will state that identity has been demonstrated and an analyst can confidently report that a biological specimen originated only from a specific individual."

"So, with that information, who killed Jaime Herrera?" Zack asked as he tried to process the information they were just given.

"Good question. And one that I can't answer."

Chapter Eight

Wednesday – 10:00 a.m.

It was a bright sunny day as two black stretch limousines pulled up behind a black-and-silver hearse parked in front of the Cathedral of Our Lady of the Angels in downtown Los Angeles. Calvin House faculty, students and parents inched their way into the church for the funeral of Jaime Herrera. Everyone was given a little brass key, representing the key to the door of heaven. In lieu of flowers, the Herrera family had requested donations to Violent Crimes Against Kids, but the church was covered with roses, lilies, carnations and a plethora of other arrangements. Classmates wept and sobbed as parents comforted them; some clung tightly to one another.

Tracey and Zack entered the cathedral and sat in the last row.

"Tracey," Zack whispered, "we've got to find out who killed this boy."

"It's puzzling. What's the motive for his murder?" Tracey whispered back.

"Yeah, that is something that has kept me up at night. I just can't figure it out," Zack expressed as he observed the students and parents throughout the church.

"I know, I've lost sleep over this one. Don't worry, we will figure it out. We just have to keep digging. Not just for Jaime but for Wendall now, too."

The service commenced with an organist playing Ave Maria. Jaime's parents sobbed the entire time. As Jose Herrera walked toward the casket, holding a white handkerchief, his hand shook noticeably. Yolanda Herrera reached out and gently clasped his hand in her own.

"That's a shame this boy was murdered. I'm sick just seeing the look on his mother's face," said Tracey.

"It tears me up, too. We've got to find this perp," replied Zack.

"No kidding, pardner," Tracey said quietly.

***

Wednesday – 12:30 p.m.

Chelsea Timberlin, owner of the New York-based Jules Kate handbag line, was a vivacious and sophisticated woman whose family owned several fashion magazines and reaped tremendous financial gains from their share of holdings in Dolce & Gabbana. Sweetly spoiled but responsible, she lived with her fiancé, hedge-fund guru, Lincoln Madden, in the SoHo neighborhood of Lower Manhattan. She's proven to be a no-nonsense businesswoman at the bargaining table, and in the boardroom.

Chelsea unsaddled herself from her horse at the lavish acres Mashomack Polo Club in Pine Plains. She desperately needed a shower. While she walked toward the club's spa, she phoned Lincoln on her cell.

"Hey, babe!"

"Hi, sweetness."

"Have you eaten lunch yet?"

"No. I can't eat right now."

"Why not, babe? What's going on now?"

"This economy depresses me. I don't feel like eating."

"Stop! It'll get better. It takes time. At least that's what the experts say."

"Chelsea, I'm losing money fast on these hedge funds."

"Don't worry. I'll support you." She laughed trying to make light of the situation and hoping to get Lincoln to relax.

"No way. I need to make this all work. Some way, somehow," Lincoln stated, making it clear that he wasn't about to let his fiancé worry about their finances.

"Have you called Forbes yet? Were you able to talk to him to let him know what's going on?"

"No. I don't have it in my heart to tell him."

"Lincoln! You've got to talk to him. He's your brother and might be the closest match. If no one else is a match, he's your only hope."

Lincoln sighed in response.

"Cheer up! I'm just finishing up here and will be heading home soon. I think you should give Forbes a call. You will feel better once you do."

"Yeah, you're probably right. Drive safe on your way home and I will see you later, sweetheart. Love you."

Lincoln Madden was the complete opposite of his older brother, Forbes: young, hip, stylish, and a magnet for women. Standing at six feet two inches tall on the hoof, he looked like the older brother. His closet was filled with stylish business suits and sweaters by Dolce & Gabbana, Prada, Calvin Klein and Sean John. He swam and played squash at the New York Athletic Club daily. During the summer months, his boat, *Monday Sparkles*, moored at the New York Yacht Club in Newport, Rhode Island, left the boat slip and headed out for day-long excursions.

Lincoln also had a tough, cunning edge to his personality. Many investors characterized him as savvy and ruthless. Everyone knew his hobby was money. Yet he lived by the motto: *Money, greed and power cannot buy happiness. Or health.*

Lincoln had heard Chelsea loud and clear. It was time. He picked up his cell and phoned Forbes.

"Hey, bro, what's going on?"

"Lincoln—what a surprise!" Forbes exclaimed, clearly excited to hear his brother's voice on the other end of the phone.

"I know, I know. I've been traveling lots and this economy is killing me. I finally had a free moment so I thought I would give you a call. See how you have been and what you have been up to," Lincoln said as he eased into the conversation since it had been some time since he'd talked to his brother.

"What's wrong, Lincoln? I can hear it in your voice."

"Nothing is wrong. Well...ok...I take that back. You know me better than I thought, even after not having talked for so long."

"Well enough. Is it Chelsea?"

"No. She's fine and I mean fine, literally."

"All right. Enough, man. What's going on?"

"I've had some doctor appointments and some blood tests run. It's nothing."

"That somehow doesn't sound good, Lincoln. What is really going on with you?"

"I have some kidney problems. Probably not drinking enough water."

"Huh! What does that mean?"

"They're doing tests on my kidneys."

"Um, if they are doing tests on your kidneys, it is more than not drinking enough water. What's really going on? Will you need a new kidney?"

"Hey! Hey! Don't you go worrying about me. They don't know yet. I'll stay in touch and let you know what the final analysis will be."

Forbes' stomach felt like it had suddenly plummeted to his feet. Just the thought of something happening to Lincoln made him sick.

"What's going on out there?"

"You don't even want to know. It has been a super crazy week. We had, what appears to be, a murder at the school last Thursday evening and another student has gone missing. I tried phoning you, but your voice mail was full. I didn't want to email you."

"A murder! Are you serious? Forbes, why didn't you try harder to get a hold of me? Who was murdered? And what do you mean a student is missing?"

"A student, Jaime Herrera, was found dead. He was a troublesome kid. As for the other missing student, well, we have no idea where he's gone. There is no sign of him anywhere."

"Wow! I'm sorry to hear that, Forbes. How are you doing? Are you dealing with it all okay? Do you need anything from me?"

"Yeah, I've got a lot going on out here in L.A. I'm handling it all as well as can be expected. Not sure what I would need from you but I wanted to let you know about it for sure. Thanks for offering."

"Well, that is what brothers are for. Seriously, let me know if there is anything I can do to help out," Lincoln said as silence overcame the conversation. "Hey, listen, Forbes, I've got a meeting in fifteen minutes that I need to prepare for. Can we talk again soon? I hate to leave you hanging but the meeting is important."

"No worries, I understand. Yeah, stay in touch and take care of yourself."

"OK, bro."

Lincoln hung up knowing full good and well that he hadn't told Forbes what was really happening and what Chelsea was suggesting. With all that was going on for Forbes, he just couldn't bring himself to tell him.

As the line went dead, Forbes started reading through papers on his desk. The phone rang startling him slightly. He pushed the papers aside and answered the phone.

"Forbes Madden."

"Mr. Madden! This is Boston Buckman. Chase's father."

"Of course, Mr. Buckman, I know who you are. How can I help you?"

"Well, you know I am cutting back on my law practice…"

Forbes immediately became disturbed by the conversation. In his eyes, Boston Buckman was a narcissistic, opportunistic attorney and negligent father who never had time for his son.

"Yes, I heard you're running for re-election to Congress," Forbes stated with an edge to his voice.

"Oh, you know. Then this will be easy. I know this is a bad time with my son and all, but I need an endorsement. I was wondering if —"

"Not right now, Mr. Buckman!" Forbes cut him off. "I actually thought you were calling about Chase. This is a difficult time for him, and for Calvin House."

"What do you mean this is a difficult time for Chase? From what I understand, nothing is wrong, my son was just questioned like every other student in the school. I'm concerned about Chase, of course—"

"Mr. Buckman, perhaps you should pay closer attention to what is going on. There *is* something wrong…a student was murdered and your son has been more than questioned. He had a DNA test as well."

"Of course his DNA is all over the room, he was Jaime's roommate. Would you expect anything different?"

"Mr. Buckman, it is more than just that. If you don't see that as a problem, you need to pull your head out of your ass. There will be no endorsements, Mr. Buckman." Forbes slammed down the phone without waiting to hear Boston's response. Forbes was furious. He sat at his desk with his head in his hands for several minutes trying to calm down.

As Forbes tried to relax, he kept thinking about his grandmother's diary that remained on the edge of his desk from the last time he'd looked at it. Suddenly, anxious to read the diary, he leaned back in his chair and opened the black leather-bound book. He continued to read the words his grandmother had written within the pages of the diary.

Once dinner was finished, I called Brinks and Frank to come eat. Frank was as hungry as I had ever seen him and practically grabbed two helpings of food at one time. Shortly after sitting down to eat there were three loud knocks on the front door. The sound of the knocks startled all three of us.

Brinks, after looking at the two of us briefly, got up from the table and walked over to the door and opened it. On the other side of the door were two men dressed in black suits with matching black wool hats. Frank and I just sat at the table and stared at the men. We had no idea what was going on. The men identified themselves as homicide detectives. They asked Brinks if he was Brinks Madden. Brinks confirmed that he was indeed Brinks Madden.

Forbes closed the book abruptly. He had a sinking sensation in the pit of his stomach that to read further would be to entertain some kind of certain madness. Perhaps another time he could endure more, but for today—and until the murder of Jaime Herrera was resolved—Forbes Madden would not delve further into his grandmother's past. Not today.

Not now.

Chapter Nine

Wendall Dobbs awakened to a dark room, black as the pit from pole to pole. The small brass lamp, sitting atop the wood table in the corner of the room, cast a dim yellow ambient light, making it hard to see anything in any great detail. He was groggy, with blood smeared on both of his arms. His hands wrapped in white latex gloves tied to the back of a chair with a piece of straw rope, began to perspire and itch. He couldn't muster the strength to untie the rope; in fact, he had little strength to do anything short of blinking his eyes.

He turned his head in response to whispers he could hear from an adjacent room. The voices were so faint that he couldn't make out anything from the conversation. Wendall heard his every breath as his chest moved up and down with consistent rhythm; he feared it might stop suddenly in response to his frequent panic attacks, but he continued to breathe as his eyes came into focus.

Across the room, a heavy metal door with a large brass handle slowly opened; beyond it stood what appeared to be a large bank vault. A tall man in a dark, long-tailed suit, with a hood covering his head and a black mask covering his face, stood quietly in the doorway. Suddenly he walked toward Wendall, a chain at his waist clanging against his belt buckle as he moved.

Wendall squirmed nervously in his chair. Beads of sweat rolled down his face as each breath came and went with uneven rapidity. Fearful of who was approaching, he closed his eyes tightly. The man grabbed Wendall's hair in a tight grip and forced his head backwards while pouring liquid down his throat. Wendall gasped and coughed spitting up some of it. Wendall had no idea what he swallowed. His body suddenly jerked spasmodically and then devolved into convulsions. At last, the struggle for life ceased and Wendall moved no more.

The man picked the boy up and threw his limp body over his shoulder and returned to the vault.

***

Thursday – 7:00 a.m.

Tracey arrived at the precinct feeling irritable and tired. He grabbed his regular mug, filled it to the top with freshly brewed coffee and waited for Zack's arrival. To kill time, Tracey read thoroughly through the DNA report.

About thirty minutes later, Zack trudged into Tracey's office, coffee cup in one hand. He stood over Tracey's desk looking at the reports his partner was sifting through. "Well, looks like you've had some time to review everything. Hoping that means you know what we're doing from here on."

Tracey looked up at Zack setting the report to the side on his desk. "Jesus, Zack, you look awful! What happened to you last night?"

"Well, the woman wore me out when I got home," Zack said with a shrug and a grin. "Man! Did I get it last night!"

"Spare me the details, Zack. I don't have time to listen to your priapic antics. We've got a decision to make."

"Like I said, I was hoping you already made such a decision. I say arrest both of them," he stated unequivocally as he sipped his coffee.

"Funny, Zack. Not an option."

Tracey scratched his head, pulled his chair closer to his desk and read the DNA findings again.

"Forbes' DNA is so close. It just can't be. Forbes was there at the school the entire time. He had motive, but we've got no concrete evidence to arrest him for murder," Tracey stated as he turned a few more pages of the report.

"Chase shared the room with Jaime and his fingerprints were on the apple juice box. We're not sure if they really got along with each other or not. His DNA is even closer, but it's similar to Forbes'," remarked Zack.

"That is what's got me so bothered. The DNA for Chase and Forbes is nearly identical. The only evidence we have is from the fingerprints on the juice box that contained the cyanide. And those prints belong to…"

"Chase…" Zack finished the sentence for Tracey then turned, scratched his head and sat down in the chair across from Tracey. "We should arrest Chase Buckman. Probable cause, based on the evidence. What do you think, Tracey?"

"My final answer: Chase Buckman. Chase could have put the cyanide in the apple juice before he left for the trip with his parents," Tracey said ruefully.

He picked up some other papers from his desk. "So, I called the phone company to check on Jaime's phone. They said it can't be traced because there is no signal to it. The last call was made a day before he took off with his parents."

"That seems to be a dead-end then. What about Wendall's phone? Did you find anything out there? Every time I've tried to call, it goes to voicemail."

"Same thing, no signal going to the phone. Seems the phones are dead-end clues. Come on, let's go to Calvin House."

"Why?"

"To see if we can satisfactorily arrest a viable suspect," Tracey said. "That would make my day."

***

Thursday — 9:00 a.m.

Tracey and Zack arrived at the Calvin House campus to find some students between classes: a few boys studied underneath a tree while another group sat off to the side under the pergola and played dominos, while others played basketball. Tracey was reminded of his childhood so very long ago. The thought momentarily depressed him—he was getting older and there was no getting around mortality.

In the administration building, Tracey and Zack took off their sunglasses as they approached Forbes Madden's assistant.

"Hi, Balian. Do you remember meeting us earlier?" Tracey asked as Balian nodded in acknowledgement. "We are the detectives investigating the Jaime Herrera murder. We need to speak with Mr. Madden. Is he available?"

"Of course I remember you gentlemen. Forbes is in his office. Let me tell him you're here."

Balian knocked and then opened the door to Forbes' office. Forbes lifted his head from his desk where he had been napping, and motioned with his hand, inviting Tracey and Zack inside. Clearing papers from his desk with one hand, he leaned forward and looked to the two detectives.

"Another good morning to the two of you. What's going on now?" he asked, the exhaustion from the past days' events marring his face with bags under his eyes and wrinkles around his mouth.

"Well Tracey paused. "The DNA results are back. We have read and re-read the results trying to make heads or tails out of it. The analyses tell us that your DNA and the DNA of Chase Buckman are identical."

"Identical? What do you mean identical? How's that even possible if we are not remotely related by blood?"

"We're not quite sure, but the results from the tests show the DNA profile is close. Additionally, forensics found cyanide in the apple juice box that we collected as evidence from Jaime's nightstand," Tracey shrugged.

"Cyanide? In the apple juice?" Forbes asked incredulously. "Where did that come from?"

"That is one of the questions we are asking as well. Maybe a science class?" Zack suggested.

"Where can we find Chase?" Tracey asked.

"He's in class. The period ends shortly. What makes you think Chase is a truly viable suspect?"

"His fingerprints were on the apple juice box. Period, end of story."

"And you think that Jaime's prints weren't on there, too?"

"Well, of course they were, Headmaster. Jaime is the victim in this scenario. Thus, although his prints are on the box, we can't arrest him for murdering himself."

Forbes tried to compose himself. Turning to the side of his desk, he picked up the phone and dialed Brolin.

"Chapman," Brolin answered his phone.

"Brolin, do you know what class Chase Buckman is in currently?"

"Yeah, he's in English. Why? What's wrong?"

"The detectives handling this case are back. They need to speak with Chase again."

"Are you serious? What does he have to do with all this?" Brolin's voice could be heard by Tracey and Zack as the man was fairly yelling from the other end of the line.

"Brolin," Forbes said clearly frustrated with all of the questions. "Just get him for me, please."

"Of course, I'll get him. Do you want me to bring him to your office?"

"Yes, please. Make it as discreet as possible so everyone doesn't start talking," Forbes urged.

"Right," Brolin said and abruptly hung up.

Forbes turned to face Tracey and Zack. "Brolin is on his way to get Chase. I assume you plan on arresting Chase? If that is the case, I would prefer that you don't handcuff him in front of all his peers."

"It's standard procedure, Mr. Madden, but we can bring the car around to the back of the school," Tracey offered.

"Please! Save us all of the embarrassment." Forbes sighed in response then leaned back in his chair and closed his eyes for a few moments.

In the meantime, Tracey and Zack, flipped through the Calvin House newsletter. Neither knew what it was like to attend a private school, but reading about the football team wins, dances and scholastic achievements allowed them to at least dream and imagine the life of a wealthy child. Not every child at Calvin House was wealthy and they knew that but they also knew that the students at Calvin House were presented with opportunities that students at other schools were not afforded.

Brolin arrived at the office with Chase five minutes later. Forbes sized Chase up then sighed.

"Hello, Chase," Tracey greeted the youth. "What's going on?"

"You tell me," Chase replied churlishly.

"You're under arrest for the murder of Jaime Herrera," Tracey said without preamble.

"What? Did you call my parents?" Chase asked as his face turned white.

"Yes. My partner is phoning your parents as we speak."

Chase lowered his head in despair and cried aloud as Tracey began to read him his rights.

"You have the right to remain silent. Anything you say can and will be used against you in a court of law. You have the right to have an attorney present. If you cannot afford an attorney, one will be provided for you."

Forbes and Brolin stood side by side as Tracey and Zack escorted Chase out of the administration building. Just before Chase ducked into the sheriff sedan, he turned his head and took one last look at them. Forbes knew that look, the look that said: How could this happen and why me? What's coming next?

A few students ran to get a glimpse of the black sedan with tinted windows as it pulled away, but it quickly reached the end of the school's long driveway, and then it was gone.

Chapter Ten

About an hour after Chase's arrest, the Buckmans returned to their house. Boston went straight to his office located adjacent to the living room and poured himself a scotch from the bar. With hope of the alcohol calming his nerves, he nestled into the leather chair by the window with his cell phone in one hand and the scotch in the other.

Boston called all of his friends in the highest of echelons of business: contacts at the city, contacts at the county, colleagues at major law firms who owed him favors. Just as he swiped his phone to make yet another call, it rang. He looked at the number on the display and frowned.

"Hello, this is Boston."

"Hello, Mr. Buckman, this is Forbes Madden."

"Yeah, what do you want?" Mr. Buckman replied angrily.

"Listen, Mr. Buckman, I care deeply about Chase's welfare. I've been thinking about Chase ever since the detectives showed up here at the school. I don't think that he could have had anything to do with the murder and I wanted you to know that and that I'm here to help."

"Help? How do you think you can help, Mr. Madden? My son has been arrested for the murder of his roommate, for crying out loud. As the headmaster of the school, you should have never allowed any of this to happen." Forbes could hear the anger in Boston's voice and he understood where he was coming from.

"Look, I am not calling so that you can be an ass to me. I am calling because I have a friend that is a fantastic criminal attorney. Not only that, she cares."

"Really?" Boston took a drink trying to register what Forbes was saying and trying to calm himself down. "So, what's her record like? I want someone who is going to be able to do the job that needs to be done. I don't need some ambulance chaser for this situation."

"I understand, sir and I wouldn't be calling if I didn't think she could help. She has a winning record: only two convictions overturned during her twenty-year career as a criminal attorney. She was the most sought-after criminal attorney in Los Angeles County. A woman charged with drug trafficking, sales and transportation—all charges were dropped and a deal was cut for three years' probation. Harianne gives eloquent opening statements and brilliant closing arguments in trial."

"Harianne DeCanter?" Boston said.

"Correct," Forbes said, mildly surprised that Boston would have heard of her.

"I know this woman. Not personally, but by reputation. Very well. She sounds like just the person I should probably be calling if she's that good."

"Yes, I promise you, she is that good."

"Ok, you've got me sold."

"Hold on while I find her number for you." Forbes said as he was flipping through his phone and address book that he had in his desk. "I really need to update my outlook contacts instead of flipping through this old fashion address book. Oh wait, here it is. Are you ready with pen and paper?"

"Ready when you are."

"This is her cell 310-555-0102. She can sometimes be hard to reach. Leave her a message if you get her voicemail. She'll call ya back."

The other end of the line was quiet for a while then Boston finally spoke. "Thanks, Mr. Madden. I guess I should have listened to you earlier about the seriousness of all of this."

"Give Harianne a call. Hopefully she can help."

Forbes didn't say goodbye nor did he wait for Boston to reply. He hung up the phone without ceremony.

Boston Buckman may be a grieving father with an attitude and Forbes could be sympathetic.

But nothing in the rule book could force him to like the man.

***

Thursday – 2:30 p.m.

Pamela Buckman pulled at her hair with one hand and held a Kleenex to her eyes and nose with the other. She walked into the den, gently closed the door until she heard the lock engage, and then phoned the sheriff station.

"This is Pamela Buckman. My son, Chase Buckman, was brought to the station about an hour ago. May I speak to him?"

"Hold on, Ma'am," replied the operator.

There was a long pause as she listened to music that was half static on the other end of the line. She remained patient, tapping her fingers on the table beside her, wiping her eyes with a Kleenex as the tears rolled down her cheeks. All she could think about was her son being behind bars with murderers and rapists and what not and how bad it had to be for him.

Pretty soon the music stopped and Chase's voice tuned in. "Hi, Mom!"

"Hello baby! Are you okay?"

"Mom. I'm alright. It's kind of scary in here with some really creepy guys around but I'm okay. Just get me out of here. They're accusing me of killing Jaime." Pamela could hear Chase's voice shake as he spoke. He was obviously scared and she knew she had to do what she could to keep him calm.

"Trust me, this will be over soon, Chase. Your father is doing everything he can to help you. We aren't going to let you be there any longer than you have to be."

"Thanks for being there for me. Mom…" Chase's voice trailed off.

"Yes son, what is it?"

"I love you, Mom. I just want you to know that."

New tears flowed from Pamela's eyes. "I love you, too, Chase. Stay strong. We will work through all of this. Your father has been on the phone all day and there will be a lawyer by the name of Harianne DeCanter in to meet with you soon. Give her whatever she needs," Pamela urged. "We're told she's the best in town for a case such as yours."

"She'd better be." Chase said. "Or I'm a dead man."

***

Thursday — 11:30 p.m.

By the time Tracey got home it was nearly midnight and he couldn't wait to see Harianne. He ascended the stairs and slowly opened the door. Harianne was waiting for him in a sexy, black negligee. She was carefully positioned in the middle of the bed with her legs wide open, anticipating Tracey's caress. Tracey lay down beside her, pulled her toward him and kissed her neck.

Harianne grabbed the tie from Tracey's shirt, and threw it to the floor. She slowly unbuttoned Tracey's shirt, one button at a time.

"Do you want a glass of wine first?" Tracey whispered.

"Just fuck me, baby," Harianne said. "That's what I need now."

Then she loosened his belt, unzipped his pants and grabbed his hard penis firmly with one hand and started rubbing it up and down slowly between her thighs and toward her moist vagina. She carefully placed his penis inside of her and let out a moan of commingled desire and pleasure.

They made love for an hour and Harianne finally fell asleep on Tracey's chest. They slept through the night dreamlessly.

***

Friday — 6:00 a.m.

Austria made a large pot of coffee and began preparing the batter for her Swedish pancakes. She set the kitchen table for two then poured herself a second cup of coffee.

Just as Austria lifted the last pancake off the griddle and stacked it with the rest on a plate beside the stove, Tracey and Harianne trundled into the kitchen. They headed straight toward the fresh brewed pot of coffee. Harianne poured the cups, while Tracey grabbed six pancakes, three each per plate, smothered them in maple syrup and dusted them with powdered sugar.

Harianne sighed in pleasure with each bite and sent Austria a thumbs-up. Tracey ate steadily, only taking a few sips of hot coffee.

"I don't want either of you to worry about the house. I'll babysit the silly contractors. They are worse than those fellas' in *Green Acres*! That used to be one of my favorite television shows." Austria snapped.

"*Green Acres*, Austria! You remember that; you're so funny," Harianne said.

"I really do remember that TV show. These contractors are just like those nitwits on that show."

"As for babysitting them, that's really not necessary, Austria," Harianne said. "We'll do it."

"When will you have the time? I know you, Harianne. I won't take 'No' for an answer."

Tracey rubbed Harianne's back and kissed her on the cheek; just being next to her brought out an irresistible urge to make love to her. He wanted more of her, but he had to get to the precinct.

"We'll let you deal with the contractors," Tracey assured Austria.

"But Tracey—," Harianne protested.

"Shush! No worries. I can handle the contractors," Austria said as she sipped her coffee. "Besides, the two of you are busy so there is no reason why you should be bothered with the construction work here if I can take care of it. Trust me, Harianne, I can handle these boys." Austria smirked at Harianne before heading to the sink to clean up the dishes from breakfast.

"Thanks, Austria. We'll leave it in your hands, then." Turning to Tracey Harianne said, "Oh, meant to tell ya…"

"Yeah, what is it?" Tracey said.

"I received a phone call last night," Harianne said. "For representation on a case you are working on."

Tracey was reluctant to hear what more she had to say about the call. He sensed Harianne knew about the arrest.

"What case?"

"Come on, Tracey, the biggest case you are working right now, the murder at Calvin house. You know, the one with Forbes Madden."

"Oh, right, what about it? Wait, we didn't arrest him."

"When were you going to tell me?"

"I wasn't. Well...I would have but, later. As in much later, because I know you have lots going on and I didn't think you would care to know or need to know. Guess I was off on those thoughts, huh?"

"Yeah, you were. And you're right, Forbes wasn't arrested but Chase Buckman was," Harianne stated, proving to Tracey that she definitely knew what was going on with his case.

Tracey continued to focus on his breakfast before him. He chewed nervously, nearly biting his lip. Tracey wasn't disturbed, just frustrated because this case was complicated.

"Honey, I'm confused," Tracey responded. "You mentioned days ago that you knew Forbes but I don't think you gave any details. Or if you did, I don't recall. Where is it you said you met him?"

"We met at a fundraiser for homeless boys on the Westside, at Shutters Hotel."

"Seems like a putz to me," replied Tracey sarcastically.

"Tracey, stop that! No, he's not. He's a very nice man, a gentleman. He's an educator." Harianne said defensively as she observed Tracey with a look of question on his face. "Honey, you know it's my job to defend people; it's my world. I thought we were a team?"

"I'm sorry, babe. I love you. Come here." Tracey took both of her arms and placed them around his waist.

"Forbes called me yesterday afternoon. He asked if he could pass my name on to the Buckmans and I would be willing to meet with them and possibly represent their son. Don't worry, I already know what you're thinking."

"Oh really? And what is it that I am thinking?" he asked teasingly.

"Here we go again, another case together," Harianne said, grinning right back at him.

"Yeah, well, I guess we better get used to working together once more," Tracey conceded.

"For some reason, I don't think that is going to be a problem for me. Oh, and just so you know, Mr. Buckman phoned me shortly after I spoke to Forbes. He has officially retained me. I've got a meeting with Chase Buckman this morning to prepare him for his arraignment."

"That's great. And I am not just saying that. Looks like we are together again."

Harianne owned a white 2009 Jaguar XF that she treasured. She needed to head downtown to meet Chase at the detention center and hated driving the Jag in the bumper-to-bumper traffic but Tracey assured her before she left that she shouldn't worry and it would be fine. She left the house taking the 101 Freeway to the 5 Freeway and arrived at the Central Juvenile Hall on Eastlake Avenue in downtown Los Angeles. Driving her Jaguar in the crazy traffic was something that she despised doing but she knew that she didn't have a choice. She knew she needed an economy car, but never got around to it and didn't take it seriously. The area near and around the detention center had trash scattered at the curbs. Harianne saw a number of homeless people pushing carts on both sides of the street, while stray cats and dogs roamed around looking for their next feast. The rotten food smell overwhelmed her when she opened her car door and exited her vehicle. The stench was so horrible that she had to actually work to keep from throwing up prior to getting into the building. The inside décor was simple: gray chairs sat up against the beige walls.

Harianne checked in at the desk and was escorted to a small room used for questioning where Chase was waiting for her. When she looked in the room, she could see a young man sitting at a small table dressed in an orange jumpsuit with his hands cuffed in front of him. He appeared to be uncomfortable in the jumpsuit and clearly the handcuffs weren't his favorite addition to his sartorial attire.

Harianne opened the door to the room, approaching Chase from behind and placed her hand on his shoulder.

"Hello, Chase! I'm Harianne DeCanter. Your parents have hired me to represent you."

"Yeah. I know who you are. My parents told me you would be coming to speak with me. I didn't have anything to do with Jaime's death. You know that, right?"

Harianne just looked at him not saying a word. She sat across from him, removed her iPhone, and retrieved the California *Penal Code* App, a legal pad, a red pen, a blue pen, a sharp pencil and a tin box full of winter mint Altoids. She brought her chair up closer to the dull wood table, straightened out the minimal wrinkles in her black wool skirt and leaned forward, looking Chase straight in the eye.

"You said you didn't do it? It seems the investigators have put together evidence to the contrary," she said evenly.

"I didn't do anything; they've got the wrong person," Chase burst out clearly upset that even the attorney his parents hired to represent him seemingly, on first blush, didn't believe that he was innocent.

"Several boys saw you and Jaime in a verbal altercation in the schoolyard," Harianne said. "You threatened to kill him."

"I was pissed at him," Chase said quickly. "He was a sloppy bastard and always left shit around the room, never cleaning up. I told him as much and he told me to go to hell. I pushed him. He pushed me back. And I blurted out I was gonna get him?"

"No, you specifically blurted out you were going to kill him," Harianne corrected."

"Whatever. I didn't mean it," Chase was almost sobbing. "I didn't kill him."

"Chase, I have seen cases like yours in the past and they usually don't play out well in the Juvenile Court. After the arraignment, the prosecutor could initiate a fitness hearing, but not when it involves murder. You understand that you are going to be tried as an adult, not as a juvenile, right?" Harianne stated looking questioningly at Chase for confirmation of his understanding.

Chase stared at her, his eyes blinking wearily. She went on to read out of her notebook to help him better understand. "Under the Welfare and Institutions Code 707(d)(2), the prosecutor can direct file against a minor, if—"

"Wait," Chase cut her off, "what does 'direct file' mean? This lawyer speak is way over my head. Help me understand."

"Direct file means the prosecutor can request that you be tried as an adult. Which I am pretty sure is what he is going to do. The code states that if the minor 'is 14 years of age or older and is alleged to have committed an offense which, if committed by an adult, is punishable by death or life imprisonment' then the minor can be tried as an adult. Since the offense is a murder with special circumstances, the prosecutor is alleging that you personally killed Jaime Herrera, and that means you are able to be tried as an adult."

"I didn't do it," Chase stated without any hesitation.

"Okay!" Harianne paused. "Chase, let me ask you a few questions if you don't mind?" Harianne said, getting a nod from Chase to ask away. "First of all, when was the last time you saw Jaime?"

"I left the school Thursday afternoon with my parents. I for sure saw him at lunch time but I may have seen him after that as well. I really can't say for sure."

"From what I understand, forensics found footprints near where Jaime's body was found. What kind of shoes do you wear, if you don't mind me asking?

"Ya know, I was looking for my shoes the other day but couldn't find them. I let Brolin know a week or more ago that I thought someone had stolen them." Chase said while Harianne gave him a dubious look.

"So if I talk to Brolin about it, he will tell me you reported your shoes missing?" Harianne asked.

"Yes, he should. I haven't been able to find my Converse tennis shoes for a few weeks now. They were black. I just figured one of the other guys at school took them which is why I reported it to Brolin."

"So, what else can you tell me?" Harianne asked.

"I don't know; you tell me," Chase retorted. "You're the expert here."

"Cut the sarcasm!" she said curtly. "If you are as innocent as you say, then we need to work together to make our case. I can't do that with the attitude you are directing toward me at the moment."

"I'm sorry but...well...I don't even know what happened to Jaime. How did I supposedly murder him? Can you tell me what happened to Jaime?"

"He died of cyanide poisoning."

"Of what? I don't even know what cyanide is much less how to poison someone with it."

"Apparently, they found cyanide in the apple juice they took from the nightstand beside his bed; he must have drank it. And your fingerprints were all over it."

The room suddenly became quiet. Chase lowered his head, staring down at his feet. When he returned his gaze to Harianne, she saw tears on his face; he clearly did not know what had happened to Jaime, and was in despair at the loss of his friend and roommate.

Harianne was puzzled. She was beginning to realize that this wasn't going to be as cut and dry as she'd first thought.

"My fingerprints may have been on the juice container because he kept it in our fridge and I probably moved it when I was getting something else out. I didn't poison my roommate," Chase stated without hesitation.

Harianne scribbled some notes on her note pad while Chase sat with his head in his hands in silence. After a few minutes, she asked Chase a few more questions about his relationship with Jaime and about school. She needed to get to know him better to help her make his case. Whether he was guilty or not didn't matter at this point. She was hired to represent him, and represent him was just what she planned to do.

"Chase, we need to talk about your arraignment."

"Okay. I'm telling you, Miss DeCanter—"

"Call me Harianne," she broke in.

"Harianne...I'm...scared." Chase hesitated, tears cascading down his face.

"I know you are, Chase. And you have every right to be. The charges being filed against you are quite serious. But, I am here to do what I do best." Harianne said holding his hand across the table.

"So, this arraignment, is it a hearing or what is it? I know nothing about courts and charges and what not. I haven't been to a court hearing previously so I have no idea what to expect," Chase said, clearing his throat in an effort to recover from his crying jag.

"Yes, it would be considered a hearing. It's a formal reading of a criminal charging document in the presence of the defendant of the charges against him or her. They will read through what you are being charged with and then you will make a plea of 'guilty' or 'not guilty.'"

Chase looked straight in Harianne's eyes and stated, "Not guilty is my plea."

"That's exactly what I wanted you to say. And with such conviction, good." Harianne smiled.

"So, exactly what are the charges against me?" Chase questioned.

Harianne looked at the documents in front of her and then up at Chase. "You are being charged with murder and possession of a weapon of mass destruction."

"I didn't kill Jaime," Chase reiterated.

"I hear what you are saying, Chase, but the evidence seems to be showing otherwise. Forensics ran tests on the apple juice box and your fingerprints were all over it. They also ran a DNA scan and it returned positively."

"What the hell is that supposed to mean?" Chase asked.

"Your DNA matched that of the DNA found on the apple juice box."

A look of bewilderment came across Chase's face.

"Is there anything else you can tell me now that might help me?" Harianne asked.

Chase only shook his head.

"Okay. So, now we wait. I'm sure a fitness hearing will happen. We'll prepare for that accordingly," Harianne said, standing.

"What am I supposed to do until then?" Chase asked.

"What else can you do, Chase?" Harianne asked. "Just stay well-behaved, wait—and pray."

Chase nodded. "Good advice, counselor."

Harianne reached out and squeezed his hand then turned and left the room.

Chapter Eleven

Friday – 10:00 a.m. – Manhattan, New York

Chelsea packed two Louis Vuitton bags with enough clothes for a weekend getaway to the Hamptons while Lincoln loaded his new white BMW 750i with a picnic basket chocked full of food. The lunch fare included two chicken Caesar salads, two apples, an assortment of cheeses, accompanied by a package of RyKrisp crackers and a bottle of Chateau Saint Michelle Cabernet Sauvignon wine. An exceptionally good year, Lincoln noted to himself.

Once everything was loaded in the car, the Lincoln and Chelsea departed for their mini-vacation. They drove for two hours and turned onto Gin Lane, the Hamptons' finest East End roadway. Georgian-style mansions and opulent estates bordered the road. The area screamed unbelievable wealth. They took time out for a half hour lunch, then once more hit the road to their final destination.

The drive had taken longer than expected with Chelsea stopping along the way to admire the majestic homes that littered the landscape. They finally arrived at their Sag Harbor Bayfront "cottage getaway"—in their opinion, a mini mansion—with two large decks facing Noyac Bay on seventy acres at the edge of Sag Harbor Village. It had been renovated by the previous owner and now had Lincoln and Chelsea's style consisting of a more modern décor, with metal name plaques over every room in the house. Chelsea loved the stylish kitchen with its white marble and white granite countertops that complemented the cherry wood cabinets.

As they unloaded the car, they took in the fresh ocean air. It wasn't like taking a vacation to Hawaii or Europe, but it was better than nothing with their demanding schedules. Sag Harbor was a short sojourn from New York City, and they relished the tranquility of the bay blessed with spectacular sunsets that captivated all who beheld them.

Lincoln felt Chelsea's excitement as she planned the meals and outings for the weekend. However, before they could fully immerse themselves in her plans, she wanted to hit the boutiques in town, perusing the selection of handbags by her competitors. She was determined to keep Jules Kate handbags as the frontrunner. A pair of Cesare Paciotti pumps called out to her from the window of Collette's, her favorite designer consignment store. Just down the road on Main Street, she visited another favorite outlet, Calypso St. Barth, which she considered the *Rolls Royce* boutique of designer-looks in Sag Harbor.

Chelsea loved Sag Harbor. She was in the company of the A-list—a major feat on her part. She walked for blocks in her ballerina flats and searched out all the designers and their new styles for the upcoming season.

It was 4:30 p.m. by the time Chelsea arrived back at the house. She called out for Lincoln, but there was no response. The French doors to the back deck were wide open. The distant sunset glowed a redolent orange-purple as she looked for Lincoln on the wraparound deck, brushing her right hand along the top of the smooth wood railing. There was no sign of him.

Inside the house, she turned down the hall and looked to the bathroom at the end of the corridor.

"Oh, my God," she groaned, as she stared at Lincoln collapsed halfway out of the bathroom entrance.

She ran over to him, knelt down and looked at his face; his eyes were half open and his breathing was clearly labored. "Hang on, baby," Chelsea said. "I'll get help."

She ran to the living room and retrieved her cellphone from her purse. Crying hysterically, she dialed 911.

She stated the nature of her emergency and found the calm in her voice to provide the 911 operator with her address and detail the nature of Lincoln's state, which was prone and in distress. 911 assured her that help was on the way.

"Hurry, please," Chelsea sobbed.

Chelsea saw the flashing red lights as a paramedic truck entered the driveway. The paramedics rolled out a stretcher and ran to the door. Chelsea directed them to the bathroom upstairs.

The paramedics checked Lincoln's pulse and immediately gave him oxygen.

"He's still breathing, ma'am," one of the paramedics informed her.

"Thank God! What's wrong with him? Why is he convulsing like that?"

"He's having a seizure."

"A seizure?" Chelsea asked with confusion as she watched the paramedics tending to Lincoln.

"I can't tell you what the cause is as yet, it could be anything. We've got to take him to the ER now!"

The paramedics moved Lincoln to the stretcher, rolled it outside and loaded him into the rear compartment. They started the sirens and sped down the road adjacent to the bay. Chelsea locked up the house and followed them in her car to Southampton Hospital.

ER at Southampton at this time of day was blessedly unoccupied. Lincoln was attended to by two first responders and three nurses, as they attempted to stabilize the disturbing seizures. He was then remanded to ICU. Hours passed into the evening and Chelsea was allowed to stay in the room overnight with Lincoln. She pulled his covers up higher, making sure he was warm enough. She rested her head on his chest.

"Lincoln, I love you so much. Please hang in there. You've got to wake up. Please!" Chelsea cried softly.

But Lincoln's unconscious state disallowed him the opportunity to reply.

For the moment, he was literally dead to the world.

***

Saturday – 7:30 a.m.

The next day, still unconscious, Lincoln was put through a battery of medical tests. Chelsea met with Dr. Adam Smith and his medical team specializing in nephrology.

"Ms. Timberlin. Mr. Madden will wake up soon, but he is seriously ill," Dr. Smith admitted.

"How serious?"

"He has chronic kidney disease or polycystic kidney disease, better known as CKD and PKD, with a GFR level of 18."

"What do you mean a GFR level of 18? What is that? And what should his level be?" Chelsea asked Dr. Smith as she held Lincoln's hand tight sitting next to his bed.

"A GFR stands for Glomerular Filtration Rate. A normal GFR level is greater than 60 to greater than 90 to 100. Lincoln has stage 4 CKD with GFR levels at 15-29. Which means his kidney function is severely reduced, thus he is in jeopardy of end-stage renal failure."

"He's had high blood pressure for years, but I could never get him to stabilize his diet or succumb to good eating habits even though he's not overweight. He loves the salt and is a moderate drinker—wine," Chelsea sniffled, wiping the tears from her face.

"Well, he's in extremis; he'll need two kidneys. There is not much we can do. We're putting him on kidney dialysis right now. He'll need a kidney transplant as soon as possible. Dialysis will postpone the inevitable but it is not a cure-all for his current condition."

"A kidney transplant? That means we'll have to find a donor?"

"Yes."

"Can I see if I'm a match?"

"You can. But you must know that the likelihood of you being a match is remote."

"I understand that. But I have to do something. What does the testing involve?"

"A number of things: A blood test to determine blood type and tissue compatibility; an interview with the social worker to ensure there is a healthy motive to donate; blood, urine and viral testing; a complete history and physical exam; a chest X-ray; and a CT angiogram of the kidneys, as well as an X-ray of the blood vessels of the kidneys." Dr. Smith looked at the chart in his hands. Are his parents living, does he have any living siblings or other family members?

Chelsea paused before answering. "Yes. He has a brother, Forbes Madden, he lives in L.A."

Dr. Smith closed his file folder. "Are you guys married?"

"No. We've lived together for fifteen years."

"If Lincoln wants to go through with the kidney transplant, his brother is going to be the most likely match, but his brother has to be willing. It's a lot, both mentally and physically."

"But Lincoln needs two kidneys, right?" Chelsea asked.

"Ideally, yes, but the body can sustain itself with only one kidney," Dr. Smith said through a tight, professional smile.

"I understand. I know they have a close relationship, but they live very different lifestyles." Chelsea got tears in her eyes thinking about the seriousness of the situation.

"Is he healthy?" Dr. Smith asked as he jotted down some notes in Lincoln's file. "Lincoln's brother, I mean."

"Oh, my God, yes! He's a health nut, well…other than he's slightly overweight."

"Well, it's definitely a possibility. However, we'll have to give Lincoln the bad news when he wakes up. This includes telling him about the decline in his health and having to be on hemodialysis. It's hard to say how long that will be required; a question that will have to go unanswered for now. If there is no donor match, then there is a time sensitive issue. The nephrologist will be able to explain it in more detail." Dr. Smith paused before continuing with a concerned look on his face. "I have to be blunt with you, Chelsea, this isn't going to be easy and it is certain to take a toll on you as well. Both of you will have to decide what type of kidney dialysis will fit your lifestyle: home hemodialysis or in-center hemodialysis. This is a serious and crucial decision both of you will have to make. While he is on hemodialysis, we can place him on the kidney wait list if there is no donor match. However, he really needs a kidney in order to live."

"I understand, Dr. Smith. So much information to take in. I wish Lincoln was awake to hear all this."

"Chelsea, it's a great deal to take in and you have a lot of decisions to make. Hopefully, Lincoln will wake soon and the two of you can start discussing where to go and what to do from here."

Chelsea stared at the doctor prior to him exiting the room and then turned toward Lincoln as he slept quietly.

"Babe, this is it. We'll get through this. I believe in you and we've got to do this. Please wake up," she pleaded through a whisper.

Her man was dying.

And inside, a piece of Chelsea was dying as well.

***

Saturday – 10:00 a.m.

When Chelsea returned home, she opened all the doors to the house in an effort to air out the place. She couldn't stop thinking about Lincoln as she entered the kitchen, filling the tea-kettle with water then waiting for it to boil. After the kettle whistle, she poured the hot water over the Oolong tea bag in her white porcelain cup.

Chelsea settled into the camel beige pillows embedded in her dark brown wicker sofa, opened her MacBook Pro, and logged on to Facebook. She posted a special living donor page, reaching out to all of their friends and family. "It's better than nothing," she told herself. Trying to hold back her tears, she phoned her mother, father and brother, giving them the news. They wanted to help and immediately agreed to a donor evaluation.

Her final phone call, and the hardest of all, was to Forbes. She dialed his number with deliberate slowness. Forbes answered after the second ring and she wasn't sure what to say and at first said nothing. He almost hung up the phone then she found her voice.

"Hello, Forbes," she said in a quavering voice.

"Chelsea?" Forbes said.

"Yeah, it's me. How are you?" trying to keep her voice in check and keep from crying right off the bat.

"Pretty good. It's a little hectic out here at the school. They arrested one of our students for murder yesterday and another student has gone missing. No sign of him anywhere. So, kind of nutty."

"Really? I heard about the murder on the news. Lincoln filled me in on the few details he knew. Sorry you're having to deal with all that."

"It's unbelievable."

A moment passed.

"Forbes…ah!" she said, choking back a sob.

"What's wrong, Chelsea?"

She sniffled. "I'm sorry."

"Chelsea, is everything ok?" The concern in Forbes' voice made the tears fall faster as Chelsea fell apart.

"Yes, I'm crying. No, everything isn't okay. It's Lincoln. He's extremely ill."

Chelsea felt faint and queasy. Her stomach churned as she sipped some tea from her cup.

"What do you mean he's extremely ill? Last time we talked, he mentioned that he'd had some medical tests but made it sound like it wasn't that big of a deal. What is wrong with him?"

"He did have medical tests done, but something else happened. We went on a little get away. I went out shopping and..." Chelsea started crying harder and said between sobs, "when I got back, I found him having seizures on the floor. The paramedics came and the ambulance took him to the ER. The doctors said he is suffering from renal failure and needs a kidney transplant."

Chelsea could hear Forbes breathing deeply. He was in shock.

"A kidney transplant?" Forbes repeated, as he tried his best to concentrate on what she was saying.

"Yes."

"But, he isn't a heavy drinker; just wine. Why are his kidneys failing on him? I don't understand."

"You're right, he doesn't drink a lot, just red wine and the occasional white wine in the summer, but he has had high blood pressure for a while now. Try as I might, he wouldn't change his eating habits even though he knew he needed to make changes," Chelsea sobbed almost uncontrollably.

"He is going to be Okay, Chelsea! When is the transplant supposed to take place? I assume he is still in the hospital?" Forbes asked as he looked at his calendar and mentally started preparing a trip to see his brother.

"Yes, he has been admitted and when I saw him last he was sleeping. I haven't spoken to him yet. As far as when the transplant is going to happen, well, that all depends," she paused.

"On what? For crying out loud, if he needs a transplant then they need to make it happen as soon as possible, right?" Forbes said frantically.

"We have to find a donor. Someone who matches. Family

members usually have the best chance of matching." Chelsea was trying her hardest to keep it together. Then she went on to ask, "That is part of the reason that I am calling. I have arranged to go through the testing to see if I would be a match but I have been told the chances of me being a match for Lincoln are slim. Since family has the best chance, I know it is a lot to consider but, would you be willing to go through the testing to see if you would be a potential donor?"

"Of course I would! That's an absolute no-brainer. He's my little brother. I just need the details about where I need to go and what I need to do to find out if I am a match."

"Forbes, thank you so much! I'm so upset." she paused.

"Chelsea, it is going to be okay. I understand that you are upset but we both need to remain calm. As soon as I get off the phone I will get a flight out today. I will send you the itinerary when I get it. Once I get there, I will schedule the testing." Forbes felt like he could sense Chelsea's relief through the phone. "I'll see you soon."

Forbes hung up the phone and wiped the tears as they rolled down his face. He just kept thinking that he should have asked Lincoln more questions about how he was really doing when he called the other day. What was he thinking? The murder investigation had his mind so preoccupied that he hadn't even taken the time to find out why his brother was really calling him.

After regaining his composure he got online and booked a flight for New York leaving first thing that afternoon at 5:00 p.m.

***

Saturday – 3:00 p.m.

Lincoln was airlifted from his current location to New York-Presbyterian/Weill Cornell Medical Center in Manhattan. He and Chelsea were met by the chief nephrologist, Dr. Cameron Kale, and his team. Lincoln was placed immediately on hemodialysis. Shortly thereafter, he regained consciousness and was even fairly articulate.

Chelsea sat on the side of Lincoln's bed and stroked his arm, giving reassurance to him.

Dr. Kale knocked on Lincoln's door.

"Hi there! I'm Dr. Cameron Kale."

Lincoln and Chelsea replied simultaneously, "Hello."

The doctor walked over and shook Lincoln's hand. "Lincoln Madden, correct?"

"That's me. And this is Chelsea Timberlin."

"Nice to meet you both. Well, I'll level with you," he paused as he looked at Lincoln and continued, "From my understanding, Dr. Smith was not able to discuss the extent of your medical situation prior to you coming here. Is that correct?"

Lincoln looked at Chelsea and then at the doctor. "No, I suppose not. The way you say that, it doesn't sound good?" Chelsea squeezed his hand to comfort him.

"Actually, Lincoln, you are right, your situation isn't good. It seems you are suffering from renal failure which is quite serious. In speaking with Dr. Smith, we both agree that your best, and perhaps only, option is a new kidney. What that means is that you will need a kidney transplant which will need to take place as soon as we can find a donor."

Chelsea looked very concerned, lowering her head to conceal a new torrent of oncoming tears.

"When Dr. Smith and I talked, he said it was serious and that it needed to happen soon. But, can you tell us what sort of time frame we are looking at?" she inquired.

"Six months at best. Renal failure is not something to take lightly. We are going to have to keep a close eye on you until we can find a donor."

"Is that it? Six months?" Lincoln asked as the reality of the situation loomed large and terrifying.

"Yes. I'm sorry. We can't waste any time. Dialysis will help but if a donor is not found soon, the dialysis can only do so much. It's essentially a band-aid to a terminal situation."

"Wow! That's a lot to take in," replied Lincoln.

"I'm well aware of that and I think both of you should take time in processing all this. I'm always here if you need me. Here's my cell phone," he said, handing a piece of paper from a prescription pad folded in his hand. "Your name will be added to the donor list to hopefully help with finding a donor more quickly."

"A donor list?"

"Yes. However, I understand you have a brother. Is this correct?" Dr. Kale asked.

"Yes, that is true."

"You do know that family members will have the best chance of being a match, right?"

"No, I guess I didn't know that for certain but it does make sense. Chelsea contacted my brother, from what I understand, and he is on his way here."

Dr. Kale smiled, placing his arm on Lincoln's shoulder, "That's great news. We will look forward to meeting with him to answer any questions he may have and I can provide him with all the details when he arrives." Dr. Kale turned and walked out the door shutting it softly behind. him. Chelsea turned to Lincoln and reached out to caress his face.

"Well," he said through a lopsided grin. "Helluva vacation, right?"

"We're gonna get through this, babe," Chelsea said. "I promise."

***

Saturday – 5:00 p.m.

Forbes flew out of LA late afternoon and arrived in New York just after1:00 a.m. on Sunday morning. Chelsea met him at the airport after watching his plane land and they immediately drove to her house and got Forbes settled so he could relax a little. Neither of them could sleep, so Chelsea made a pot of coffee. They got caught up until it was time to go to the hospital.

Chelsea showed Forbes to Lincoln's room. Forbes opened the door to the room slowly hoping not to wake his brother if he was sleeping and walked to his bedside. Lincoln was awake, reading a magazine. From the look on his face, Forbes could tell Lincoln was worried but at the same time glad to see his brother.

"You look like an octopus," Forbes joked, indicating all the tubes pumping fluids into Lincoln's veins from a central console and IV stands. "How are you feeling?"

"I'm feeling about as good as I probably look," Lincoln said, keeping his eyes fixed on his brother. "Honestly, I am just okay. I'm scared shitless, but maintaining an air of courageous calm."

"I know you are, Lincoln," Forbes said.

"Well, here's what the doctor told us this morning, Forbes. We have to find a kidney donor," Lincoln said as his eyes started to glaze over with tears.

"That's what Chelsea told me before I came. I've already scheduled an appointment to go through the donor evaluation process, as will Chelsea and her family. We'll see what happens, okay?

Lincoln looked at Chelsea and then back to Forbes.

"If we can't find a donor, I'm going to die," Lincoln said matter-of-factly.

Chelsea walked to the other side of the bed as Forbes shook his head. He didn't wish to admonish his brother, but felt he had to express some frustration. "Lincoln. Man, I thought you were eating healthy. You work out every day, but—"

"He drinks moderately, but his food is high in fat and he loves meat," Chelsea replied.

Lincoln turned his head toward the window and locked in a long stare of the outside view. He knew he was partially to blame for his kidney condition because he had an affinity to fried food. Late nights, stress and a non-stop travel schedule didn't make it easy and convenient for Lincoln to eat a well-balanced meal on a daily basis.

"It's hard sometimes. I try my best to eat healthy, but sometimes it's not possible," Lincoln said defensively.

"We have to think positive about the donor, whomever that may be, and persevere. Are you guys with me?" remarked Forbes.

"Yes," Chelsea and Lincoln replied simultaneously.

Forbes nodded in seeming satisfaction.

But deep inside, he was dying. If he lost his brother, Forbes Madden knew he would never recover from the grief.

***

Sunday – 7:00 a.m.

Forbes spent most of the morning visiting his brother at the hospital. In the back of his mind he was thinking about Chase's arraignment the following morning back in California. Shortly after 7:00 a.m., as he was waiting to meet with Dr. Kale regarding the donor evaluation, he received a call from Brolin letting him know that Chase would remain in custody and that the hearing date had been set. Forbes couldn't help but think about how it must be for Chase being in the detention center.

Although he knew that he was doing the right thing by being in New York with his brother and going through the testing to see if he was a prospective donor, Forbes couldn't help but dwell on all the responsibilities he'd left behind in California.

Dr. Kale entered the room startling Forbes out of his thoughts. He introduced himself, told him a bit about the donor evaluation procedure, and then started asking a few questions.

"How long will you be in town?" inquired Dr. Kale.

"Only a few days. I have to get back to California. I understand it takes a matter of hours for the results to come back. I plan to return if I'm a viable candidate for Lincoln." Forbes said.

"Yes, the results usually take about 24 hours or one to two days. If you choose to do the test today, I'll put a stat on it to obtain the results today. If you're a match for your brother, we can schedule the surgery."

"What's the recuperation like?" Forbes asked.

"Mr. Madden, let's find out if you're a match and go from there. If it turns out you are, we will discuss what you can expect during the surgery and what recuperation will be like. We need to take one step at a time."

After meeting with Dr. Kale and discussing his health history, Forbes went to the ninth floor of the New York-Presbyterian/Weill Cornell Medical Center and entered the front door of the transplant office. Frazzled, worried, and nervous, he walked up to the front counter where he was greeted by a pretty receptionist, who, according to her name-tag, went by the name of Sage.

"Hello! I'm here for a donor evaluation to determine if I'm a match for my brother who is hospitalized here."

"That's great," Sage said smiling. "I'll need to ask you a couple of questions before you complete the questionnaire. Can I get your name and your brother's name so I can find your file?"

"Of course, Forbes Madden is my name and my brother is Lincoln Madden."

"Perfect," she said as she pulled a manila file from the stack of files on the desk. "Do you live within 75 miles of the hospital?"

"Actually, no, I'm from L.A."

"Okay. So are you staying near the hospital?"

"Yes, I will be staying here for a few days," said Forbes, sighing.

"That's perfect. Since you're here we'll get going on the bloodwork and start the testing here if that works for you." The receptionist looked up with a practiced smile. "Here's the questionnaire. Please complete the entire form in blue ink," she continued, handing him a clipboard with a number of sheets of paper clipped to it along with a blue ink pen. "Let me know if you have any questions."

Forbes paused, looking at the clipboard and the extensive questionnaire. He then found a seat in the corner of the adjacent waiting room, and started completing the form. It took an hour for Forbes to finish the paperwork. By the time he was done, he felt like he'd felt years ago after completing a final exam in college. He walked back to the front counter and handed the clipboard to Sage.

She smiled. "Thank you. Have a seat. The nurse coordinator will call you in a few minutes."

Forbes scratched his head, clearly nervous and returned to his seat. He waited about twenty minutes before he heard his name called.

"Forbes Madden!" hollered a petite Puerto Rican nurse with black hair cut very short.

Forbes stood, placed the magazine he was reading on the table, and walked towards her.

"My name is Noreen. I'm the nurse coordinator. We'll be testing your blood type, antigen match as well as a crossmatch with the recipient."

"What do you mean by crossmatch?"

"Oh, I'm sorry. A crossmatch will tell us whether the recipient cells will react well with the donor cells."

"Okay. So, I've been told getting the results back can take 24 hours or one to two days, is that correct?" Forbes questioned as he fidgeted with something in his pocket to try to calm his nerves.

"Yes. It usually takes about 24 hours. A nurse coordinator, like myself, will call and inform you of the results," she smiled as she held open the door leading back to a number of small rooms used for exams. Forbes shot a smile back as he walked through the door.

"Wow! That seems like a long time." Forbes remarked, puzzled.

"If you're a match, the nurse coordinator will ask if you are interested in further testing."

"I see. I'm doing good to just get this done at this point."

"I understand." She raised her hand and placed it on his shoulder. "You'll be fine. Follow me."

Forbes walked behind her until they came to one of the small compact rooms, sparsely furnished with furniture more appropriate for an Army barracks. The nurse coordinator motioned for him to enter the room and then she closed the door behind them. Forbes waited patiently for the nurse to draw his blood. He was glad he was doing this for his brother and was glad to know that Chelsea's family would be doing the same the next day.

***

Sunday – 5:00 p.m.

The afternoon was drawing to a close as Forbes sat in the chair in the examination room anxiously waiting for the doctor. He worried about his brother as he awaited the results of his donor evaluation. He knew he had a weight problem, but his heart was strong and he didn't have any serious diseases that he was aware of anyway.

Finally, the door opened and Dr. Kale entered.

"Hello Mr. Madden. Nice to see you again," Dr. Kale said as he shook Forbes' hand.

"Nice to see you again as well, Dr. Kale. Hoping that you have some good news to share with me today," Forbes said with anticipation. As soon as he said it, the look on Dr. Kale's face said it all.

"Well, I'm sorry Mr. Madden but the results aren't what we were hoping for. You're not a match."

Forbes' heart sank and the first thought to come to his mind was that his brother was going to die.

"No, that can't be. I'm his brother. We were told that the best chance of someone matching would be a family member. Why is it that I don't match? What happened?" Forbes inquired.

"It's true. Typically speaking family members have a better chance of matching. However, in this case, that doesn't ring true. There is another option which is called a 'paired exchange.' Paired exchange requires finding another donor-recipient pair who has incompatible blood types, but your blood type would, in fact, be compatible with the other recipient and the other donor's blood type would be compatible with the potential recipient's blood type. In that situation, you would donate to the other recipient, and the other donor would donate to the recipient, your brother."

"Sounds complicated and like a very long process. Is that the only other option?"

"No, there is another option which is called plasmapheresis and involves the transplant recipient undergoing a special medical process that will remove the blood's incompatible antigens. After the removal of the recipient's antigens, the donor is then able to donate. There is a web page that contains additional information about this process. I can have the nurse write it down for you if you want to do some of your own research."

"Yes, that would be good. But, is there anything else we can do? These options don't sound very promising."

"No, I'm sorry, Forbes. Those are the only options for helping your brother unless someone else would be found to be a match. Please be aware that plasmapheresis is still an experimental procedure and medical insurance sometimes does not cover this expense. Be sure to check with your medical insurance provider before you proceed with any of the options available."

"None of Chelsea's relatives and friends so far were donor matches. Anything else?"

"I'm afraid not. Lincoln has been placed on a high priority list to help with finding him a donor. Until then, we will do what we can to help keep him as comfortable as possible."

"That could take years!" Forbes protested loudly.

"Yes, that is true. And in this case, I hope not. I'm really sorry for the disappointing news. We'll keep the faith and proceed with the next donor evaluation," Dr. Kale said as he exited the room.

Forbes went into a small, adjoining room, closed the door, put his hands over his face and cried. He was beyond disappointed that he wasn't a match for his brother and was having a tough time coming to grips with the reality of the situation. He walked to the lobby, took the elevator to the eighteenth floor and made his way to Lincoln's hospital room. Chelsea was sitting in the chair by the window at Lincoln's bedside.

"Hey, big guy!" Forbes greeted his brother. "How ya doing?"

"OK. Been waiting for you to visit. So what's the word, are you a match?"

Forbes covered his entire face with his hands, and then let them drop.

"I'm afraid not," he said as he watched Lincoln's expression turn from hope to gloom. "Lincoln, don't worry, buddy, we'll find a donor. Hang in there."

Lincoln started to tear up. He was a true cutthroat in the hedge fund business, but when it came to matters of the heart, medical issues or death, he was very sensitive, especially when they involved his own medical issues and potential demise.

Forbes leaned over and embraced him tightly. Lincoln hugged him back and Forbes could tell that Lincoln's state of mind was deteriorating quickly with the news he just received.

"Lincoln, I love you, big guy. Like I just said, don't worry, we will keep looking for a donor until we find one. I hate to say it but I've got to get back to the airport for my flight. I wish I didn't have to leave already but with everything going on at the school, I have to get back. I love you." Forbes stood up, grabbed his coat and left the hospital.

Chelsea and Forbes made their way to Chelsea's black S class Mercedes Benz. As Forbes put his bags in the trunk, Chelsea got into the driver's seat. While waiting for Forbes, she looked at herself in the mirror. Her mascara was smeared under her eyes from another day of tears so she attempted to make herself look presentable again.

Forbes got in the passenger seat and sat silently watching Chelsea fix her makeup. As soon as she felt like her face looked better, she put the car in reverse and headed toward the airport. Most of the drive to the airport was quiet. Neither one of them knew what to say about the results of the evaluation.

They passed the sign for the airport terminal and came to a stop in the passenger drop off zone where Chelsea was lucky enough to get a spot right in front of the doors going to the airline for his Red-eye flight.

After they stopped, Chelsea looked into his eyes. "I'm trying really hard to be strong. I'm just so scared. I wasn't a match and I'm not ready to lose him."

"Listen to me. You're not going to lose him. We'll get through this. When will your family be hearing back on their evaluations?"

"As you know, my mother, father and brother went in for evaluations and blood tests a few days before you did. Got their tests results back and they were not a match either…"

"That's good news. Stay positive, Chelsea. I'll stay in touch and will return as soon as I can."

Forbes pulled her towards him and embraced her petite body, feeling every bone in her back.

"Chelsea, you're not eating enough," Forbes said as he held her tight.

"I know. I can't. But I will." Chelsea knew she hadn't been eating enough and that it wasn't healthy but she was so worried about Lincoln she never made time for eating.

Shaking his head. "You'd better. You won't be any good to Lincoln if you don't stay healthy. You know that, right?" He felt Chelsea nod her head against his chest.

Forbes solemnly stated, "I'll be back to see him soon. I've got to return to Calvin House to find out what has transpired since I left."

"Is it about—"

"The murder. Yeah. One of the students was found dead on the construction site of the school, buried in the dirt. Then another turned up missing. The last month has been a whirlwind." Forbes paused to collect his thoughts then said "I'm really upset about Lincoln. I was hoping that I could help to be a part of the solution. That I would be a match and we could all move on with less worry."

"I know. I was too. Thanks for coming Forbes. It means a lot to him…and me. I'm glad you went through the evaluation to try to help him."

"Yeah, I'm glad I did, too.

Forbes sighed and looked out the window at the kids playing and laughing as they made their way into the terminal.

"You know, we used to be like those kids, playing, happy and not a care in the world."

"I think we were all like that. Life can be tough and sometimes we don't get to choose our hand. We've got to take the cards we're dealt."

"You're right, Chelsea. Sometimes that hand isn't exactly what we expect or anything that we know how to deal with...but, we will get through this," replied Forbes.

"Do you think we'll find a match? Do you think Lincoln is going to be alright?" An inquisitive Chelsea asked with tears filling her eyes.

"I don't know but I am not giving up hope. Besides finding a match, it will have to be a person with a big heart."

"That's true it will. We'll have to keep trying and not give up," Chelsea replied with a sniffle as a tear dropped down the side of her face.

Chapter Twelve

Monday, September 15, 2008 – 8:00 a.m.

Eleven days after the murder of Jaime Herrera and just four days after arresting Chase, Harianne arrived at the Los Angeles County Central Juvenile Hall on Eastlake Avenue for the detention hearing/arraignment of one Chase Buckman.

As usual, TV crews surrounded the front entrance of the Juvenile Hall courthouse. However, with the high priority of the case, it seemed there were more than usual. Harianne felt the heat from the media lights as reporters conducted one-on-one interviews with the seasoned prosecutor, Gaston Reeves, just before the security entrance. She paused momentarily to take in his attitude and demeanor.

After three marriages, and the victim of an attempted murder by a young ex-girlfriend, Gaston Reeves had his way with the ladies, regardless of his profession. In the courtroom, he gave transparent and important opening statements and jaw-dropping, heart-throbbing closing statements. Watching his reaction to all the reporters was too much for her to handle so she continued on, pushing and shoving her way through the rest of the crowd, to get to the security clearance so she could arrive on time for the arraignment.

Gaston Reeves walked down the street headed to the front entrance of Juvenile Hall courthouse. As he walked, he flirted with all of the female reporters before he opened the glass doors to the courthouse.

"Hello!" Gaston exclaimed as he reached out with his hand,

waving to a female reporter.

"Hi There!" he said to some of the other reporters as he passed them by.

Walking past the journalists he continued scanning the crowd. There was one reporter in particular he was searching for, one that he favored more than the others. She was the blonde that stood out from all the others with her tight fitting black stretch dress. Taylor Banford was her name and she was extremely thin, with very pale white skin.

Gaston sauntered his way to the front entrance of the courtroom doing his best to make sure he was the last to arrive. He wanted badly to visit with Taylor. Just as he reached for the door, she nudged his arm, motioning him to the side for a quick interview. Afterwards, he whispered at a very low decibel to Taylor, "You should call me later." He winked at her and passed through the courtroom doors.

Harianne marveled at the way the man worked a crowd...and the women. She had to give him credit—he was a ham sandwich, made to order. She turned and moved toward the courtroom.

Inside, the detention courtroom the atmosphere felt gloomy to Harianne as she approached the haggard and apathetic court clerk. She showed her I.D., then signed in on a billboard. She then took her seat at her table and opened the file marked "Buckman, Chase – Criminal-C10."

The Bailiff brought out Chase Buckman, who appeared bewildered and grief-stricken, into the courtroom and seated him next to Harianne DeCanter.

"Hi, Chase," she leaned into him.

"Hi, Harianne," Chase responded in a whisper.

Ten minutes later, the Honorable Jack Stein entered the courtroom. Slightly gray, fifty-three years old and approaching early retirement, he sat down and took in the view of his courtroom.

"Case Docket No. 55-333888, People v. Chase Buckman," the court clerk announced. "Will the defendant please stand and state and spell your name for the record, please?"

"Chase Buckman," Chase stood and said his name, then proceeded to spell his name slowly for the Clerk.

Judge Stein apprised Chase of his rights to a court-appointed attorney, and then addressed the crucial charges at hand.

"Would counsel please state appearances," the Judge said, staring pointedly at both Harianne and Gaston.

"Harianne DeCanter representing defendant, Chase Beckman," Harianne declared.

"Gaston Reeves representing the people of the State of California," Stated, almost theatrically, and Harianne lowered her head momentarily to conceal her smile.

Judge Stein proceeded to read the charges aloud.

"Gaston Reeves, Los Angeles County District Attorney's Office complains and alleges, upon information and belief that said defendant, Chase Buckman, did commit the following crimes in the County of Los Angeles, State of California: Count I – Murder, violation of Section 187 of the California Penal Code, Count II – Weapon of mass destruction, violation of Section 11417, 11418, 11418.1, 11418.5 and a special allegation, alleging that the defendant acted intentionally, deliberately, and with premeditation."

"How do you plead to the criminal charges," Judge Stein inquired.

"Not guilty," Chase stood and replied.

Harianne stood up with direct eye contact on Judge Stein.

Gaston stood, following Harianne's lead and cleared his throat slightly before speaking. "Your Honor, at this time I would like to make a 707 (c) motion under the Welfare and Institutions Code for purposes of a Fitness Hearing?"

"Ms. DeCanter, any objections?"

"Your Honor, I have no objections as this is the first time the Defendant has been arrested for any crime and is under the age of 16 years old." Harianne stated.

"Very well. Defendant shall continue to remain in custody and shall return to this courtroom in 5 days on Monday, September 22, 2008 for the Fitness Hearing."

"Thank you, Your Honor," Harianne said equitably, offering Gaston a victorious wink. Gaston frowned, but gave her the courtesy of a cursory nod.

Harianne leaned in to Chase. "Good news, my friend. Trust me."

He nodded uncertainly. "I hope you're right."

"I am. Hang in there."

"Like I have a choice?" Chase offered through the first grin he had ever given her.

Harianne sighed. *No, son. You have no choice whatsoever, I'm sad to say."*

She placed her hand firmly on Chase's shoulder and gazed into his eyes. "Don't worry, Chase, we'll beat this. Stay strong and be patient. I'll be in touch with you soon."

Harianne gave Chase a reassuring look before he was escorted out of the courtroom. She then exited the court at a leisurely pace. She was more than aware that every set of male eyes were on her as she moved down the main aisle; she could not help but smile ever so slightly.

"Whewy…look at her!" Harianne's clothes complimented her impressive figure with rare perfection.

"It's all about the walk and glide," remarked Gaston to his associate, Tom Garland, as they both watched her until she was out of sight. "Yesterday I was doing some research on her to prepare for today so I pulled up her website. She changed it. It's completely different. You should see it," said Gaston.

"Really, why what did she alter?" Tom asked.

"Better graphics. It shows the prisoners behind bars in a continuous image marquee that states: *'THE VELVET VOICE WINS.'"*

Harianne has been known to carefully vet out her cases thoroughly. The cases she's accepted in the past had elements of drama, trauma and intrigue and her clients, in the end, had so far been proven to be innocent. Her nickname had indeed become the 'Velvet Voice.' While she continued to hold that title, she always blew up the prosecution's case.

Harianne worked the remainder of the afternoon. She tightened up her witness list, and reviewed the toxicology report as well as Calvin House's list of daily dinner attendees.

Time had gotten so far away from her that when she looked out the window, it was already dark.

She sighed. And found herself looking forward to the end of this prospective trial before it even began.

Chapter Thirteen

Monday — 5:00 p.m.

When Harianne arrived home at the end of the day, she was greeted at the front door by Austria and the general contractor, Christophe Dubois. Christophe, a French immigrant from Cognac, France, had a keen eye for design, and his work was popular, particularly with the Beverly Hills elite. But he did have a reputation for being slow in finishing projects.

"What the hell's been going on here today? Looks like someone trashed my house. What's the status on your project, Christophe?" Harianne asked, disgruntled, as she slowly took in the ladders, paint-stained drop cloths, caulking tubes and cans of latex primer in disarray across the expanse of the house. The smell of paint and lacquer thinner was overwhelming. "I literally can't tell where this project starts and ends! And if I don't see some sort of progress in the near future, I'm not sure what I will do."

"Well…we ran into a few problems and I have to go to the city to get more permits, Miss Harianne." Christophe stumbled around knowing that his words were not going to go over well with her. "But, don't worry. We should be finished in three months."

"Don't you 'Miss Harianne' me!" she shouted taking a step closer to Christophe.

Christophe took a few steps back before saying, "I understand your frustration, Miss Harianne. But the project is coming along although it may not look that way from the mess you are seeing. Three months and we should be done."

"Three months? Is that some sort of joke, Christophe?" Harianne fumed. "Three months?" she questioned again in disbelief.

"Well…we're…" Christophe threw up both hands, frustrated, finding no more words in hi defense. He was well aware he was behind schedule and he sympathized with Harianne's ire, but there was little he could do to improve the situation.

Austria suddenly entered the room, arresting further discussion or ass-reaming from Harianne. Austria could feel the thick tension in the place and knew that it would be wise to try to diffuse it somehow. One quick look in Harianne's direction and she knew Harianne was ready to rip someone's head off, if she hadn't already done so.

"What's wrong, Harianne?"

"What do you think is wrong? Look around. The house! It's a disaster. At the rate Christophe is going, he'll never be finished with this project. It's frustrating!"

"Now, now! Harianne! Calm down. He's been working hard. I told you I would oversee the project while you and Tracey were at work."

"I know but you're-"

"Busy?" Austria cut in. "No, I'm not. I'll oversee the contractors just like I said I would. Don't worry about the project, please."

"The house is a mess."

"These things take time. And it will likely get messier before it gets better. Stop your worrying and leave it to me."

Trying to gain their attention, Christophe cleared his throat.

"Um…I just thought I would remind you, you'll have to remove all of the furniture from the house so I can complete the rest of the project."

"I know," Harianne said wearily. "We'll take care of it."

Harianne then remanded herself to her office, closing the glass, French doors behind her to silence the noise from the ongoing construction work.

Settling in, she grabbed some bottled water from the small stainless steel fridge located under her desk. After seeing Chase at the arraignment earlier in the day, she knew that she needed to be doing more digging to make her case stronger. She grabbed her smartphone and started scrolling through contacts until she found the number of a private investigator.

Harianne listened as the phone rang twice before being answered, "Clarence here."

"Clarence James?"

"Speaking," the man on the other end stated.

"Hi Clarence, this is Harianne DeCanter. How are you? It's been a long time."

"It sure has. What's up?"

"I need your help on a case involving a minor."

"Sounds like something I might be interested in, can you give me any more details?"

"I'd rather meet you in person to discuss the case," Harianne said pausing hoping that he would have time to meet soon.

"I'm available tomorrow."

"Great. I'll call you tomorrow morning to set up a time. Bye!"

As Harianne was hanging up from the call with Clarence, Austria opened the doors slightly to Harianne's office trying not to interrupt her. When she saw she was not on the phone she said, "I'll make dinner tonight: green salad, fish and garlic risotto in truffle sauce. Or we could do breakfast for dinner; I want to try a new recipe for banana walnut French toast with maple syrup and brandy."

"Yum! Either of those sound delicious. You're making me hungry just thinking about the choices. But let's save the French toast for tomorrow's breakfast and do the risotto for dinner. Tracey should be home soon."

"OK. You keep working." Half an hour later, Tracey stumbled into the foyer, carrying two boxes. He waved his hands at Harianne who he could see to be hard at work and slowly slid the glass doors open.

"Hey, babe! What happened in there? Looks like a tornado," Tracey said as he gestured toward the living room.

"The living room? Ah, I like to call that Tornado Christophe. Not to mention the fact that he reminded us today that we will need to empty the house. You know, like pack everything up?"

"Yeah, I was thinking about that today. That's why I brought home some boxes. At least we thought to cover the furniture and other items in the room they are currently working on."

"Looks like we'll have to bunk with Austria. I know how much she likes her quiet time so not sure how that's all going to work out," Harianne said as she shook her head.

"No worries. Relax. It's only for a short time while Christophe and crew finish up the project."

Tracey sauntered over to Harianne and kissed her. He placed his big, firm hands on her shoulders and gently massaged her neck working each finger in a round circular motion, pressing each muscle with his thumbs.

"Aw, Tracey…" she quietly moaned. "Don't stop. Keep going," she sighed with relief.

Tracey leaned over Harianne looking toward her desk as he continued to massage her tight muscles. "What are you working on?"

"What else? Chase Buckman's defense, of course."

"Do you really think he's innocent?"

"Yes. Someone else did it. He wasn't even at the school. I'm preparing a pretrial motion now stating that he was on vacation with his parents for the weekend. You were there today. Did he look like someone who murdered his classmate to you?"

"Well…uh…" Tracey stuttered thinking the same thing but not so sure he was ready to admit it. "Maybe he put the cyanide in his juice before he left for vacation? They were roommates ya know?" Tracey said as he sat in the wingback chair in front of her desk.

"Yeah, I know. But I don't think that's what happened. The vial of cyanide was never found in the boys' room. Just Chase Buckman's fingerprints on the juice box, along with a plethora of hair fibers and clothing fibers. Let's be sensible here, Tracey."

He stared at Harianne hard. "I'm trying." He rubbed his eyes. "But he's the strongest suspect out there for our murder."

"Is he?" Harianne said and it was clear to Tracey that the question was completely rhetorical. She didn't need an answer from him.

To her credit, she believed her young client was completely innocent.

Tracey found himself hoping for her sake that she was right.

***

Tuesday – 11:30 a.m.

The next morning Harianne ate breakfast with Austria and Tracey then headed off to her office. She made a quick call to Clarence with the two of them agreeing to meet around lunch time to discuss the case.

Arriving at The Grill On The Alley in Beverly Hills just before noon, Harianne found Clarence sitting in a booth in the back of the restaurant with a notepad and pen in front of him on the table. He was talking quietly on the phone as Harianne approached the booth. Gesturing for her to take a seat, he ended his phone call and gave his undivided attention to Harianne.

"Harianne," he said with a big smile on his face. "It's been a long time since you've contacted me. Seems you've found a way to do your own investigative work on some of your past cases."

"Yep, I tend to find my ways of getting info when I need it. This case is a bit different. My fiancé is working the case so I have to be careful how much digging I do, if you know what I mean."

"Oh definitely. I totally understand. Well, how can I help you today?"

With that, Harianne gave him the details of the case. She asked him if he might be able to find some more out about Forbes, look into Chase's background and parents a bit and perhaps find more out about the school. She really wasn't sure what she was looking for but she felt like there was a great deal of information that she, and the investigators on the case—one being her fiancé—were missing.

Clarence threw out some thoughts about where to start and what all he would do with regards to the case. They enjoyed a leisurely rest of their lunch and exited the restaurant together parting ways with plans to touch base with each other as information became available...if there was any information to be found.

Harianne knew she could probably acquire any additional information on Forbes Madden, the school and Chase's parents, but she wanted a third eye on this particular case. And there were fewer eyes in the city than those of Clarence that she trusted to turn up buried treasure.

***

Tuesday – 3:00 p.m.

Harianne had not yet met Chase's parents in person other than seeing them briefly in the court room the day before. After leaving the restaurant, she got in her car and drove out to visit with Boston and Pamela. Harianne arrived at the Buckman residence in La Canada Flintridge surrounded by other similarly opulent homes just after 3 o'clock. She was concerned she might not catch either of them at home but she was in luck as Pamela Buckman greeted her at the front door.

"Hello, Mrs. Buckman," Harianne said standing on the front steps of the house. "I'm Harianne, Chase's attorney."

"Yes, of course. Please, come in."

As Harianne walked down the long, high-ceilinged hall, she admired the *Blue Nude* Picasso artwork, the English-style furniture, the huge Provence-style kitchen off to the side, and beautiful ornate artifacts by famous designers. In the family room she was greeted by Chase's father, who stood to shake her hand.

"I'm Boston Buckman."

"Good afternoon, sir! According to the polls, sounds like you may be slated to be our next congressman."

Mr. Buckman smiled and directed Harianne to take a seat on the sofa. "I guess time will tell on that one. Let's cut to business, what can you tell us?"

"Of course, first, let me start by saying that I met Chase in person a few days ago. He made it clear to me that he is innocent and we prepared for the arraignment that took place yesterday, as you well know," Harianne said. "He seems to be well adjusted—and, after meeting you, I can see why."

"He's very bright, well-mannered and an honor student," Pamela remarked. "Jaime and Chase were just roommates. Sharing a room together doesn't make him a killer."

"Our kid is a practical joker, not a killer," Boston asserted strongly.

"He's a practical joker? I don't know that I was aware of that. What do you think drives him to do that?"

They looked at each other briefly before Pamela replied, "We both are professionals and our schedules are demanding."

"What does that have to do with being a practical joker?"

"He's harmless, but a little hyper at times. We try to spend as much time as we can with him. However, it doesn't always work out that way. We think he has resorted to the practical jokes as a means of getting attention, good or bad."

"Harmless? We're dealing with a real murder here! And *your* son has been charged for that murder! Both of you need to get your priorities straight. Your son's welfare is at stake."

Harianne stood preparing to exit frustrated with the lack of concern that Chase's parents were showing regarding the seriousness of the situation.

"Look, our priorities are straight. You came here to visit with us and more than anything what I want to know is if you will be able to help our son?" Boston asked as she made her way back down the long hallway.

Harianne stopped walking momentarily and turned to face Boston, "Mr. Buckman, it appears as though you are more concerned about your political race than you are about your own son. I will do what I am paid to do, and that is to defend your boy. I think for your son's sake, the two of you should show more concern and pay more attention to what is going on. He's being charged with murder! That's no small charge in case you are not aware."

With that, Harianne turned around and continued walking down the hallway and out of the house. She made her way to the car, peeved for reasons she was not completely sure of. She drove down the long driveway towards the street wondering how people like the Buckmans could be so oblivious to such serious matters as their own son's murder.

Chapter Fourteen

Tuesday – 4:00 p.m.

Driving away from the Buckman home, Harianne called the Calvin House from her cell phone.

"Calvin House, Balian speaking."

"Hi Balian, Harianne DeCanter here. By any chance is Forbes available?"

"I'm sorry, he's out of town right now. I can transfer you to Brolin if you would like, he is the one accepting any calls for Forbes."

"Actually, I would like to visit with someone from the construction company. Do you know if the crew is still working?"

"Yeah, they should be. They usually leave around 5:00."

"Ok, thanks. I'll be there shortly."

Harianne headed out south on Gould to Foothill Boulevard, passing La Canada High School. She crossed the overpass above the 210 freeway, stopped at the stop sign and turned right. She took the back way along Linda Vista Avenue and followed the street for less than a mile, parallel to the 210 West, and then veered left up the hill to Calvin House. She walked to the administrative office where Brolin met her outside of Forbes' office.

"Hi, I'm Brolin. I understand you would like to talk with someone from the construction company?"

"Nice to meet you, Brolin. Yes, please."

"Sure, I'll take you to the foreman."

"What about my stilettos?" Harianne chimed.

Brolin smiled. "The office trailer is on a cement surface. Good thinking, though. Follow me."

Harianne followed Brolin across the campus toward the construction site. The construction cranes were operating at maximum speed, and cement trucks were churning steadily. Steel saws and heavy equipment created so much noise that Harianne could hardly hear.

The foreman, Varner Davis, emerged from a large elevator lift and met them away from all the equipment. Brolin introduced Harianne to Varner who then escorted her to a dingy trailer off to the side of the construction site. Inside, papers were scattered across a desk, and the smell of old, burnt coffee engulfed the room. Harianne seated herself in a metal chair and pulled a gray lined legal pad from her briefcase.

"Hi, Mr. Davis."

"Please, call me Varner."

"Sure, Varner, I have been hired as an attorney in the murder case. I have a few questions I would like to ask, if you don't mind?"

"Well, I will do my best in answering them. What do you want to know?" Varner asked.

"Do you recall about what time it was when you found Jaime Herrera?"

"I don't know exactly. It was early in the morning. I know that much."

"Did you find him or one of your workers?"

"One of my workers found him. But I was notified immediately. News about the discovery traveled fast. Everyone on the site was pretty shook up."

"Do you know, when they found him, was his body completely covered in dirt?"

"Yes. They were digging and noticed his feet first and then his hands surfaced."

"Was he lying on his back face up or face down?"

"If I recall correctly, he was found to be face up."

"Had you seen him around the construction site before?"

Varner scratched his head and took a sip of cold coffee from his white, stained cup. He leaned forward with his arms on his knees.

"Yes. He came to the site every morning and just kind of stood around."

"Did he cause trouble?"

"He liked to kick the dirt with his shoe. That's about all. He never bothered us. Just watched us work."

"Did he ever bring a friend?"

"No. He was always by himself."

After a few more questions, Harianne flipped her notes to the beginning and placed her pad back in her briefcase. "Thank you for your time, Varner. I'll be in touch."

As Harianne strode away from the construction site in her black pencil skirt and black patent stilettos, Varner leaned against the trailer door and silently enjoyed the view.

***

Tuesday – 7:00 p.m. – New York

Forbes spent as much time as possible visiting with his brother in the hospital. He knew that his time in New York was going to be short lived and wanted to take advantage of being with his sibling. Lincoln spent a good amount of time sleeping as he was both weak and depressed about the current state of his health. When he was awake, they laughed and talked about old times. They shed some tears here and there when they thought about their parents and how much they missed them.

Forbes left his grandmother's diary at home even though he really would have liked to discuss what he had read with Lincoln. He knew that Lincoln had more important things to be worried about than what had happened at the school and what was currently happening.

As his last night with Lincoln was quickly coming to an end, Forbes worried that he may not get to see his brother again. If the tests didn't come back showing that he was a match, and another donor was not located soon, Lincoln may not make it until the end of the month. Forbes tried not to make his thoughts obvious but apparently he wasn't doing a very good job.

"Forbes, I know what you are thinking," Lincoln said as he looked wearily at Forbes. "We will see each other again. You said you are coming back for the test results, right?"

"Yeah, that's my plan. I wish I could stay here but with everything going on at the school…"

"I understand. You need to get back to take care of all the boys. Don't worry, I am going to do what I can to be strong and continue to hold out hope that a donor will be found." Lincoln said glancing over at the window to try to hide the tears that were welling in his eyes. "I had a thought the other night that I am going to share with Chelsea. Hopefully it will end up being a useful thought."

"All your thoughts are always useful," Forbes joked giving Lincoln a slug in the arm. "Chelsea is taking me to the airport so I am going to have to get going. I will be back here in less than two weeks. We will talk more than. Keep your head up, say some prayers and follow the doctor's orders. I love you, brother. Don't forget that either, ok?"

"I love you too, man! Travel safe and I will see you again soon. Can you let Chelsea or I know via text that you made it home safely?"

"You bet."

Forbes walked to the door, looked back at Lincoln prior to walking out the door and made his way to the lobby where he met up with Chelsea. The two of them walked in silence to her car and traveled to the airport. At the airport they said their farewells before Forbes grabbed his small suitcase and disappeared into the busy hustle and bustle of airport travelers.

Chapter Fifteen

Wednesday – 1:00 p.m.

Forbes wiped the sleep from his eyes four short hours after crawling in bed the night before. He hit the shower then put on a white shirt, trousers and a black blazer. He wasn't in the mood for a tie to his neck after his travels and such little sleep. He made a hot pot of coffee and filled his travel mug, then grabbed a carton of yogurt, some cheese and crackers before heading to Calvin House.

As he pulled his car into his marked parking space, he spotted who he believed to be, Harianne parking her car in front of the building. As she got out of her car she motioned to him which confirmed that it was indeed her.

"Hey Forbes!" Harianne hollered as she approached him. "Are you just getting here? Where've you been?"

"Yeah, a bit of a late start today. I was on the East Coast. A quick trip; Just got back last night."

"East coast, huh? On vacation doing something fun I hope."

"Not exactly but not a bad trip either. I got to spend some much needed time with my brother."

The two of them walked through the front door down the long entrance hallway. The walls on both sides of the hallway were decorated with historical pictures dating back a century and more: Calvin House in 1868…a 1900 portrait of the California Supreme Court Justice Thomas P. White…the 1911 Pep Club…the Calvin House Dramatic Society on Grand Avenue in downtown Los

Angeles in 1911…the first classroom at the Highland Park campus in 1913…the school's 1916 varsity football team…the class of 1918…the 1960 faculty.

World War II photos hung on the opposite wall in antique wood frames held by a gold clip and gold chain on the beige faux walls while the recessed lighting above highlighted the war veterans during combat.

Harianne stopped in her footsteps to look at them. "Some of these photos depict a very volatile time."

"Yeah, they do. That was a horrible war, but we'll never forget it. Look at us now! We are trying our best to get our men out of Baghdad and bring them home."

"I know. It just sucks to see all of those men killed every day. I just stop watching the news when they talk about the casualties. I sometimes feel guilty when I'm enjoying a meal and the thought of them over there dodging bullets every minute comes to my mind. Makes me sick to my stomach."

Forbes pointed at another group of photos and explained, "These photos are of some famous African Americans, the Tuskegee Airmen, also known as the 'Fighting 99th.' 1n 1942, Eleanor Roosevelt flew with Charles Anderson, a flight instructor at the Tuskegee Institute, a black university in Alabama in his twin-seat Piper Cub. Her Secret Service agents protested, but she went anyway. She was surprised to learn that black men could fly just like white men. She was in favor of the Tuskegee project."

"Tuskagee Airmen," Harianne said as she continued taking in the photos. "Ya know, I remember hearing about them, but I never knew the full history. Wow, I had no idea Eleanor Roosevelt really discovered them. I somehow missed that piece of history." Harianne started reading the plaque below the photos. "It says here that 'they had to battle both adversaries: the enemy and the racism at home and that they were ready to fight.' This is great history. Fun to be able to see all these photos, but I must admit, the photos make me realize how much I cannot stand racism. It really upsets me."

"Me, too, Harianne," Forbes stated with a look of sadness showing on his face.

"Impressive photos though. Really," remarked Harianne as they continued toward Forbes' office.

A little further down the hall they entered his office and took their seats.

"How have you been, Harianne? It's been a long time."

"I'm good. And yes, it has been a long time."

They both let that hang in the ether for a whole minute.

"Thank you for taking Chase Buckman's case," Forbes said.

"You're welcome." Harianne shook her head from side to side. "I'm still shocked about the situation. It's not every day there is a murder at a school." Harianne paused and then said, "Which of course that is good that it isn't every day but, the murder of Jaime Herrera is just so unbelievable. It just doesn't seem possible."

"I know. I've been struggling with the situation from the day the body was found. It just pulls at my heart strings."

Forbes got up from his chair and began pacing the floor. He pulled the wrinkled white handkerchief from his pocket, leaving the gold lining of his pants half out. Tears had formed and were slowly falling from his eyes. He wiped the tears from his face as he looked at Harianne. "Like you just said, it is so very surreal. At times I feel I'm living a dream. I've made my life this school and the students that attend. They mean the world to me. The future of every one of them is important to me and I want them to be successful men."

"I know how you feel. Sometimes people don't know how other people feel when they lose someone they love, someone who was close to them. I think what you're saying is this school, Calvin House, is your family?"

"Right!" he immediately agreed.

Harianne glanced out the nearby window at the media camped out on the front entrance lawn. "The media folks are always hanging out, looking for a story. Looks like Calvin House is the story for the time being. I was here yesterday and talked to the construction foreman, Varner. He seems like a nice guy. Sounds like the crew was pretty shook up when they found the body. Do you know, how is the investigation going? Are they making any headway?" Harianne asked the question knowing that Tracey and Zack did not have all that much to go on.

"Not exactly," Forbes stated as he returned to his chair behind his desk.

"Really? I would have thought by now that they would have leads of some kind," Harianne said as she pulled out her notebook.

"Yeah, I was hoping we would have known more by now as well. I am just really hurting for those boys. I just can't believe this. I'm responsible."

Harianne stood and walked over to Forbes placing her hand on his shoulder hoping to give him some comfort. "Forbes, I know you are hurting but it isn't your fault what has happened. Things will work out one way or another."

"I sure hope so, enough of this, what brings you to Calvin House on this beautiful day?" Forbes said focusing on Harianne.

"Actually, I needed some information about the boys."

"Of course, what sort of information are you looking for?"

"What are the ages of the boys?"

"Fourteen to seventeen. Ninth to twelfth grade. Eighty applied, but we did not take all of them. We've got seventy boys attending the school."

"What is an average/typical day like here?"

Forbes smiled. "Every day is different, but it can be typical.

"Breakfast is served every morning from 6a.m. to 8a.m. Lunch is served from 12p.m. to 1p.m. and dinner from 6p.m. to 7p.m. Attendance is taken at every meal to account for all the boys. Between meals the boys attend the classes in which they were registered for at the beginning of the year." Forbes paused and looked at Harianne. "For the most part, behavioral issues at the school are kept to a minimum. They all know the rules and we try our best to make them follow them."

"That's quite a day," remarked Harianne. "When you refer to 'we,' who exactly are you referring to? The teachers and yourself or does your administration staff help as well? Does everyone work together to keep the students in line?"

"Yes, of course the instructors are part of keeping kids in line. However, in addition to myself, there is an administrative team consisting of three assistant principals. One deals with the curriculum and scheduling, another deals with the supervision of faculty and technology; and the other deals with everything that is non-academic including the clubs, the sports and any other activity not related to academics."

"That sounds like a rather extensive administrative staff. Is there anyone else involved?" Harianne said looking up from her notebook.

"There is one other key person here at the school. The Dean of Men, Brolin Chapman, who is in charge of attendance and discipline. He seems to get the raw end of the deal as it seems every bad thing comes his way. Anything the students do not like about the school or activities, etc. is dumped on Brolin. He does a phenomenal job at what he does." An odd silence overcame the room as both Forbes and Harianne sat thinking. "Basically, we all come together and do our job to help the lives of the boys attending the school."

"In the end, you're a team with ideas and solutions."

"Yes, that's a good way of looking at it." Forbes said with a proud smile that was quickly interrupted with his cell phone ringing. "Excuse me, let me take this call. It shouldn't be long and we can continue where we left off."

Forbes answered the phone. Harianne sat silently listening to just one side of the conversation.

"Are you sure?" Forbes said, clearly agitated, while he listened to the other person on the phone.

"Have you talked to the other boys?" A short moment of silence followed by "Okay, I will be right there." Forbes hung up the phone and set it on his desk.

"Harianne, I am sorry but it looks like my presence is needed elsewhere. Can we finish this conversation another time?"

"Yes, of course, that isn't a problem. Sounds like you need to get going." Harianne said as she grabbed her stuff and headed for the door. "Thanks for your time."

Harianne left, walked down the hall and pulled her cell phone from her pocket. She called Tracey. No answer…straight to voice mail.

The call had been from Brolin and, as soon as Harianne was out the door and out of earshot, Forbes called him back.

"Brolin, please tell me you found him?" Forbes said with desperation in his voice.

"We haven't. We are still looking."

So there it was. Garrett Medford, another student at the school, had gone missing. Brolin told Forbes on the phone that he couldn't find him anywhere but that he was at lunch and then went back to his room. After lunch he was supposed to be in study hall with another student but never showed up. Forbes tried Garrett's cell and it went straight to voice. As soon as Forbes heard the news, all he could think about was the fact that another student was missing, another set of parents would need to be notified, and the media people who were camping out in front of the school certainly weren't going to be leaving anytime soon.

***

Wednesday – 6:00 p.m.

Forbes called Tracey and Zack one minute after he had spoken to Brolin. They arrived within the hour and combed the premises for the missing boy. They, like Brolin, failed to find the new missing person. Garrett Medford was gone but this time, unlike the other two boys, his phone was found sitting on his desk in his room.

After several more hours of fruitless searching of the premises, Forbes and Brolin phoned Garrett's parents and asked if they could meet with them right away. Two hours later, they arrived at Garrett Medford's home. They were greeted by Mrs. Tricia Medford at the front door. She led them wordlessly down the hall to the living room.

"Where is Mr. Medford?" Tracey asked.

"He's upstairs; he's coming," Tricia responded in a lackluster voice.

Tracey and Zack heard Adam Medford's sluggish footsteps echo on the tiled floor leading to the living room. Within minutes, Medford entered the living room. He remained standing as he sized up the detectives.

"Well?" he grunted at the two men.

"Mr. and Mrs. Medford. I'm afraid I've got some bad news," Forbes began softly.

Tricia broke into tears. "It's Garrett! What happened?" she cried.

"Where is Garrett?" Mr. Medford inquired tonelessly.

"Well, we're not sure. We're looking for him as we speak," Forbes responded carefully.

"I thought the murder was an isolated incident. Obviously not," Mr. Medford stated sarcastically. "My son makes for one more student now missing. You'll locate him before he ends up like Jaime

Herrera, right? Promise me that…"

"We have no evidence that your son is dead," Forbes said. "He's just off-site at this point in time."

"Did you check the entire campus and his room?" Tricia asked, now a little less agitated. Apparently, Forbes' reassurance of her son's disappearance not necessarily linked to homicide, had calmed her.

"We did a thorough search, Mrs. Medford," replied Zack. "But it simply means he's not on the campus. He's a young man and young men are prone to impulsive actions. He may very well be taking a kind of holiday for all we know."

"What's next? What are you going to do to find my boy," Adam asked trying to keep his composure.

"We'll keep looking for him. We'll keep you fully informed of the situation," Zack stated looking Adam directly in the eyes.

As the Medfords sat side by side, Forbes walked towards Adam and placed his hand on his shoulder. Two minutes later, he clasped Tricia's hand and followed Zack and Tracey as they exited the house.

***

7:00 p.m. – Forbes' Office

Forbes sat in his office watching the clouds roll in over the foothills, creating within minutes, a misty fog that covered the entirety of the school grounds. His mind was whirling from the latest events at the school. He settled in his chair and opened his grandmother's diary that continued to loom in the back of his mind. He flipped to a particular page wherein he found a letter taped to a page. He buried himself in the words as he read:

Before the detectives said anything more, Brinks held up his hand to Frank and I, gestured toward Frank and then down the hall. From the look on Brinks' face, I assumed whatever was about to be said, or done, was something that he did not want Frank to hear so I sent Frank to his room. I didn't want him to see or hear what was going to happen with his father and the two men standing at our front door.

As I write this, I think about the swarm of feelings that rushed through my body while everything was happening. I hated Brinks but at the same time I loved him. With the reaction from Brinks, I knew what was coming, wasn't good. Brinks was my husband, the father to my son. We'd had our differences but that didn't mean I wished for anything bad to happen to him. My emotions were swarming and my stomach was queasy, sinking to the floor. I'll never forget the words from the detective.

'Brinks, we're arresting you for the murder of Thomas Peyton,' the detective stated. 'His body was found in the woodshed outside the main building on the Calvin House school grounds this morning.'

As I stood looking toward the door, I nearly fell to the floor hearing the words. I looked at Brinks. The look on his face was one of shock as he stood holding the door handle of the front door. Initially I thought he might pass out. The officers stepped just inside the house, asked Brinks to turn around, and then handcuffed him, as they read him his rights. Before walking out Brinks looked back at me with loving eyes, but the pain was so evident in his face. He blinked a few tears away and mouthed 'I'm sorry' as he was escorted out the door by the detectives.

Forbes paused briefly before turning the page to the next entry. He wasn't sure he was ready to continue on but the urgency in his mind and soul to know more was only getting worse by the day so he forced himself to read on.

September 19, 1941 – After yesterday's events I have been trying to come to grips with what is going on. I talked to Frank about his father being arrested and, as expected, he is not handling it very well. He has been locked in his room crying since I told him.

I wasn't surprised to see the newspaper this morning. The Los Angeles Times, and I am sure other papers, ran an article about the murder. It is four pages long and the title reads 'ONE OF CALVIN HOUSE'S BOYS MURDERED.' The gist of the article says that the son of the affluent tobacco tycoon, Clay and Talia Peyton is believed to have been murdered. His cold, lifeless and naked body was found lying in a bed of autumn leaves near the woodshed on the Calvin House campus.

As the news has spread around town, the school and our home have been inundated with horrible telephone calls and nasty hate letters from unknown people on a daily basis. Reporters are looking to get a statement from someone from his family. I have resorted to taking the phone off the hook. We haven't left the house all day and the blinds have been pulled. It has been a horrible day.

Sweating, Forbes took a couple of swigs from a bottle of water on his desk. His father had told him about the murder, but not the woodshed. It was, eerily, the same spot where Jaime Herrera's body had been found—only without the woodshed as it had been removed from the construction site at the start of work.

So many ghosts, Forbes kept repeating to himself. *So many…*

Chapter Sixteen

Chelsea arrived at New York-Presbyterian Weill/Cornell Medical Center just in time for Lincoln's breakfast. Rubbing his head, she took a seat beside him and absorbed the view of him lying in the bed, moribund and listless. She tried not to think of the worst, but her fears lurked in her psyche as she sat next to him.

Lincoln kept his head turned toward the window as Chelsea placed her hand on his shoulder; he shrugged it off, but she took no offense. She could sense that he had something on his mind but she wasn't sure what it might be. Aside from the immutable fact that he may die in the near future if a suitable kidney could not be found. It was a gallows-humor thought, she realized, but it reared its ugly head nevertheless.

"I don't know if you're thinking what I'm thinking," he said.

"I'm not a mind reader, honey. What's wrong?"

"Chelsea, I know that years ago we made a decision that was not easy for either one of us. However, it seems it may have been easier for you than for me."

"Lincoln, what are you talking about?"

"Fifteen years ago a decision was made, one that very nearly cost us our relationship. Now, I am lying here in this bed and that is all I can think about."

Chelsea looked at Lincoln and wasn't sure what to say to him. She knew exactly what he was talking about and what he was thinking.

She paused and took a deep breath without making eye contact with Lincoln.

"We haven't contacted the adoption agency in years. We agreed that certain decisions would need to be made and we were okay with what the agency staff decided was best."

Lincoln looked at her and sighed, with tears in his eyes, "Chelsea, you do realize contacting the agency may be my only hope of survival."

"Lincoln, your brother is still waiting to find out if he is a match. Making contact with the agency may not be necessary. Don't get so down. We'll find a donor."

"You have that luxury to be so selfish! I do not."

His eyes moistened as he turned back toward the window.

"Stop being so mean/ I'm not selfish!" she yelled. "I love you more than ever and we'll keep looking for a living donor. It's going to work out! You've got to believe that."

He cocked his head slightly in her direction.

"Am I even on the donor list? Or are the doctors just telling you that to make us happy?" he rolled his eyes and turned away.

"Of course you're on the list. Why wouldn't you be?"

"I will die at this rate. You know that, right?"

She moved to the foot of the bed and stood there, not sure what else to say.

Glaring at him, she asked, "Where do you propose we start?"

"Well, considering we really only have one place we can start, let's go with the adoption agency," Lincoln said wearily. "Like I suggested," he added.

"Fine, I'll call the agency today," Chelsea surrendered.

"No. I don't think you understand. I want answers. I want you to *go* there today. Not call, but go, do you get it?" Lincoln said petulantly.

"All right, all right. Trust me, I do understand. I'll head there now. Please stop worrying. Everything has to be all right."

"This isn't happening to you, Chelsea. It's happening to me. You would probably understand better if you were lying in this bed instead of me." With that, he closed his eyes and acted as if he were going to take a nap. Chelsea left the room with tears in her eyes.

***

In a private room, adjacent to the hospital lobby, Chelsea pulled out her cell and Googled, the New York Foster Family and Adoption Agency in Manhattan. She found the phone number and punched it into her cell, not sure what exactly she was going to say.

The phone rang several times before giving the directive prompts. Chelsea pressed one for the director of the agency. She got the receptionist first and, after answering a few questions, was then put through to the Director of Adoption.

"This is Honore Sinclair."

"Hello Miss Sinclair. My name is Chelsea Timberlin. You probably won't remember me."

"Well, I suppose that depends. How long has it been?"

"Fifteen years ago," Chelsea said holding her hopes up that maybe this woman would remember her.

"Sorry, I wouldn't remember you after all, I wasn't the director then. But maybe I would still be able to help you?"

Chelsea sighed. "Well, I'm not sure if you will be able to help or not."

"Let's start here, were you adopted?" Miss Sinclair asked puzzled.

"No actually I am calling with regards to an adoption I was a part of fifteen years ago. I'm calling now because I need to make contact. My boyfriend has fallen extremely ill and this may be his only hope for survival." Chelsea's voice cracked as she said the last sentence.

"Oh, that doesn't sound good. I would love to meet with you first. Let me look at my schedule. Is there a time that might work better for you?"

"I was hoping that maybe I could meet with someone this afternoon?" questioned Chelsea anxiously.

"Looking at my schedule, I would be available any time after 2 o'clock. How does 2:30 p.m. sound?"

"That sounds great!" Chelsea said excitedly. Is the address correct that is listed on the internet?"

"Yes. 555-888 East 8th Street, New York. Do you know how to get here?"

"Yes, I can find my way. See you later today! Thank you so

much!" Chelsea said as she ended the call.

Chelsea decided not to tell Lincoln about her call to the agency. She didn't want to get his hopes up. Instead of going back to the hospital, she got lunch at the small café on Bleecker Street at a Starbucks then waited until 2:00 p.m. before she walked to the office of the adoption agency.

She didn't really believe Honore could help her…but perhaps Lincoln was right.

At this stage of the game, no stone should go unturned in the effort to find a viable kidney for her man's life.

***

Thursday – 7:30 a.m. – California

Forbes woke up after only a few hours of sleep due to anxiety about everything that had transpired and was continuing to transpire at Calvin House; the situation with his brother, and the murder history he knew nothing about until only a few days prior and now the missing boys all occupied his every waking moment. The day's packed schedule weighed heavily on his mind as he stumbled into his kitchen only half awake. His feet blasted him fully awake from the shock of the cold tile floor.

Each morning he concocted a smoothie for breakfast; he did this with the fervent hope that such a recipe would contribute to robust good health. Grabbing some kale, fresh berries and cranberry juice from the refrigerator he chucked them into his blender before slicing what was left of a banana in a straw-lined wicker basket on the counter. With all the veggies and fruit stuffed into the blender, he added a few ice cubes, pushed the start button, and returned to his bedroom for a pair of socks at the foot of his bed. With his feet cozy and warm, he walked back into the kitchen and poured the resulting smoothie into an ice-cold mug, taking care to scrape all the good bits from the bottom of the blender. He drank the smoothie slowly while reading a newspaper at the kitchen table.

The headline in the *California Section* of the *LA Times* in big black bold letters immediately caught his attention.

"PRESTIGIOUS CALVIN HOUSE FALLS VICTIM TO A MYSTERIOUS MURDER FOLLOWED BY A MISSING STUDENT."

Jesus. Did I have to see this first thing in the morning? he mused to himself miserably. But this thought was immediately eviscerated as he forced himself to read on.

"Less than a week after the body of Jaime Herrera was found, Chase Buckman, Jaime's roommate, was arrested for his murder. Chase is the son of a publically celebrated and wealthy attorney, Boston Buckman, who is also running for Congress. The arrest came as a shock to many.

As Chase prepares for his trial date, investigators have found themselves back on the school grounds scouring for clues to lead them to another student, Wendall Dobbs, who has mysteriously disappeared from the school grounds.

Faculty sources admit they don't know if he left on his own free will, disappeared through kidnapping or if perhaps he was drugged and forced to leave the school grounds by the same perpetrator who murdered Jaime Herrera."

Forbes sat back in his chair and collected his thoughts. He wanted to reach out and call his brother but decided better of it, since he knew Lincoln was in no condition to discuss the matter with him. He sat there for another ten minutes before he made the decision that he would not let the article, or the ongoing situation here at Calvin House, consume him to the point of a nervous breakdown. He had students at school that he needed to be there for and a student who was presently in absentia.

After finishing up the smoothie, he headed upstairs where he donned his usual attire: a white shirt, some dark trousers and a thick leather black belt to hold up his bulging stomach, which refused to slim down regardless of his healthy diet plan. He slipped on a pair of black loafers with a plastic shoe-horn and left the house.

Forbes parked in his normal spot and made his way to his office where he was greeted by his assistant, Balian, who was standing beside her desk with some telephonic messages in hand.

"Congressman Buckman phoned again," she informed him. "He wants a meeting."

"Did he say what he wants to talk about?"

Balian sighed. "Yes. With all that's going on, he doesn't seem as concerned about Chase and the day to day activities but he would rather tell you about his campaign ideas."

"Fine," Forbes replied. "Clear my calendar and tell him I'll meet with him tomorrow—let's say, 2:00."

She returned to her chair, phoned Mr. Buckman's office to confirm and entered the meeting in the black leather calendar on her desk nearby. Knowing Forbes was a stickler for a paper trail she turned to her computer and entered it in her Outlook program.

"While there were many attempts to go paperless, Calvin House would probably be the last," Balian silently wisecracked to herself.

Forbes sat down immediately and dug into a stack of files by his telephone. He swiveled his chair to the computer keyboard and began inputting information. As he grabbed another file, he was startled to see Balian standing beside his desk.

"Oh geez! You scared me. I didn't hear you come in."

"They're back."

"Who?" Forbes said, confusion showing on his face.

"Detectives Sanders and Grimes."

Forbes tossed the file aside, removed his glasses and sighed. "What do they want now?" he asked. Balian merely shrugged. "Send them in," he told her.

Balian escorted the detectives into his office.

"Good morning, gentlemen! Can I get you anything? Coffee?" Forbes asked.

"No, we won't be long," Tracey replied. He paused, as Zack looked around the room and surveyed the walls.

"So we didn't know that Calvin House had such a rich history," Zack said as he made eye contact with Forbes.

"What is that supposed to mean? You've seen the historic photographs lining the walls here. What are you getting at?"

Tracey cleared his throat. "I mean this," he said, pulling a newspaper and some other papers from a leather folder in his hand. Forbes knew in seconds the newspaper was likely the same newspaper article he found in his grandmother's diary. Tracey handed him the papers.

Forbes looked at the papers and then tossed them back toward Tracey responding, "So, what does this have to do with me?"

"Looks like Calvin House has some history that may be of interest to us. You told us before that the school has been in the family for years. I'm thinking you may have forgotten to mention to us what happened in 1941. Now I think that's somewhat symbolic of the school's history. Don't you?"

Forbes glanced down at the papers that he had tossed back to Tracey and then replied, "It's our family business." He was fuming, but doing his best to keep calm and collected.

"You never shared it with us," Tracey said.

"No, I didn't. It's a long story that I don't wish to discuss. And, quite frankly, falls under the purview of ancient history," Forbes stated as he threw a pen on top of his desk. "What do you want from me about something that happened more than 60 years ago?"

"Answers. Did you and Jaime have a fight the night before his death?" Tracey asked.

"Yes, you already knew that. He was out of control."

"Would you say you have anger management issues, Mr. Madden?" Zack asked pointedly.

"No!" Forbes replied, his voice rising—which he realized belied somewhat his conviction of temper control. "Look, yes, there is some family history here at Calvin House, though I didn't know much about it until I was older. My father told me." Forbes didn't mention his grandmother's diary as he hadn't read it all and wasn't sure what else it may contain. He thought it would be better to know the history first, before the detectives.

"And your father would be…?" Zack said quietly after remaining silent for most of the discussion.

"Frank Madden, son of the deceased Brinks Madden. My grandfather left Calvin House to my father in his will. My father wasn't interested in running the school, but did it out of responsibility and the legacy of his father; he wanted nothing to do with scholars or anything scholastic. My brother Lincoln wasn't interested either and left me his share in the school. Now, does any of that information make me a killer?"

"Well, I don't think we have an answer to that at this point."

Tracey stated then picked up the papers that Forbes had tossed on the desk. "And you're under no suspicion of murder at this time, Mr. Madden. We are simply following through on due process vis a vis questioning. I'm sure you understand this."

"We're still trying to put the pieces together, Mr. Madden," Zack added. "Your DNA was similar, but your fingerprints weren't on the apple juice box that contained the cyanide. Skin particles and fibers were found underneath Jaime's nails. Yet similar fibers were found all over Jaime's body that appear to belong to Chase."

"Jaime and I were engaged in a heavy argument but we did not physically engage one another, gentlemen." Forbes glanced at his grandmother's diary and rose abruptly. "Is there anything else? I've got a lot of work to do."

"It seems you had more than just the one altercation according to your students. They mentioned something about you throwing a chair during a morning argument with Jaime as well." Zack added. "Is there anything else that you aren't sharing with us Mr. Madden?" Zack said sternly.

"Will that be all gentlemen?" Forbes asked, not answering Zack's question.

"We'll be leaving now," Tracey nodded. "Just thought the murder of the past is something you probably should have, better yet, *would have* told us about when we questioned you the first time. As they say, history has a way of repeating itself." Tracey and Zack stood up and departed the office.

On his way back to the car, Tracey called the Los Angeles County Sheriff Department, requesting a search of the entire school grounds by the L.A. Sheriff.

Chapter Seventeen

Thursday – 2:00 p.m. – New York – Adoption Agency

Honore Sinclair greeted Chelsea in the lobby. Honore was a statuesque woman of Irish decent with medium-length brunette hair and flawless fair skin. She was tastefully attired in a tailored black coat dress.

"Hi, I'm Honore Sinclair," she said extending her hand.

"So nice to meet you. And thank you for being able to make time for me today," Chelsea smiled, taking the proffered hand.

Honore walked Chelsea back to her office, which was decorated in a Kate Spade décor. A cluster of black and white polka dot bowls sat on a round table by the window.

"Can I get you anything: coffee, tea or water?" Honore asked as she gestured Chelsea to take a seat in one of the chairs on the opposite side of her desk.

"No, I'm good. Thanks. I love your décor. I'm really into Kate Spade. She's one of my favorite designers."

"Thanks, she is obviously one of my favorites as well. So, you said on the phone that you want to make contact. I assume you are referring to a child that you gave up for adoption?" Honore asked as she sat behind her computer.

"Well, actually there are two kids I'm looking for," Chelsea said quietly.

"Okay, well, in order to see if I can help you find them, I will need to know the name of the father?" Honore said.

"Lincoln Madden," Chelsea almost whispered his name.

"Have either of you changed your name since then? As in, have you had regrets you had taken such options to surrender your children?"

"No."

Honore typed both of their names into the computer. After a few seconds elapsed, Honore sighed and looked to Chelsea.

"Due to the date of the adoption, the records have been sent to the archives. I will have to go to another computer to retrieve this data. Do you mind waiting here while I try to retrieve what I can?"

"Not at all." Chelsea said as Honore stood up from her chair and left the office.

Chelsea tapped her pen continuously on the table beside her, nervous and preoccupied. It seemed like she'd been waiting forever when really it had only been about ten minutes when Honore returned to the office.

"Okay, good news," Honore said as she walked in the office with some papers in her hand. "So, from what the records show, the children would be fifteen years old today. There was a note placed in the file by you and Lincoln Madden and the adoptive parents. The adoption was considered an open adoption."

"Great! So that means you can tell me where they are? What city they are living in?" Chelsea exclaimed.

"Well, not exactly. Given the length of time that has passed, as the director of the agency, I am not allowed to give out the adoptive parents' personal contact information to you or Mr. Madden." Honore stated seeing the disappointment in Chelsea's eyes. "You still have their names, don't you?"

"Yes. I have their names, but not their home addresses and telephone numbers."

"There are other alternatives?"

"Like what?"

"As the director and Licensed Clinical Social Worker, I can act as the mediator/facilitator in connecting you with the adoptive parents. There is a lot involved here. According to your file, your children were split and adopted by two different families. Some parents only want one child and are unable to take a second one."

"Yes, I'm aware of that and I also knew that they were split up at some point. Can you tell me where they ended up at the end of the day?"

"Looks like one was adopted by a family here in New York and the other went to California," Honore perused the paperwork.

"Can you tell me what they were named?"

"I cannot give you that information. There is a certain protocol I have to follow. I have the telephone numbers, but I will have to contact them for you," Honore said, sincerely disappointed by the restraints put upon her by professional guidelines.

"Fine. That works for me. Can you contact them now?" Chelsea asked, the sense of urgency in her voice palpable.

"Here is my card with my contact information," Honore said, handing over a business card. "I understand that their father is not well and this may be a life or death situation. I will contact them as soon as I can." Honore said apologetically, upon seeing Chelsea's disappointed expression.

"That's it. You're giving me your card, a thank you and a good-bye. This can't be happening. Did you even hear me? My boyfriend is very ill. We need to find a kidney donor for him, ASAP!"

"Chelsea, I heard you. However, there are protocols that I must follow. If you don't mind me asking, can you tell me a bit more about Lincoln's condition?"

"He needs a kidney, as I just said. I was hoping that one of the kids might be a match." Chelsea said through trembling lips.

Honore grabbed the Kleenex box behind her desk and handed some tissue to Chelsea, as the latter began to cry.

"I see your urgency. But there is really not—"

"Anything else you can do, right?"

"That's right. Chelsea, you'll have to be patient. I know how hard it is given your circumstances."

Chelsea cried aloud. "It's really hard. The whole thing is really hard for me." She sniffled, wiping her face with one hand. "The decision to put the children up for adoption wasn't an easy one. It was one that took me years to get over. I would have never imagined I would be put in this position," Chelsea mewled.

"Chelsea, you and Lincoln need to know that some parents will be reluctant to give you information and will be unresponsive to your needs, even if they are for medical reasons. It's been a long time," Honore said as gently as possible.

"I understand that but this is serious. Lincoln doesn't have time on his side. Are you sure you can't make some calls now? I really need to find these kids."

Honore could sense the tension in the room rising, as she took mental note of the look on Chelsea's face, along with the anxious movement of her legs from side to side.

Sighing with frustration, she tossed her pen on the desk and closed the file. As she deadlocked her eyes with Chelsea's she said, "Keep in mind, the adoptive parents have not requested or asked anything of you regarding medical records according to this file. And the kids are not looking for their biological parents so far as I know. Since there were notes from both sides—the birth parents and adoptive parents—that the only contact would be for medical emergency purposes, I will make the call."

"You just said this was considered an open adoption? I don't understand why you are getting all pissy with me. I just need to find the kids to hopefully help their dying biological father," Chelsea persisted.

Honore insisted, "Yes, it is an open adoption policy. I said I'd make the call! But I am not going to do it while you are sitting here in my office, I'm sorry."

Chelsea stood up, frustrated and running on fumes in the patience department. "Fine, When can I expect to hear from you?"

"Probably tomorrow," Honore stated as she set the folder aside.

Chelsea, taking that as her sign to leave, turned and left out the double glass doors of the adoption agency.

One hour had passed before Honore Sinclair had calmed down enough to phone one of the families. Honore phoned them and left a lengthy message with her contact number.

With that, Honore hung up the phone. Sitting quietly and reconsidering her seemingly intractable position with Chelsea, Honore decided it was probably best to get in touch with Chelsea as soon as possible. Turning to her computer, she pulled up her email program.

Chelsea:

I contacted the adoptive parents of one of the children shortly after you left my office. I explained that, per the open adoption agreement, either party is allowed to contact the other when a medical emergency exists. I told them that there is a medical emergency currently with their child's biological father and that you would like to speak to them to provide them more details. I left my phone number with them and let them know the matter was time sensitive. However, I left it up to them to decide if they will help you. I asked that they please get back to me either way.

It was nice meeting you today and I will be in touch after I speak to the other adoptive parents. Until then, best of luck with your situation.

Sincerely,

Honore Sinclair

Later that afternoon, Honore picked up the phone and dialed the parents of the other adopted child. The number had been disconnected and was no longer in service. Honore hung up the phone with a sigh and wondered how she was going to break that news to Chelsea. That was a message she was not looking forward to delivering.

By evening, Honore wrote another email to Chelsea.

Chelsea,

I reached out to the other family and the phone number was disconnected; no forwarding number.

Best regards,

Honore Sinclair

***

Thursday – 10:00 p.m.

Calvin House, a durably prestigious place of learning for these many decades, having enjoyed many visitors throughout the years, had stories that had been spread about it since its inception—many occupying the realm of urban legends and even tales of ghosts that wandered the grounds even still. As had been told as early as the 1800's, when the lights went out and the rooms and halls turned to silence, the echoes of the past dead scholar's voices and footsteps could be heard haunting the halls, classrooms, and attics. Some students attending Calvin House had accustomed themselves to hearing creaks in the walls, unidentifiable moans and whispers in the halls, and footsteps heard where no footsteps should be, while other boys simply found it difficult to fall asleep each night, convinced that restless phantoms of the past were lurking nearby, winikins of some nameless history, ready to possess or terrify some hapless youth in the dark.

Garrett Medford, sitting naked in a wooden chair in a room with Arroyo rock walls surrounding him, and no windows, could hear voices and footsteps…perhaps the ghosts of past petulant scholars. That would be the welcome preference for Garrett. The alternative was far more frightening—that he was being held captive by some living psychopath for some nefarious purpose that might end up leaving him dead—or worse.

The area he was currently being held in, felt like a dungeon. His knuckles bled from the thick wire-like rope which bound his hands behind his back, and goosebumps covered his pale, white skin across his entire body. He shuddered due to the coldness of the air that enveloped him like a death shroud. Fearful of where he was and who was holding him, he imagined the worst. He knew what Jaime's fate was and didn't want the same for himself. Every ten minutes he would lift his head slightly then lower it again, as it felt like it weighed a ton. It took enormous exertion to even lift his head for a few seconds and there was nothing but rock walls to look at anyway.

He heard a door open and someone enter the room from behind him. A straw was suddenly forced into his mouth and he took a big drink from the container because he hadn't had anything to eat or drink for what seemed like days. It was an instinctive reflex and not an unwelcome one. He sucked down the contents of the container. It was filled with apple juice. Not long after he swallowed the contents of the container, Garrett drifted in and out of consciousness, unaware of the potent GHB drug he had just ingested, until he finally passed out completely.

***

Wendall heard the sound of some kind of noisy machinery approaching him, as he lay on the cold concrete ground. His mind was foggy, his vision blurred and unfocused, yet he was able to make out the rear tail-lights on what appeared to be a black SUV. From his vantage point, he saw a tall man in dark clothing and black leather gloves walk quickly to the back of the SUV and open the doors; a body on a stretcher was carried out, completely covered with a black blanket.

Wendall's vision began to fade in and out at this point. He vaguely perceived an unidentifiable individual approaching him, and felt his limp body being placed on the stretcher and being moved. He heard the sound of an engine starting and heavy metal doors slamming shut behind him as he slipped once more into a deep, drugged sleep.

Chapter Eighteen

Singing birds, street traffic and bulldozers at the school construction site could all be heard outside, signaling that morning had arrived. But inside, Wendall couldn't see whether it was sunny or cloudy in the outside world. He had awakened in a metal chair wearing only his underwear. His feet, although enveloped in white socks, were bruised and sore. As he looked down at the floor, observing his feet through afflicted visual acuity, he could discern yellow puss and a few blotches of blood oozing through the white cotton that created a pattern not unlike an animal paw print. His head felt like it had been a piñata kicking bag for a baby mule and he could feel a large aching bump on his forehead. He tried his hardest to recall what had happened but the memory wouldn't immediately surface.

Wendall slowly raised his head up toward the white bead-board ceiling. A tall, dark figure in a black hooded robe hovered over him, his face obscured by a black cloth. Wendall's goose bump-covered body began to tremble.

"Who are you?" Wendall cried out in panic.

The figure's only response was to wrap a long, black blindfold tightly around Wendall's head, obscuring his vision. Then he left the room to return a few minutes later carrying a plate of food. He walked over to where Wendall was sitting and grabbed his hand, guiding it to a sandwich on the plate.

"Here! Eat this now!" said the deep, oddly distorted voice.

Wendall felt large, rubber-like hands embrace his own; he wanted

151

to puke from their horrible, foul smell. He took a few bites of the sandwich, chewing slowly. He tried to identify who it was that stood in front of him watching, him in silence as he consumed the sandwich. He wanted desperately to figure out who it was who was holding him hostage.

Within minutes of finishing the sandwich, Wendall could feel a cold malaise come over him; he recognized immediately that he'd been drugged. His eyes began to flutter, and then consciousness suddenly abandoned him. Once he passed out, the figure walked to the heavy, wooden door, pulling it open and closing it behind him. He locked the door from the outside with the turn of a key and departed.

***

Friday – 10:00 a.m. – New York

Honore Sinclair arrived at her office, grabbed a cup of coffee from the kitchen and proceeded to her office. The first thing on her agenda was to phone Chelsea Timberlin and give her the bad news. Honore dialed Chelsea on her cell, dreading the call.

"Hi, this is Chelsea!"

"Chelsea! Honore Sinclair."

"Hi Honore! You found them?" Chelsea said with excitement in her voice.

"Well, yes and no," Honore admitted ruefully.

"Well, what does that mean?" Chelsea inquired.

"I was able to get in touch with one family as I stated in the email I sent to you. I haven't heard back from them but hope to hear something in the near future. When I phoned the number in the file for the second family, the phone number was disconnected."

"No way. This is supposed to be an open adoption. How can that be?" Chelsea responded incredulously.

"After years of being together, oftentimes when families move around, they don't always think about contacting the adoption agency to update their contact information," Honore explained as gently as possible.

Chelsea's silence confirmed her disappointment.

"So, now what? How can I get in touch with the second family? Can you at least tell me what city they lived in last you knew?" Chelsea found her voice finally.

"Chelsea, I understand your disappointment. Unfortunately, the Agency is unable to do much more. I can tell you the last known contact, the second family was living in Los Angeles. You can search for them yourself, if you want, and wait for the one family that I was able to reach to respond to our inquiry."

"Seriously, that's like finding a needle in a haystack. Los Angeles is a huge city. I need more to go on than that."

"That's true but unfortunately I don't have anything more than that in my file. I'm sorry we were not able to help you further. I will be in touch when I hear back from the other family."

"Thanks," Chelsea said as she hung up abruptly.

Honore stared out the window in silence. She wished she could do more to help this woman, but her hands were tied on so many levels. And she prayed she would not in some way be responsible for a man's death by lack of luck and persistence.

***

Friday – 2:00 p.m.

Boston Buckman arrived at Calvin House in his 550 SL Mercedes and parked in the guest parking lot. He was dressed elegantly in a black Tommy Hilfiger suit, a white shirt and black tie. He strode into the administration building and stridently entered Forbes' office.

"Good morning, Mr. Madden," Boston said in a full Stentorian voice.

"Hello, Mr. Buckman," Forbes replied wearily.

"My wife and I wanted to extend our gratitude to you for recommending Harianne DeCanter. She's an excellent choice for Chase and a highly experienced criminal defense attorney. I like her," Boston said with all the equanimity he could muster.

"I'm glad you're pleased. She's one for the books! How's Chase holding up?"

"I was just there to see him last evening. He has his moments…good and bad. He's coping and doing the best that he can, given the circumstances," Boston stated as he approached Forbes' desk.

"Hopefully all this will be over soon. And you? How are you handling all of this?" Forbes asked, genuinely concerned.

Boston clearly hesitated. At last, he sighed heavily and nodded.

"I'm...well, I'm okay. It's hard at times. I'm worried about him. May I?" he pointed to the chair on the opposite side of the desk.

"Yes, of course. Forgive me. Take a seat. Can I get you anything?" Forbes asked as Boston motioned for him to stay seated that he didn't need anything. "How is Pamela doing?"

"Work consumes her or should I say she consumes the work. She stays busy trying not to think about Chase. Like I said, it's been hard for all of us," Boston admitted.

"Yes, I understand completely. Calvin House is on overload with problems right now. It started with the discovery of Jaime's body and then the other boys that have gone missing. As you said, it's hard for all of us right now."

Boston cleared his throat. "Well, if there is anything that you need, please let us know. We've always been there for Calvin House in terms of donations. The Buckman family has contributed to Calvin House with a consistent cash flow for many years and will continue to do the same for many years to come."

"Of course, Boston. I am well aware of all the contributions you have made. I gather this is your annual visit to ask for contributions for your campaign even though your son is sitting in jail awaiting a murder trial?" Forbes inquired bluntly.

"Forbes, I'm well aware of where my son is right now. I don't need you reminding me. I know you think it is cold of me to be here looking for contributions for my campaign but I have a life to carry on with while we wait."

"Right, right! Of course. Don't worry, I haven't forgotten. You pay me a visit every year. I'm not surprised to see you today," Forbes said as he glanced over at his computer.

Boston sat silently thinking to himself how much he would really like to put a price tag on the contribution to be made. However, he knew that Forbes was under tremendous stress. Boston didn't care. He was smart, astute, wealthy, and selfish at times and liked by many of his constituents. He knew that Forbes could afford it, but would always remain a modest man.

Forbes leaned forward, hands clasped. He was angry and this feeling was difficult to dispel at the moment. He looked Boston in the eyes and said, "Let me think about it. I'll have to get back to you. Right now, my biggest concern is the student body of this school. I need to focus on what is going on here and with your son rather than your campaign," Forbes dropped his eye contact before saying. "Now, if you don't mind, I have work I need to tend to."

Boston stood up and left the office without a word. He was furious and couldn't believe that Forbes hadn't issued him a check to put toward his campaign.

Forbes leaned back in his chair for a moment, and then reached for his grandmother's diary. Inside, he found a letter taped to a page. He buried himself in the words as he read:

Lauren, my love. You are my heart and soul, my world. I love you more than words can say. I know you are worried but you must stop. We'll be together soon. Brinks has no idea what he's lost. You're my most treasured gem and I'll take good care of you.

Soon you'll leave Brinks. I bought a little chateau in Paris. We'll move to Paris and live a wonderful life. I love you, my sweetness.

Love to you always,

Clay

Underneath the letter was a small diary entry that read:

Clay Peyton is my heart and the love of my life. How could I have been so stupid to believe that Brinks would stop treating me badly-his evil rages and the cheating. Now it's my turn and my future.

***

Friday – 8:00 p.m.

After his meeting with Boston Buckman, and then trying to get through the pile of paperwork that he had been putting off for days, Forbes found himself sitting silently at his desk deep in thought. He wanted to continue reading his grandmother's diary, but his eyelids grew heavier and heavier until they eventually closed. He was startled awake by the loud ringing of his telephone.

"Forbes? It's Chelsea," Forbes could hear her voice was tremulous.

"Hi, honey, how are you? How's Lincoln?" Forbes asked.

"Taking things one day at a time," she said solemnly. "Baby steps."

"What's up?"

"I just landed in L.A."

"What? What are you doing here? Do you need me to come get you? You can stay with me."

"No. That won't be necessary."

"I won't take no for an answer."

"Afraid you are going to have to this time. It's a long story, Forbes. Are you free for lunch tomorrow?"

"Yeah, of course."

"Ok, I'll see you tomorrow," Chelsea said and then abruptly hung up.

Well, this can't be good, Forbes thought.

Bad news was coming, he mentally sighed.

Chapter Nineteen

Friday – 6:30 p.m.

Harianne stopped at the storage facility on her way home and purchased twenty large boxes for packing. She pulled into the driveway with Tracey pulling up right behind her. They both exited their vehicles at the same time, excited to see each other.

"Hi, babe," Harianne beamed as she threw her purse over her shoulder. "Don't suppose you could help me with all these boxes I paid high dollar for from the storage place?"

"Well, I guess it depends on what's in it for me," Tracey remarked with a giant grin on his face.

"I'll have to see what I can come up with," she smiled back, giving him a kiss before he grabbed some of the boxes from her trunk. "What a day!"

"I hear ya'. Mine probably wasn't much better."

"Really? Do I dare ask what now?"

"Zack and I heard from Forbes and another boy has gone missing," Tracey said through a weary sigh.

"Wow! Another one? So who was it if you don't mind me asking?" Harianne anxiously replied.

"A student by the name of Wendall Dobbs. He's been missing for a few days. They have no idea what happened. All of a sudden, he was gone."

"Any clues? Did you talk with anyone else? Any of the students who saw him last?"

"Forbes talked with the other students. But he came up short. I'm afraid the boy may be gone for good."

"Oh, no! Don't say that."

"Either he left on his own recognizance or has fallen victim to foul play or is somehow annexed to this case in a felonious manner," Tracey said. "He could, I suppose, be our killer and fled the scene for obvious reasons."

"This is just crazy." said Harianne shaking her head.

"It is at that," Tracey said."

"So how is Chase?" Tracey inquired.

"He's a normal kid and he's scared like anyone else would be. We're working well together and he gets how serious his situation is," Harianne said.

"This boy going AWOL puts a whole new twist on the murder of Jaime Herrera," Tracey said.

"I know you don't like to tell me everything, but could you keep me posted on what happens?"

"No worries. I will."

***

In the kitchen, they found Austria cooking pasta with a very fragrant lemon sauce to accompany it. She drained the rigatoni in the colander over the sink and spooned the contents into the pasta bowl nearby. Tracey retrieved a beer from the refrigerator as Harianne walked briskly to the wine cooler for a bottle of Pinot Noir on the other side of the kitchen.

"Hey, guys," Austria called out. "Are you ready for dinner?"

"You bet!" Harianne replied. "I'm starved."

The three of them sat down at the island in the middle of the kitchen and ate quickly before returning to their packing project. Austria boxed up items from the kitchen, living room and dining room, while Harianne and Tracey packed the bedrooms, bathrooms and the office.

They worked diligently until midnight. They wanted to move to Austria's cottage over the weekend and time was of the essence.

***

Saturday – Calvin House – 8:00 a.m.

The next day, Harianne drove back to Calvin House and met with Wyatt Nance in his room. Tracey had filled her in on Wyatt, describing him as "an extremely intelligent kid and good-natured to boot."

Wyatt was of interest to her because Tracey, perhaps by accident, had mentioned during one of their conversations that Wyatt talked about a fight he had witnessed with Forbes and Jaime. She knew her client was innocent and wanted to determine who was guilty and Wyatt might be able to help with that. She decided that it would be best if she sat down and spoke with him directly. Prior to going to Calvin House, she called Forbes to set up a time to meet with Wyatt. When she got to the school, he was waiting for her in front of the entrance.

Harianne walked up to Wyatt and introduced herself.

"Hi Wyatt. Thanks for meeting with me. Let's go over to that table and talk," Harianne pointed to a table adjacent to the front entrance, conveniently attended by two chairs."

Harianne and Wyatt walked over to the table and sat down in the wicker chairs. With a small notepad in her hand, Harianne looked to Wyatt.

"I'd just like to ask you a couple of questions."

"OK," Wyatt stated nervously.

"Can you tell me how long you knew Jaime Herrera?"

"We met in our freshman year."

"Were the two of you close?"

"We studied together three days a week. Spending that much time together we got to know each other pretty well," Wyatt said neutrally.

"So you had a number of classes together?" Harianne asked.

"Yes, we had some of the same classes so we saw each other a lot. He used to complain to me a lot about Chase Buckman. I suppose he needed someone to complain to and I just happened to be that person," Wyatt shrugged.

"What do you mean he would complain about Chase? What was Chase doing that was worth complaining about?" Harianne asked.

"Chase never let up with the practical jokes. He's like that 24/7. I think that Jaime was tired of it and didn't know how to deal with it."

"Was Chase in the same classes as you and Jaime?"

"Yes."

"Did Chase and you ever argue?"

"No. I get along with Chase. Actually, I get along with pretty much everyone."

"Did Chase and Jaime argue?"

"Heck…all the time. Like I said, Chase liked to play practical jokes on him constantly. As I am sure you can imagine, there is only so much a person can take when it comes to practical jokes. Some days Jaime could take more than others. The days he couldn't take it, him and Chase would argue."

"Did you ever see Chase lose his temper?"

"Yeah. In the schoolyard awhile back. Chase threatened to kill Jaime. No one thought much about it—just a dumb fight and a dumb thing to say," he said."

"Yes, I'm aware of that incident. Just one more question if you don't mind," Harianne said. "Can you tell me what classes you had together?"

"All three of us or just Jaime and myself?"

"All three of you, please."

"Yeah sure. English, music appreciation and chemistry. I'm pretty sure those were the only three."

"Thanks for meeting me and answering my questions, Wyatt. As things progress with this investigation, I may be back in touch with you. Here is my business card in case you think of anything else that you think might be worth telling me about."

Harianne handed him her card, shook his hand and headed for her car. Wyatt sat at the table and watched as she walked away, his eyes focused on her shapely backside.

Nice ass, he noted absently to himself.

***

Saturday – 9:00 a.m.

Zack lingered in bed with Eve, knowing full well he'd be late for work. He had fallen in love with her all over again and it was difficult for him to detach himself from her on any given occasion, especially post-lovemaking. He pulled her toward him, turned her over in the bed and kissed her nipples until they were erect and hard. He moved his lips to her arms and shoulders pulling her fingers to his mouth, then sucking them like a lollipop.

"I love you so much," he murmured.

His hands traveled toward her vagina until he felt her wetness. Shifting positions, he caressed her belly then embedded his head between her legs and went to work. She came almost immediately. Eve continued to moan with pleasure as Zack turned over on his back and sighed.

After lying in bed for a few more minutes with her, Zack crawled out of bed and finally hit the shower around 9, while Eve slept. After he got dressed he leaned over the bed, and kissed her on her forehead.

"What time is your class today?"

"Two o'clock, in Westwood."

"Have a splendid day," Zack whispered to her.

"How could I not?" Eve teased. "I got a heck of a wake-up call."

***

10:00 a.m. – Precinct

Tracey and Zack arrived at the precinct at the same time. They ran to the elevator and hurried into it together.

"I know why I am late, so what is your excuse?" Zack said.

"Awe! Harianne had me up late."

"Yeah!"

"Packing boxes. I told you we're moving to Austria's house. The construction will take a long time. What's your excuse?"

Zack laughed loudly as the elevator doors opened and they made their way to Tracey's office. As they approached the office door, they could hear the phone ringing from inside. Tracey threw open the door and grabbed the phone.

"Detective Sanders," Tracey answered.

On the other end of the phone was Randy Yew, the lead crime scene investigator. "Hey Tracey, it's Randy."

As soon as Randy identified himself, Tracey motioned for Zack to close the door and hit the speaker button so they could both hear the conversation.

"I wanted to get in touch with you right away. There was a shoe found by one of the construction workers early this morning. I'm not sure where they found it but we sent out one of our guys to collect it. It went through security when it arrived and was sent to forensics where I performed a preliminary examination," Randy paused briefly.

"And?"

"I wiped the shoes for prints or anything else I could find. Came up dry. It could belong to any of the boys—missing or still at the school for that matter."

"Shoot," Zack muttered.

"Thanks, Randy! For a moment I thought maybe we would have something more to go on. Apparently not!" Tracey hung up the phone and regarded Zack with clear frustration.

"We're going nowhere mighty fast on this case, pardner," he said dejectedly.

"No shit, Sherlock," Zack agreed. "But the fight ain't over yet, pal."

"Got that right," Tracey said.

***

1:00 p.m. – Old Pasadena

Forbes met Chelsea for a late lunch on Green Street. Chelsea, wearing a short-sleeved black Prada dress, greeted Forbes with a hug and a kiss at the table of a restaurant called Mi Piace.

"Chelsea, I am so glad you called and we were able to meet for lunch. I was shocked to hear that you were in town. What brings you here?"

"Forbes, Lincoln isn't getting any better and we haven't heard anything on a donor match yet," Chelsea said trying to contain her tears.

"Oh, Chelsea," Forbes said as he reached across the table grabbing her hand to comfort her. "I was hoping maybe you were here to say a donor had been found. How long can he hold out according to the doctors?"

"I don't know. That's the problem. The doctors said that we needed to find a donor as soon as possible but that every day with no donor is one day closer to…" Chelsea's voice drifted off into a sigh.

"There has to be something else we can do. We can't just let him die," Forbes stated, as a single tear ran down his face.

Chelsea regained her composure and sat up straight, looking Forbes in the eyes. "Forbes, I've come to…for a reason. I'm on a mission and hopefully that mission will be one in which a donor match will be found."

"Wait a minute. What do you mean you are 'on a mission?' Do you know someone that you think will be a match that lives here?"

"Yes… Well, I am hoping this person is a match. Actually, I am hoping I will be able to even find the person to speak with them to convince them to go through the testing required to determine if they are a viable candidate or not."

The waiter arrived and they placed their order quickly. The food was brought to them almost immediately and for a while, Forbes and Chelsea simply ate.

"So, are you going to tell me who it is you are trying to find or how you know them? Or are you going to leave me hanging?" Forbes said at last, pushing his plate away.

"I'm sorry, Forbes. Right now I will have to keep that information to myself. I hope to know more by the end of the day but that may not even happen. I just want you to know that I am doing everything I can for your brother. No matter what happens, just know that I love him and would do anything for him." The tears were running down Chelsea's face by the time she was done talking and Forbes wasn't really sure what to say. He knew if he said too much or pressed too hard that it probably wouldn't go well but he was also very curious as to who she could possibly know in LA that could be a match. She picked at the last of her food then pushed the plate back impatiently.

After much personal contemplation, Forbes said, "Chelsea, I know how much you love Lincoln. I am not sure who you are going to speak with but I am hoping beyond hope that you are able to say the words required to make them understand the importance of being tested to determine if they are a donor match for Lincoln. But even more so, I hope that you are able to find them."

"Forbes, thanks for being so understanding with my lack of providing further information. I know it must be hard for you and confusing that I am unable to share more with you right now.

"I just want you to find a donor and if you have a lead, I want you to follow it. Admittedly, I would feel better if I knew more but hopefully in time that will change," Forbes said through a friendly smile.

Polishing off the glass of chardonnay in front of her, Chelsea rose from the table, wiped her eyes and kissed Forbes on the cheek.

"I'll let you know how things turn out, I promise. I won't leave without saying goodbye." Chelsea grabbed her purse and headed toward the restaurant exit leaving Forbes still sitting at the table. Forbes watched her walk out the front door before finishing the rest of his iced tea. He left a tip at the table for the waitress and headed home.

Chapter Twenty

Sunday – 10:00 a.m.

Sunday…a day in which Forbes normally looked forward to because it was a day that he was able to relax and take a bit of time for himself. It was a day where he normally wasn't burdened with Calvin House drama because, oftentimes, the students at Calvin House were able to visit with their families or would spend the day relaxing themselves.

Forbes found himself sitting on his couch at his place in silence. No radio, no TV, no noise of any kind. He was deep in thought. So deep that he didn't even realize that several hours of the day had passed by and he hadn't accomplished a single thing.

It had been over two weeks since Jaime's body had been found at the construction site. Since then, two other students—Wendall and Garrett—had gone missing within days of one other. Sheriff had scoured the property, interviewed staff, students and even parents of the students. Even with such comprehensive procedural action, the case of Jaime's murder and the missing boys remained insoluble.

Forbes continued to pray and hold out hope that the boys were still alive and would be found. Soon. If they were not found alive, Forbes was not sure how he would be able to handle two more tragic deaths. He wasn't sure he would be able to live with the guilt that he should have been able to keep them safe because they had been under his watch while attending Calvin House. They had been his responsibility. He already felt like he had failed miserably with Jaime; he didn't want the same to be true for two more students who had been attending his institution. A school like Calvin House should be safe for all the boys.

As these thoughts invaded what little peace of mind he had, Forbes suddenly blurted out, "No! This can't be happening to me. Those boys have to be okay. They have to be found alive…and soon."

He got up from his couch, walked over to his kitchen and grabbed a soda, then returned to the living room. On his way by the table, he paused momentarily before picking up his grandmother's diary that he had been staring at for hours while thinking about the boys, about the past two weeks and the events that had tragically transpired.

Forbes nestled into his recliner before opening up the diary to continuing reading the words his grandmother had written.

It's been two weeks since Brinks was arrested. Things have settled down with the phone ringing less all the time. Frank and I have been able to leave the house for brief periods of time. We get nasty looks from the locals as if they think we had something to do with the murder. Frank is taking it hard, not sure how to deal with all the emotions he is feeling.

I spoke to Clay earlier today. With everything that has happened, he has asked me to leave Brinks. Since Brinks is still in jail, I am realizing how poor our relationship actually is, and has been for a while.

My feelings for him have faded away, although he is the father of my child, I no longer possess the love for him I once did. Frank is young and right now his welfare is what is most important to me. The arrest of his father has made it such that I am all that he has. I love my son and could never leave him behind.

During our conversation today I asked Clay about his wife, Talia. He told me he hasn't been happy in his marriage for years. She spends money whenever she wants on frivolous things. He has only stayed because of his son. He is ready to file for divorce to be with me. The two of us will talk to Frank together to break the news. Clay has always wanted to have a law firm in Paris. He thinks business will be good there.

I love Clay to death and I know this is what is going to be best for both Frank and I. I need to be happy again too.

Forbes closed the diary and sat quietly in his chair, thinking about the ancient past. The more he read the diary, the more he learned about his grandparents; and at the same time, the more he started to wonder if he really wanted to continue reading—because learning the truth may very well be hard to accept.

Forbes could feel a palpable darkness begin to come over him, as black as the pit from pole to pole.

His final thought before closing his eyes to nap was: Please let the boys be alive. Please, God…

***

1:00 p.m.

After meeting with Forbes Saturday afternoon, Chelsea made some calls to private investigators in the area. She knew that trying to find her kids was sure to be a challenge, but she was determined to do as Lincoln asked. After all, he had been right; relatives were the most likely to be viable candidates. She loved Lincoln; she needed to do what she could to find the children.

As Chelsea sat at Starbucks, waiting for Anderson Finn to arrive, she already could feel tears forming in her eyes. She hadn't seen Lincoln for a few days and was ready to get back to New York to be with him. She was hoping the private investigator would be willing to take on the job.

Taking a drink of her iced coffee, Chelsea she saw a tall, slim man walk through the front door. She made eye contact with him about half way across the room as he slowly walked to her table.

"Chelsea?"

"Yes, that would be me. Are you Mr. Finn?"

"Nice to meet you. Please, call me Anderson."

"Hi, Anderson! Thanks so much for meeting me on such short notice. I really appreciate it."

"Really, it isn't a problem. I am glad to try to assist. As I understand it, you are searching for some children that you gave up for adoption years ago?"

Chelsea and Anderson talked for about two hours. She provided him with all the information that she had about the kids, let him know they had not been in contact over the years and that Lincoln was not well and a donor really needed to be found. By the end of

the two hours, he agreed to take the case giving Chelsea some hope
for the first time in days.

***

1:15 p.m.

Garrett Medford awakened, startled and disoriented, and quickly
turned his body to the right and then to the left. With his hands still
bound together by the thick prickly brown rope, the red sores on his
hands oozed yellow puss and blood. No one was in the room. He felt
his body temperature massively drop as the cold air consumed his
frail and fragile body. He yearned for a warm blanket, but there was
no furniture or bedding in the room. Not that he could get to it even
if it was available.

As the heavy metal door abruptly opened, Garrett was
overwhelmed with terror and uncertainty as the frightening figure
made his way towards him. A mask covered the individual's face,
making it impossible for Garrett to identify his captor.

The individual rubbed his hand vigorously through Garrett's hair
and placed the other hand on Garrett's penis and then stroked it
violently. Garrett felt overwhelming fear and disgust, but was unable
to find his voice to protest such a violation.

The figure abruptly ceased the penile abuse and walked quickly
across the room and returned waving two syringes in Garrett's face.
Garrett feared for his life and had no idea what was going to happen
to him.

The individual continued to wave the odorless syringes under
Garrett's nose and then abruptly injected one into Garrett's neck and
the other one into his arm. Garrett fell to the floor, realizing
immediately that he was dying.

From a poem he had been forced to read back at Calvin House,
he recalled T.S. Elliot's fateful verse: "This is the way the world ends,
not with a bang—but with a whimper."

A single tear rolled down his cheek as he welcomed the
painlessness of oblivion.

Chapter Twenty-One

September 22, 2008 – Monday – 7:00 a.m.

Forbes was scheduled to meet with his administrative staff within the hour, but he couldn't wait to read the rest of his grandmother's diary; her story was tasking him on multiple levels. He grabbed a cup of coffee, added his favorite French vanilla creamer and settled into his plush office chair. He opened the leather-bound book and resumed reading about Lauren and Clay Peyton's affair.

"I just received a letter today from Brinks."

Forbes saw a letter taped on the opposite page. He hesitated before slowly unfolding it and reading the scribbled words on the paper.

Dear Lauren,
  As I sit in this cramped jail, I remember the good things, and how much I loved you. You were my angel. The trial will be over soon and I'll be convicted for the murder of Thomas Peyton. I'm so overwhelmed and depressed. The death chamber couldn't come quickly enough for me.
  I really wanted Clay Peyton to die. But I thought to myself, the best revenge is to make Clay hurt as much as I do—by taking someone very close and dear to his heart away from him. What better way than to

*murder his son, Thomas? I hate him for taking you away from me. It's his
fault. I hope both of you rot in hell! I love you, Lauren.*
   Good-bye Lauren, My Love.
   Brinks.

Balian suddenly appeared at the doorway.

"Sorry to bother you but the staff meeting is scheduled in five
minutes. Are you ready to meet with everyone?" she asked
tentatively.

"Yes. And Balian, thanks for your hard work and dedication,"
Forbes said as Balian smiled sympathetically. He knew that things
had been difficult for him the past few weeks and assumed they
weren't much better for Balian. Recognizing her for her hard work
was the least he could do.

"Thank you," Balian said gratefully. "I'll get the rest of the staff."

***

Calvin House had regular staff meetings to discuss pertinent
information about the school, staffing, and students. The attendants
at a typical meeting consisted of the headmaster, three assistant
principals, and the Dean of Men. This particular staff meeting was an
urgent one called by Forbes making it such that it wasn't a "typical
meeting."

Brolin entered the conference room of the administration building
in a dark suit, white shirt, and black loafers. Although he was in
charge of attendance and discipline, Brolin took his real role quite
seriously, which consisted of being a second father to the boys. While
the boys were at Calvin House, the visits with their family were
sometimes quite infrequent. Those infrequent visits meant that often
times they would be looking for a shoulder to cry on, an ear to bend,
or some arms to embrace them. Brolin filled all of those roles on a
regular basis. He was, in essence, the Dad By Proxy of Calvin House,
and as such, much beloved by the student body at large.

After acknowledging the three other men in the room, Brolin took
a seat at the opposite end of the table. The assistant principals looked
anxious as they fiddled with their pens or tapped their fingers waiting
for the meeting to start.

Forbes was the last one to enter the room. After greeting everyone, he took a seat at the head of the table.

"Thanks for changing your schedules and making time for this meeting. As you are all very well aware, one of our students was murdered, another was arrested for that murder and is sitting in jail waiting for his hearing, while two others have gone missing," Forbes stated matter-of-factly. "The media continues to do an excellent job of providing negative press for the school making things difficult for all of us to continue to stay upbeat and positive."

Forbes looked at the four men sitting at the table and observed them all as they nodded their heads in agreement about what he was saying. "We're in crisis management mode. We need to continue to move forward and thus, I've decided to contact someone from a public relations firm."

The principal of curriculum piped up, "A public relations firm? I'm confused. What are you hoping to accomplish?"

"As I said, the negativity focused on the school right now needs to change. We need to do some damage control. Calvin House is not the school they are making it out to be. If we don't do something soon, our attendance is going to drop and we won't have any students at all. We've got to portray to the general public that Calvin House is still one of the finest boarding schools in Los Angeles County. Let's be smart about this—change their perception of us back to the positive side. What has happened at the school is not shedding a very bright light on us. We need to change that. Which is why I hired a small PR firm, with fresh ideas to get us through this nightmare."

Further discussion ensued with a few arguments creating a bit of tension briefly in the room. After some hesitation and reluctance, everyone agreed with the idea of working with the public relations firm and the meeting ended.

As everyone filed out of the room, Forbes remained seated. As the last principal departed, Forbes swiveled in his chair and stared out the window.

His overriding thought this morning was filled with portents of doom. He knew well that if this case was not soon put to rest—and that the mystery of the missing boys was not resolved—that Calvin House would soon cease to exist.

***

September 22, 2008 – 7:30 a.m.

Harianne traveled down the crowded freeway, inching her way through the bumper to bumper traffic to the exit. She arrived at the Central Juvenile Hall, parked her car in the designated spot and headed to the courtroom.

Gaston and Harianne regarded one another coldly as both approached the door to the courtroom.

"Good morning, Harianne!" Gaston remarked with a smile as he opened the double doors.

"Hello, Mr. Reeves," Harianne said, returning a tight smile.

Gaston continued smiling but to Harianne it was more of a self-satisfied smirk. She took the lead and walked in front of Gaston to her counsel table. They both settled in and removed documents from their briefcases.

Chase, accompanied by the Bailiff, walked to the table where he was seated next to Harianne.

"Good morning, Ms. DeCanter! How are you?" Chase inquired neutrally.

"Good morning! I'm real good. How are you feeling?"

"Well let's say I'm better than last time; trying to remain optimistic."

Pamela Buckman had a firm grip of Boston's hand as they entered the courtroom, taking the empty row just behind Chase. Pamela laid her head on Boston's shoulder as her lips trembled noticeably. It looked to Harianne that the woman was about to collapse in tears.

"I'm really nervous. I don't like this. This whole thing is getting to me," Pamela whispered to Boston.

"Chase is strong and we have to remain strong as well," Boston patted her hand.

Judge Stein took the bench and after all of the formalities by the Court Clerk were articulated, the Fitness Hearing commenced.

Gaston stood with a swagger and let out a measured breath. "Your Honor, this kid is playing with fire. Chase Buckman knows right from wrong. He's savvy, sophisticated and intelligent. That level of sophistication and advanced knowledge sets him apart from the average 15 year old boy." Gaston let that hang for a moment, then continued unabated. "The Defendant had motive. He had access to the apple juice at all times. He is known in school as a practical joker although this time he went too far with his jokes. Given the Defendant's socio-economic status, he had friends outside of school that illustrated a high profile social circle which allowed him to gain access to drugs and other illicit chemicals."

Harianne eyeballed Gaston with clear heat. Gaston merely smiled, before continuing.

"Even though he has a squeaky clean record, and given the severity of this crime conducted by a minor, the Defendant Chase Buckman cannot be rehabilitated," Gaston said in a tone of voice that left little room for debate. "And with that—the prosecution rests," Gaston said with the equanimity of a skilled politician.

"Ms. DeCanter. Please present your evidence," the Judge said. "Any motions?"

Harianne stood elegantly in a black pencil skirt and a short matching black jacket. She pointed her hand towards Chase, who remained impassive and expressionless.

"You know, I'm asking myself the following questions. How could a student, who typically gets good grades, with no prior criminal history and with ostensibly no hatred towards the victim, would suddenly and wantonly and with violent malice aforethought, suddenly take to murder his roommate? Yes. He's a practical joker, but not a killer."

Harianne paused, letting the preamble hang in the air for a moment, before continuing.

"The crime scene was at the Alcott Construction site. The victim was found on the construction site, not in his room. The search warrant was for the room, not for the construction site. Why wasn't a search warrant issued at the construction site? What prompted the homicide detectives to seek out a search warrant on the room shared by the victim and the Defendant? The cyanide may have been placed in the apple juice box by the victim as the ultimate suicide. To make my point here, the bottom line is the fact that it could have been anyone in that room. It just so happens that my client's fingerprints were the last ones detected prior to anyone else. If the victim did commit suicide, he would be shamed by his family after his death for such a cowardly act. Therefore, the victim knew that he shared a room with someone and that someone was the Defendant Chase Buckman who happened to be in the wrong place at the wrong time. The boys at Calvin House are rushing to complete homework, some last minute tie-ups which leads to tardiness in class. Chase Buckman had just returned from spending the weekend with his parents and that makes this whole case suspect. After he got home, he could have moved the apple juice box in an effort to grab a book. Does that make him a premeditated killer? I don't think so."

After a lengthy presentation by Harianne, Judge Stein inquired. "Any motions at this time?"

"I would like to keep my client in juvenile court," Harianne said quietly.

"Motion denied." Judge Stein remarked slamming down his gavel. "After careful evaluation of the five fitness criteria, I find the defendant not found to be fit to be a juvenile. The severity and brutality of the crime and the fact the Defendant had full possession and access to the cyanide chemical which falls under the parameters of California Code, Penal Code – PEN § 11417, this case will be transferred to Adult Court where the Defendant will be tried as an adult. Even though the Defendant had no prior offenses that doesn't lessen the degree of severity of this particularly heinous crime. I feel that the Defendant Chase Buckman must be remanded to the Adult Court at this time, despite no prior serious malfeasance. Defendant is to remain in custody and the transfer effective immediately. No bail set. The arraignment is set for September 24, 2008," Judge Stein decreed.

The Judge stood and exited to his chambers.

Harianne turned and looked to Gaston. Gaston was also attending to his material. They walked together silently for a few moments down the aisle. Once outside of the courtroom, Harianne turned to Gaston and offered a weary smile.

"Are you on the vertical for this, Gaston?" she said tightly.

He gave her his best telegenic smile. "I'm in the tank on this all the way, Harianne. Your boy is going down."

"Remains to be seen," Harianne said, turning on her heel, and walking away. What she wanted to say but held back: *You sanctimonious bastard. I'll see you in court.*

As she exited the building, she congratulated herself on her self-restraint.

***

10:00 a.m.

Wendall Dobbs awakened later that morning, groggy and just as disoriented as he had been the last time he was conscious. He was still blindfolded and tape still muffled his mouth. He tried desperately to determine where he was by odor or familiar sounds but he still didn't know where he was being held captive. The one thing he was fairly certain of is that yelling would do no good; it seemed no one would be able to hear him. From what he could determine, there were no windows in the dark, cement-floored room. Minutes had turned into hours, hours had turned into days, and days had turned into weeks as he remained locked in a chamber in and out of consciousness with some unknown individual occasionally feeding him and giving him something to drink.

His hands chafed against the rope that tied him to his chair, and he shook his head in despair. Every day became progressively harder as he prayed to God that someone would find him and save him from this living hell. His mind wandered with thoughts of the past days, how he got here, who had kidnapped him, and why someone would do this to him in particular. Bewildered, nothing came to his bludgeoned mind.

The heavy door suddenly opened. He strained to see through the blindfold but his vision was completely obscured. The sound of keys dropping on a hard surface near the door could be heard prior to the footsteps as someone walked towards him. Wendall could only assume it was the same person who had been there previously when he was somewhat conscious. He jumped as he felt a hand touch the side of his cold face. Goosebumps ran up and down his arms as the person in front of him rubbed their fingers through his dirty flaking hair, evidenced by Wendall's poor hygiene of not having showered in a number of days.

As the individual continued to play with his hair, Wendall moved his head to try to get his tormenter to stop. The blindfold across his face slipped slightly giving Wendall a marginal view of the person in front of him. The tape on his mouth was ripped from his face causing Wendall to scream in pain. The figure partially adjusted his mask to allow Wendall to see his mouth. It was a creepy smile and before Wendall knew what was going on, the figure's hands moved towards Wendall's crotch to stroke his flaccid penis. The figure unzipped Wendall's pants with one hand. Wendall squirmed and tried to prevent further invasion. But the figure was too strong and aggressively grabbed Wendall's thigh, squeezing it hard enough to make Wendall cry out softly in pain.

"No! Leave me alone. Don't!" Wendall pleaded as the figure continued to play with various parts of his anatomy.

The figure bent down and placed his mouth on Wendall's penis and took the shank fully in his mouth. Wendall tried to move but was completely immobilized. He screamed, "Stop it! Leave me alone, you pervert."

The figure stopped momentarily and looked to Wendall. "Have you ever been fondled?" he asked Wendall. "Has anyone ever touched your dick?" As he took a firm grip and started stroking his penis up and down, Wendall squirmed as the goosebumps returned and coldness enveloped his entire body. There was nothing pleasant about what was happening to him and he was disgusted to his very core. He wanted to vomit and expiate this degrading experience forever.

"What?" Wendall whimpered. "What do you want?"

The figure stopped stroking Wendall's penis and walked behind him. He yanked him up into a standing position.

"Have you ever had anal sex?" he whispered in Wendall's ear as he pulled the boy's pants down. Startled and scared, Wendall started to shake uncontrollably. He could barely stand up. He couldn't speak. He just stood there mortified.

"You heard me. Answer my questions. Was the sex good or what? How did it make you feel?"

Wendall's mind did the funky chicken. What was currently happening to him was out of some kind of freakish nightmare.

"No!" he yelled, trying to work his fingers through the ropes that bound him. The figure came around to face him directly once more.

"Who are you?" Wendall pleaded. "What do you want? Why are you doing this to me?"

"Shut up!" The figure angrily snapped. "I don't want to hear you speak. Shut up!" He yelled again as Wendall mewled hopelessly.

The figure continued to speak. "My older brother touched me down there and put his mouth down there on my dick," he said as he reached for Wendall. "He wouldn't stop. It was every day, nonstop." Wendall froze as he felt the figure's grip tighten on his pathetic manhood. "His fingers were firmly wrapped around my dick as he ran his fingers through my hair, constantly moving my penis up and down." As the figure described what his brother had done to him, he performed the same actions on Wendall. "He wouldn't let me go. I looked up to him. I've tried to forgive and forget, but I can't erase him from my mind! I see the visions so vividly; they never end."

The figure broke out crying and wiped his eyes abruptly. As Wendall considered the figure in front of him, he began to realize that there was something odd about him. It was as if he had two different personalities. The person crying in front of him was not the same person who had just finished molesting him.

Suddenly, the conversation and crying stopped. The figure pulled Wendall's pants back up but did not fasten them, He grabbed a small bottle of apple juice from a refrigerator in the corner of the room, and turned back towards Wendall. "I have something for you."

He walked back over to Wendall.

"Drink this," he said as he shoved the bottle to Wendall's mouth.

Wendall tried to make out the voice, but he couldn't think straight. It was somewhat familiar, but he couldn't place it.

"Stop it!" Wendall yelled. "I don't want anymore!"

"Drink this!"

"No, I…!" Wendall screamed but before he could finish the word, the figure removed the thick black leather belt from his pants and slapped Wendall's face.

"Stop!" Wendall cried out as tears flooded his eyes.

While his mouth was open, the juice drained into his mouth as the figure held Wendall's head fast. He had no choice but to swallow or choke on the fluid, so he swallowed without further protest. Within a minute, Wendall's eyes started to flutter shut. As hard as he tried to stay awake, he couldn't. From somewhere deep inside his battered psyche, Wendall knew he had been drugged. He tried to fight against the liquor's foul intent, but within a few seconds, the blackness overcame him. He welcomed oblivion.

The figure watched as Wendall's head slumped on his chest. Walking towards the heavy metal doors, he started to sob as he glanced back at Wendall before opening the door and exiting the room.

Chapter Twenty-Two

Tuesday, September 23 — New York — 9:00 a.m.

Dr. Kale made his morning rounds as usual. As he was heading into a patient's room, his pager went off and he headed immediately to the nurse's station who directed him to Lincoln Madden's room. Upon arrival to the room, the nurses were frantically updating him on Lincoln's vitals as he started making his own assessments.

Lincoln had been dialyzed, but the intrinsic failure of both his organs was not keeping up with the protocols in place. He had taken a turn for the worse.

"We're losing him, doctor," one of the floor nurses whispered to him.

"I know," the Dr. Kale responded. "Not much more we can do."

With Chelsea out of the state, Dr. Kale knew he would need to get a hold of her as soon as possible. He asked the nurses to find her contact information so that he could give her a call once he had looked in on the last two patients for his morning rounds.

***

Los Angeles — 7:00 a.m.

Dressed in her sweats and clutching her red Apple laptop, Chelsea headed for her hotel's Garden Café, where she took a corner table by a pond that housed a variety of koi. A waiter brought her a huge cobalt blue bowl filled to the rim with a cinnamon latte designed with a dog's face on top. Chelsea gazed into the latte, and then looked at the waiter.

"Never seen this before, but I like it."

"The puppy face is a nice touch, I think," the waiter agreed.

She lifted the cup to her lips and sipped slowly. She flipped open her laptop and checked her email hoping to have received a message from Honore regarding the one family that she was able to communicate with vis a vis Lincoln's condition. Much to her disappointment, there was nothing on her email. It had already been a few days since Honore let her know the mother of one of the children would need to speak with her husband first before agreeing to speak with Chelsea. Due to the circumstances with Lincoln, she sent Honore an email hoping to try to keep things moving along.

Hi Honore!

I was just touching base to see if you heard back from the family you were able to get in touch with. Lincoln isn't getting any better and I am really hoping you will be able to help me locate the children.

Thanks for your help!

C

Chelsea signed the email with a 'C' as she signed most of her emails knowing that Honore would recognize her email address as soon as she saw it.

Chelsea was using next to no information when it came to the search for her children. She knew that years ago one of them might have lived in the L.A. area so that is what brought her to the west coast. Having hired a private investigator, she was hoping that some progress would be made, and soon with this outside assistance.

After contemplating sending the email to Honore for a short period of time and reading and re-reading what she had typed, she finally hit the send button. After this, she stared at her computer for an extended period of time as if she was instantly messaging Honore expecting an immediate reply. Chelsea's cell phone rang, causing her to jump. She looked at the screen and recognized the number.

"Uh-oh," she mused to herself, recognizing the number to Lincoln's hospital.

"Hello?"

"Chelsea? This is Dr. Kale."

"Hi, Dr. Kale. Is everything okay? Is Lincoln alright?"

"Actually, that is why I am calling. I am afraid I've got some bad news."

Chelsea felt like her stomach sank to the floor.

"Did he die?" That was all she could think of was that he had passed away while she was on the other side of the country.

"Oh, no! I'll be honest with you, though. He's had a tremendous setback that could lead to a coma. Right now, he's fully conscious, but he's unable to speak."

"He can't speak at all?"

"No, I'm afraid not. Have you had any luck with finding a donor? Although he has been placed on the donor list, nothing has come through yet on our end. I was really hoping that you might be having better odds. Lincoln suggested that you were looking to find some children that the two of you gave up for adoption years ago. Any luck?"

"I'm still searching. I have very little information to go on but I am hopeful. I have hired a private investigator to help with the search. If Lincoln has taken a turn for the worse it would probably be best if I head back to New York, right?"

"In the end, it's your call. But if I had to advise you, Lincoln would probably feel better having you by his side."

"Yeah, I am sure you are right. Thanks so much for calling me. I will likely be seeing you soon."

Chelsea ended the call with Dr. Kale and pulled out her plane ticket from her purse. She contacted the airline to change her flight. She gave Anderson a call and let him know that she was going to have to head back to New York but that she would stay in close contact. Heading back to her hotel room she was in a daze, concerned that if she was unable to find her children that Lincoln would not make it.

After packing her bags, she called Forbes and asked if he could meet her at her hotel. Chelsea sat in silence in the lobby area of the hotel, tearfully remembering when she first met Lincoln. The rush of fond and passionate memories firmed her resolve to find a donor.

Within about thirty minutes of calling, Forbes arrived at the hotel, shuffling through the front doors and appearing to be in a bit of a panic.

"Chelsea, hey. Is everything okay? You didn't sound quite yourself on the phone and you look like you have been crying," he said with clear agitation.

"Forbes," she said as she stood up hugging him. "No, It's Lincoln. He had a setback. He can't speak anymore."

"Oh no! What happened? Is he conscious?"

"From my understanding, yes." Chelsea started crying harder. "Sorry. I'm just surprised because I myself just found out. Dr. Kale called me earlier this morning."

"I assume that you are planning on heading back to New York to be with him? Do you think I too should go?" Forbes anxiously inquired.

"Yes, I'm headed back. That's why I called and asked if you could meet me. My flight is in a couple hours. Thing is, I got the feeling Dr. Kale wasn't telling me everything, but... I just don't know. So I have to go to be with him. Might be best if you let me get back and find out what is going on before you travel as well. I will definitely let you know once I get home." Chelsea paused briefly then looked at Forbes. "We've got to find him a donor or he isn't going to make it." Chelsea reached in her purse for a tissue and wiped away a steady stream of tears.

"We will. You said you were looking for someone here. Did you find them?"

"Not yet. I hired a private investigator so hopefully he can help."

Just then her phone chimed, letting her know that her ride was pulling up in front of the hotel to take her to the airport.

"Looks like my ride has arrived. I need to get going. Forbes, thanks for meeting me on such short notice. I will call you as soon as I know more."

Forbes gave Chelsea a hug and she walked out the door. He watched as she climbed into the black Toyota and drove away.

You're a lucky man, Lincoln, my dear brother, Forbes thought to himself. You have a woman who loves you without reservation.

If anyone could produce a miracle, it would be Chelsea.

Chapter Twenty-Three

Wednesday – September 24 – 7:00 a.m.

As the rays from the morning sun penetrated the windows of Austria's cottage, Harianne was getting ready for another long day of preparations for the hearing that would transpire on the following day. She had a lot on her mind with the different facets of the case. As everyone in town knew well, she did her own investigating and she was feeling like she hadn't done enough for this particular case. She wanted badly to visit with Forbes Madden one last time before the hearing. To that end, the first item of the day would be a stop off at Calvin House in hopes of shedding some light on something that would be helpful to her client. Tracey had already left for the precinct so Harianne gathered her paperwork from the makeshift desk that she had been using, shoved it into her briefcase and headed out the door.

9:00 a.m.

The tall, dark hooded figure, wearing a mask, opened the door to the room where Wendall was tied to the chair. He removed the blindfold from Wendall's face and showed him pictures of toddler boys being molested on ten black canvas boards, one right after another.

"Why are you showing these to me?" Wendall yelled. "I'm tired of being in here. Who are you? What do you want from me?"

The figure did not respond but rather just stood in front of Wendall forcing the pictures in his face.

"Stop it!" Wendall yelled again.

Wendall writhed in his chair, trying to free himself. The figure slapped him three times with a leather belt, creating fork-like marks across his cheeks. The figure struck him several more times, until Wendall's face was covered in blood and the boy devolved into soft sobbing.

The figure placed the blindfold back over Wendall's face and left the room.

Wendall's mind was at a breaking point. He knew he would die at the hands of this madman, it was only a matter of time. He wished desperately before he expired that he might free himself long enough to inflict some pain on his tormenter. Even if that exertion would be met with instantaneous retaliation of a lethal kind.

Just give me a moment with this bastard, God. Just one moment, is all I ask...

But he realized his entreaties fell on deaf heavens. This realization made him cry once again.

Shortly after 9:30 a.m.

Harianne arrived at Calvin House to find boys hustling from one building to another. She assumed it was between classes and tried her best to stay out of everyone's way as they rushed to make it to class on time. She observed the matching uniforms of the boys and how polite and respectful they seemed to be to each other. She was impressed that Calvin House was doing such a good job with all the students on the campus.

Harianne made her way to Forbes' office pretty easily to find the door to his office open and no secretary around. She found Forbes working at his computer, with a green-shaded banker's lamp offering the only illumination in the dimly lit office. She knocked gently on the open door.

"Hey!" Forbes said as he stood up from his desk. "How are you, Harianne? I understand you were here a few weeks ago to look around and ask some questions while I was out of town. How did your talk with Varner go?"

"I'm doing alright. My talk with Varner went well. He seems like a nice enough guy."

"Honestly, I only know his name. But I have never had any problems with him…" Forbes said as his voice faded off bringing unsavory memories of the day that Jaime was found.

"Forbes, is everything alright?"

"Yeah. I'm okay. Just…a lot on my mind. What brings you to my part of town?" Forbes asked.

"Forbes, do you need to talk about whatever is going on? I just stopped in to see how you were doing. With the hearing tomorrow for Chase I thought I would see if you were doing alright."

"Doing just so-so. Not only is Chase's hearing tomorrow but my brother is sick back East and not getting any better. I've had ten or more news vans camped out here since all this started weeks ago and there's a constant media feed going with live, breaking reports about missing boys. It's hell and today is exam day for the students."

"Exam day That must be why the boys were all rushing around trying to get to their next class on time." Harianne paused, taking in Forbes' forlorn look. "Forbes, I know this has all been hard, and it sounds like you have other things going on in your personal life, too, but you've got to believe you'll get through this."

"Yeah, I'd like to believe that but my father…" Forbes stopped himself from finishing what he was saying realizing that Harianne was probably not the right person to be spilling his family history to.

Harianne blinked and looked directly at Forbes.

"What do you mean?" she asked, seeing the agitation on Forbes' face.

He stumbled with his words. "I-I still can't believe it. And I am not even sure myself what happened," he said glancing at the diary tucked under some papers on his desk. "I'm still trying to put all of the pieces of the puzzle together. I probably shouldn't even have said anything."

The confusion showed on Harianne's face. "Pieces of what puzzle?" she said, hoping that perhaps this was a piece of the puzzle that she needed for her case.

"My grandparents. Their marriage and all their secrets."

Harianne scratched her head and leaned forward. "Forbes, I'm not quite sure what you are talking about but, whatever is going on, it clearly has not been easy for you."

"No, it hasn't and I'm still gathering facts. It was a long time ago, but it's my history and my family."

Forbes crossed his arms on the desk and lowered his head.

"I'd rather not talk about it anymore," he said softly.

Harianne stared at him and sighed. "Oh, Forbes. I'm sorry you're going through all this. If there is anything I can do to help, please, let me know." Harianne said as she stood up from the chair across the desk from Forbes. She walked around to the other side of the desk and Forbes lifted his head to look at her.

"Thanks, Harianne. Means a lot to me," Forbes said as he stood and she gave him a quick hug before she left his office.

After her meeting with Forbes, she made a mental note to look up who Forbes' grandparents were and what may have happened so many years ago that had left Forbes so uncommunicative and despondent.

September 24 – Second Arraignment – 8:45 a.m.

The second arraignment was simply a more truncated version of Chase's first arraignment, except that Harianne suffered from the burden of certain knowledge that Chase would be tried in adult court and stood a good chance of spending the rest of his life in jail, should she fail to persuade the jury of his innocence. The day had not started out well for Harianne. She and Tracey had quarreled about wall coloring in the living room and though it was a silly thing to argue over, given the state of incomplete reconstruction, it had soured her mood considerably. She now forced herself to concentrate on immediate matters at hand.

Gaston entered later than usual, straightening his tie. He looked somewhat rushed but did not so tarry as to fail to give her his most professional smile. She nodded back then turned her attention to Chase being led into the courtroom, cuffed and appearing somewhat exhausted.

Harianne reached over and touched Chase's arm. "Are you hanging in there, my friend?"

"God, I so want this to be over," he mumbled as he watched his parents, Boston and Pamela, enter the court and seat themselves.

Harianne had no reply she could offer or words of comfort, for that matter. These were the dark times and the cards would fall where they would, regarding Chase's destiny. She glanced over at Boston and Pamela. He looked fit as an athlete; she looked tremulous, hollow and highly medicated. Harianne couldn't really blame her; she assumed Pamela was pretty well doped up on Xanax to simply get through this whole debacle.

Her phone suddenly vibrated. Someone was texting her. She took out her Samsung and glanced down at the text.

Sorry. You're right—yellow is nicer for the wall.

Harianne tried her best not to smile—she knew Chase was watching her. She looked up and sighed, then said one word to Chase: "Courage."

He frowned and nodded.

Harianne glanced at Forbes Madden, who was dressed to the nines. He gave her a wave then searched for a place to sit. The bailiff was busy doing some procedural business at the bench and Gaston was deep in discussion with Tom, his paralegal.

Okay, game on, Harianne said to herself, and almost whispered this thought aloud.

The Judge was an attractive woman in her early fifties, who used a cane to move about. She exited chambers and moved with surprising grace to her place behind the bunch. She looked out to the court as the bailiff turned and made his prefatory statement to the assembled audience.

She listened to the merits of the case and then essentially handed down her decision, not to Harianne's great surprise.

Her client, young Chase, would be tried as an adult, per the prior Judge's decision. She glanced over to Gaston who gave her a self-satisfied smile. He gathered his papers and walked out with his paralegal, offering her a very small salute that smacked of "good luck."

Harianne signed then looked to Chase, who was already being led off by his jailers. He did not turn to look at her as he exited the courtroom.

10:30 p.m.

Wendall woke up not knowing for sure how long it had been since the last encounter with his abductor. He shuddered from the coldness in the dark room; he sensed that the thermostat had been adjusted to a lower temperature rather deliberately. He felt tightness on his face that he assumed was dried blood caked on his skin from the belting he had endured earlier, but he couldn't free his hands to wipe his face.

Suddenly, he heard the signal tones on a vehicle going in reverse. Shortly thereafter, the figure returned.

The figure carefully released Wendall from his chair and marched him down a long corridor. Wendall was extremely weak and found that he could barely walk. As they progressed, Wendall could hear the continuous sound of an automatic lift humming away. The blindfold on his eyes prevented him from being able to see anything although he could tell that he was still in a dark area. After walking for a distance, the individual leading him stopped abruptly on what sounded like a metal platform. Wendall felt the floor he was standing on begin to move as the figure lifted him up on what he assumed was the same automatic lift he heard earlier. The figure pushed him forward, forced him to sit and strapped him into what felt like a car seat. Wendall guessed it was a van or SUV. Once the figure had him settled where he wanted him, he shoved something next to Wendall's lips. Wendall tried his hardest to keep his mouth closed but his hair was yanked back, causing him to scream in pain. Once his mouth opened, a liquid was poured down his throat.

Wendall heard the vehicle door slam shut then felt it shift into gear. It only drove a short distance before stopping. He struggled to stay awake but much to his dismay, the sleep overcame him faster than he ever would have expected.

When he awoke hours later, Wendall could hear birds singing—a clear indicator that it was morning. He was tied in a chair again, and blindfolded. The approaching footsteps filled him with dead as he knew his tormentor had returned.

The figure lowered his voice to a whisper.

"Shush!!!!!"

Wendall pleaded. "Please don't hurt me."

"Be quiet. Shush!!!!"

Wendall felt someone untying the blindfold from his face, and then the rope on his hands was removed before the figure left the room. As his eyes slowly came into focus, he observed the space around him. The walls were white and there were no windows.

The figure returned reached for a plate of food which consisted of scrambled eggs, toast, juice and a banana. Starved, Wendall ferociously devoured everything on the plate. The figure spoke in a deep, distorted voice; Wendall couldn't quite make it out, but it was familiar. A glass of juice was pressed to his lips until he was forced to drink it. Wendall felt his eyelids growing heavy.

Barely conscious, he felt the figure lifting his arms and walking him across a hallway into another room that resembled a large, gray-and-brown cave. He dimly perceived lightbulbs hanging from long metal pendants and, in the center of the room, a king-size bed with white sheets. Wendall's eyes fluttered open enough to see a man in a dark business suit entering the room through a metal door. Then he felt the blindfold once more being tied around his head.

Wendall heard the door close, and sensed he was alone with the stranger in the dark suit. He heard shoes fall to the floor, and the rustle of pants and jewelry being removed. Then he felt hands picking him up and placing him so that his knees were bent and he was leaning next to the bed. He could feel legs on either side of him.

"No!" Wendall cried.

Wendall's head was shoved between the sweaty thighs with protruding moles of a complete stranger. Wendall felt the prickly pubic hairs against his dry chapped lips and the smell of the stranger's crotch emitted a horrible odor. His mouth was guided to a rock-hard penis. As hard as he tried to keep his mouth closed to prevent the penis from entering, he couldn't maintain that kind of energy, due to the man shoving his head so forcefully toward the erection. Eventually, Wendall's mouth opened as he screamed in pain and the man shoved his mouth over his erection. His mouth was around his entire penis as his head was forced up and down in a violent continuous motion. A strong stream of semen shot through Wendall's mouth in a matter of seconds.

Wendall nearly threw up as he spit the semen out and tried to get away from the bed. "Stop it! Please stop!" Wendall yelled.

The man grabbed Wendall aggressively, picked him up and threw him on the bed on his stomach. He started to cough out the remaining semen wriggling to get out from under the man who had crawled on top of him. Then the penis violently penetrated his anus with a strong force, harder and harder. Wendall felt the figure's hands up against his butt as he held his penis. He kept shoving his penis in and out quickly until Wendall's anus bled profusely. Wendall couldn't speak, almost comatose from the pain.

In a very low voice, Wendall pleaded.

"Please stop. Please."

As tears streamed from Wendall's eyes, the figure raised himself up gently from Wendall, and put his clothes back on. He departed, leaving Wendall lying naked, immersed in blood on the white sheets of the bed.

Chapter Twenty-Four

Thursday, September 25, 2008 – 6:30 a.m.

As Harianne and Tracey exited their Coldwater Canyon home at dawn, three black Ford F-150 trucks, with sparkling chrome wheels pulled into their brick circular drive.

Harianne's patience was wearing thin. This remodeling project was costly and time-consuming. Tracey didn't care about the cost; he just wanted the project finished. He missed his 70-inch flat-screen television and the lazy weekends with Harianne. He liked football, golf, baseball and basketball games on the big screen. Tracey wasn't fretting the extra time it was taking; he knew a new media room would soon be his second home. It would all work out.

Stepping out of his truck, Christophe tucked his white shirt into his tight blue jeans and grabbed his plans from the front seat. Instinct told him not to bother Harianne and Tracey. He raised his hand and waved goodbye as he walked to the company trailer parked off to the side of the house.

Walking together to the garage, Tracey whispered in Harianne's ear. "I should have been a contractor. I missed my calling, Harianne."

"I don't think so. If you decide you don't want your new Porsche 911 that was specially shipped from Germany, just let me know. I'll take it off your hands," Harianne quipped good-naturedly.

"I'm cool, no complaints," he smiled indulgently.

They kissed each other before getting into their own vehicles, both heading to the same location, the Clara Shortridge Folz Criminal

Justice Center, where the preliminary hearing for Chase Buckman would commence.

September 25, 2008 – 10:00 a.m.

Twenty-one days after the discovery of Jaime Herrera's body, the preliminary hearing of Chase Buckman at the Clara Shortridge Folz Criminal Justice Center, was on schedule for 10:00 a.m. Harianne parked across the street in the underground structure designated for staff and visitors. She grabbed her briefcase and headed toward the courthouse, her pace brisk.

Harianne wore her signature attire—black leather stilettos, a black blazer, a black pencil skirt and a white blouse adorned with gold-buttons. She headed to a Starbuck's coffee cart in the corner section of the courthouse, grabbed a Grande Caramel latte and sat on a bench outside Department A3, waiting for the courtroom doors to open. The waiting was always tedious even if only moments away. She hated sitting on the hard wooden benches (which seemed more like bedrock) and hoped that things would proceed on time to limit her duration on the bench and give her poor butt a break.

After twenty minutes of eternal waiting, and her behind hurting like hell, the bailiff finally opened the courtroom doors. Harianne polished off the last of her latte and dropped the cup in the trash and wiped the foam from her mouth. She checked in with the court clerk, found her designated seat, and began organizing her notes and documents in preparation for the hearing.

The courtroom filled up with Calvin House faculty members, neighbors and parents—all for the most part quiet and orderly. Harianne turned around and took in the arriving people into the courtroom. Boston and Pamela Buckman, clearly distraught and agitated, sat directly behind the counsel tables in the second row. Forbes sat in the first row behind Harianne's table. He made eye contact with her but did not attempt comment. The seeming madding crowd remained discreetly quiet, waiting for the judge to enter.

Gaston Reeves seated himself at his designated table and removed files from his briefcase. He felt Harianne's presence, but did not look her way, preferring to keep his head down and focused on his files.

He then proceeded to write on a long yellow-ruled legal pad for about ten minutes before turning his head to acknowledge Harianne.

"Harianne, how are you?" he said with forced equanimity.

"I'm fine. Seems like old times," she replied evenly.

"One could say that, yes."

And that was that. Bullshit banter finished and done with. Time for war. A war, Harianne feared, she would at this stage of the game, lose.

A door in the corner of the courtroom opened, and the bailiff escorted Chase Buckman to the defense table beside Harianne. Everyone in the chamber stood as Judge Aaron Portola entered the courtroom. A no-nonsense Italian-American man of around 70 years old, who had been on the bench for more than twenty years, Judge Portola took his seat and looked to the crowd, his pellucid eyes razor-sharp and incisive. The shuffle of the rest of the courtroom audience could be heard as everyone resumed their seats. Judge Portola glanced at his laptop and perused the files before him. The courtroom was silent aside from a quiet sneeze heard from somewhere in the back of the room.

The Judge began his standard prefatory litany: "This is the time and place for the preliminary examination and hearing in the case of the People of the State of California versus Chase Buckman. Case No. EA4953388. Would each Counsel state their names and appearances for the record, please."

Gaston stood and spoke in a tone of voice he was certain commanded respectful attention. His arrogance was palpable but Harianne felt it wasn't really off-putting. Amusing at best.

"Gaston Reeves, People of the State of California."

Harianne stood next. "Harianne DeCanter, attorney for defendant Chase Buckman. He is present, Your Honor."

The Judge nodded in approval.

"Thank you. Are Counsel ready to proceed?" he asked.

"Yes," Gaston said.

Harianne cleared her throat and pushed a paper on her table for no reason other than to give her some time for verbal preamble. "At this point, Your Honor, I would like to make a motion to exclude."

The Judge nodded then looked to Gaston. "Mr. Reeves, would you please approach the bench."

Gaston stood, adjusting his suit as he walked quickly toward the judge. His Honor leaned in a bit to speak with him.

"Mr. Reeves. Do you have any potential witnesses subject to exclusion?" inquired Judge Portola.

"No, your Honor."

"Thank you."

Gaston returned to the prosecution's table.

The Judge looked out to the courtroom. "Mr. Reeves does not have any witnesses for exclusion." He took a moment to glance at his papers then looked up to Gaston.

"Would the People call their first witness."

"The People call Dr. Cole Peduska," Gaston spoke out, perhaps too loudly.

Dr. Cole Peduska, sitting in the third row behind the prosecution, stood and moved along the aisle toward the witness stand. She wore an impeccable two piece suit and her hair was tucked neatly into a bun, befitting the occasion. The tapping from her heels as she walked toward the stand resonated in the room, the only discernible sound in the place for several seconds. The clerk at her desk to the left of the stand, stood, pro forma, looked to the good doctor and spoke.

"Please raise your right hand and repeat after me. You do solemnly swear the testimony you may give in the cause now pending before this court shall be the truth, the whole truth and nothing but the truth, so help you God?"

As serious as a heart attack, Dr. Peduska responded, "I do."

The clerk resumed her seat and Gaston walked towards the witness and stood at her side.

"Please state your name for the record, spelling your first and last name for the Court." he said once more in a voice that he hoped resonated with sheer authority.

"Cole Peduska," the doctor said and then proceeded to spell her name.

"Please state your position."

"I'm a Medical Examiner for the County of Los Angeles."

"And you are a doctor of pathology, correct?"

"Yes."

"Are you Board Certified?"

"I am," she said.

"Thank you. When did you first observe the body of Jaime Herrera?" Gaston asked.

"September 5, 2008 at Calvin House Preparatory School."

"What time would you say you observed the body?" Gaston asked.

"According to my report, just before 7:30 a.m."

"Where was the body located?"

"It was located near the dig site where Alcott Construction was working. To be exact, the body was lying next to the bulldozer that unearthed it. It was face up in the dirt."

"What do you believe the time of death to be?" Gaston asked.

"Judging by my analysis, it would have been between 9:00 or 10:00 p.m. that same evening."

"Were there any marks on his body which might have shown a struggle?" Gaston continued.

"None whatsoever."

"Would you please describe your findings?"

"We found the body completely naked and buried in loose dirt. No hemorrhages were present, although superficial abrasions were found on the arms and tibia surfaces, indicating that they probably occurred post mortem and may have occurred in the process of transporting the body to the eventual grave site."

"Objection," Harianne said. "Lacks foundation and is conclusionary."

"Sustained," the Judge said.

Gaston frowned at both the Judge and Harianne.

"For the record, can you tell us what rigor mortis is?" Gaston asked.

"Rigor mortis is a state in which the body musculature contracts, primarily in the large muscle groups of the shoulders and large muscle groups of the upper and lower limb girdle, making the body rigid. The process begins 6 to 8 hours after death and extends 8 to 10 hours thereafter. The condition was still present in the corpse at 8:30 a.m. The approximate time of death was, as I said, about 10:00 p.m. The temperature was 68 degrees during the night and was 68 degrees Fahrenheit when the body was discovered."

"Was there anything else unusual about the body?" Gaston asked.

"Yes. The color of the body was a bluish gray and it emitted a semi-sweet odor—sweet, like honey, yet somewhat acrid as well. I guess a sweet and sour smell is the best way to characterize it. From colleagues who have had first-hand experience with cyanide poisoning, this odor is described as the aroma of bitter almonds."

"Was there evidence of cyanide in the body itself?" Gaston asked.

"Yes. We performed a spectral scan on the blood to confirm the presence of cyanide. The scan revealed at least 10 times the non-toxic level of cyanmethemoglobin. Cyanide combines with hemoglobin to prevent the transport of oxygen to the tissues and vital organs. There are spectral peaks which indicate cyanide binding, also known as CN Radical. According to toxicology, there were no signs of alcohol or other drugs indicative to the cause of death."

"So in your expert opinion and from your autopsy results, what was the cause of death?" Gaston asked.

"The cause of death is clearly cyanide poisoning. There is the possibility that rigor mortis may have been accelerated by the toxin," the doctor replied.

"Thank you, doctor," Gaston said and then turned to the judge. "No further questions, Your Honor."

The Judge turned his attention to Harianne.

"Cross-examination, Ms. Decanter?"

Harianne nodded. "Yes, Your Honor."

She walked over to the witness stand and leaned both hands on the banister, facing the examiner.

"Dr. Peduska, you just testified that cyanide was present in the body of Jaime Herrera. Did the toxicological study reveal that Mr. Herrera had any medical condition prior to the presence of cyanide?"

"There is always a possibility that a medical condition might have been present. It is very unlikely, though, and I saw no evidence of medications or other chemicals that would have contributed to the cause of death.

"How much cyanide was in the body of Jaime Herrera?"

"It was substantial. It was in granular form, like salt, and it was detected in the apple juice carton."

"From your observation, could you tell if the body was placed there in the face up position, dragged to the construction site or simply dumped?"

"Objection," Gaston said. "Compound."

"Sustained," the judge said. "Ms. DeCanter, please ask another question that is not compound."

Harianne took in a breath then looked to the Medical Examiner.

"Doctor, please tell us if the body was placed face up, to the best of your knowledge. Can you say that with any degree of certainty?"

"No."

"Can you say with any sense of certainty that the body was dragged there?"

"No."

"Or that it was dumped?"

"No." But the body was handled with some obvious care, no marks or bruises. From the looks of it, Mr. Herrera was moved to the construction site in some manner, but then carefully placed in that position before he was covered up."

"Thank you," Harianne said. "Now how much would you say Jaime Herrera weighed prior to his death?"

"Maybe 125 pounds."

"Would you agree that when you factor in rigor mortis, it would be difficult to move the body by carrying it from inside the building to the construction site?"

"Yes, that would be a reasonable assumption," the doctor said, nodding.

Gaston glanced to the Judge. "No further questions, Your Honor."

"Then please call your next witness, Mr. Reeves."

"The People call Detective Tracey Sanders," Gaston said.

Although Tracey and Harianne had not discussed the matter, she had a feeling he was going to be required to testify. She moved her legal pad to the side and focused intently on the testimony Tracey was about to provide.

The clerk once again stood and repeated her mantra to Tracey.

"Please raise your right hand and repeat after me. You do solemnly swear the testimony you may give in the case now pending before this court shall be the truth, the whole truth and nothing but the truth, so help you God?"

Tracey gave a slight nod. "I do."

"Please state your name for the record, spelling your first and last name for the Court," Gaston said.

Tracey complied, spelling it all out.

"Please state your position," the clerk said.

"I am a Homicide Detective with the Los Angeles County Sheriff's Division."

"Detective Sanders. We have located your notes that you made in the course of your investigation in the murder book at pages on 00501 through 00602 and photos taken by the crime scene investigators. Did you write these notes?"

"Yes. I did."

"Are you familiar with the notes you wrote?"

"Yes, but I've not referred to them in a while."

Gaston gave a sigh that seemed to say 'figures'. He said, "If I show you the notes, would it refresh your memory?"

"Yes, of course."

Gaston walked to his table and pulled out a set of documents from a three ring binder. He returned to the stand to hand the notes to Tracey who perused the material without comment. After several minutes Tracey looked up at Gaston indicating he was ready to continue with his testimony.

"Do you feel your memory is now refreshed, sir?" Gaston asked.

"Yes, thank you," Tracey replied.

"Having looked at the notes, what time did you arrive at Calvin House?"

"At or near 7:00 a.m." Tracey said.

"What did you do upon your arrival?"

"I spoke with the responding First Officer at 7:05 a.m. He informed me that the body of a dead juvenile male around 15-17 years old had been found at the construction site located on Calvin House property."

"What was your first observation?"

"Upon examining the body, I noticed that it was grayish blue. The boy had been dead for a matter of hours. There were no other people in the area other than the construction workers and the foreman in the trailer," Tracey said without emotion.

"Did you see any other people around the CSI site that might be persons of interest other than the foreman and the construction workers?" Gaston asked.

"No."

"We've already established that the cause of death was cyanide poisoning, but from your initial examination of the body, was there any indication that the boy had been shot?"

"No indication," Tracey said evenly.

"Had he been stabbed?"

"No."

"Did you find a weapon at or near the body?"

"There were no weapons at the crime scene."

"Did you notice any vehicles?"

"No, other than the white Chevrolet Tahoe that was parked by the trailer. The Tahoe belonged to the foreman."

"Did you notice anything else unusual at the crime scene?"

"No."

"Were there any fingerprints on the body itself?"

"Yes, several, including those of the defendant. Our fingerprint analyst was able to determine that much. It's a difficult process because we deal with powdering wrists, ankles, face or breasts and any prints that are developed are photographed and lifted accordingly. The fingerprints of the defendant were also on the apple juice carton that we found in his room as well."

"Let's back that up a bit. The carton was actually found in Jaime's room?"

"Correct. In the room shared by Jaime Herrera and the Defendant, Chase Buckman."

"And they were roommates?"

"Yes. So the headmaster of the school confirmed," Tracey replied.

"And to confirm further, the fingerprints on the carton matched with those found on the deceased?"

"Correct. Yes."

"Can you account for how the fingerprints might have been on Jaime's body?" Gaston asked.

"Any number of ways. They were roommates, no doubt there was physical contact to some degree or another," Tracey said.

"Was the deceased homosexual? That would also explain the prints."

"Perhaps. But I have no idea of what the sexual orientation of the deceased might have been, nor the defendant, for that matter. In any event, though, Headmaster Madden never indicated as such about the two boys," Tracey replied.

"Where on the body were the fingerprints located?"

"Arms, wrists and hands," Tracey said.

Tracey glanced at Harianne. Harianne lowered her head momentarily, and the look on her face bespoke true concern.

"No further questions, Your Honor." Gaston said.

Harianne focused intently on the documents in front of her. She was trying to quickly review her notes and the information she had obtained throughout the weeks prior to the hearing.

Judge Portola cleared his throat quickly catching her attention and continued, "Cross-Examination, Ms. DeCanter?"

"Yes, your Honor."

Harianne smoothed her skirt, took on a serious demeanor and looked directly at Tracey as she approached him.

"Detective Sanders, when you arrived at the crime scene, did you notice anyone or anything unusual at the construction site?"

"No."

"Was there any evidence of footprints in the dirt prior to the body's discovery?" she asked.

"No There were no traces of footprints."

"Any tire markings?" Harianne said.

"No."

"You stated that there were no weapons found. Did the crime scene investigators sift through the dirt thoroughly to ascertain if weapons were on site?"

"According to the report, a thorough search was completed for the presence of weapons," Tracey said.

"Let's shift gears. How do you suppose the body got there?"

Gaston called out as Harianne had anticipated. "Objection. Calls for speculation,"

"Ms. DeCanter, can you rephrase the question, please?" the Judge said.

Harianne took a breath and nodded. She gave a tight smile to Tracey.

"You mentioned the white Chevrolet Tahoe. Was that vehicle examined thoroughly for weapons?

"Yes. Nothing was found," Tracey said.

"No further questions, Your Honor."

Judge Portola looked over to the Prosecutor.

"Mr. Reeves. Any further witnesses for the prosecution?"

"No, your Honor. But I would like to admit some exhibits as evidence, if you would allow?"

"Proceed," the Judge nodded.

While Gaston admitted his various exhibits, which included chemist and toxicology reports, along with relevant photographs, Harianne vigorously proceeded with her objections that the information was privileged and consistently made motions to suppress evidence and motions to dismiss. She knew that no matter how hard she tried to prove the credibility of Chase, the Judge had his mind made up that her defense was going south which was pretty much par for the course. She would have to agree. Chase's fingerprints on the deceased, the fingerprints on the cyanide-laced apple juice carton and the fight witnessed by boys in the schoolyard, plus Chase's declaration of "I'm gonna kill you, Herrera," were fairly damning and the Judge would surely quash she had to dismiss the case in its entirety.

Her best chance would be at the trial level and that's where she would shine most brightly and would get what she wanted—a fair trial with an end-verdict of "not guilty." Of course, what one wanted and what would prevail in the real world were two different bears and right now Harianne did her best not to think about this.

Judge Portola listened patiently to all the stipulations, motions to admit evidence, motions to suppress evidence and all the predictable objections.

Finally, Gaston sighed, looked up at Judge Portola and said, "Prosecution rests."

"Ms. Decanter would you like to make any further motions at this time?"

"Yes, your Honor. For the record, I would like to make a motion to dismiss for insufficiency of evidence."

"Motion denied," Judge Portola stated unequivocally. "Ms. DeCanter, the defendant was heard threatening the deceased, his fingerprints are all over the planet in terms of the body and the apple juice carton, I mean really... I believe there is reasonable suspicion and cause in this case to warrant trial proceedings. Counsel, you are held to answer in Department B-8, 15 days from today, October

10th. Defendant is to remain in custody with no set bail. Court adjourned."

Judge Portola brought his gavel down on the block and stood to exit the courtroom. All those present quickly came to their feet as they watched him walk through the door to his chambers.

Pamela, Chase's mother, dressed in a black coat dress and low heels, broke down in tears. Boston pulled her towards him doing his best to comfort her, giving her a kiss on her forehead.

Chase, slouching in his seat after the door to the judge's chambers closed, fought the urge to cry, but the salty tears rolled down his face, ignoring his will to remain stoic. Harianne knew she had to remain strong for her client; she pulled a small package of Kleenex from her purse and handed it to Chase. She clinched his hand, a tactile gesture of moral support.

"Chase, I'm sorry. I know this isn't what we wanted but please know that I am still fighting for you. I believe, now more than ever, that you are innocent and I am going to do everything in my power to make this right. You have to stay strong."

Chase looked at her, tears still streaming down his face, with an expression that held a mezzaluna of devastation and hopelessness.

She saw the despair in Pamela's face as she wiped away tears with a crumpled piece of Kleenex. Boston stood strong, and concerned himself with consoling her. He glared at Harianne before exiting the courtroom with a look that said clearly "you're failing, counselor."

Salty tears continued to stream down Chase's cheeks despite all best efforts to arrest their torrential flow. The bailiff walked over to Chase, handcuffed him and led him back to the jail. Chase turned back to look at Harianne. She gave him a "chin up" sign with her hands.

A rough first day, Harianne thought to herself. But not entirely a surprise. Of course the Judge was going to rule for the continuation of a trial. The evidence, notwithstanding her motion to dismiss, was rather damning on the surface. Gaston gave her a perfunctory nod as he packed his paperwork into his briefcase then also exited without a word.

Tracey glanced at her for a moment, then walked over and gave a slight nod. There would not be much to discuss tonight regarding this stage of the case.

Not yet, anyway.

The fun had not yet really begun.

"Wanna grab some lunch?" Tracey asked.

"I'm for that," Harianne said, bunching her papers into her own briefcase. "Let's get the hell out of here."

Chapter Twenty-Five

Thursday – 6:00 p.m.

Back at the precinct, Zack knocked on Tracey's office door. Tracey, preoccupied with paperwork, jolted out of his concentration and snapped. "What do you want?"

Zack opened the door and peeked in at Tracey.

"Hey, what's wrong with you, sourpuss?"

Tracey relaxed and shook his head wearily. "Nothing. Just whipped."

Zack frowned dubiously. "Doesn't sound like nothing, pal."

Tracey offered a grim smile and stretched his arms, letting out a tired groan. He suddenly thought of how good a drink would be just about now.

"Just thinking about today's hearing," he said.

Zack stepped into the office proper, one hand holding a Coke can, and nodded.

"Yeah. Looks like the prosecution has a solid case against Buckman," he said matter-of-factly.

Tracey sniffed diffidently, almost derisively. "We'll see. I dunno. Sure, the kids were roommates and the apple juice carton with the cyanide residue is pretty damning, but I still have my doubts."

Zack let a dubious whistle-sigh. "Okay. I'm pretty sure we have the killer, but…"

Tracey let that hang in the air for a moment but said nothing. He suddenly wished that Zack would just leave; it felt he had a thousand more important things to do at the moment than shoot the shit with his partner on a case he was coming to detest on a minute-by-minute basis.

"His family is really taking it pretty hard," Zack said at last. He grabbed a metal chair, turned its back toward Tracey and sat down, legs spread out. He eyed Tracey evenly. "So, what's eating you about all this?" His tone was sympathetic, not pushy.

Tracey chuckled humorlessly. He abruptly stood and walked over to the window overlooking the parking lot. Two cops on either side of what appeared to be an agitated junkie walked toward the booking offices. Another point for justice being served, he noted. Tracey thought back distantly when he wore a uniform and worked the streets. Seemed so long ago. *In the days when the fish were thick and he was young and strong.* The sea-faring ditty came out of nowhere and he smiled inwardly.

He shook his head, as if in answer to a piece of self-questioning then turned back to Zack. "I want to go back to Calvin House."

Zack raised his eyebrows in clear surprise. "Why the hell?"

"I want to look at the rooms of the other boys again."

"Okay," Zack said, still clearly a bit confused. "Do you know something I don't know or is this a gut-hunch Hail Mary in finding new shit?"

"I know as much as you do and, yeah, I'm not quite sure so I'm following my gut. I feel like we're missing something."

"We have two more boys missing and the person we think murdered Jaime is behind bars. Any other reason you want to go back to the school?"

"Yeah, Forbes Madden."

"What about him?"

"He and Jaime Herrera didn't get along. And his DNA was a close match."

Zack took a drink of the soda then nodded. "Yeah, but Chase had motive and they didn't get along, either. Besides, his fingerprints were all over the apple juice carton."

"I think both of them had motive."

Zack didn't seem to want to argue that and conceded. "Maybe. But, again, the fingerprints…the boy, not Madden."

Tracey nodded in agreement but then made a smacking noise with his lips that all but screamed 'I'm still not sure.'

"I wonder if he's hiding something," Tracey mused.

Zack shrugged. "Maybe. But it doesn't point to him being the killer."

Tracey sighed, acknowledging Zack's point wearily. "We're going back to Calvin House. I want to make sure that we've got all of the facts straight."

"Fine, but I'm calling it a day. We zap the Calvin House again, no problem by me. See you in the a.m." With that, Zack flipped his chair back around and left the office, dropping the dead soda can in Tracey's trash basket on his way out.

"This whole case stinks," Tracey said aloud and scratched his head with both hands, despite the lack of an itch. Something *was* missing—he felt it deep in his gorge. It was the feeling one gets with the surety that something bad was going to happen, an unspoken and undefined notion of rot in the making.

Think, he said to himself. What to do next?

***

After Zack left, Tracey picked up his phone and punched in some numbers. The voice on the other end answered almost immediately.

"Hello?"

"Dr. Peduska, Tracey Sanders."

"Hey Tracey, how are you?" The doctor's voice was congenial yet maintained professionalism.

"I'm good, thanks—still working the Herrera case. I'm wondering if you might be able to help me out with a few answers to some questions."

"Of course, shoot."

"I've been looking at the DNA results. Curious, just how close were the Restriction Fragment Length Polymorphisms, you know, the RFLP's, on the DNA profile for Forbes Madden?"

"These can be separated into different bands. These bands are scored as if they were specific genes. To the point, in the examination of Forbes Madden's DNA, there were remarkable similarities to those of Chase Buckman. Like the separation in the procedure of the alleles and their assortment."

"I'm sorry," Tracey interrupted. "Can you say that in English—

I'm just a dumb cop. What the hell are alleles and assortments?"

The doctor laughed good-naturedly.

"Okay, sorry. Alleles are one of two or more alternative forms of a gene that arise by mutation and are found at the same place on a chromosome."

"Got it," Tracey said, though in fact, he really only understood the mutation part—that the genes had substantively transformed. "Go on, please."

The good doctor continued obligingly. "On the other hand, there were several significant bands that were specific to Mr. Madden. In other words, the bands are kinda like genetic signatures. Like your name. In any case, these would tend to rule him out as a suspect, by rule."

The doctor heard Tracey's long sigh. "Since Chase's fingerprints were on the apple juice box and he shared a room with Jaime, it was only logical that Chase was the killer. Why are you asking?"

"I'm skeptical, is all. Could there possibly be two killers, doctor?"

"Possible, but not likely. Why?" A slight pause, then: "What are you thinking?"

"I'm just finding it hard to believe that Chase was the killer. It may sound logical but yet I'm not so sure."

"Predicated on what, detective? What are you not sure about? The science doesn't lie," the doctor said, as if there was little room for any kind of reasonable doubt on the matter.

Tracey could discern the tone of slight annoyance in the doctor's voice. But he'd gotten what he needed. Ok, doc, thanks so much for your time. If I have more questions, I may be contacting you."

"I'm always available," Tracey said equitably and hung up.

Tracey leaned back in his chair.

The mouse in his gut was still gnawing away at him.

"This case stinks," he said again aloud.

***

At day's end, Forbes remained in his office, eating from a small carton of blueberries. He stared off into space, his mind wandering, swiveling right to left in his chair. The hearing was a man-bitch to sit through and he just couldn't shut his mind off. His grandmother's diary was lingering in the back of his mind; once again he found himself being drawn to what she had written so very long ago:

Trial had commenced. I watched as Brinks, dressed in dark gray jail attire, took the stand. I could tell that he was a nervous wreck. I had no idea that his testimony would be what it was.

I sat in the courtroom today and listened to my husband talk about murdering an innocent boy because of an affair I had with the boy's father.

During his testimony he talked about how he had asked Thomas Peyton to go to the woodshed that evening and get some more kindling for the school fireplace. Once he left, Brinks said he covered his own head and entire body in a priest's robe, pulled the hood over his head, and placed a black mask over his face as a disguise. He followed the boy to the tool shed. He admitted that the boy was of small build and that he only weighed about 80 pounds.

As I listened to him testifying, I sobbed uncontrollably with tears running down my face. I couldn't believe what he was saying. I couldn't believe what he had done. And it was all my fault. He did what he did to that child because of me.

Brinks talked about how he snuck up behind him and pushed him head first into a hole that he had dug earlier that day inside the shed; where no one would notice him digging. On the way down into the hole, he said he heard a loud crack as Thomas' head hit the arroyo rock. He went on to say he didn't mean to kill him; he just wanted to scare him.

It seemed like his testimony was never going to end. I was having a hard time listening to what all he was saying. As he was describing the events he kept his head down. He didn't look up; he just looked at the wood in front of his chair. He continued his testimony talking about how he jumped into the hole immediately and tried to revive him, but he couldn't. 'By the time I realized what I had done, the boy was dead so I tried to make it look like an accident by moving the body to the pile of leaves. I felt helpless, and deeply saddened,' he said. As he looked up, making eye contact with me from across the courtroom where I was sitting he continued, 'I even cried, but it didn't take away my anger with Clay and the betrayal by my wife.'

I will never forget those words. He stated them so clearly, in front of everyone in that courtroom. My affair caused Brinks to go off the deep end;

to murder a poor innocent child. He just sat there on the witness stand—
no remorse, no movement and no emotion. He'd had his revenge against
Clay Peyton and me. He shuffled his feet, bound by metal chains, as the
bailiff removed him from the courtroom. He was convicted of the murder of
Thomas Peyton and sentenced to life in prison without parole. It was the
ultimate revenge against revenge. Thomas Peyton was an innocent child
used as a weapon of hatred and jealousy.

Forbes involuntarily shuddered. His grandmother's words were haunting in the extreme. The magnitude of evil that was manifest, not only back in the day when his grandmother was passionately cavorting about with Clay, leading to murder, but also the more recent homicidal malfeasance, boggled the mind of one Forbes Madden. Christ, he thought; humanity could be a foul lot on occasion. Strike that, on *most* occasions. How this current case might resolve itself was anybody's guess…but Forbes had the lurking feeling that it would not end well. Correction, had not ended well for the poor victim already.

Another shudder, this time followed by a wave of nausea.

He glanced at the blueberries he was munching.

And then he thought of the boy's corpse, described in horrible forensic detail on the stand today by the medical examiner and the detective in charge.

He rose suddenly and fled to the bathroom.

The yarking seemed to go on forever.

Afterwards, he still felt ill.

That poor kid, he couldn't help repeating in his mind. *That poor kid…*

Chapter Twenty-Six

Thursday Evening — 7:00 p.m.

Tracey and Harianne arrived home at the same time, the sun well over the horizon, but its light still polarizing the sky with an azul blue and orange veneer. The outside driveway and path leading up to the house proper had been transformed into a virtual construction zone home littered with cement containers, trash bins, canvas and workhorses. Paint cans lined the perimeter of the path, as if there was some concerted effort to at least appear organized, with a polite concern for the owners perception of work performed and executed.

They parked side by side in the wide driveway. Austria waved from the living room window. When they walked into the house, she greeted them in the foyer, two bottles of wine in either hand—one a Chardonnay and the other, a Pinot Noir.

"Hi, guys! How was your day? Are you hungry?" Austria machine-gun queried them, her indelible smile fairly infectious.

Harianne grinned back at her. "Kind of," she replied, looking beyond Austria at what appeared to be some arrested construction a few yards yonder in the living room. "What's going on back there?"

"Is that a hole in the wall?" Tracey asked, incredulously, staring at a black gaping maw toward the rear of the room.

Austria nodded vigorously. "Christophe's worker hit the wall by accident. He didn't mean to do it," she explained. "Just one of those things, right?"

"Um…yeah, I guess," Harianne said rather cynically.

"Christophe came to me immediately to let me know what had

happened and assured me that they would be fixing it. He said that once the room is completed, you'll never know the wall had been damaged."

"That's comforting," Tracey said sarcastically.

Harianne sighed wearily. "I don't understand...how could he not see that he hit the side wall of the dining room?"

"They're demolition happy!" Tracey yelled from the kitchen, more irritated than he had been previously in terms of how the construction project was going. "I hope they're not deliberately creating more work for themselves, hoping to bill us through the room. Trust me, we won't be paying for the hours it will cost to fix that hole issue."

"I've got this all under control," Austria assured the disembodied voice of Tracey. "I'm working with Christophe so let's leave it at that. I know you both are busy and ready to have your home back but getting irritated with the contractor isn't going to make it happen any quicker."

After a cursory investigation of the progress with the house, the three of them made their way back to Austria's cottage. They settled into the kitchen, where Austria dished up a flank steak salad. A piping hot loaf of pumpernickel bread followed forthwith, served on a wood platter with a ramekin full of honey butter. The *coup de gras* was a bottle of Syrah. They enjoyed their meal for several minutes in silence.

Tracey cut another piece of bread and finally broke the quiet. "So, I gather you're already preparing for trial," he said to Harianne. "I'm going to assume that, as always, you don't think your client did it?"

"You bet I'm preparing, pal. How could I not? I *know* he didn't do it. The facts just don't add up."

Tracey looked into Harianne's eyes and considered her words for a moment. She was voicing what he himself was feeling. "Would you mind pouring me some more wine, please?," he said with a smile. Harianne smiled back, reached for the Sirah close to her and complied.

"Actually, the facts *do* add up, at least to this poor old beat cop," Tracey said casually. "The cyanide in the apple carton, the DNA and the absence of any other credible suspect—this all tells a guy like me that your boy is guilty as hell."

"He isn't," Harianne said simply, sipping her wine.

"Based on what? Spiritual intervention—little voices telling you that he's as innocent as the day is long?"

"You don't have to be so rude," she said easily. "No, I'm saying it's a feeling I have—the kid's not a murderer. Come on, Tracey, I know you. You have doubts, too. I can see it in your eyes."

He considered her for a moment without comment. Then: "I'm going back down to Calvin House tomorrow with Zack. Gonna nose around some more."

"So, I'm right," Harianne said victoriously. "You're not completely sold that Chase is the bad guy either. Little voices?" she teased.

"A gut hunch, lover," he smiled back.

Austria regarded the byplay between them and smiled. She could see they were having fun with one another, despite the seriousness of the subject matter.

When Harianne finished her meal, she yawned and signaled Tracey that she was heading to bed. He soon followed but not until he had cleared the table and helped Austria in the kitchen.

Friday – 9:00 a.m.

A heavy rain fell the next morning, and traffic was jammed on the 210 East into La Cañada Flintridge. When Tracey and Zack finally arrived at Calvin House, they found Forbes standing under the arched corridor, his hands behind his back as he watched the rain soak the Calvin House grounds. The rain had a tremendous effect on the number of media vans at Calvin House. When the rain arrived in the early morning hours, the media vans were gone. It was a nice break for the students and faculty at the school and especially for Forbes.

"Good morning, gentlemen," he called out to the detectives as they made their approach.

"Good morning, Forbes," they both said in unison.

The look of confusion spread across Forbes' face as he tried to figure out why the detectives were back. After a few seconds he asked, "Did you forget something?"

"Not exactly," Zack said as he pulled a pen and paper from inside his coat. "We're going to need a head count of the boys attending Calvin House."

"Uh, Okay," Forbes said hesitantly. "Our enrollment currently is 287 boys. That includes Chase who, as you know, is in jail."

"Thanks, that's what we had in our notes as well. Just wanted to make sure."

"By any chance does the school use any kind of tracking devices on the boys, kind of like GPS? Something that helps to keep track of where they are or for any boys who may try to leave?"

"Unfortunately, no, we don't. There has been discussion about using some sort of tracking device in their back packs, but from my research, they only last a day. The batteries need to be recharged daily and many of the boys would remove them. However, had we done it, maybe we wouldn't be in the situation we are in now."

"We'd like to take another look around the grounds again, if you don't mind," Tracey said.

"Not at all," Forbes answered. "Go ahead. I've got to return to my office for a meeting. If you need anything, you know where to find me."

***

The rain had cancelled all work for the day at the Calvin House construction site. Zack followed behind Tracey as they stepped in enormous amounts of mud that completely covered their rubber shoes. There wasn't much to see at the spot where Jaime's body had been found other than puddle of rain and mud. The rain came down harder as they moved toward the rear of the property. Tracey's gut told him there was more to the boys missing and he welcomed a media break as they had been camping out across from the school daily. He needed more time to figure out the conundrum.

After reaching the wrought iron and flag stone fence at the back of the property, Tracey and Zack heard a crashing noise. They stopped in their tracks to listen to the noise as it suddenly stopped.

"Was that an earthquake, Zack?"

"I don't think so. The buildings aren't shaking, and nothing else is moving.:

Tracey placed his hand on the ground, but felt nothing.

"Could have been a big rig out on the street, or a sonic boom," Zack suggested.

"I don't know what that was, but we're going to find out," Tracey said.

Forbes had just completed his meeting, when his cell abruptly rang loudly.

"Hey Forbes! It's Chelsea. I'm back. How are you?"

"I'm good. The important question is how are you and my brother?"

"It's day by day, but we're coping. Lincoln is not eating much, but other than that he's good from a health standpoint."

"Chelsea. What's really going on with Lincoln?"

"Bottom line. We still don't have a donor."

"Damn!" angrily remarked Forbes.

"It's been awhile I know, but we've got to bring out patience to the doctor and deal with it."

"How long does he have?"

"I'm not quite sure because he gets better and then he gets worse. Go figure!"

"I see. So day by day?"

"Yes."

"Is there anything I can do to speed up the process?" Forbes asked hopefully.

"No. I tried searching for donors on my own, but it's still a long process."

"How does he look?" Forbes asked, dreading the answer.

"His color is not the greatest. You can tell something is wrong."

"Waiting is the hard part. I really wish I was a match and you would not be going through this."

"The doctors tell me every day to be patient and a donor should come through."

"How are you with that?" Forbes asked softly.

"I have no choice, but I just push through it. The better question is how are you? I catch the news mostly while I'm sitting with Lincoln in his room, and the media is crazy. Are they there all the time?"

"Mostly. It's a media circus."

"I really try to hide it from Lincoln so that he won't worry about you. It's hard because he's so inquisitive."

"Well, call me with another update when you get one. Just check with me."

"I will. Love you." Chelsea said blowing him kisses over the phone.

12:30 p.m.

After combing the Calvin House grounds for two hours, trying to locate the large sonic boom, Tracey and Zack came up empty.

Chapter Twenty-Seven

Friday – 3:00 p.m.

Soaked from their foray at Calvin House, Tracey and Zack headed straight to the locker room at their precinct. They each took a hot shower, washing off the L.A. acidic rain assiduously, then quickly changed into fresh clothes. Zack made his way to the kitchen, grabbed two mugs from the shelf and filled each to the brim with hot coffee. He handed one to Tracey on the fly as they headed to their desks.

Tracey sunk into his chair, accompanied by a sigh. He ran his fingers through his hair, looking out the window at the L.A. skyline. It was morosely gray and the inclement quality of the outside downpour matched his current mood of pell-mell missing facts or evidence to support his gut-hunch doubts of this case.

"Wow! It's coming down cats and dogs now," Zack commented through a whistle. He sucked at his coffee—a habit Tracey silently loathed, but didn't mention this to his partner. Instead, he sipped his own brew with the silence usually attributed to a grave.

"Yeah," he agreed. "We missed the heavy shit of it only by a few minutes."

Zack turned to him, a frown furrowing his brow. "What the hell do you think caused that explosive sound out there? I haven't been able to get it out of my mind."

"I don't have a clue. There's probably a logical explanation that we just didn't come to at that time being pelted by acid rain and all." He chuckled at this and Zack agreed.

"Yeah," Zack quipped. "Or thermobaric gophers with a grudge, preparing to nuke the place."

"Thermobaric," Tracey nodded. "I'm impressed. Where did you learn a word like that?"

"All the new Tom Clancy knock-off novels," Zack admitted. "I eat that shit up like ferrets going after bleeding roadkill."

"Gotta use that word one day on Harianne," Tracey said. "Make her think I'm smarter than I am." He laughed at his own joke, shaking his head in private mirth.

"You fooled me—why not her?" Zack came back without losing a beat.

"Yeah, I walked into that one, didn't I?" Tracey said. He placed his hands on his forehead and leaned back in his chair with another sigh—his litany of late. The Sigh King.

His cell suddenly rang. He glanced at the caller ID and winked at Zack.

"Hey baby! How are ya?" Tracey boomed into the phone.

"I'm good, lover," Harianne replied. "And you'll never guess where the hell I am right now."

"Okay. Where the hell are ya?"

A sexy purr Harianne did offer. "In your lobby, doll."

"Get out of here! So get your tush in here, babe!" Tracey chortled seductively.

Harianne walked into the outer office a moment later. She wore a beige leather sleeveless dress with matching beige heel-out pumps. Her moves were feline, gracefully executed for the benefit of all male personnel in the desk pool. She was inwardly pleased with the attention given to observant eyes to her tight behind, fairly teasing one and all as she walked, and her buttocks shimmying playfully away like two frisky puppies padding to and fro under taught fabric. She glided down the aisle of desks on either side of her and noticed with quiet satisfaction the admiring coterie of attentive detectives taking in her presence, as she approached Tracey's office.

When you got it, flaunt it, she teased herself inwardly.

Harianne gave a little knock on the crenelated window to the office. She then unceremoniously entered. She carried in one hand a large brown paper bag with handles, marked *Portifino*.

"There you are!" she smiled at Tracey. "Hey, Babe!"

Tracey stood up and hugged her, following this with a more than affectionate kiss that made Zack quip: "Get a room, guys!"

"Oh, hush, Zacky." Harianne waved at him in playful dismissal.

"Wow! Look at you!" Tracey said to her, ignoring his partner completely. "Did you just come from court? What's in that Portifino bag?"

"Heck, no! Silly! I just wanted to surprise you with an early dinner." she grinned from ear to ear. Tracey turned to Zack in mock pity.

"You poor bastard. See, I've got a good woman here! Man oh man!"

Zack nodded in acquiescence, secretly hoping he would be asked to partake in the festivities (he loved Portofinos). He watched as Tracey removed the boxes of food from the bag. Tracey noticed Zack fairly salivating and asked casually: "Zack, would you like to join us? There's enough here for one and all."

"Well, maybe some garlic bread if you have it, then I'll be off," Zack said, licking his lips.

Tracey handed him two slices of bread and Zack took the proffered treasure. He got up quickly. "You guys enjoy," he said and made a speedy and discreet departure.

"Let's dig in," Harianne said, taking the chair where Zack was seated.

***

They ate in relative silence, Tracey mentioning about his trip to the school grounds again and Harianne barely uttering a word about the Chase case. Tracey didn't' mind; he relished the quiet time with Harianne, which they didn't have much of too often especially when they were both working on high-profile murder cases together. Harianne stayed for what seemed like hours to Tracey, but he didn't have the heart to end their meal unilaterally. When Harianne was ready to leave, she'd leave, Tracey figured, and far be it from him urging her out first so he could get back to work.

His desk phone abruptly rang. He hit the speaker button, still chewing an errant piece of chicken and mumbled, "This is Sanders," he said, gulping his bird.

For a moment, there was only dead space. A vacuum of sound. Then, they heard it: deep breathing, ragged, almost feral. Then the phone went dead. Harianne looked at Tracey. "Weird. A breather." He replaced the phone on its cradle. "Wrong number, I –"

The phone rang again. The voice this time, male, held no perambulatory breathing.

"Detective, I'm hoping you might have a contact number for Harianne Decanter,"

"I know the lady in question and speak of the devil she's sitting only three feet away from me. And who might this be?" Tracey asked, all friends.

"We'll get to that, detective," the voice said in a clearly patronizing manner. Then: "I really like what you wore today, Harianne! You look hot and sexy. So sexy I could just eat you up, pussy, clit and labia. I want to put my penis between your wet thighs, feel that soaking velvet stitch –

"Hey, hey, hey," Tracey fairly roared at the phone. "Who the hell is this?"

The disembodied foul voice pressed on, as Harianne's expression darkened with horror. "And then I want to suck your tits until you scream like a bitch, hot with desire. I want to soak into you until you howl my name. I want your wetness to drench my face with your cunt cum!"

Tracey couldn't help himself. "Listen, you son of a bitch –"

But the caller hung up in a New York second. Tracey's impending invectives were stultified from the get-go.

Harianne was visibly shaking—with rage—having been verbally defiled in Tracey's presence. She looked to him but she could find no words.

Tracey reached out and took her hand. "You okay, baby?"

"Sure, fine. Except I have an obvious sex pervert as a stalker now," she said, recovering somewhat. "As if I need *that* in my life at the moment," she sighed in surrender.

The phone rang again before the issue could be further discussed. Again, there was no visible caller ID. Tracey hit the speaker button once more and the voice began talking immediately. The voice's timbre this time was low and preternatural in tone—distorted, obfuscated either by the speaker utilizing a device to alter it or by deliberately disguising it without mechanical means.

Harianne visibly shuddered as the first words were uttered.

"This is the Whisper. I'm watching you very closely, Harianne. I know every move you make, where you go and where you *live*. You need to drop this case and drop it fast!"

"Who is this?" Tracey snapped.

"Shut up, cop!" the voice snapped back with equal force. "Listen and learn what you're dealing with. Like right now! If you don't drop the case, Harianne, you and your loved ones will die one by one. Horribly—and in agonizing pain. I will bleed you and them—you will watch in awe at your own exsanguination. Heed my words! Watch me! I am The Whisper."

The phone went as dead as yesterday.

Tracey watched Harianne as she trembled; she looked like she was about to burst into tears, but she stopped short of this and took a deep breath before speaking.

"That's it. This has to be the killer. It's not Chase, clearly, since he's in jail."

"That's total supposition and you know it, Harianne. This could simply be a prank call," Tracey said dismissively. "Some weirdo getting his rocks off talking to you vicariously through my office."

"What makes you so sure of that? He asked for me—by name! And he had the nerve to call here!"

"This kind of thing happens a lot," Tracey said. Not strictly true. They don't usually call asking for your girlfriend and then levying a host of verbal filth across the phone willy-nilly.

Tracey frowned inwardly, thinking.

"The Whisper—who says he knows both of us and where we live." Harianne said in a voice heavy with portent.

"He could be lying," Tracey said, not really believing that at all.

"He knew what I was wearing," Harianne said.

"No, he said he *liked* what you wore," Tracey said. "He didn't go into specifics."

"Well… I do look hot today," Harianne said through a slight (very slight) smile.

"Yeah, you do."

They both went silent after that.

Harianne stood and began to pace. "Wants us to drop the case.

How could any rational individual expect me to do that?"

"You heard the voice," Tracey nodded to the phone. "Did that sound like a rational person?"

"No," she admitted. "Far from." She looked to him in silent supplication. "So…what do we do now?"

Tracey stood as well. "We wait."

"Wait. For what? Love letters next? Flowers?"

"If this guy is a real threat, he'll make some kind of move. He'll make a mistake," Tracey said, with practiced ease.

"Yeah. I only hope that move and mistake are not mutually exclusive and get you or me killed," Harianne voiced what Tracey himself was thinking. She kissed him quickly and walked out the door without a word.

Shit. Tracey pounded the wall in frustration.

God, he hated this case.

8:00 p.m.

The fog had settled over Downtown Los Angeles like a murky shroud, tinctured with an ocean spray fifteen miles away to the west. A breeze accompanied the dewy mist, just enough to scatter fallen leaves across the smooth sidewalks, settling there like motes of colorful arboreal shrapnel. A red brick building not far from the Calvin House and lighted from within by failing fluorescents and surrounded by an 8 foot black wrought iron fence, seemed to defy the encroaching fog with its ambient presence.

Within the generally darkened halls of the place and inside of one of the small rooms, a man in a hoodie, naked from the waist down, was engaged in some rather fierce and vigorous anal assault on young Wendall Dobbs. He had supplied the boy with a generous amount of GHB by way of fine wine and P-Daddy rap deployment and the drug had effectively rendered the lad insensate to the current piece of buggery.

Sweet bleeding Christ, this boy's ass is like velvet, the man mentally notated with lust-laden appreciation. He was pumping the unconscious youngster like a well-oiled derrick; he had briefly—but only briefly—considered donning a condom for this festivity but decided against it at the last moment. The kid's a virgin, after all—no danger of disease in this pert little poop chute. AIDS was a distant remote possibility, like one of those newly discovered exoplanets by SETI, its devotees claiming the possibility of habitability by alien life.

Fat chance of that. Same for Wendall's rectum harboring any secret suppurating disease lurking therein, waiting to devour this man's cock like some predatory flesh-eating bacteria housed on Level 4 of the CDC. Nah.

He'd go in bare and it would end beautifully.

Somewhere deep behind this predator's immoral decision-making to rape Wendall, the more rational, more adult voice of his better nature admonished him for the foul deed-in-making. *So wrong,* the voice repeated over and over, matching each mindless thrust of his drug-induced tumescence (thank you God for Viagra). Of course, it was wrong, he countered as he brought himself closer to climax with each thrust.

That's what makes it so good.

Young boy. Tight ass. Forbidden fruit.

He screamed as he ejaculated his penile sludge deep into Wendall's colon. His body shuddered with the terrific climax, which seemed to go on forever. As he recovered, he already was making preparations for getting rid of the kid, oozing semen like puss from an open sore.

Recovering from the hot shot of his load, the rapist stood and looked down at Wendall, splayed out on his belly like a dead mackerel on some nameless dock.

"Okay, kid," the man murmured. "Gotta get you the hell out of Dodge."

This is where things could get dicey—deciding where to dump the blissfully unconscious human receptacle of his mucilaginous love-crap. He smiled at his own verbal imagination (not to mix metaphors, he quickly amended) then dressed quickly. A strong man by nature, he pulled Wendall up like a sack of potatoes and cradled him in his arms, opening the front door and heading toward the barely operational elevator adjacent to the building.

Once he arrived to ground level, he walked a few yards down to where his vehicle was parked. Now he was breathing heavily from the burden of Wendall's weight.

He arrived at the vehicle, hit the remote in his pocket while lowering Wendall onto the hood, then gave a cursory glance around.

No one lurking about, he noticed with zero surprise.

All in all, he thought, a perfect night for young-boy and a swift, deft departure from the scene of the crime. He dragged Wendall's body to the back of the vehicle, shoved him in and slammed the door shut. "There we go," he muttered satisfactorily.

Life was good.

But that voice in the back of his head simply couldn't resist: *You're gonna get it in the ass because of this, you nasty cum-guzzling poof...from here to eternity...*

He got into the vehicle, turned on the ignition and screeched away.

Chapter Twenty-Eight

Friday – 8:30 p.m.

Tracey and Zack committed several hours researching as to the identity of The Whisper. The customary attempts, pro forma, were made in tracing the calls, but the caller had probably used a burner phone that was identity proof. Besides, no one had expected the call and thus there was no official trace team in play. Tracey phoned the contact person for all the surveillance cameras at or near the Sheriff's Headquarters, located at the Hall of Justice, but no video was found to be suspect, no strange individuals lurking near Tracey's precinct and/or the Hall. Tracey and Harianne had already both called Austria, alerting her to a possible intruder menace on the property, but Austria said everything was fine, no peeping toms, perverts, mullochs or other gremlins lurking about their home property. Tracey had taken no chances, though, and had ordered a drive-by from patrol cars in the vicinity. He and Harianne were not terribly paranoid about this nebulous Whisper entity trying to force his way upon their property, but, hell, it didn't hurt to be ultra-cautious when dealing with possible nut-jobs.

"If I see anyone suspicious, I zap them with my taser," Austria bellowed over the phone to Tracey. Tracey and Zack smirked at this, and Tracey simply replied: "Nice, but I'd prefer you simply lock the doors and call 911 if you run into anything worrisome."

"Oh, you're no fun, honey," Austria replied with a snort.

"Comes with the job," Tracey agreed.

Harianne informed him via email that she had questioned guards near her office, reception personnel, even the next door coffee-jockey at Starbucks if they had seen anyone loitering around or near her offices. All responses were in the depressing (yet relief-giving) negative. If the Whisper had wanted to remain more hidden, he could have bought beachfront property in southern Botswana.

In short, there was simply nothing of substance to latch onto…and this was something both Tracey and Harianne couldn't abide—yet they were helpless at the moment to do more. Though Harianne had left already, they had exchanged half a dozen phone calls and emails. Tracey was right: they would have to let this creep make the next move and attendant to that make a mistake. And this…if truly this guy was the real deal—a potential murder suspect—with truly perilous designs on both Tracey and Harianne. So far, there was only a lot of telephonic sound and fury but nothing in the way of tangible danger.

Zack made himself and Tracey a cup of coffee from the new *Keurig* Zack purchased a couple of days earlier, thinking it was a good idea not to waste coffee anymore. Zack noted Tracey's anxiety level rising and could palpably feel the man's anger evolve into something volcanic—yet Tracey did not blow. He worked methodically, if not a bit frenetically, but Zack could tell that his partner was working on an *uber* level of adrenalin.

"How's it going, pal?" Zack chanced, half expecting to have his head bitten off by an increasingly frustrated detective. And he was half right. Tracey ignored Zack's query, but snarled aloud, with some decent volume attached: "Damn it! This perv is a ghost. I've got *nada*."

Zack waited a moment before responding. He knew that in part Tracey's fury was being generated by a very deep instinctual fury—which his woman had been so humiliated with sexual invective by a voice in the wilderness that he could not lash out at and take the mats proper. It was this masculine impotence, Zack recognized, that fueled most of his partner's seething antipathy.

"Like you said, he'll surface again, if he's a real player and not some loon trolling your line for shit-giggles," Zack said reassuringly.

"I know," Tracey capitulated, tossing his pen on the desk. "And that may still be a possibility."

"Patience, old friend," Zack said. "That's what we're best at."

"When my woman's not involved, I agree," Tracey reasoned. "But right now I'm on fire and wanna kick ass and take names."

Zack said nothing to that. Because there were no words of comfort he could offer. He knew Tracey, though…sooner or later, the older man would pull out of the loving embrace of protracted offense by way of Harianne and recline more logically into the world of police due process.

9:30 p.m.

The fax machine in Tracey's office bleeped and clicked, announcing in its mechanical rote way that an incoming message was in process. He glanced at Zack, who was as alert as a greyhound anxious for the starting gate. One piece of paper slid out of the machine. Tracey grabbed the fax (more like snatched it, Zack noted) as it barely exited the tray. Tracey read the message aloud.

"The Whitmore Corporation recently purchased a building not far from Calvin House Preparatory School. That's all for now. Chew on that, Detective Sanders. Stay tuned."

"What the hell does that mean?" Zack blurted out the obvious.

"A lead? To what? Something germane to the case? Or more bullshit from some clown playing with us?" Tracey ruminated.

"How about all of the above?" Zack said rhetorically. "At least it's not filled with bullshit sex blather."

"For this relief much thanks," Tracey muttered. "My fax number anyone could get, including Elsie the Cow, if she wanted. It's not that hard. Call LAPD and it's done."

"Granted. Want me to do some digging on the Whitmore angle?" Zack asked.

"Why not? If it ties into the Chase case, it's something more concrete than we've had thus far," Tracey said.

Zack wheeled around on his chair and hit some keys on his computer. "I'm on it."

An exasperated Tracey wanted to check in on Harianne again, but he'd already called her four times in the past hour. He knew she was hard at work on her case and his worry wart communications, while loving and caring in nature, were sure to be an annoyance after a while. He knew he was tired, functioning on anxiety fumes and he forced himself to relax.

The fucker had talked about her pussy…

…son of a bitch…when I get your ass, I'm gonna get Roman evil on you…

"No number of origination on the fax," Tracey remarked evenly, pulling himself up by the mental bootstraps from his verbal byplay promises of death by way of agonizing pain on Whisper.

"Did you really expect one?" Zack gave an ugly chuckle.

Tracey didn't bother to reply but his mind started in on some hard analysis, just the facts, ma'am kinda stuff.

Fact: Chase was the logical suspect in this murder—DNA on an apple carton and just probable cause. Moreover, no other viable suspects on this side of the known galaxy. What would be the reason for anyone wishing Harianne and himself to simply 'drop the case'…as if this was even a remote possibility right up there with raising the dead using owl's entrails and garlic beads?

Fact: If the Whisper really was for real, he wanted Chase exonerated. But why? If the Whisper *was* the murderer, he most certainly would want someone else to take the guilty fall and all attention away from any other possible suspect. Which meant that Chase had a secret ally. Which meant…

No, it didn't wash. The lack of logic was damning. Someone calling himself the Whisper was just blowing farts in the wind, seemed most like to Tracey with each passing moment. Yet, this foul-mouthed creature could not be ignored.

"Whitmore Corporation is the real deal," Zack said tonelessly. "Offices here in Los Angeles. No listing of a CEO or a website."

"A shadow entity?" Tracey offered curiously.

"Could be, or a dba for something else," Zack replied, scanning his computer screen intently. "I'm checking the Secretary of State website now."

The team in charge of installing tracing mechanisms for Tracey's phone entered a moment later, two guys who looked like they'd be comfortable flipping burgers or tacos someplace south of the border, down Mejico way.

"Evening, Tracey," a guy called Mack said through a grim smile. "Got some porno girls calling you eager? Russian trim wanting to pay *you?*"

"Good guess, Mack," Tracey grinned. "How long will this take?"

"Two shakes of a lamb's tail, boss," the other fellow named Wilson replied.

They went to work on Tracey's phone as the latter stepped to the side.

Tracey glanced at his watch.

This night, he thought, was never gonna bloody end.

The tracing boys came and went, more coffee was brewed, Maalox was gobbled for heartburn and the clock slowly rolled into the Devil's Hour (3 a.m., boys and girls – when He With No Name and pitchfork blazing looms large) – time for all good children and exhausted cops to be beddy-by, not researching the whereabouts of a vile phone marauder.

Tracey muttered at the bottom of the hour, "He's gonna call," he said softly to Zack, whose eyes were closed in forced or genuine meditation.

As if on cue, the phone rang, jolting Zack out of his seat. "You're kidding me. Right?" he muttered, zapped back into reality. Tracey took the deepest breath in the world and expelled it through a tooth-whistle.

They both stared at the phone.

"Showtime," Zack whistled. "Want me to get it?"

"Not a chance, pal," Tracey said decidedly.

He stared at the phone for another moment. It glared back at him: NO I.D.

He picked it up. "Sanders," he said tonelessly.

"I see you received my fax. Detective." the Whisper said enigmatically.

"Look, you shitbird! Who the hell are you? What's your game, what do you want?"

"I recognize a good investment," Whisper replied, chuckling.

"How so?" Tracey inquired as patiently as possible.

"It's personal and involves my reputation," Whisper said in a serpentine voice that made Zack, at least, visibly shudder. The guy sounded like a serpentine, effeminate Grinch, Zack pulled from cartoon memory—slimy, gross, shtink, shtank, shtunk.

Tracey hit the mute button. Looking to his partner.

"I need to keep him on until we get a trace."

"So talk to the prick," Zack said, as he hit the door with his knuckle and caught the trace boys' attention out in the detective pool. They nodded, and returned their attention to Tracey's call.

Tracey hit the mute button and began speaking. "Did I lose you, Whisper?" he asked.

"You'll never lose me, Detective," Whisper replied in a seductive tone of voice. "I'll give you just enough time to chat before your trace is completed."

"Is that what you think I'm doing, buying time?" Tracey rolled his voice.

"I would if I were you," Whisper accommodated him with a lisp.

The prick is playing with me. Tracey said quietly in his mind.

"Must be nice to be fucking that hot Harianne," the Whisper chortled. "Fine piece of snatch, I'll bet —"

"Fuck off," Tracey said.

"Okay," Whisper said and hung up.

He looked to Zack, who glanced out of the office at Wilson and his partner. They both nodded in the affirmative. Zack gave a thumbs up and said, "We got the sucker."

Wilson handed Tracey a piece of paper through the half-open door. Tracey snatched it and read aloud. "18-4433 Dorothy Drive, La Canada, Flintridge, California. Okay, then."

They both fairly bolted from the detective pool, down to the parking area.

"Your car or mine?" Zack asked.

"Mine," Tracey said. "You drive like Batman on meth."

"We'd get there faster, old man," Zack quipped, opening the passenger door to Tracey's car.

"But with me driving, we'll get there alive," Tracey grinned.

Despite his pretentions for cautious driving, Tracey tore out of the garage like a bat out of hell. Zack let out a small 'whoop' of glee and turned on the siren.

Tracey focused on surface streets, avoiding the usually congested 110 interchange around the 101 which was still ongoing even at this ungodly time of night. He was in no mood for delays—with stealth and divine guidance they'd be in Flintridge within 15 minutes.

The siren whined its immutable klaxon as they weaved in and out of traffic. Tracey could imagine the leopard-like hold Whisper's ass in his jaws, chewing him into a fine bony mess, drilling him for answers and locking him up for the next century, even if he was innocent of nothing more than telephonic harassment.

"If he knew about the trace, he could be on the move, you know that," Zack pointed out the obvious.

"Yeah, but let's not go there," Tracey said dismissively and shoved his foot further on the accelerator.

They arrived at the trace address in twenty minutes and Tracey was out of the car before it even came to a stop. He had his .9 millimeter out and Zack exited, following suit. They glanced up at what appeared to be tinted windows splattered unevenly on a concrete brick building that was both ugly in appearance and non-descript, an odd paradox to the contiguous landscaping of symmetrical architectural landscaping. There was an underground parking garage.

Tracey wondered vaguely from a thousand miles away how this area looked during the day. Probably shitty, he answered his own question…if only based on this tortured building in front of them.

They looked to the front door, waited for a moment, guns up. Then Tracey tried the handle. It opened easily.

They both entered, at the ready.

The stench of mold and acrid air filled their nostrils and motes of cancer-causing asbestos ash filled the air. Zack gave a cough as Tracey ascended a stairwell directly ahead.

"Sheriff, anyone here? Clear."

Silence greeted his invocation. "Hello?"

A voice behind him, elderly in tone, spoke out. "Ain't no one there. Not now, anyway," a man in his late 60s spoke from the front entrance. Zack turned to the gentleman as Tracey descended the stairs and then stopped and turned.

"He left, ran out of there fast," the old man said. "About half an hour ago. Was watching him from my porch, yonder." He pointed at a small ramshackle house, ill-kempt, with a porch light indicating a terrace laded with Budweiser crates stacked against the outer wall.

"Can you describe him, sir?" Tracey asked, putting his gun away.

"Can't really," the old man shook his head. "Too far away. Just know he was in a hurry."

"Young or old?" Zack tried.

"Young, I think. Yeah, youngin'. 20 something, maybe. Maybe 30, but moved like a kid."

"Did he have a vehicle?" Zack asked.

"Nope. Just ran into them thickets," the old man obliged them with another wave of his finger. "Sorry, boys. Used to be a guard at Chino Corrections. Know he must be wanted for something."

Tracey nodded, frowning.

"Thank you, sir," he said. "Have you seen this individual here before, in this building?"

"Can't remember. Ain't young anymore. Know what I mean?"

Sure do, old timer, Tracey thought wistfully. *I'm getting older by the minute...*

"Thanks, again," Tracey said, shaking the man's hand.

Both he and Zack walked dejectedly back to their vehicle. Tracey looked to Zack and shook his head. "Don't even say it."

Zack didn't need to but kept his conviction in silence. *Old buddy, he knew he was being traced, was banking on it, and played us like the proverbial fiddle.*

3:30 a.m.

Boston Buckman arrived home and got out of his black *Mercedes* 550 S, feeling about one hundred and six years old, if a day. He lumbered to the front door, mouthing a silent prayer to the deaf heavens above that his wife was asleep and would not be up waiting for him like some nocturnal bird-of-prey, waiting to swoop in for the kill. He recognized she was under extraordinary pressure (me, too, dear) but he simply didn't want to engage in one of her miffed debates as to where the Sam Hell he'd been without notifying her of his every move. Please, God, let her be blissfully unconscious and quiescent tonight. Please.

He turned the knob as quietly as he could—opening the door only a few inches. A light came on from someplace within. Oh, well, he thought—so much for prayer, trans-substantiation and whatever gods may be. Pamela was up, probably ready to tear into him for his recent non-communication.

The *Robert Louis Tiffany* lamp was lit in the family room adjacent to the kitchen. He knew that Pamela had a remote switch to it from anywhere in the house. She loved that goddamn lamp and needed access to it constantly, like the Pale Rider needing his title of Death.

Boston entered the house and could, without even looking up to the top of the stairwell, feel Pamela's accusatory gaze upon him—the apotheosis of conjugal disapproval heavy in the atmosphere.

Pamela Buckman, dressed in a sheer white negligee did indeed stand at the top of the stairway, gazing down at him, an unmistakable look of curiosity and annoyance in her expression. She wanted him at this moment, to feel him inside her, to provide comfort to her pain…but his frequent disappearances of late were vexing to her, at best. Could it be possible he was seeing someone else? Another woman…at this particularly agonizing time in their lives? No, he couldn't be that unfeeling, that cruel, she castigated herself immediately; not my Boston. Other men, maybe. But not him.

Still…

"Where have you been? You didn't even call, text or leave a voicemail!" she heard her voice from some distant place, sounding shrewish and old—anti-diluvium old.

"I know. I was remiss," Boston replied, a tired, feeble tone in his voice.

"To say the least! What the hell is going on with you?" Pamela snapped, again sounding inordinately shrew-like, in her own mind, anyway.

"Nothing! I got caught up with a case at the office," he said, not even glancing up at her for a few moments. Christ, woman…lay off.

Pamela's expression became crestfallen despite her annoyance. She tried to suck it up and adjust her tone a bit (something a bit less like Bitch Of The Universe, hear me roar).

She tried to sound pouty. "Well…okay. But next time you could at least let me know. I was worried sick. I texted you several times, no replies. The calls I made went immediately into voicemail which means you turned off the phone."

He now looked up at her, his eyes hooded in a kind of dog-weary way that made Pamela feel trivial and insubstantial.

"I got it," was all he could muster.

"No. You don't got it. Our son is in prison. You should be available by any means, 24/7," she snapped back—realizing that she'd reverted back to Wicked Witch of the West mode with absolutely no trouble at all. She'd gone to the trouble of looking dick-hard sexy for the man and all he could do was grunt at her with clear disinterest and insensitivity.

Oh, screw it, she thought. He's under pressure, so am I. Who am I kidding that anyone wants to make love under these depressing circumstances.

"Good night," she said, turning on her heel and heading back to the bedroom.

***

Boston watched his wife move morosely off to their love abode (what a joke, he snickered inwardly) and let out a rather audible groan. He simply wasn't in the mood for Pamela's pre-menstrual bullshit. Still, what he wanted now was some degree of comfort and a world without pain and if she could provide it with a minimal amount of nagging once he came to bed, he'd offer her some degree of affection. A kiss on the cheek, a soft murmur of apology for being so negligent to her worry, maybe let her blow him to show her how much he loved her. Actually, the thought of a good sucking from Pamela (then she couldn't nag) was not unwelcome when you got right down to it.

With that, he started the Olympian-like journey up the staircase. His legs ached as did his back. It had been a long, hard night. He wasn't young anymore, he thought ruefully (fossil-like)? He chuckled at the thought. He made his way to the bedroom and slipped in quietly, like some errant, guilty phantom unsure of the welcome his supernatural presence might invite.

"Sorry, again, Pam," he whispered. He could feel that she was still awake, pouting, feeling ignored, neglected. Unloved. He made his way into the bathroom, but left the door open as he stripped himself naked and turned on the shower. He knew Pamela's gaze was on him—watching him nude as a jaybird—tormenting her, possibly? But he didn't care.

The shower spray cascaded over him like a welcome shroud of liquid love. He closed his eyes, doing nothing more for a moment than feeling the heat from the water and steam pour over his face, hair and shoulders.

He opened his eyes in surprise as Pamela was suddenly next to

him, in the shower, holding him, her belly up against his ass—
holding him the way a child might hug a tree with its little arms—or
mommy or daddy when the day had been particularly cruel.

"Sorry, too," she kissed him on the back. "I just feel horrible, is
all. This whole trial, Chase…" she trailed off as water doused her face
as well when he turned to look at her. He nodded in understanding
and kissed her forehead.

"I love you," he said. "And we'll get through this, babe."

He began to soap up his balls, but then Pamela took the bar of
Irish Spring from him and fondled his nuts in both hands. She
looked up at him.

"Do you mind?" she asked, her eyes doe-like, supplicating,
wanting…

He nodded that he minded nothing at the moment as she took
him into her mouth. Boston closed his eyes and welcomed the
oblivion of sexual release. He surprised himself at how quickly he
came but Pamela seemed not to mind a bit. She gobbled him down
obligingly and then kissed his still-rigid rod.

"Let's go to sleep," she said and he nodded.

What a day, he thought to himself, as she dried him off with the
only available towel in the bathroom and led him to their bed.

Saturday – 4:30 a.m.

Tracey arrived home to find Harianne buried knee-high deep in a pile
of books (not to mix metaphors, he thought to himself). Papers were
stacked high on a large round mahogany table in the living room,
with binder clips and file folders strewn haphazardly around the floor
nearby. She was so absorbed in her work that she did not
immediately notice his entrance. Tracey could not help but smile at
this. Lost in her own zone, the words loomed prominently in his
mind. Just as well, he thought. It meant she was focused on other
things aside from the Whisper crap that had slid through the life-
goose's gullet as slick and disgusting as an oil slick in the Gulf.

He tossed his keys, cellphone and wallet on the table with a
resounding clatter that forced Harianne to take note of his presence.

"Hi," she said wearily. "I didn't even hear you come in."

"It's because I've discovered the secret to invisibility and Kung Fu rice paper soft-footedness," he smiled back at her. "And hi yourself."

He walked over to her, kissed her on the lips, then fell into the camel cashmere wingback chair beside her. They regarded one another in silence for a moment. A universe, a chasm of welcome emptiness—of simply appreciation in being together again.

"How goes the case of the century?" he asked through a yawn, stretching like an exhausted Cheshire cat.

"It goes," she said nodded, yawning herself. "Trial is October 10. Still a ton of stuff to do."

"I'll bet," he agreed.

"You're back late," she said.

"Yeah well, been a busy night. I had a lot of surprises after you left," he said.

"Surprises?" she was suddenly interested.

She took her glasses off and rubbed the space between her eyes, but her gaze remained fixed on him.

"The Whisper phoned me today," Tracey said. "Again. And sent us a fax."

"Ah. Well, don't keep me in suspense," she said, leaning forward, pushing some extraneous notes to the side. "Are we smarter than earlier?"

"No, not a wit," Tracey admitted ruefully. "He led us on a wild goose chase but we came up empty."

"And it's been as quiet as the grave here," she said. "No bad guys, ghosts or other beasties muddling about."

"I'm beginning to think that this Whisper is just a troll," Tracey said. "Has a branch up his ass with me over something or has been hooked into this Chase matter and just somehow wanted to become involved."

"That's comforting," Harianne nodded. "So we just forget about him?"

Tracey smiled then lunged forward and drew her close to him. "For tonight, let's forget about everyone and everything."

She smiled at this and kissed his nose. "That sounds like an unsubtle preamble to sexual gymnastics."

"Why, fair lady, after our kind of day, where would you ever get such a notion?" he teased.

She gave him a lingering look and then kissed him, insinuating her tongue deftly into her mouth. "Why, sir… I don't have the faintest clue."

She pulled back for a moment, another expression of concern on her face that she could ill-conceal. "But I'm still worried, love."

"Me, too," Tracey said as he began to unbutton her blouse.

Chapter Twenty-Nine

Monday – 7:00 a.m.

The overcast did little to elevate Forbes' disconsolate mood. Even while the sun was battling for supremacy against the cloudy muck, it was clear the day would remain pretty much occluded and depressing. Forbes walked like a truculent ghost into his office, barely nodding to a passing associate, his mind light years away on the planet Lake Woebegone or some other place where the trouble of this world of wrath and tears could not immediately assault him as the week began.

Once in his inner sanctum, he took his chair and gazed vacantly out the window. A sparrow showed amazing audacity by flying on the exterior window ledge and took to a staring contest with Forbes, its little black eyes fixed on him in avian vapidity. Lucky little bastard, Forbes thought to himself. Fly off whenever you want to wherever and not have a lick of worry for the recent past or an uncertain future.

He glanced at the diary that had haunted him of late—his familial bailiwick of drama and angst. He half considered simply consigning the thing to his drawer, never to be viewed again, but dismissed the thought in a nanosecond.

No, it *would* be read—correction, it *had* to be read. It cried out to him, like some tortured phantom, pried from its grave, resenting its reintroduction into a world without reason or rhyme.

Forbes took a deep breath and reached for the diary. He held it for a moment, turned to the window once more. His feathery little friend had flown off, no doubt doing very sparrow-like things in the beginning of this new day. He looked down at the diary, and then opened it slowly to where he had last left off perusing it.

The words were almost palpable in their personal outreach to him; he was at once drawn into the universe of a distant past. It was not exactly a welcome invitation.

As my stomach swarmed with muffled sounds of a monster within, I was feeling sad for Frank. In many ways, I thought it was my fault; something I could have prevented? I had my doubts. A part of me thought it was selfish of me to engage myself with this lustful and blissful affair, love like none other was lacking in my life, but after so many years of being tormented with vicious verbal abuse, the discernible marks on my body and exploiting myself as the perfect housewife, it was time to terminate my marriage.

It was the 1940's and divorce was present, but unheard of, especially if the woman initiated it. The misbegotten people took a cowardly position, but they never wished me well from the start. I had to weather the storm of humiliation, resentment and backlash it would have on Frank. For weeks I gave myself to Frank, making every attempt possible to console him with his incessant crying, but to no avail, I failed. He couldn't stop. Frank's face began to change with red blotches that blanketed his entire face, while the swelling, which resulted in an absorbent amount of puffiness, made for the backdrop. Frank resembled the horrible character in "Beauty and The Beast 'the Beast'." His eyes were red which diminished the true color of his blue eyes. Frank's hygiene had diminished and deteriorated. His breath wreaked of a sour, foul smell from not brushing his teeth on a daily basis. The mere mention of taking a bath threw him into a state of denial and he was obstinate in obliging me on this.

He just sat there, staring at the door waiting for his father to come home. The real truth is that door would never open again with a daily vantage point of his father in his dark gray suit, a matching black and white stripe tie and a gray wool brim hat surrounded by a black band bestowed on his head. That vision was one of the past. I fully knew that Brinks was gone forever and that he would never walk through the door again

I never told Frank about the affair because the real truth would destroy him. I couldn't bear to see him sink into another layer of anguish over my choice, but that choice cost him his father. I was scared for Frank, but I had to prepare myself for the worst and live with that for the rest of my life; a better life that was needed, that I was entitled to for so long due to Brinks' madness. It could be a choice or a mistake, but for now it was a choice. Frank cried for days non-stop unable to go to school.

Forbes closed the leather bound book, shook his head and whispered to himself. "That's my father, Frank Madden!"

Christ on a pony!

Forbes continued to ruminate internally, *He never uttered a word to Lincoln or me. Wow! This is deep, unimaginable shit. It actually pisses me off. I wonder what's next? Maybe I should simply save my soul, burn this diary and go off and live happily ever after. Yeah, like that's gonna happen.*

His internal mind's eye was now set ablaze. He couldn't help but create a distorted mental image of his grandmother—wizened, tortured, clearly sexually unstable and…

…stop it. She was not unstable. She was an unhappy woman that was all. She had acted in a very human way and unfortunately for her and her husband, the consequences of her affair resulted in tragedy…

Forbes sat quietly for a moment until the prayer and class bells rang. He roused himself momentarily, wondering briefly if it was worth the effort to begin his rounds of the premises. This was his daily routine—insinuating himself into the school interior—the titular leader of all things good, great and profound to higher education and the development of tomorrow's leaders. The urge to stand was suddenly arrested as a sensation coursed through his entire being—a tsunami of emotion and confluence of feelings he could not pinpoint exactly, but which caused within him an overwhelming sense of grief and poignancy.

Forbes Madden began to cry.

And the tears did not dissipate for over twenty minutes.

When he recovered, he stood slowly and cleared his throat—as if he was preparing for some piece of oratory to God himself; an apology for abject weakness and an ill-controlled emotional meltdown. He took a step toward his door, then stopped.

He turned slowly and looked back at the diary of his family's past—the smoldering pyre of angst, horror and death.

God damn you all, he thought.

As he reached for the doorknob, he heard the same litany running over again and again in his head.

The evil that men do…the evil that men do…the evil…

1:00 p.m.

Harianne DeCanter arrived at the Los Angeles County Jail, her mind focused on her client rather than the past few days of anxiety vis a vis one Whisper Sonofabitch Whoever You Are. Her mind had always been keenly disciplined, her emotions held in careful and balanced check, even in the face of adversity and crisis. Whisper had unhinged her on a deep level…but Harianne was not your average bear…and she knew it. She was made of sterner stuff than most and she admired that quality of immutable strength within herself. She would not waiver from her primary goal: saving her young client's life. To that end, she stalked into the halls of the correction facility with a determined purpose. The outer guard desk and its sole gatekeeper, a fellow named Byron, glanced at her I.D. perfunctorily, looked to her and merely nodded. His eyes were red and rheumy, denoting that young Byron had probably had too much vino the night before. He nodded her toward the door that separated the outer world from the inner maelstrom of evil and wrongdoing—the cells to those who were held for various levels of malfeasance and crimes against humanity.

A guard she recognized and knew well by the name of Gibson smiled at her warmly."Morning, Ms. DeCanter," he said, his smile revealing two gold teeth on his upper incisors. "How are you today?"

"Trying to save the world one heartbeat at a time, my friend," she grinned back. Gibson was around 60 years, and 6 foot 4 on the hoof, with a voice that sounded like that of a bass baritone. Gibson Jones had once, a long time ago (when fairies and little men went up and down the mountain and through the running glen) been a rather celebrated beat cop. He had been part of a tortured police force that battled many of the Watts gang wars in the 1960s and 70s and had seen some things, paraphrasing Charlene's famous song that a man just ain't supposed to see. He had endured and could have retired years ago but felt that 'an idle man retired is a dead man aspired.' It was an original Gibson quote, but younger officers were known to repeat this mantra for survival through the halls of the academy and Rampart all too often.

He had taken on his role as Chief Warrant Officer for this particular jail and ran the joint with the precision of a captain of a Los Angeles Class nuclear submarine—by the book, tight and trim—always seaworthy and on watch.

"You here to see your boy Chase, I'll bet," he surmised, folding his arms almost theatrically.

"Yes, sir, I am indeed. Can you lend a hand with that?" Harianne asked.

"Yes, ma'am," Gibson replied cheerfully. "You head to that room down the way and I'll see the man is brought to you direct."

"Thank you, Gibson. By the way, how's Meredith? She getting stronger?" Harianne asked of his wife. His look suddenly changed—from crestfallen to simply sad.

"No, Ms. DeCanter, thank you for asking but the cancer came back," he said dejectedly. "They ain't even bothering with chemo. Done deal." He could not bring himself to look at her.

She reached out instinctively and touched one of his massive forearms. "I'm so sorry, Gibson. Please let her know I asked about her."

"I will indeed, ma'am. Let me go get the boy," he turned and Harianne could have sworn he wiped a tear from his eye as he pivoted toward the cell hall.

She walked into a room marked Interview Area No. 1. She sat in one of the three utilitarian fold-out metal chairs and put her briefcase on the extended table. She closed her eyes and counted to ten and then allowed herself a few moments of meditation in the dark void of her consciousness, trying to fend off the innumerable worries in her life.

A noticeably subdued Chase, wearing the bright orange jail attire, padded into the room, hands bound by the deliberately constrictive metal handcuffs and sat in one of the two remaining chairs across from Harianne. He was clearly despondent (Harianne forced the phrase from her psyche "clinically suicidal"), distant and lethargic; his entire appearance reminded her of a mentally ill patient doped up with thorazine. He did not look at her immediately, keeping his head down and shoulders hunched. He looked vaguely like an errant schoolboy about to be chastised for pulling Kathy May's pig-tails in math class.

"Chase, look at me, please!" Harianne said evenly.

Chase did nothing of the sort but merely shook his head and mumbled, "I can't. I'm ashamed. I don't care anymore." He began to sniffle and rubbed haphazardly at a line of snot that had begun to icicle down one nostril.

Harianne was in no coddling mood. "Look at me! You have to care. You have to help me help you," she said in a cold, Arctic voice.

Chase then slowly raised his head. The snot under his nose began to bubble and Harianne pulled a handkerchief from her purse. She leaned in and wiped his nose along with two tears in avalanche-mode streaming down his cheeks. She gazed into his big brown eyes, lined with the two rows of brown freckles underneath. He reminded Harianne of the teen heart-throb film star, Ashton Kutcher.

Chase took a breath that lasted from here to eternity before exhaling and rubbing his eyes, suddenly focused and attentive.

"Okay. What do I have to do?"

Harianne placed her hand under his chin. "We'll beat this. You've got to work with me. Deal?"

Chase studied her momentarily and nodded.

"Deal." He managed a very slight grin.

"I need to ask you a few questions and I need one hundred percent honesty from you," she said, her tone now warm and comforting.

"Sure," Chase said, wiping his nose again.

Harianne gave the boy a moment to collect himself. This also gave her time to push the record button on her cell phone. He then nodded to her.

"When was the last time you saw Jaime alive?" she asked.

Chase's response was immediate. "That day in Chemistry Class. Even though we were roommates, we only had one class together."

"Do you know how the apple juice got into your room?"

Chase snorted. "Well, yeah. Jaime or his parents bought it for him and it was left there. Jaime didn't take it home with him."

"Did you drink it, too?" Harianne asked.

Chase frowned and gave an impatient sigh. "No. I don't even like apple juice. Jaime drank apple juice. He loved the shit!"

Harianne nodded and smiled grimly. "So you don't drink apple juice at all?"

"No." He again winced, as if in physical pain.

"Then you would have no reason to touch the apple juice bottle, right?"

"Not to drink the crap. But I did touch the apple juice box because Jaime would leave it in different places in the room. It might be on my nightstand, on top of our refrigerator, on the coffee table by our little sofa."

"How many times that day, Thursday, September 4, 2008, did you move the apple juice box? Think back for a moment."

Chase shrugged. "I don't remember. Maybe once. I was packing my clothes."

"Once?"

He simply nodded in the affirmative.

"Okay. Where did you move it to?"

Chase scratched his head in thought. "I don't remember. Probably put it back on his nightstand or my nightstand, just to get it out of the way. I get a little clumsy and always thought I would spill it." Chase suddenly sounded exhausted.

"Good. We're making progress here. Hang in there with me. Then what happened?"

"I packed my clothes for the weekend trip with my parents."

"And when did you return?"

"The next day-Sunday. Sometime in the late afternoon, evening; can't remember."

Harianne nodded and then proceeded to outline what he should expect from the trial. This included jury deliberation and possible sentences being handed down, based on evidence the prosecution would emphasize could leave no doubt that Chase was the bad guy and guilty as hell of Murder One. She emphasized that he must do his best to show as little emotion as possible on the various testimonies that would come into play. When he asked about the duration of time he might have to serve if found guilty, Harianne did not immediately reply.

"Seriously, how long?" Chase pushed.

"Pretty long, contingent on the judge and jury together," Harianne admitted.

"Can you define pretty long?" Chase asked.

Harianne bit her lip but her gaze did not waver from his. "Life. You could spend the rest of your life in jail," she said in a low voice.

She wondered if she could have handled being the messenger of doom a little more elegantly because again Chase began to tear up.

"For the rest of my life," Chase said, the dawning horror of this possibility hitting him like a mag truck. "Jesus," he muttered and wiped the tears away. He looked to her plaintively. "But I didn't do it! Can't they see that?"

Harianne's response was measured. "The jury is looking at evidence only, not your emphatic declaration of innocence. They'll hear about your DNA and they'll come to conclusions. My job will be to spin that another way."

"How?" Chase asked pointedly.

"You'll see," Harianne said and abruptly stood. "I have to go."

Chase stood as well and abruptly handed her a white-ruled paper note with blue ink. Harianne took the note then put her hand on his shoulder.

"Are you gonna get me off?" Chase asked.

"That's the game plan, my friend," Harianne said with a tone of confidence she did not remotely feel.

***

Harianne walked to her car, and leaned against it, closing her eyes for momentary personal solace. The Chase interview had drained her more than she had expected and she realized that she had become emotionally involved with the boy's case. She trusted her gut hunch and she had defended true murderers in the past—it was part of the job description—and she knew that her client was not the devil incarnate in this case. Someone else (don't know why, don't know how) had murdered Jaime. Period.

Completely famished, she got into her car and drove down Hill Street into Chinatown. Traffic was predictably hopeless but she didn't mind today—it gave her time to ruminate on her case. But she did realize that someone needed to be contacted and rather immediately. She speed-dialed on her cell phone and waited for the three rings before Austria picked up.

"Hi, there!" Austria chortled. She always sounded so festive, Harianne thought; like every day was Christmas Eve.

"Hi, Austria! Hey listen, I just finished with my meeting and am going to chow down at Ching Lee's tonight. Sorry. I forgot to tell you earlier. So no need to go three-course on me."

A disappointed Austria replied, "Okay. No problem. But what about Tracey?"

"I'll call him, find out what he wants to do about food and call you back."

"Gottcha! Drive safely," Austria's perky voice returned.

Harianne found a parking place in front Ching Lee's adjacent to Temple and 1st Street, near downtown. Ching Lee was famous for its shellfish cuisine and was usually packed at this hour, even on a Monday night. Harianne turned the motor off and dialed Tracey on his cell. After five rings, his familiar voice mail greeting sounded off.

"Hey Babe! I just left the jail and am in Chinatown at the Lee. I'm dying for Chinese tonight for some reason. And no! I'm not pregnant. Call me back so that I can tell Austria what to do for you re dinner."

Harianne then called Austria back.

"That's fast. Is he coming home for dinner?"

"We never spoke. I don't really know where he is or what he's doing. Eventually he'll surface. Austria, don't fix dinner for either of us; just enough for yourself."

"That works for me." Austria laughed.

8:00 p.m.

An hour later, Harianne had finished her large order of crab's legs but still had not heard back from Tracey. She paid the bill and left the restaurant, walked out to her car and started it. Her feet ached for her tennis shoes, a pair of *Nikes*, with *Velcro* straps and she decided she simply refused to be uncomfortable on the drive home. She hit the automatic trunk lever, got out of the car, and walked to the rear of the vehicle.

That's when she noticed him. A tall man dressed in a black suit wearing sunglasses stood on the sidewalk fifty feet from her, staring. He looked like one of those nutty characters in Men in Black, a favorite film of hers from the 90s. He made no threatening moves, nor spoke...he simply stood there, obviously gazing at her.

"Can I help you?" Harianne asked him pointedly, reaching for her shoes from the trunk.

The man in black was unresponsive.

Harianne's internal weirdometer kicked in and she decided it was high time to get the hell out of here. Whisper's perverted phone call to her the day before raised alarm bells in her that suddenly caused her bladder to fill. At first she thought of approaching the man and confronting him, inquiring as to the reason he had taken to staring at her, but she quickly thought better of it. No, if this weirdo was Whisper, best not do anything that might piss the fruit-loop off.

She got into her car, jammed the ignition on and pulled out of the parking space with a screech. She headed back up Hill Street, towards downtown L.A. and turned right on Fifth Street. From there, she navigated to Fifth going west, crossing over Figueroa Street and entered and emerged onto the 10 Freeway, her speed approaching 70 miles per hour.

She checked her rear-view mirror. No reason that anyone could be following her, but the presence of the man in black five minutes earlier had unnerved her. What she saw in the mirror now increased that sense of unease.

A black vehicle was accelerating on her, approaching so close that she feared the vehicle would slam into her rear-bumper. She turned on her right blinker and crossed over to the right lane. The vehicle followed.

"You fucker," Harianne hissed to herself.

She turned on her left blinker and transitioned into the parallel lane. The vehicle mirrored her exactly. "Okay, what is this bullshit?" she murmured.

She exited Robertson north and took it to Burton Way. The car from behind her punched the accelerator, keeping apace. It finally caught up with her at the signal light on Burton Way and Doheny. Harianne hung a fast right, heading north on Doheny to Santa Monica and turned left. There was a normal steady stream of traffic and then suddenly the vehicle behind her had seemingly ceased its pursuit. This gave her little cause for comfort as she turned right onto Canon Drive in Beverly Hills going north.

Got you, she thought with inward satisfaction. *Ran you out, whoever you are.*

She dialed Tracey, but the line abruptly died.

"Shit," she mumbled.

She realized he was in a bad zone for cell phone coverage. She pulled the car over to the curb, engine still running and tried his number again. This time he answered, but in a disjointed muffled voice that she could barely recognize. Doggone cell phones.

"Tracey! Are you there? Can you hear me?" she spoke out in an elevated tone of voice. She hoped she stopped short of panic.

"Yeah. I'm—"

The phone again died a horrible death and this time Harianne yelled at it: "Shit!"

A silly reaction, she thought suddenly. Irrational rage at inanimate objects. Dumb, dumb, dumb. But she forgave herself quickly because she realized one immutable fact this moment.

She was terrified.

***

And then, as if out of a nightmare, the car reappeared and slammed into the back of Harianne's car. The jolting impact slammed her chest against the steering wheel, knocking the breath out of her. Gasping for oxygen, she lunged for her glove compartment and uttered the voice recognition deactivation mechanism. The glove compartment door popped open and she reached in and grabbed the pistol within.

Shaken and trembling, Harianne looked in her rear view mirror at the attacking vehicle. She couldn't see the make of the vehicle.

"Bastard," she whimpered, but still had the presence of mind to throw the car into drive. She tossed the pistol on the passenger seat, realizing she was in little position to use it. Besides which, her gut hunch told her that a direct weapons confrontation would not be in her best interest. Punching the gas pedal, her car lurched forward with an audible groan and she slammed the pedal to the floor. Not bothering to see if she was being pursued by her tormenter, she raced up Canon Drive to Sunset and took a hard right on that main artery to Coldwater Canyon. She made an arguably suicidal left turn and exceeded every safe speeding precaution on her trek home. Even while driving this wildly, she tried Tracey again on the cell.

He picked up this time, the reception much clearer now.

"Harianne," Tracey responded in clear agitation.

"Tracey!" And this time, she could hear herself screaming.

"Yeah, Babe! I'm here! I'm here," Tracey responded, his voice calming. Mainly for her sake, she made a mental note.

"Stay on the phone!" Harianne screamed. "He hit my car!"

"Who—what?"

"Someone slammed into me, deliberately," Harianne forced herself to calm down. "I don't know who it was, but it was a shoot to kill hit!"

But as if the gods of GPS technology were personally out to get her, the phone again bleeped out.

Of course, Murphy's law in perfect cause and effect, she lost Tracey just as her nemesis again appeared in her rear-view mirror. She punched speed dial with one hand, weaving up the canyon unsteadily with the other.

"Harianne!" Tracey now yelled. "What the hell's going on?"

"Tell you in a few," Harianne said, her voice now calmer. Fear was being replaced by fury. "I have a son of a bitch matter to take care of. Meet me at the gate. Bring a gun."

The pursuing car again accelerated toward her like some predatory panther bearing down on its prey. Tracey's voice went in and out intermittently but she had no inclination for conversation at the moment. She was in survival mode. She slowed to approach her driveway, the appearance of the automatic gate giving her immediate comfort. As she turned into the driveway, Tracey was already outside, standing near the open gate, gun in hand, pointed directly at the vehicle behind Harianne. The car moved on up the road, screeching into acceleration, clearly in no mood for an angry cop with a weapon at the ready.

Harianne sped through the open gate, kicking up dust onto Tracey's new sweat suit. She slammed on her brakes and turned off the engine. *Jesus H.* She sat there for a microsecond, took a breath, then exited the car.

"Did you see that?" Harianne yelled at Tracey.

He ran up to her, nodding. "Yup. You okay?"

She simply gave a curt nod. "Someone wants me out of the way," she said, her nerves returning to normal.

"Did you see the car when you left the restaurant?"

"No. When I left, I had zero company."

"Okay. Okay," was all a shaken Tracey managed.

"Someone took a big chance trying to take me out," Harianne sighed.

Tracey pulled her towards him and kissed her forehead.

"Are you okay?"

"I hit my chest up against the steering wheel, but no permanent damage. At least I don't think so," she said with uncertainty.

"Let's head inside."

Austria greeted them as they approached the front door of her cottage.

"What happened?" Austria queried, noticing Harianne's ashen expression.

Harianne took a breath, then looked to Tracey. "I revise my statement, Your Honor. Now my chest hurts."

"I think we should have it looked at," Tracey said. "ER? Now?"

"Okay." Harianne responded, fighting back tears.

Tracey U-turned Harianne on her heel and glanced back at Austria. "I'll call you from the hospital," he said.

"Ya, ya," Austria said. "Hurry!"

***

Tracey drove like a madman, occasionally glancing at the still shaken Harianne next to him. He did not try to engage her in conversation. Almost defying Newtonian physics and the laws of gravity, he literally flew down Coldwater, negotiating his way to Cedars Sinai near La Cienega within ten minutes—twenty minutes less than the Google map indicator would have denoted.

He exited his car and yelled out at an orderly who was exiting the South Tower.

"You, there!" Tracey pointed. "I've got a situation here. Get some help!"

The orderly to his credit did not hesitate. He re-entered the ER doors and within sixty seconds, three attendants were jogging toward Tracey's vehicle as Harianne tentatively exited her vehicle.

Two hours later, after being quickly processed at the front window, the ER doctor determined that Harianne, based on X-rays, Cat scan and an MRI, had simply suffered some bruising to her ribs but no internal injuries. Harianne could feel her pain diminishing somewhat and again the anger welled inside of her at the assault she had sustained. She looked to Tracey, who refused to leave her side through the entire examination procedure and smiled bravely.

"Let's go home," she said softly.

Tracey glanced at the doctor who nodded without a word. Tracey took her hand and kissed it. "You're the boss, boss."

***

Tuesday — 12:00 a.m. — Midnight

As Harianne sat quietly on the edge of her bed in their new bedroom, Tracey finished up some work on his laptop at the nearby desk. Harianne stood, feeling her bruised chest gingerly and walked over to her purse, lying on an end-table not yet properly placed near the bed's edge. She removed the handwritten note Chase had slipped to her earlier in the day.

Tracey glanced over at her. "What's that, babe?"

"Something Chase gave me today." she said. "A note, I guess."

"Have you read it?" Tracey asked, approaching her.

"No. Not yet. I was going to read it now," she answered quietly.

Harianne returned to the bed and sat there, as Tracey followed suit, like a loyal greyhound.

"Well, open it. What's stopping you?" Tracey almost sounded like he was teasing her.

"I'm afraid. It might be another unwelcome surprise," she replied drearily, then grinned at him.

"Harianne! Open it."

She faked an expression of horror then opened the napkin. Gingerly, as if it was sacred rice paper created by monks who revered holy relics.

"Read it," Tracey gently nudged her.

Harianne complied, clearing her throat theatrically.

"12-1, 12-2, 8-1, 8-2, 14-1, and 14-2 with an historical annotation: 1920's cold brick, newly restored building that once belonged to an old jewelry company was moved there. Today it resembles a private home now owned by the Whitmore Corporation."

Harianne sighed. "Not exactly monolithic in nature," she quipped.

"Yeah. Cryptic at best." Tracey remarked without expression.

"What do you think it means?" Harianne said.

Tracey rubbed his eyes in weariness, trying not to look at her, giving way to his investigation of the Whitemore Corporation.

"Who knows?" he said then leaned in and kissed her. "Let's get you naked."

"And?" she teased.

"None of that after your day," Tracey chided kiddingly.

Tracey helped Harianne remove her clothes and slipped on her night gown. She allowed this gentle treatment, occasionally kissing him when he got close, but he was on a mission to get her ready for sleep and swatted her nose gently. He literally then tucked her in, pulling the sheets over her, taking particular care with covering her feet.

"Gotta keep those tootsies warm," he smiled.

"Why do you have to be so wonderful?" she asked softly.

"Years of training and duty," he whispered back, kissing her gently on the lips.

She closed her eyes and forced herself to relax. Tracey watched her, a panoply of uneasy thoughts swirling in his head.

He thought back suddenly to his ex-wife. Murdered, taken from him all too soon. He could not bear the idea of losing Harianne. He again leaned in and kissed her gently on the forehead.

"Sleep," he said softly.

But Harianne was already gone to the world and Tracey smiled as he heard her soft snoring begin.

Tuesday – 1:30 a.m.

The artist moved about the room with a portrait on the art easel, as graceful as a ballet dancer performing *Swan Lake*. He had committed

Harianne's walk to memory and the way her ass shimmied to and fro.

Like a sidewinder snake, the artist thought figuratively. *A fine piece of ass in full-tilt boogey.*

The artist began to unconsciously fondle his groin, not with a deliberate attempt for nutting…but more of a relaxed, casual caress, which to a fly on the wall would have appeared oddly discomfiting, even by a fly's non-discriminating perspective.

The artist began to draw Harianne with a very fine charcoal pencil detailing every anatomical part of the developing female form. The breasts were supple, which in the artist's estimation, only enhanced the perfection of her posterior.

Ass gotta be perfect. Maybe like J-Lo.

He then took particular care with her hair, draping it down her back like fine silk thread, extolling every strand.

Like a lover, the artist thought poetically with a sudden sense of romance. *She should be so lucky…*

The hair alone took thirty minutes to complete and he stood back for a moment to assess his work. The breasts had come out well (no pun intended) and he was not displeased with his execution of Harianne's muscular legs and accentuated pubis.

Hmmm. Pussy. Detail. Shaved or unshaved. Decisions, decisions…

The artist decided on simply a small tuft of fur on her pubic area. *Just a touch. I mean it's a pussy, right? It's not Dr. Evil's cat, after all…*

He giggled at his imagined cleverness.

He then carefully crafted a blanket around her exterior which of course obfuscated all the work he had done in creating a vision of naked feminine beauty.

The artist chuckled to himself. For him, this was an act of love and seduction. First get the girl naked, admire her, imagine him inside of her. He had drawn Harianne in a way where she was slightly angled to the right—as if she was looking back at the painter. Seductively, of course.

A come-hither look, the artist giggled to himself. *Fuck me now,* her expression radiated to the artist.

The time had arrived when the artist realized the portrait was complete. He leaned in slowly and licked Harianne's chalked image. He then unzipped his pants and let his penis dangle momentarily in front of the painting. Then slowly—very slowly—he began to stroke himself, his breath growing ragged and uneven.

When the moment came his ejaculate splattered forth like a geyser and, splattered the portrait with seminal fluid that somehow, almost mystically, hit Harianne's face dead center.

Spent, the artist looked down at his cock and smiled. Then back up at Harianne's wet face.

"Good for you, too, bitch?" the artist quipped rhetorically.

Harianne's expression remained predictably unchanged.

Figures, the artist thought contemptuously. All women like spunk in their grill, plain and simple. Whores, all of them.

He wiped his dick clean with his trousers then turned and exited the room.

Not bad work, he thought, whistling all the way.

Chapter Thirty

October 8 — 5:00 a.m.

Harianne woke up ahead of Tracey but lay in bed for half an hour, staring at the ceiling. Tracey snored quietly and she smiled at this; even troubled souls find solace in rest, she mused. Her thoughts upon awakening consisted of the realization that Chase's trial was only two days away and there was still a lot of prep work to be done. Two days. Not a lot of time, she thought dismally; not a lot of time to do battle with a prosecution determined to consign her client to life imprisonment.

She rolled onto her side and sat up, feeling her ribs. The pain from the vehicle attack from the preceding week had all but vanished; what she felt now was only a twinge now and then in the morning, particularly upon awakening. She wandered to the kitchen and fixed a fresh pot of French Press coffee and a bowl of cereal topped with fresh fruit. When the coffee finished brewing, she poured it into her cup embossed with the words "Win, Win, Win" and read her newspaper in silence. Such silence was brief as Tracey entered the kitchen, yawning and groaning at the same time.

"Morning, baby," he smiled at her, his eyes still droopy from post-sleep.

"Give me a kiss, handsome," Harianne said.

Tracey padded over to her and complied. She hugged him fiercely, reveling in the strength and comfort of his muscular body. They stood there for a moment, just holding onto one another, two ships in peaceful anchor before the rising sun of the day ahead reached its zenith.

"Ready for trial?" Tracey whispered into her ear.

"I'm ready for battle," Harianne replied confidently.

He kissed her once more, then turned around and headed into the bedroom. Fifteen minutes later, he returned to the kitchen, dressed and looking as alert as a falcon. He poured some of Harianne's coffee, kissed her once more, then walked to the front door. He turned and looked her.

"I'll see you later," he grinned.

"Okay. I'll call you," she replied.

He left and Harianne repeated the words aloud that she had spoken to Tracey.

"I'm ready for battle," she said, followed by a sigh.

It would be a bloody battle to be sure.

8:00 a.m.

Zack and Tracey arrived to the station at roughly the same time. They changed into civilian clothes, jeans, t-shirts, sunglasses and tennis shoes. Once finished with the sartorial street transformation, they both looked like musicians in *Coldplay*. They took Tracey's car and headed directly to the Whitmore Corporation on Dorothy Drive. They drove slowly up the street and located the target building. During the day, the light reflected just how dark the tinted windows really were. The building in Tracey's mind was a behemoth of ugliness—large, modern cement building with a subterranean parking garage, unusual for a residential area and unwieldy, secretive. And he hated secrets.

Tracey and Zack remained parked near the building for about two hours. It was a long shot that anyone remotely suspicious would either come or go, but due diligence needed to be observed. At length, they walked around the block and entered the back alley to the loading zone area. There was a garage attendant in the underground parking structure. A three mangy dogs and two feral cats occupied the alley.

A large black unmarked delivery truck suddenly pulled into the back alley. He glanced furtively to the two officers, nodded and drove into the underground parking structure. The attendant stopped him and wrote down his license plate on a clipboard. The driver parked the truck but he remained inside, not in a hurry to pick up or offload anything for around fifteen minutes. At length, a large burly man on the wrong side of fifty with an ill-kempt beard exited the vehicle, opened the rear container doors and carried three large crates to the loading zone platform where he deposited them on the platform ledge. Then he quickly got in the truck and exited the alley.

Tracey and Zack glanced at one another. The alley apparently held little in the way of interest for them and they returned to the front entrance and examined the directory enclosed in a cracked glass panel. Tracey scanned the personnel to various companies until his eyes came to rest on a number sequence at the bottom of the roster.

"Hey! Those are the numbers that were on Harianne's note!" Tracey exclaimed.

"Note. What note?" Zack said, puzzled.

"Chase gave Harianne a note awhile back with those same numbers," Tracey explained. "Last week.

Zack read the number sequence aloud.

"12-1, 12-2, 8-1, 8-2, 14-1, and 14-2."

Tracey nodded. "They're identical to the ones on Harianne's note, I'm certain of it.

Zack shook his head and gave a humorless chuckle.

"Man! You never mentioned that to me. I thought we're a team," Zack said evenly.

"We are, Zack. It just slipped my mind. At the time, the numbers meant nothing to us and it had already been a bad night with the car incident, remember?" Tracey said defensively.

Zack nodded, not really perturbed. Harianne's run-in with the mystery vehicle more than a week back had been traumatic, to say the least. This note deletion from Tracey's recollection was more than understandable.

"Let's head back to the precinct and run this info," Tracey said.

"I'm for that," Zack agreed.

Returning to their car, they observed a black Escalade enter the underground parking structure off the alley.

Zack nodded to Tracey. "That seems out of place. Why not enter from the front?" he said.

"No shit. The garage attendant is also out of place." Tracey agreed.

"Worth a further look?" Zack asked.

Tracey weighed the question fairly. Then shook his head. "Based on what? Nah. Let it go for now. If it had been a Mercedes, then we'd be barn-storming."

"Copy that," Zack said. "But I memorized the plate. Hope you don't mind."

"That's why I keep you around," Tracey quipped. "Run that on the way back, won't you?"

"Yes, sir, captain, my captain," Zack chuckled.

As Tracey and Zack drove back to the precinct, and as they got closer to downtown, they noticed a throng of young people crowding the sidewalks, parading up and down the street contiguous to the local sidewalk cafes and *Starbucks*. This was a popular part of town where local business owners boasted small art galleries and historic museums extolling the grand past of the City of Angels. High end New York style restaurants and boutique clothing stores had also just commuted to the downtown area, adding to the local appeal. Little by little, Los Angeles development cartels were catering to an increasing population of international diversity, all of which spelled higher employment and revenue production. But it also spelled a possible increase in crime amidst so much genesis affluence.

Tracey and Zack returned to their detective pool where they met with Chief DeMille Stanford. Stanford was their stellar chief, one of a kind. A bit of an icon, and veteran of forty-five years on the force, Stanford had negotiated his way up the career latter with enviable skill and political aplomb. Standing six foot, three inches tall, Stanford had a full head of white hair, much like the color of marshmallows. He combed it back and it had been remarked more than once that he resembled the television star, Ted Danson. He wore black jeans, a crisp white shirt and some lace up black shoes, which looked similar to black army boots, except much lower with black socks peeping out from the top of the shoe rims. In conversation, he was controlled and articulate, combining a sense of field leadership and experienced bureaucracy. When pressed as to why he had never married, his reply was deliberately consistent: "Too much work and I never did toller to honey do's and don'ts by the wife." Everyone knew Stanford enjoyed the company of women immensely—he simply didn't subscribe to eternal matrimony and conjugal constraint.

He greeted the two men gruffly. "Okay. What did ya find? Anything?"

Tracey nodded. "Nothing tangible as yet, but there's something there."

"Like what?" Stanford asked dubiously.

"A black *Cadillac Escalade* went into the underground parking structure," Zack said, glancing back to Tracey. "Could be something. Looked gangsta'," Zack added.

"Did you run plates and a VIN number?"

"Yep. Plates. I.D. says it belongs to the Whitmore Corporation," Tracey said matter-of-factly.

"You'll need to find out who the President of Whitmore Corporation is, along with the officers of the firm."

"Yeah. I know. We're on it." Tracey confidently replied.

"Did the driver see you apes?" Stanford asked.

"No." said Zack. "Not a chance."

"Could you see inside?"

"No," said Zack.

Stanford nodded for a moment before signing off. "Find out everything about the Whitmore Corporation and keep me apprised," he said, moving back into the sacrosanct interior of his office.

8:30 a.m.

Wendall Dobbs was barely alive, much less awake. He grimly regarded his crenellated, encrusted hands; they resembled artisan bread or decomposing cabbage. He also noted the veteran sores that oozed of yellow puss and blood. All he could recall from his immediate past was that his blindfold or mask or whatever it was had been removed. As he moved his fingers over his face, he could feel a sticky wetness; he pulled his hands back from his face, and saw that they were bloody. Weakened and dehydrated, he couldn't walk or speak. Hell, he could barely breathe.

He regarded the room around him. It had black walls and the one dark gray door with a metal handle was at the furthest point of the

room. The place resembled a meat locker or a large dreary cold
chamber while the large slabs of cement comprised the bottom as the
floor. There was a space heater in one corner, providing some
warmth, but not much. There were no windows.

The sound of the door opened and the tall dark figure in the black
hooded robe approached him. This memory also loomed large in
Wendall's assaulted psyche. His tormenter, the devil.

He opened Wendall's mouth as far as it would go, forcing a steady
stream of water from a glass. Wendall choked, coughing up green
goo.

The devil suddenly spoke. "It's time for me to get rid of you.
You've tortured me enough. I hate you for everything you've done. I
just wanted us to be close, but you can't do that."

Wendall could hear himself release an ugly and sarcastic laugh.
"You're tortured? You son of a bitch!" Wendall choked.

"Shut up!" the devil hissed.

Wendall recognized the voice but his assaulted mind could not
place that voice to a face. He squirmed in his chair, trying to remove
his hands from the tight wire-like rope and chain held together by a
padlock. He then attempted to rise up from the chair. The figure
produced a syringe and injected Wendall's arm with it. Within a few
seconds, Wendall entered the never-never land of black
unconsciousness.

11:00 a.m.

Tracey dug up the corporate records and went to Chief DeMille
Stanford to give him the news. Zack joined his partner in Stanford's
office.

"Yeah. What did ya find?" Stanford barked.

"Boston Buckman is the President of the Whitmore Corporation."

"Are you sure? Congressman Boston Buckman?"

"Oh, yeah. We're sure." Tracey said assuredly.

"Get out! Tell me you're kiddin?" Stanford leaned back in his
chair and gave a mirthless chuckle.

"No shit, sir Sherlock," Tracey scratched his head, leaned forward
and tapped his pencil.

"So the black *Cadillac Escalade* is registered to Whitmore

Corporation?" said Chief Stanford.

"Yes," replied Tracey shaking his head.

"Are you shocked?" Chief Stanford inquired.

"Yeah!"

"I'm not; he's a shady man. Loved by many and hated by more. I want you and Zack to do a surveillance of the Congressman. Follow him from his law office to his home and get inside his playground. Find out who his playmates are. I'll notify our homicide team."

The search for the missing boys increased with intensity, hour by hour. Tracey was becoming sure of one thing as well: There was someone out there taking these boys and it wasn't Chase Buckman. Chase Buckman committed his own murder of a fellow schoolmate.

But some other nefarious party was culpable of these other abductions.

12:00 Noon

Tracey and Zack obtained a search warrant and left the precinct immediately, heading for the Whitmore Building. They casually walked into the underground garage and entered the security office. They presented the warrants to the garage attendant for surveillance footage of the subterranean parking garage and a warrant to place a GPS Tracker, with an extended battery under the vehicle. Zack placed the GPS Tracker into a waterproof Pelican magnetic casing and mounted the GPS Tracker underneath the rear bumper of the Escalade. The head of security returned with the required footage.

Thirty minutes later, Tracey and Zack returned to the precinct and viewed all of the surveillance tapes. The resolution was dim, downright murky and shitty. It was hard to make out any significant detail.

"I can't see at all. It looks like a person on the right side is getting into the Escalade, but there's a blind spot," remarked Zack.

"Damn! I can't believe we can't see these people," said Tracey.

"All you can see is the front of the Escalade. See, the license plate? Damn!" yelled Zack.

The GPS Tracker suddenly started pinging, alerting them that the Escalade was now on the move, destination unknown.

"What now?" Zack excitedly remarked.

"We've gotta see what location the Escalade arrives at."

They opened the GPS app on the cell phone to obtain the location of the vehicle.

"Where do you think he's going?" Zack mused to no one in particular.

"I don't know, but I want to make sure it's him. This has to be Buckman!"

A half hour later, the GPS indicated that the vehicle arrived at the Buckman residence.

"Bingo. We definitely know now that he owns the Escalade," Tracey deduced proudly. "Cops 1 – Buckman 0."

4:00 p.m.

Tracey and Zack arrived at Murphy & Arbuckle and were in time to observe Boston Buckman drive his black Mercedes 550 SL out of the underground parking, down Glendale Boulevard. They followed him up the 2 Freeway, headed North to the 210 East, exited Gould Avenue and turned left from the exit. They went three intersections up and turned left on Frances Lane and the house was on the right side.

The garage door opened and Buckman pulled his Mercedes inside. Tracey recognized that the vehicle resembled the one that had tried to run down Harianne, but he wasn't sure of the make. The black Cadillac Escalade was not parked inside the garage. It was gone. Within seconds, the garage door closed.

"So, Buckman drives the Mercedes," Tracey surmised.

"But who drove the *Escalade*?" Zack countered.

"Don't have a clue. But I'm calling in a search warrant for the Whitmore Corporation subterranean garage. We're going in hard!"

7:00 p.m.

Forbes Madden returned to the school that evening and opened the leather bound book of his family's haunted past.

"I had just got Frank settled and he was asleep. Poor little boy cried all day. He couldn't go to school because of the depression. I am so worried

about him. I sat down with a glass of wine and the phone rang. The police chief informed me that Brinks hung himself in the jail. My whole world crashed and it was my fault. I lost my son's father all to a frivolous affair that led to nothing. It wasn't about the money. Both families had money, I just wanted to feel alive again. I wanted fun. There I was a single mother with a son to raise. I made the necessary funeral arrangements but very few attended. I was ashamed. His father's death was my fault. I lost my son's father and also lost the love of my life. But then I thought how selfish can I be. As time went on, I had moved on and Frank was fine in later years. He adjusted very well and grew to be a wonderful, intelligent young man, much like his father. Brinks to you, I'm sorry. Lauren."

Forbes laid his head on his desk.
Jesus, Joseph and Mary.
So much senseless death…all for nothing, he thought miserably.
Forbes sighed deeply and welcomed oblivion.

Chapter Thirty-One

11:00 p.m.

Tracey had nodded off into a catnap while Zack maintained his vigil on the Buckman residence. Fifteen minutes later, the garage door opened. Zack nudged Tracey with his elbow.

"Tracey, wake up! He's leaving!" Zack snapped, starting up the car.

"The garage door isn't open. Why is the GPS Tracker pinging?"

"I don't know. But now it stopped."

"But the Escalade never left the garage nor did the Mercedes."

Zack looked at Tracey, clear puzzlement in his expression.

Let's go to the Whitmore Corporation." Tracey said.

"Tonight?" Zack questioned in surprise.

"No time like the present," Tracey countered.

Zack shrugged. Twenty minutes later, they arrived at the Whitmore Corporation. Zack and Tracey moved quietly to the front gate and looked inside the garage. Their eyes came into full focus as they noticed the Black Escalade parked inside. The Whitmore Corporation was across the street, two addresses down from Calvin House Preparatory School. Zack sighed in confusion as they walked back to the car.

"I'm tired. I think we should call it a night? What do you say?" Zack inquired.

"No. I already served the warrant. We're staying." Tracey replied firmly.

"Staying for what?"

Tracey's jaw clenched and he shook his head, glancing at Zack. "Something isn't right."

The Calvin House was beautifully lit in the distance, a monolith of learning and mystery that Tracey was coming to hate—a place of too many secrets and unanswered questions. When midnight rolled around, there was still no pinging.

"Let's get out and go inside the garage," said Tracey.

Zack exited the car quietly and walked behind Tracey towards the garage. When they arrived, they couldn't see a thing. It was black as pitch, visibility zero. Tracey removed his flashlight and pointed it at the dark interior of the garage and towards the rear entrance and exit to the alley.

"It's gone!" Zack muttered.

"No. It's still in there somewhere."

"We didn't fall asleep and miss the Escalade leaving, did we?" Zack inquired.

"Hell, no!"

"And he's running for Congress?"

"I know. Tell me about it!" Tracey said dryly. "Go figure, huh?"

A noise from inside the garage silenced them both. As they flashed the light around the abyss, the Escalade reappeared in the corner. It was on a lift rising up from beneath the flooring. The vehicle was empty.

Zack glanced at Tracey, "What, ghosts?"

Tracey frowned. "I wish it *were* ghosts. Less problematic than the living."

"So now what?" Zack asked.

Tracey took a deep breath and nodded, looking to his partner. "Whoever drove that thing is long gone. We go home."

October 9 – 2:00 a.m.

Tracey arrived back at the house feeling beat, tired and sore. He walked quietly into the bedroom and slipped into bed next to Harianne.

"I'm not asleep," she whispered.

"Hi, babe! I didn't mean to wake you."

"Sure you did," she said and chuckled.

"No. I'm so tired." Tracey yawned. He looked to her. "What's up with the case?" he asked softly.

She frowned abruptly and gave him a knowing nod. "I knew you were going to do this."

"Do what?"

"Start in on me with questions which you know are highly confidential."

"Look, this case has become important to me –"

Harianne threw back the covers, turned on the light and glared at Tracey.

"And this just happens to be my case, too!" she said, her voice rising.

"Stop! You'll wake up the whole neighborhood along with Austria! Come on."

"Okay. Let me calm down. What's going on?"

"I'll tell you. But you'll have to promise not to say anything. I'm not sure if this deals with your client or not. I still think Chase killed Jaime Herrera."

"You do?"

"Yes. But, I'll tell you. I have Mr. Buckman under surveillance."

"Why?"

"We're not sure yet. He might be involved with the missing boys."

Harianne mumbled. "Yeah, right. I want to go with you on the next stake out."

"I knew it!" Tracey chuckled humorlessly.

Harianne decided to let that hang in the ether for a moment. Silence being golden and all.

"I'll take you, but it's very dangerous and you've gotta stay quiet about this whole thing or the case is dead in the water! Understand?"

"I will. I promise." Harianne smiled and hugged Tracey. How well she knew her man. Let him work things through mentally for a few seconds and you win every time!

"Besides, you'll be in trial soon," Tracey shrugged.

"I'll leave the office and cut out early today," Harianne teased.

He kissed her and for the rest of the night the screaming was confined solely to that of a loving nature.

October 9, 2008 – 3:30 p.m.

Tracey phoned the Whitmore Corporation and informed the garage attendant that they would be stopping by at 8:00 p.m. that night. Later in the early evening Harianne continued to her office to prepare for trial. Today, her case in particular was deeply disturbing her, both mentally and physically. She couldn't sleep, even after some robust lovemaking, and her stomach felt as if pirates had knotted her intestines like pier ropes. Deep in the back of her conscious legal mind, she knew Chase Buckman *was* innocent. He was still a child in every sense of the word. He was everyone's son, boy or baby, Harianne thought to herself dismally. And it was her job to elicit a Not Guilty verdict from a jury comprised of mainly parents.

She worked diligently through the late afternoon into the evening preparing her *voir dire* questions for the jury. The first day was challenging. In Harianne's mind she needed the best jury in the world—a jury that was fair and saw her client's childlike face with those rosy cheeks, radiating innocence.

This was a hope devoutly to be wished for, Harianne thought poignantly.

That, and a lot of luck.

October 9, 2008 – 7:00 p.m.

"Hi, Austria! How are you?" Harianne spoke into her cell.

"Fine. Are you heading back this way?" Austria asked.

"Tracey and I are both on our way home. We've got a date tonight."

"Sounds like trouble to me," Austria said through a chuckle.

8:00 p.m.

Harianne and Tracey picked Zack up at his house and headed to the garage at the Whitmore Corporation.

When they arrived the place was empty—not one single vehicle in the garage.

"The perfect storm," Tracey remarked with a smile as he phoned the garage attendant alerting him of their arrival.

"Let's go," said Tracey.

Zack, Harianne and Tracey walked single-file to the front of the garage gate. The gate slowly rose up and the garage attendant stood before them.

"I remember. I spoke with Lt. Sanders today. The place is yours."

The three of them split up and searched the garage for 45 minutes before Tracey found a large cement slab with a square rim around it that was even on all sides. It was pretty hard to detect except for the extra black line around the rim. Tracey motioned for Harianne and Zack to join him.

After another hour, they found the electronic lift.

"What's that?" inquired Zack.

"A hydraulic lift," replied Tracey.

"What's it used for?" Harianne asked.

Tracey looked around at the bottom of the lift and saw the tire marks near the edges of the lift.

"The Escalade drives on and off this lift." Tracey remarked. "Look here. See that extra black rim mark around the cement slab?"

Harianne stared at it. "I still can't see it! Where is it and what does that mean?" She spoke in a frustrated voice that Tracey knew all too well.

"There is something underneath that slab. But this slab is not stationary."

"Now what?" Zack said.

"We have to open it," Tracey replied.

"How?" Zack asked.

"We won't physically open it ourselves. We have to find the person who *is* opening it," said Tracey.

Zack and Tracey continued to talk while Harianne wandered off to the other side of the garage. She noticed a metal box with a padlock in the corner. It was bolted to the floor of the garage. She looked at it silently.

Tracey glanced around the dark interior and found Harianne. Tracey and Zack approached her.

"What's this?" Zack indicated the box.

"We need to get into that. There could be something of interest in there," Harianne said hopefully.

"Okay. Hold on *Nancy Drew!*" Tracey remarked. "This box has a padlock on it. We need to get it off," said Tracey.

"Use two nut wrenches," Zack offered. "They're in the car. I'll get them."

Zack ran back to the car and returned with the wrenches in hand. He then placed the nut wrench on each side of the hook and then brought the short blades together. The lock was quickly dismantled.

"Great job, Zack!" Tracey remarked as he reached for a long white rolled up paper bound by a single rubber band. "These look like architectural schematics."

He slipped the band off, and opened the document. He studied the diagrams then looked to Zack and Harianne. "This is a map of Calvin House Preparatory School."

"Really! What's it doing here?"

"Good question, Zack!" said Harianne.

The garage attendant watched from a distance, but didn't seem much interested in what Harianne and Company were up to. He nodded his head to and fro as he listened to his iPod.

"We're done here," Tracey said decisively.

9:30 p.m.

Harianne and Tracey arrived home, their drive marked by a deliberate silence. They had hardly spoken during the trip back, both preoccupied with their own thoughts on the case. Harianne, though quiet, was inwardly pumped up with energy and it was hard to quiet her agitation. Her mind was focused very much on Chase's innocence.

The days passed, mainly in the preparatory phase for Harianne. By the time October 10 rolled around, she felt that she was fully prepared to go into battle with the People against Chase Buckman.

That morning, multiple news vans filled with hungry reporters camped out in front of the Clara Shortridge Foltz Criminal Justice Center. A virtual wave of news people approached the favorably infamous Harianne DeCanter, but she declined any interest in interviews. Hand up, as she made her way to the front door, she simply said to one and all: "Not today, ladies and gentlemen."

After going through security, Harianne walked down the hall and entered the courtroom marked Department B-8. She wore her black

Prada power coat dress and black Manolo Blahnik stilettos and sat at the defense table.

Gaston Reeves, representing the prosecution, sat across from Harianne dressed in a black *Tommy Hilfiger* suit accompanied by a pair of black Calvin Klein loafers. He looked at Harianne and smiled, signaling the green light for the courtroom carnage in the offing. These two were cordial, but when it came to trial and winning, they always went for the jugular. All bets were off in courtroom combat. They had won and lost to one another many times over. Every new trial had different characters, different players and a different courtroom. They were both up for the battle.

Harianne perused her papers in silence.

Forbes Madden sat three rows behind Harianne. He left Brolin Chapman in charge of Calvin House until his return to the school that afternoon. Forbes knew the anxiety and nervousness of every boy at Calvin House, all concerned for Chase's immediate judicial destiny.

Boston and his wife sat in the first row behind Harianne. Pamela wore a black suit with dark glasses to hide the tears rolling down her face—all too appropriate for this, the darkest day of her life so far.

Tracey and Zack entered the courtroom and sat in the row of chairs behind the prosecution desk.

Calling the court to order, the bailiff instructed everyone to stand, as Judge Chester Hamlin took the bench.

"We are on the record. Case No. 55-222-5555, People versus Buckman. Counsel is present. Please proceed with the jury selection."

Due to the high publicity of the case, the selection of a good jury was problematic to the Court and Counsel. After several days of the *voir dire* jury selection and peremptory challenges, a very ethnic diverse jury was chosen which consisted of seven men and five women: Seven whites, 3 blacks and 2 Hispanics. They had an array of occupations: nurse, massage therapist, toy designer, taxi cab driver, process server, C.P.A., chiropractor, funeral home director, librarian, school teacher, human resources director and clothing designer.

Now the fun was to begin.

October 13 – 5:00 a.m.

There was no coffee time together. Tracey went in early to the office, while Harianne got dressed for court. It was a bleak Monday, the clouds above obscuring nearly every part of the sky—the sun too shy to show his head. There was a slight chill in the air—a foreboding coolness which Tracey felt almost immediately when he awakened. He chugged down some semi-old coffee from a few days back, then headed into the precinct.

Upon arrival to the office, Tracey scanned some preliminary paperwork on his desk, then looked up as Zack entered, holding up a folded document.

Tracey nodded. "Let's go!"

They exited the office and headed for Zack's car. "I'm driving."

"Like hell," Tracey grinned. "Calvin House, get ready. Here comes a pale rider!"

"Muy Biblical," Zack chuckled and started the car.

***

October 13 – 6:00 a.m.

The morning was cloud-covered and before departing for the courthouse, Harianne walked into the foyer of her newly remodeled home and looked up at the second floor addition. It was all coming together: stairwell-riverfront buff with trim, crystal wall sconces on the walls gave light up the stairwell, brass door knobs on the upstairs bedroom doors and master bedroom suite, hardwood maple floors throughout the entire home, varied room colors gave each room its own theme along with a host of other fixtures, designs and additions to the home.

"Christophe! Christophe!" Harianne yelled.

"Right here, Miss Harianne! How do you like?" Christophe appeared.

She yelled. "I like it very much! It's kinda happening!"

"I think it is very romantic," Christophe agreed.

"I'm sure you do. It sure took long enough for this romantic home; you think?"

"I will finish soon," Christophe promised.

"I hope so."

But Harianne was not displeased. Her abode was going to indeed be a thing of beauty in the near future.

She left the house and got into her car.

The courthouse was thirty minutes away and in that span of time, Harianne went over all the details of her defense.

***

The courtroom was filled to capacity when Harianne arrived and seated herself at the defense station. Wearing a classic dark blue suit and tie, Chase Buckman was escorted into the courtroom by the bailiff who then turned to the courtroom audience.

"All rise!" said the bailiff.

Judge Hamlin assumed the bench. The preliminaries of "all rise" came and went quickly.

Judge Hamlin then stated: "We're on record. Counsel is present?" Both Gaston and Harianne obliged simultaneously with an affirmative, "Yes, your Honor."

The judge nodded to Gaston. "Begin, Mr. Reeves."

"Ladies and Gentlemen of the jury," Gaston said. "Here we have a minor who appears to be an intelligent, loving and caring individual. He enjoys good grades in school and is the best at everything he does. He comes from a wealthy family and in his mind, money can buy you anything. Ladies and gentlemen, the people will show that Chase Buckman is not whom he appears to be. You will hear evidence this young man has fine grades, is well-liked by his peers, and enjoys a superior academic record. But the darker reality is that this young man committed a violent and willful crime against a fellow student. We are dealing with a person who has no heart, and basically is a cold blooded killer with zero conscience. Sometimes the most promising are the most dangerous. And killing an innocent roommate in cold blood…a scholarship student who had a bright and noteworthy future is criminal in the extreme."

The jury turned their collective head to regard Chase, who was sitting motionless, head down, eyes closed. Harianne stole a glance of the boy, feeling an immediate and overwhelming sense of pity for the young man. Gaston's presentation of him to the jury was merciless…but then again, that was his job.

The Judge looked at some papers in front of him, scanned the room then looked to Gaston.

"Counselor, would you please proceed with your inquiry," the Judge said dryly.

Gaston gave a curt and unnecessary nod. "The People call Detective Tracey Sanders," he said ceremoniously.

Tracey stood and approached the stand and was sworn in. He nodded briefly to the bailiff—an unspoken gesture of thanks.

"Please state your name and spell your name, and state your title and occupation for the record," Gaston Reeves spoke in a crisp tone, bordering on military precision.

"Tracey Sanders," Tracey said evenly and spelled out his name accordingly.

Gaston took a moment, allowing the jury and the courtroom to focus on the handsome detective.

"Detective, when you arrived on the crime scene, what did you find?"

"A dead fifteen year old boy on the construction site at Calvin House Preparatory School." Tracey said.

"And what ethnicity was the boy?" Gaston asked.

"Hispanic," Tracey said.

"What did you determine was the cause of death, initially, that is?"

Harianne spoke up: "Objection, foundation."

"Sustained. Please rephrase," the Judge said.

"What's the name of the company on the project at Calvin House?"

"Alcott Construction," Tracey replied.

"Did you question the construction workers and foreman of Alcott Construction?"

"Yes. Standard procedure."

"Did you question all of the boys before deciding that Chase Buckman was a person of interest?"

Harianne said, "Objection. Foundation."

"Sustained," the judge said. "Counsel, please pursue another line of questioning."

Gaston nodded in compliance. He looked to Tracey, gave a tight smile that was more perfunctory than sincere.

"Based on the information reviewed, was there anything you felt was significant when you questioned other students?"

"Objection, calling for an opinion," Harianne said, injecting a tone of deliberate bitchy weariness.

Gaston turned to her as the judge spoke quietly. "Counselor. Move on, please."

Gaston again nodded obsequiously then looked back to his witness.

"Detective, what led to the arrest of Chase Buckman?"

"The DNA Test."

Harianne studied the jury closely as Tracey's testimony continued for another twenty minutes, trying to gauge the collective reactions of the members. Several jurors had turned to look at Chase during Tracey's testimony. Their gaze seemed to Harianne to be disconcertingly unfriendly. Not a good sign, but then again, not entirely surprising, either.

She gritted her teeth. Gaston's initial foray was damning, as usual, objectifying her client as a kid-gone-bad, a born killer who had simply been waiting for a perfect opportunity to murder a fellow classmate.

And she didn't like that one little bit. She now glanced at Gaston as his eyes met hers.

"No further questions," Gaston said.

"Ms. DeCanter, cross-examination?" the judge asked.

Harianne smiled wanly at him. "Yes, your Honor. Thank you."

Harianne straightened her blazer as she walked over to Tracey.

"Detective Sanders, would it be fair in your investigation that you questioned quite a few boys?"

"Yes."

"How many boys, precisely?"

"Sixty," Tracey replied.

"And how many Buccal Swabs were conducted?"

"Two."

"Who was the other person aside from Chase that the smears were taken from?"

"Mr. Forbes Madden."

"Would you please describe to the court Mr. Madden's title and affiliation?"

"Forbes Madden is the Headmaster of Calvin House Preparatory School."

"Why did you choose him for the Buccal Swab?"

"We had reason for doing so. The victim and Mr. Madden were close in that they had numerous conversations in person. Some were of a confrontational nature."

"So several of these controversial conversations led you to conduct the Buccal Swab for DNA evidence?"

"Objection. Leading," stated Gaston.

"Noted. I'll allow it," the judge said quickly.

"Mr. Madden and the victim had some explosive conversations, so, yes," Tracey said.

"What was the result of Mr. Madden's test?"

"It was remarkably identical to the defendant. However in addition to the DNA test, we collected fingerprints and the fingerprints of the defendant were on the apple juice box we obtained in the defendant's room."

"Where was the apple juice box precisely?"

"On a table in the boy's room."

"To be clear, this was the same room that Chase Buckman shared with Jaime Herrera?"

"Yes."

"No further questions." Harianne nodded to the judge.

Gaston called his next witness, Dr. Cole Peduska. The good doctor was tailored meticulously in a pant-suit, entirely appropriate for the occasion. Her expression was inscrutable, though the bags under her eyes, artfully camouflaged as much as make-up would allow, belied the truth that this woman enjoyed very little sleep in her profession. She entered the witness box and raised her hand as the court clerk swore her in.

"Do you solemnly swear to tell the truth, the whole truth, so help you God?"

"I do," she replied through a sigh.

"Please state your name and spell your name for the record and state your occupation."

"Cole Peduska. I am a Los Angeles County Medical Examiner from the County Coroner's Office," she said and then spelled out her name.

Gaston leaned on the stand railing. "Doctor, what did you find at the scene of the crime at Calvin House?"

"When I arrived, I found the body of a boy approximately fifteen years of age. He was of Latino background."

"What was the cause of death?" Gaston asked.

"Cyanide poisoning."

"How could you make that determination?" Gaston pressed.

"We did a hemoglobin analysis and determined that there was a high level of oxygen obstruction. The red blood cells were afflicted, consistent with cyanide poisoning. On a more pedestrian level, the bluish cast on his body and the aroma of bitter almonds was indicative as well."

"Was there anything noticeable on his body? Tattoos, piercings, stuff like that?"

"A birth mark only," Peduska said, almost dismissively.

"Can you provide the court with the DNA evidence, specifically, the DNA profile?"

"After conducting the Buccal swab on the defendant, the DNA profile was conclusive and very close in terms of the RFLPs."

"Would you please explain for the jury what RFLPs are?" Gaston said, glancing at the courtroom at large.

"Restriction fragment length polymorphism, or RFLP, is a type of DNA profiling based on the coding of the four chemicals called bases that make up DNA. For every person, there is a one in three-billion-base sequence consisting of guanine, cytosine, adenine and thymine (g, c, a and t). Since it is impossible to compare sequences of this size, snippets of DNA are compared. These snippets do not contain coding for traits like eye or hair color. Instead, the test seeks out places on the DNA strand where patterns of bases repeat themselves over and over. This part of the strand is sometimes called and also known as junk DNA because it does not carry information tied to specific human traits. From person to person, the number of repetitions varies greatly. On one person, a certain pattern may repeat itself 25 times; on another, it may repeat 50 times."

"That's a mouthful," Gaston said, turning to the jury and smiling.

Harianne fumed in silence. *He was trying to charm the jury, the clever bastard.*

"Dr. Peduska, would you please explain the test for the RFLP?"

"Yes. RFLP testing compares four or five such locations, using DNA probes. The test is conducted as follows: blood samples are collected from the victim, the defendant and the crime scene. RFLP requires a sample about the size of a dime. Secondly, the white blood cells are separated from red blood cells. Thirdly, the DNA is extracted from the nuclei of white blood cells. Then a restriction enzyme, which looks for specific chemical sequences in the DNA strand, cuts the DNA wherever it finds those sites. The amount of material between cut sites varies, so the fragments vary widely in length. After that the DNA fragments are put into slots in a slab of gel that has electrodes at either end. Then an electrical current draws the negatively charged fragments toward the positive end. The shorter fragments move more quickly through the gel. Within hours, the fragments are sorted by length. Lastly, a nylon membrane, placed over absorbent paper, soaks up the DNA and secures the imprint of the sorted fragments. It is radioactively treated and then developed. The film is called an autoradiograph. Our analysis would be that the jury is expected to see evidence similar to the autoradiograph at right from a murder unrelated to the Herrera case. This portion compares four DNA probes. For each probe, the pairs of bands are studied for matches. For instance, at Cellmark Diagnostics, the proximity of bands must vary no more than one millimeter to be considered a match. When a match is found, a database compiled from genetic types in blood bank pools is consulted to determine how frequently the DNA profile would be expected to occur in the general population. In this case, therefore, the DNA profile would be found in one in a million people."

Gaston smiled slightly, almost indulgently. "Doctor, that is a comprehensive and detail-friendly description of this process. But could you put it in more simplistic terms for this old country boy prosecutor?"

A small titter of subdued laughter rippled through the room. Harianne glanced around humorlessly.

Peduska looked to be blushing and she smiled as well, though controlled. "Yes. "RFLP analysis is a specific technique that exploits homologous DNA sequences."

"Homologous?" Gaston pressed. "What does that mean?"

"It means a similarity in structure and quality," Peduska explained, as if to a child.

"Thank you. Please continue," Gaston nodded.

"RFLP exploits the difference between DNA molecules from different locations. Through this breakdown, we could determine cyanide incursion into the boy's body."

"So, to be very clear—you're saying that the victim, Jaime Herrera, was indeed poisoned?"

"Yes."

"How would this poisoning be accomplished?" Gaston asked.

"Well, the cyanide in powder form can be placed in the apple juice box with a spoon. If the cyanide is in a vial or tube, that dispenser can be shoved into the hole of any container, like a carton, and deployed likewise."

"Thank you. That's all. No further questions, Your Honor."

"Thank you," the judge remarked dryly. He glanced over to Harianne. "Cross, Ms. Decanter?"

Harianne cleared her throat and nodded. "Thank you, Your Honor, yes."

Harianne moved toward the doctor and rested her hand on the stand banister. "Dr. Peduska, in what way was the DNA of Forbes Madden and the defendant similar?"

"The DNA of Mr. Madden and the defendant was almost identical, but with a slight differential."

"Can you account for this differential?" Harianne asked.

"It would be on an infinitesimal level," Peduska said dismissively.

Harianne nodded to Peduska. "Something seems funny to me, doctor. Could the test have been conducted incorrectly? From my point of view, a differential to me spells 'funky and discountable.'"

The courtroom tittered once again—this time in favor of Harianne's casual humor.

Dr. Peduska bit her lip. "No, highly—it's highly unlikely that the analysis was performed erroneously," Peduska said, though her response was far from emphatic.

"Highly unlikely still denotes room for the possibility of error. Wouldn't you agree, doctor?"

Gaston called out. "Objection. Leading."

The judge took a breath then held up his hand. "I'll allow it for now."

Harianne took a deep breath, realizing the judge had just given her some leeway. She looked to Peduska. "The DNA evidence seems to me to be very weak, given that there is DNA of another person out there that's very similar almost identical to my client."

"I wouldn't characterize it as weak."

"I would," Harianne said.

"Objection, move to strike," Gaston snapped.

The judge looked to the jury. "Sustained. Motion granted. Counselor, please—another direction."

Harianne took a moment.

"Any more questions, Ms. DeCanter?" the judge prompted.

"No," Harianne responded softly. "I don't wish to belabor the obvious."

The judge looked to the doctor. "You're excused, doctor. Thank you."

Dr. Peduska rose gracefully from the stand and moved silently out of the courtroom as the judge nodded to Gaston.

Harianne regarded the jury in triumph. She had introduced the element of doubt and she could tell that she had hit her mark in terms of logic.

She had won round one.

But the fight was far from over.

Chapter Thirty-Two

October 13, 2008 – 9:00 a.m.

Forbes was notified by Balian that the detectives were on their way. That could either be good news or bad—the latter the more likely. With a heavy sigh, he put his jacket on and walked through the garden to the front doors. Zack's Suv rolled into the cul de sac near the black wrought iron gate at the school's circular drive entrance.

Zack's vehicle was a black Chevrolet Tahoe, with tinted windows blacked-out similar to a presidential motorcade and which by now had become an almost normal fixture at Calvin House. It seemed like there were police or detectives here at his facility daily, Forbes thought drearily. He realized this was a mental exaggeration, but it wouldn't go away as an overriding depressive shadow.

Forbes had by now generally accepted some kind of law enforcement presence and impromptu visits. What surprised him was the warrant they served him with, informing him there would be yet another series of investigative sweeps.

"Thank you for your cooperation," Tracey told Forbes dryly. "We'll try to make this quick."

"What exactly do you expect to find that you haven't already thoroughly investigated?" Forbes pressed.

"We'll keep you apprised on that presently," Tracey responded diplomatically.

Forbes again sighed. His litany. He nodded at the two detectives.

"Do I need to evacuate the students?"

"Yes. I want all of the students in fire drill mode and standing outside on the lawn of the school. No one is to be in their room or a classroom. Do I make myself perfectly clear?"

"Yes. I'll notify Brolin Chapman."

"We're doing a search of the entire school and it is officially on lockdown." Tracey stated in a firm voice.

"We'll search every one of the boys' rooms," said Zack.

Forbes again nodded. And the beat wore on, he thought from somewhere far away and long ago.

Fifteen minutes later, the boys were assembled in the front lawn area. There was a collective nervous titter among the group, but the Dean of Men, Brolin Chapman, held up his hand and with this single gesture, the boys went sullenly silent.

Chief DeMille Stanford had called for the Special Homicide Task Force to move in on the grounds on an ASAP basis. Ten minutes following Tracey and Zack's arrival, a parade of black Chevy Denali SUVs pulled onto the grounds, their red and blue sirens blaring out so loudly that it could be heard miles away, echoing across the school grounds. The SHTF officers exited their vehicles quickly wearing black shirts with the huge yellow letters "HOMICIDE" embossed on the back of each. They filed out of the SUV and proceeded to the boarding house. Tracey spoke briefly to the taskforce commander and then the agents were dispersed into the school proper.

The search continued for another hour. Approximately one and a half hours later, Zack found what appeared to be a small jewelry case in one of the dorm rooms. It was padlocked by a size-appropriate lock. Zack brought it to Tracey. As there was no immediate key to be found, Tracey circumnavigated this small issue by cracking the lock's hook with a letter opener that Forbes provided him.

Inside the open case was a USB flash stick. No name was attached to it and there was no indication as to whom the owner might be.

Tracey took it from Zack and they headed straight to the precinct.

Tracey and Zack walked hurriedly to Tracey's office and placed the USB Drive in Tracey's computer.

"Moment of truth, perhaps?" Zack intimated.

"In this case, everything's up for grabs," Tracey said as the stick began to reveal its contents on the screen.

***

Judge Hamlin started trial promptly that morning. Usually he was a few minutes late from appearing in chambers, but not today. Hamlin looked to the courtroom, then to Gaston specifically.

"How do the People wish to proceed?" Hamlin asked.

"The prosecution rests, Your Honor." stated Gaston.

Hamlin gave only a brief nod then looked to Harianne.

It was Harianne's turn to show the people what it took to be a good defense lawyer. She stood now silently—with a touch of stoicism and gazed at the Judge.

"Counselor. please call your first witness," Judge Hamlin directed.

"The Defense calls Forbes Madden."

Forbes slowly rose from his chair and walked over to the stand. He was dressed in a conservative blue suit—a slight paradigm shift from his traditional black. He looked exhausted, Harianne thought, but she needed him for the very specific purpose as to represent himself as an impartial, yet sympathetic witness, for her client. The court clerk swore Forbes in.

"Do you solemnly swear to tell the truth, the whole truth, so help you God?"

"I do," Forbes relied...solemnly.

"Please state your name and spell your name for the record and state your occupation."

"Forbes Madden," Forbes said and spelled out his name. "I'm the Headmaster and owner of Calvin House Preparatory School in La Canada Flintridge, California."

"Mr. Madden, how long have you been Headmaster?" Harianne said evenly.

"I've been headmaster for over 10 years. I inherited the school from my father," Forbes replied.

"Is this the first time a murder has occurred at the school?"

Forbes paused. "No."

Harianne let that hang in the air for a moment as she turned to the jury. She then looked back to Forbes.

"When was the last murder?"

"1940."

"Who was the victim?"

"Thomas Peyton."

"Were you shocked at the murder of Jaime Herrera?"

"Yes. It affected me deeply. It is still affecting me," Forbes admitted.

"How long have you known the defendant?"

"Two years now. He came to Calvin House as a freshman and now he's a sophomore."

"Would you consider Chase to be a good kid?"

"Yes," Forbes replied and held Chase's gaze. "He's a very good boy. I'm quite fond of him."

"In your opinion, is he capable of murder?" Harianne spoke slowly on this last question.

Forbes took a moment longer than probably necessary to answer. "No. I don't believe Chase killed anyone."

"Did he play practical jokes on you and the other students?"

"All the time, but the jokes were harmless. Really."

"Can you point to the Defendant in the courtroom?"

"He's right over there at the table."

"Do you think the murder was a harmless practical joke, a mistake?"

"I do not know if Chase murdered anyone. But if a murder did occur, it would far exceed that of a practical joke or a mistake."

"Agreed, Mr. Madden."

Harianne glanced over to Gaston, eyebrows raised—gotcha!

Then Harianne did something she'd never done before. She would usually never resort to this tactic, but she was up against the wall. "Mr. Madden, is there anything you'd wish to add that might provide insight as to the defendant's innocence?"

"Objection," Gaston said. "Your Honor, is there a relevant question germane to an actual murder from counsel? Or are we now going to next ask this witness what his astrological sign is?"

The Judge frowned at Gaston, but then gave a stern look to Harianne. "Would both counsel please approach the bench."

Harianne and Gaston moved to the base of the judge's table. He looked to Gaston first. "Mr. Reeves, there's no room for sarcasm in my court. Am I clear on that?"

"Understood, your Honor," Gaston said, nodding vigorously.

The judge regarded Harianne and made a clicking noise with his teeth. "And I don't recall, counselor, where asking a witness his personal reflections on a defendant is close to normal protocol as a conclusion to questioning. Do you?"

"As I said, your Honor, it was an unusual move for me," she said softly.

"Make it your last move to that effect in my court, yes?" the judge eyed her pointedly.

"Yes, your Honor. My apologies."

"I'll have a word with the jury now," the judge said. Both Harianne and Gaston returned to their tables.

The judge then looked to the jury. "Generally, I would support the People's position on this. But given the severity of the crime and Mr. Madden's unique insight into the defendant as well as insight engendered from his position as headmaster, I'm going to allow his opinion."

Forbes gave a nod of appreciation then looked to the jury. "I'm not a professional crime investigator, nor an expert in forensics. But I do believe I'm a good character study of a human being's soul. I do not believe Chase Buckman, the young man accused of murder in this room, could hurt a fly. He's been demonstrably well-behaved and assiduous with his studies. This is a crime, I believe, that he simply could not commit."

Harianne nodded to Forbes. "Thank you, Mr. Madden." She looked to the judge. "No further questions."

The judge nodded to Forbes. "Mr. Madden. Thank you. You may step down."

Forbes stood and stepped off the stand and headed back to his seat.

Judge Hamlin again cleared his throat and looked to Harianne. "Please call your next witness."

"The Defense calls Mrs. Pamela Buckman."

Pamela stood slowly from her third-row seat and it seemed that the weight of the world was on her shoulders as she padded to the stand. She was duly sworn in and Harianne commenced her inquiries.

"Please state your name and spell your name for the record and state your occupation for the record."

"Pamela Buckman," she replied and spelled her name. She added, "I'm an attorney."

"Mrs. Buckman. Was it a joint decision to place Chase in Calvin House?"

"Yes. My husband, Congressman Buckman and I jointly agreed to do this," Pamela replied wearily.

"Why did you want to place him in a boarding school?" Harianne asked.

"We wanted the best education possible for him. We felt Calvin House offered that."

"Do you see him on regular basis?"

"Yes. Once a week and we talk to him every day," Pamela said, choking on the last word.

"Was he there the night of Jaime Herrera's murder?" Harianne asked softly.

Pamela took a deep breath and momentarily closed her eyes. She then shook her head. "No. We picked him up earlier in the day and took him to Monterey, California for an attorney conference."

"Would you consider your son to be a mean-spirited person?"

"No. Not at all."

"Is he funny?"

"Yes."

"Does he like to play practical jokes?"

"All the time."

"I have no further questions, Your Honor."

"Thank you, Mrs. Buckman," the judge looked to Pamela. He then glanced to Harianne. "Counselor, please call your next witness."

"The Defense calls Dr. Paul Jameson," Harianne called out.

After being sworn in, Harianne continued with her questioning.

"Please state your name and spell your name for the record and state your occupation."

"Paul Jameson. I am a professor of pathology at Stanford University and had an appointment in the Department of Molecular Biology at John Hopkins University for 16 years. I am called upon often to testify as a DNA expert."

"Dr. Jameson, are you familiar with the circumstances of this case?"

"Yes."

"Were you asked to investigate the DNA from the defendant?"

"Yes."

"Please explain the process of this particular case."

"In this case, the DNA is somewhat ambiguous. The current

molecular techniques employed in identity testing can be used to generate genetic profiles that are so rare—1 in 3600 billion—that some laboratories will state that identity has been demonstrated and an analyst can confidently report that a biological specimen originated only from a specific individual or his/her identical twin. The DNA appears to be virtually identical. The overall homologies are close to Chase Buckman."

"Can you put that in other words more facile for the court?" Harianne asked.

"Of course. So, there are very highly conserved similar sequences in the genotypes of both Forbes Madden and Chase Buckman. There is another individual with his genotype."

"No further questions, Your Honor."

Harianne proceeded to call a plethora of other witnesses, including students and Calvin House Administration personnel. The questioning continued for the remainder of the afternoon, to no great melodramatic discoveries.

Judge Hamlin adjourned Court.

Harianne studied the jury in silence as her client was led away by a guard. The jury betrayed no collective emotion that she could tell. That was either good or bad. Only the next day might reveal more.

***

Chelsea arrived at the hospital that morning and headed straight to Lincoln's room. Nothing had changed save his condition worsened. Chelsea sat quietly in the white plush chairs, focused on Lincoln's labored breathing as his chest rose up and down. It was heartbreaking to behold. Chelsea's cell vibrated. It was Honore Sinclair.

"Hi, Chelsea? How's your boyfriend?" inquired Honore.

"Let me put it this way. Fifteen years ago, my fiancé and I gave up our children for adoption. During the adoption, they were split at birth. We left the adoption open for personal reasons. Those reasons have come to fruition."

"I feel for you Chelsea. My hands are tied," remarked Honore.

"Let me finish!" Chelsea's voice rose in agitation. "I had a very difficult pregnancy. My fiancé Lincoln is the father and in desperate need of a kidney."

"I'll have to talk to the other family. I have not been able to get in touch with them as of yet."

"Well, if and when you do find my children, they'll have to travel back to New York."

"Yes."

Chelsea continued to listen to Honore, as tears rolled down her face. She reached in her purse, pulled some white tissue out and wiped her face.

Honore heard the desperation and anguish in Chelsea's voice as she spoke.

"Our hands are tied right now. I am working on it daily."

"Have you had any luck contacting the other family members?"

"We haven't made contact yet."

An hour later, Chelsea Timberlin left the hospital and traveled back to the house. Once in the door, she kicked off her shoes, threw on her pajamas, slippers and sat at the small table accompanied by two antique chairs. Chelsea opened her file, sifted through the papers and pulled a sheet of paper from the file. Chelsea sat there, feet numb, stomach churning with anxiety and rubbed her forehead with two fingers in a continuous left and right motion. Her frustration was at full throttle and Chelsea was ready to give up.

Later that evening, she watched the news coverage of the trial. She picked up her cell and called Dr. Kale for updates on Lincoln's condition.

"I didn't want to tell you, but I'm going to tell you now," Dr. Kale took a breath from the other side.

"Tell me what?"

"I might have two donors, but it's a difficult search. I gave my babies up for adoption 15 years ago. It was the hardest thing Lincoln and I ever did in our lifetime. I was young and climbing the ladder to success. My parents are heavy socialites and my upbringing was regal, blueblood, yet I like to go outside the lines. My family adored Lincoln as he was a blueblood, but had his own successes which married our backgrounds."

"Well, that's a mouthful!"

"The most sentimental and loving aspect of this story is that we gave them both gifts with a lovely message. I have been trying to locate them for weeks and nothing."

"I understand and I hear it in your voice. Seriously, I get you. However, even if you do find them, they'll have to be tested to see if they're a match."

"I know," Chelsea sighed wearily. "I know."

***

Harianne's stomach felt like it was doing the crazy chicken dance. She couldn't tell if it was hunger or anxiety or an amalgam of the two. She couldn't wait to get home to a home cooked meal from Austria.

Harianne arrived home, dropped her briefcase in the foyer and placed the keys on the foyer table. Tracey was in the kitchen, lifting the lids of the pots on the stove. Austria cooked a wonderful *Coq au Vin* with a French *Bordeaux* wine in celebration of Harianne's first day of trial. When Harianne was a child, Austria fixed a special dinner for Harianne on her first day of school. This brought back special memories for Harianne.

Harianne was taken by the sweet French aroma and walked to the kitchen. She met Tracey at the stove, grabbed his waist and kissed him with unmistaken passion.

"How was our day?" Tracey asked.

"I'm on the stage," she kissed him again with intensity.

Harianne walked over to Austria and hugged her.

"Austria! Thanks. You always remember. I love you so much."

"Your welcome. Sit. Sit." Austria replied in her light English accent.

Austria, Harianne and Tracey sat down in the kitchen at the granite island on a large mahogany base and dug in.

"Austria. What happened to the walls in the living room? The colors were switched."

"I know Harianne. Christophe will fix it tomorrow."

Tomorrow, Harianne thought with some measure of impatience. Always tomorrow.

Chapter Thirty-Three

October 14, 2008 – Tuesday

It was another morning of dreary overcast, punctuated by rare moments of blue sky. Before departing for the courthouse, Harianne walked into the foyer of her newly remodeled home and looked up at the new second floor addition. It was all coming together: stairwell-river front buff with trim, crystal wall sconces on the walls gave light up the stairwell, brass door knobs on the upstairs bedroom doors and master bedroom suite, hardwood maple floors throughout the entire home, varied room colors gave each room its own theme along with a host of other fixtures, designs and additions to the home.

"Christophe! Christophe!" Harianne yelled.

"Right here Miss Harianne! How do you like?" Christophe called out from around a corner.

"I like it very much! It's coming together! Except for the wall colors. How did you switch the colors?"

"I know. Ms. Austria told me. I fix soon."

"Otherwise the other colors are very romantic."

"It sure took long enough for this romantic home to come together. You think?"

"I will finish soon.

"I hope so."

Harianne's cell suddenly rang.

"Hey Babe!" Tracey's voice rang out. "I just wanted to tell you good morning and have a great day. I left early this morning."

"What's up?"

"There's been some ground-breaking news on this case. I'll keep you posted."

"Wow! And?"

"Harianne. You know I can't tell you anything right now. But I've always got your back."

The clouds roiled above as cold air pushed up against the windows, giving off damp and oppressive air on the glass pane that engulfed Tracey's office. He grinned as he spoke into his phone. "I'll talk to you later, ok?"

"Talk later," Harianne replied and then hung up.

Tracey longed for a cup of hot coffee. His nostrils took in the aroma of the freshly brewed coffee in the kitchen next to his office. He walked into the kitchen, grabbed the last white cup from the shelf and poured himself some java. He glanced out into the main detective pool area and watched his Chief enter, glance around, then walked out of sight.

Chief Stanford returned to his office, closed the door, pulled the blinds shut, sat on his black leather sofa, pulled the cup of coffee to his mouth and slowly sipped. Five minutes later, there was a knock at his door. Yawning, he pulled the blinds up on the door. There stood Tracey and Zack.

"Come in!" the Chief waved to them.

"Man! You look tired!" Tracey remarked.

"I am. All I wanted was a cup of coffee and two minutes to close my eyes."

"I see. Well, give us a few then we'll let you be. We've got a serious problem on our hands."

"How so?" the Chief asked.

"The map on the USB drive is identical to the map you found at the Whitmore Corporation."

"How's that?"

"There's a specific area circled on the map from Calvin House and that same area is circled on the map from the Whitmore Corporation."

"What's the area that's circled?"

"The altar in the school church. It's known as an undercroft."

"We searched the entire school. What's different?"

"It's the maps. They match."

"So we're getting another 365 and returning to Calvin House?"

"Yep," Zack affirmed through a sniffle.

"When?" the Chief asked.

"Tonight."

"And what is the connection to the Congressman?" the Chief asked.

"I don't know," Tracey admitted. "It's a mystery."

They all let that sink in for a moment of silence. Then Tracey turned to Zack.

"We've got to move right now. Let's get the hell out of here."

"What do you need from me, detective?" the Chief asked.

Tracey looked at him point blank. "Everything, Chief. Everything."

***

That evening, the Special Homicide Task Force, with Tracey and Zack leading the convoy, drove in ten black Chevy Denalis and filed behind the double gates of the school. They drove single file one lane towards the school entrance and agents emerged from their vehicles, as serious as heart-attacks.

Forbes was in his office. A knock at his door startled him. Tracey and Zack entered his office and sat in the chairs in front of Forbes' desk.

"What's going on now?" Forbes asked, a tone of resignation in his voice.

"We need you to take us to the altar in the school church," Tracey replied.

"Sure," Forbes said, standing. "Not a problem."

Forbes led Tracey, Zack and the Special Homicide Task Force to the altar.

Once they were inside, Tracey walked behind the altar and noticed a give in the floor. The floor was covered with brown low grade carpeting. Tracey pressed his hands on the floor and there was a small brass hook, lever-like attached. Tracey pulled on the lever and a floor door covered with the carpet opened. It was completely dark. Tracey grabbed his flashlight and pointed down inside the hole. Zack ran to Tracey.

"What did you find?"

"There's an entrance to stairs down-a floor door."

"A floor door," Tracey repeated quietly.

"Let's do this," Zack said enthusiastically.

***

Tracey, Zack and the Special Homicide Task Force moved into the tunnel. They couldn't see or hear anything. They were in the middle of the undercroft. Suddenly Tracey saw a desk in the corner with a small lamp atop, dimly lit. A neat pile of papers was on top of the desk. Tracey approached the desk.

"What are these?"

"Looks like prescriptions for medicine," Zack said, examining one paper in particular.

"Insulin and GHB prescriptions. Gamma-Hydroxybutyrate," said Tracey.

"What's the name on the prescription?"

"Wyatt Nance," Tracey said.

"Look! Here's that map again, but it's in a tube holder. The top to the holder is on the shelf above."

"What does the tube say?"

"Property of Calvin House, Brinks Madden, 1940."

"That's Forbes Madden's grandfather."

"So this is the original map from back in the day?" Zack said through a whistle.

"Yeah. But the maps we found are the same as this, except for the circle of the altar."

"You got it. Someone stole the maps out of the Headmaster's office," Zack surmised and Tracey nodded in agreement.

"Someone scanned the old map onto the USB drives and also printed additional copies."

"Hey Lady Doll Loreal! Run a report on Wyatt Nance. Send the info back; don't call me on the cell," said Tracey.

"That's what I'm talk'n about. You think you got him?" inquired Loreal, the crime analyst.

"Not sure. Let me know what you find."

Tracey and Zack proceeded through the tunnel until they heard voices nearby. The tunnel temperature was dropping rapidly as they moved further inside.

Tracey's phone vibrated and the information was sent via text. He found a quiet, secure place and called Loreal.

"Wyatt Nance. He's the son of Charles and Kelli Nance of San Marino," Loreal said. "Mr. Nance owns several medical laboratories in Southern and Central California. Mrs. Nance is the Executive Director of the SIDS Foundation in Los Angeles. Mrs. Nance is the founder of this organization after she lost her baby sister to SIDS. Wyatt Nance was also known as Wyatt Lawrence in New York. Mr. Nance adopted Wyatt and changed his last name. Previously, he was adopted by Mr. and Mrs. Stewart Lawrence. Mr. Lawrence was a wealthy real estate developer. Kelli Lawrence divorced her husband, took Wyatt, moved to California and married Charles Nance. Charles Nance is a doctor, but doesn't practice medicine. He owns a medical laboratory in California. Mr. Stewart Lawrence had an older child, a son, Peter Lawrence from a previous marriage who used to stay with them from time to time. Peter Lawrence molested other boys in his school until he was caught. The Court system considered it to be mostly juvenile behavior. Because daddy was rich, he got off."

"What else?" Tracey asked.

"Yeah. It gets better. Wyatt Nance is very smart, good hearted, active in sports, religious, plays by the rules, family oriented and basically a good kid overall. However, there is a very dangerous and dark side to this story. Dr. Nance wrote prescriptions for medications that include the GHB drug for the last six months. Dr. Nance was informed by the medical board about the numerous prescriptions for the GHB drug and maintains the story to the medical board that someone forged his signature on the GHB prescriptions."

"We were given that information earlier when we started the initial investigation. Amazing! Was Wyatt ever molested?" Tracey asked.

"It doesn't say he was molested. No police reports. Nothing from social workers or child protective services."

"Go on," Tracey said.

"Wyatt is a diabetic and had access to insulin. Dr. Nance recently informed the medical board that he regularly wrote prescriptions for insulin for Wyatt Nance. Two years ago, Peter Lawrence who lived on the East coast died due to an insulin reaction. According to the medical records, his C-petide level was high which means he produced natural insulin in his body. Forensics ignored the low C-petide levels, because Peter Lawrence was also a diabetic. If a C-petide level is high, insulin is naturally produced. If a C-petide level is low, the insulin was injected."

"That explains the prescriptions for the insulin and the GHB drug. So we've got a monster on our hands." Tracey sighed with disgust.

"I think so," Loreal replied.

"Good work, kiddo," Tracey said. "And now the fun begins."

Chapter Thirty-Four

The next day Honore Sinclair phoned the Buckman residence. Pamela, feeling hungover and bereft, picked up the landline.

"Hello," she said, choking back a tear.

"Hi. My name is Honore Sinclair. I'm with the New York Foster Family and Adoption Agency. I left a message awhile back and I never received a call from you,"

Pamela's heart suddenly raced. "What do you want, Ms. Sinclair?"

"I know this is a bad time for you. I've been watching the trial on television and am fully aware your son is on trial for murder. However, I desperately need to talk to you and Mr. Buckman."

"About what?" Pamela urged cautiously.

"Your son, Chase."

"Is this about our adoption?" Pamela asked, wiping her eyes.

"Yes. But it's not what you think. Please hear me out," Honore said.

"We're not taking any visitors. We're too distraught," Pamela choked.

"I'm aware of that and I feel for what you are going through. I need to speak with you at length and if this is not a good time, what about tomorrow evening after the trial?"

"That's fine," Pamela responded, and she found herself fighting back another bout of crying.

Honore could tell Pamela had a few glasses of wine to calm her nerves.

"Why don't you just tell me now?" Pamela suddenly blurted out.

"Well-I'm not quite sure that would be helpful in your current state of difficulty," Honore said in a sympathetic tone of voice.

"Just tell me!" Pamela hissed, her patience dwindling.

Honore bit her lip. "The birth father is in desperate need of a kidney donor. He's dying."

"Well, Chase is in jail. You know I just can't—"

"Listen! This is a matter of life and death!" Honore interrupted.

Pamela slammed down the phone and looked out the window, tears again welling up once more. She looked around, momentarily dazed, then turned and headed for the bar.

***

Wendall Dobbs awakened, groggy and his eyes red with pain and fatigue. The pain hit him immediately and he felt like yarking, his world a miasma of dizziness and nausea. He was in a different room than before, this much he could discern through his veil of foggy acuity. He was in a chair, bound; he turned to the right and came face to face with Garrett Medford. Garrett's gaze was blank and vacant— the immutable expression of the dead. His face was a bluish-gray which told Wendall that Garrett had been dead at least for a day or two.

Suddenly, Wendall heard a familiar voice, as if in conversation. The voice grew louder and Wendall closed his eyes, feigning unconsciousness.

A figure dressed in a long black robe with a hood that covered his face pulled Garrett Medford's body away. Garrett was lifted and placed on a gurney. The figure then moved out of the room.

Garrett was loaded into an SUV, parked nearby. The figure removed his hood, to reveal Wyatt Nance. He turned and re-entered the undercroft proper.

Wyatt paced the cold gray cement floor. From Wendall's point of view, through one barely opened eye, Wyatt was obviously disturbed and anxious. Wendall, surprised, returned to a comatose state, pretending to still be dead to the world in an unconscious state.

Wyatt's footsteps grew with intensity as he approached Wendall. Then he changed direction and walked into another room. Wendall looked very carefully at the room he was in. It was clearly an underground facility with marble walls on one side and rock walls on the other, complimented by cold gray cement floors. A medical facility of some sort, Wendall adduced absently. Wall mount sconces lit the little hallways off of the main room. Who knew where they led or what they contained.

Wyatt abruptly returned and walked towards Wendall.

Wendall felt a needle enter his arm and then he could feel a momentary sense of euphoria, the likes of which one would feel with a shot of morphine.

I'm dying, Wendall's mind informed him from someplace far away. *I'm being murdered.* The pain was now diminishing and Wendall welcomed oblivion.

Wyatt watched Wendall's body jerk briefly then remain still. The death process took less than thirty seconds. Wyatt began whistling as he covered Wendall's body with a white sheet.

The whistle turned to humming as Wyatt exited the room.

***

Harianne DeCanter had been in trial for the past two hours, about to conclude her case and rest when Tracey sent her a text message.

"I think Chase is innocent. Talk to you later," the text read.

Harianne almost let out a yelp of glee. Then she realized where she was and who was looking at her.

"How does the defense wish to proceed?" the judge looked to her.

Harianne cleared her throat and replied, "the defense rests,"

Judge Hamlin hit his gavel on his bench.

"Court adjourned until tomorrow, October 15," he said and then stood, as did the courtroom, and headed for his chambers.

***

Harianne ran out the courtroom, turned the volume up on her cell and phoned Tracey.

"No answer. Straight to voicemail." Harianne quietly remarked to herself.

"In a stake-out. Call you later." Tracey texted to her.

Harianne bit her lip in impatient anxiety and hissed to herself, "damn!"

***

The news vans were still camped out across the street from Calvin House. The school was secure and the kids were evacuated and moved across the street out of the line of media fire. Tracey, Zack and the Special Homicide Task Force moved in full force into the undercroft and cornered a Caucasian olive-toned boy with blond hair, combed and parted to the side. As Tracey and Zack got closer to the boy, they noticed his brown eyes and how the resemblance to Chase Buckman was simply astonishing.

"Freeze!" Tracey snapped, his gun up, as Wyatt fiddled with his hands in the robe's pockets.

"Don't you come any closer!" Wyatt yelled in a panic.

Wyatt suddenly grabbed his gun in the drawer by the surgery table and pointed it at Tracey and Zack. Ordinarily, Tracey would have simply taken a shot, but he hesitated and Zack followed his lead.

Wyatt's gun shook in his hand.

"Wyatt Nance!" Tracey said evenly.

"How do you know my name?"

"Don't worry about it! Put the gun down."

Wyatt shook his head. "I can't do that."

"I know about your stepbrother Peter Lawrence, Wyatt," Tracey said softly.

"How do you know about that?" Wyatt whimpered.

"We know. Put the gun down!" Zack snapped.

"You killed Peter Lawrence with an insulin injection," Tracey said, taking a step forward.

"Shut up! You asshole cop!" Wyatt cried out.

"Jaime Herrera, Wendall Dobbs and Garrett Medford were in your little initiation club. You brought them down here to show them your little club. Jaime Herrera is the only one that got away and when he threatened your operation, you put the cyanide in his apple juice and killed him. Since Jaime shared a room with Chase, Chase was your cover. You set Chase Buckman up. Easy pickins. Chase liked to play practical jokes and you knew that."

"Fuck you!"

"After you showed them your club you drugged them with GHB

and handed them off to the Congressman. You did the torturing and participated in the molestation and other sexual encounters. The Congressman engaged in sexual acts and took it to another level. Then you finished them off with insulin injections and killed them."

The Special Homicide Task Force entered the chamber, six men total, all guns up.

"Take him!" the commander yelled out.

Before Tracey could protest, a shot rang out. Wyatt returned fire. More shots were fired and Wyatt was slammed to the ground. He clutched his chest, hitting the floor face first. He rolled over, his eyes wide in pain and astonishment.

Tracey walked over to the boy and took a knee. Wyatt reached out with one hand and clutched Tracey's jacket.

"Sorry," Wyatt whispered through a death hiss. In another second, he was gone.

"Hang on, kid," Tracey said.

"Gotta...tell you...something," Wyatt struggled. "Come closer."

Tracey leaned in closer to Wyatt as Wyatt began speaking softly.

Tracey nodded then looked to Zack. When he turned back, Wyatt was dead.

***

An hour later, Harianne parked in the front entrance way of Calvin House. Tracey was standing by his car, writing his notes. She got out of her car and jogged toward him.

"Are you okay, babe?"

Tracey looked up and smiled at her. "Yeah. I'm fine now that you're here." He kissed her. "We found a locket inside Wyatt Nance's pants pocket with an inscription inside that reads, '*Love You Forever, Mommy and Daddy*'. We phoned Forbes Madden."

"Wyatt Nance?"

"Yep," Tracey replied. "The real killer, a student here at Calvin House. Your boy is off the hook."

Harianne nodded in clear surprise. "Tell me more."

"He lived in San Marino before attending Calvin House. Wyatt Nance was paid off by Congressman Boston Buckman to get the boys to him so he could molest them. Congressman Buckman received illegal campaign contributions from politicians as well."

"Who had the cyanide?"

"Wyatt Nance. He stole it from his chemistry class. A few days ago, the chemistry teacher told Brolin Chapman that cyanide was missing from his classroom."

"Wyatt put the cyanide in Jaime Herrera's apple juice, setting up Chase Buckman."

"So he set Chase up. That son of a..."

"I know. So this case was in front of us the whole time?"

"Yep. Congressman Buckman used his son at his own expense. However, Congressman Buckman didn't know that Wyatt murdered Jaime Herrera and framed Chase. Wyatt never told him. Money was no object. He's going to jail for a long time."

Harianne pulled Tracey towards her and smothered him with little kisses.

"I'm not finished with my story."

"Yes. You are finished. Let's go home." Harianne smiled and grabbed her keys from her purse.

"I've got a stop to make before I come home." Tracey hugged Harianne and pulled her towards him.

"What kind of stop?"

"You'll see."

"Our house is almost finished and I want to enjoy it."

"We will."

Chapter Thirty-Five

Tracey arrived home two hours later. With his hands behind his back, he walked into the living room where Harianne stood, mesmerized by her gorgeous house.

"Hey! There you are. Why are your hands behind your back?" Harianne asked, a small smile forming on her lips.

Tracey kneeled down on one knee, raised Harianne's hand and brought it towards his lips. He kissed her hand.

"Harianne. Will you marry me?"

Tracey opened the black velvet box and pulled a six carat Princess cut diamond set in platinum out and placed it on her finger.

Harianne was shocked and speechless. She gasped, swallowed and then spoke.

"Yes! Yes! Yes!" she giggled excitedly.

"Thank you. I love you babe."

She smiled. "So that was the stop."

"*Arnold's Jewelers* in Pasadena," Tracey smiled and kissed her.

***

Honore watched the continuing coverage of the news about Calvin House. She then phoned Chelsea Timberlin.

Chelsea walked into the living room of her Sag Harbor home and picked up her cell, while watching the television. She had heard the news about Wyatt Nance.

"Hi Chelsea! This is Honore Sinclair from the adoption agency."

"Hi, Honore!" Chelsea responded.

"I found your son."

"You did?" Chelsea said after a long moment of silence.

"Actually both of your sons," Honore said.

"Really!" Chelsea screamed with excitement. "When can I see them?"

"Have you been watching the coverage of the Calvin House Preparatory School murders in California?"

"Yes. My pseudo brother-in-law, my fiancé's brother owns the school. Are they in that school?"

"Well both of your sons are in that school, Chase Buckman and Wyatt Nance."

Chelsea's voice dropped to a hush. "My son is dead."

"I'm sorry. The Buckmans never got back to me. The Lawrences had no current contact information and never updated their information."

"And the innocent one, Chase Buckman is my son?"

"Yes. I called Pamela Buckman and told her the situation."

Chelsea planned a careful response but that effort devolved into uncontrollable sobbing.

***

Honore's cell phone rang. "Hold on Chelsea." She picked up.

"Hi! Honore Sinclair?" Harianne's voice queried.

"This is Honore Sinclair, yes."

"I'm Harianne DeCanter. I represented Chase Buckman in the trial involving the Calvin House murder. I've got someone that wants to talk to you."

A moment of silence followed. Then Pamela Buckman came on the line.

"Honore. This is Pamela Buckman. I'm ready. Do you still need a kidney donor?"

"Yes. I heard the good news about Chase. Congratulations! You were in my prayers every night."

"Is his birth mother with you?"

"No. She's on the other line on my cell. Her name is Chelsea Timberlin."

"Please have her arrange the trip. He'll be there in six hours and I will accompany him on the plane trip. I'm very distraught, but willing to help his birth mother. I would imagine we don't have much time. My husband is being questioned by the detectives right now as we speak. He will not be accompanying us on this trip."

"Great news! I'll let her know. Thank you."

"Who's that?" Chelsea lifted her head hearing a muffled conversation on Honore's cell.

"Pamela Buckman."

"Isn't the Congressman in jail?"

"Not yet, but I'm sure he is headed there. Chase Buckman is free. Pamela Buckman gave her permission for Chase to travel to New York. She's accompanying him. What do you think?"

"Oh, my God! Awesome! I've got to call Dr. Kale. What can I say?"

"Nothing. It's all good. Good luck Chelsea!"

***

Kelli Nance was distraught over the loss of her son for many years. She sought psychiatric help, remained married to Charles Nance and continued living in San Marino, California.

Three hours later, Chase and Pamela boarded United Flight AA55 for New York. An ambulance met them, along with Chelsea at the airport and took them to the hospital. Over the last several weeks, Lincoln's condition had rapidly deteriorated, causing him to return to a comatose state.

One hour later, Chase went in for the kidney donor test, clutching a gold locket on a gold necklace. Chelsea noticed his fist was closed very tight.

"What's that in your hand?"

"Oh this. My locket. My Mom saved it for me and gave it to me when I turned ten. I keep it for good luck. The inscription read, '*Love You Forever, Mommy and Daddy*'."

Chelsea smiled with delight, cried and spoke no words as they walked into the testing room.

Chase was tested and was a successful donor match. Chelsea was forever grateful and glad to finally meet her son. Chelsea spoke for

Lincoln as well.

Forbes phoned the hospital and spoke with Lincoln.

"So how does it feel to be back?"

"It feels good. It's like I wasn't sick, but we all know that's not true. I'm grateful for my son. Chelsea told me the story."

"I feel bad for you. Because you lost a son and yet gained a son."

"I gained a son and you gained the nephew you didn't know you had."

"Detectives Sanders and Grimes explained to me why my DNA was so closely tied to Chase and Wyatt. They're my nephews. Anyway that's our past. Chase is our future."

"That's so true. I'll talk to you later."

"Sure. I'll call you later, buddy."

***

Tracey and Zack gathered their evidence against Congressman Buckman on a plethora of charges for illegal campaign contributions, coercion, sexual assault, molestation, rape and kidnapping. The list was endless. It was later revealed that Congressman Buckman purchased the Whitmore Corporation building or house five years prior to his campaign for Congress.

***

The light fog painted the sky light gray, almost mystically, as it settled over La Canada Flintridge, California. The home of Congressman Buckman stood quiet, dark and majestic in nature from a street view. The confident Boston Buckman walked to his elevator which was not the norm in every house on his street. He pushed "B" that took him down to his favorite place, his wine cellar in the basement. He combed his hand over all the shelves of his cellar. Lastly, he entered the champagne section and popped the cork to a bottle of *Veuve Clicquot*, took a sniff of the soothing aroma and settled into his burgundy velvet sofa. He had a burgundy velvet journal of the history of his wines and champagnes. He was well aware that *Veuve Clicquot* was a French champagne house based in Reims, France specializing in premium products. Founded in 1772 by Philippe Clicquot-Muiron,

Veuve Clicquot played an important role in establishing champagne as a favored drink of *haute bourgeoisie* and nobility throughout Europe. The 1811 comet vintage of *Veuve Clicquot* is theorized to have been the first truly "modern" Champagne due to the advancements in the method champenoise which *Veuve Clicquot* pioneered through the technique of reimage.

Boston poured his champagne into a Waterford crystal champagne glass. Sipping slowly, he recalled his past—Chase's childhood, the birthday parties, his wedding to Pamela and the day he was sworn in as a member of the California Bar. Beautiful memories intact forever in his mind and his heart, but the greed got the best of him which led to a devastating life of destruction. That, and his predilection for perversion. Dumb detour, he thought, nodding to himself.

He had been a man of stature and handshake relationships that made people feel warm and fuzzy with trust and concern throughout Los Angeles County. His bastard soul reached into his body and created a monster. A monster chalked full of greed, hate and revenge. The money would leave the firm, clients would substitute the firm out and pending cases would suffer immensely with no attention. The writing was on the wall. There was no escape attached with the embarrassment and shame of a fine lawyer as Boston Buckman. He help build Murphy & Arbuckle and took them over the top. And most of all, he settled with guilt and humiliation of the rise and fall of Congressman Buckman, the most prestigious position in the country.

Now it was over. Past achievements evaporated before his eyes.

He closed his eyes and breathed deeply. He slipped into a deep sleep. An hour passed and he opened his eyes. For a moment, he was unsure of where he was. Then he remembered.

Ah, yes…that's why I'm here…

He slowly lifted his hand and reached inside the drawer of the Cherry wood side table by the sofa. He then pulled out a .38 police special pistol. He stared at the barrel then allowed it to rest in his lap as he looked straight ahead.

And so this is how it ends.

He thought back to an old T.S. Elliot poem.

This is the way world ends, not with a bang, but a whimper.

Boston chuckled to himself and shook his head, thinking back on his life. So many good times, so many successes…it was all coming to a close.

Ah, well, Boston thought. Things are up sometimes, then down. Like the old Frank Sinatra song said "You're riding high in April, shot down in May."

"So. That's that," Boston said to himself.

He then raised the pistol and shoved it under his chin.

He pulled the trigger. The last thing that went through his brain aside from the bullet was the thought that he really should have purchased a little more *Veuve Clicquot.*

One can never have too much champagne, after all.

***

The detectives went to the home of Boston Buckman several times, but each time, the man was unavailable. He had apparently simply disappeared. A week later, Pamela entered her husband's sacrosanct wine cellar and found Boston curled up on his side, blood and brains fairly painting the wall. Pamela would later remember screaming hysterically as she fled the cellar, not because of the horror of seeing her husband dead.

It was the maggots crawling out of Boston's skull that sent Pamela howling for help and 911.

***

Forbes walked to the front of Calvin House and looked out over the grounds. He wondered what ghosts lurked about on this landscape; what troubled souls wandered, bereft of rest and peace. Good, bad or indifferent, they were ghosts of a distant past. He wondered what life was like in 1940. He was forever grateful for the leather bound diary of Lauren Madden. He would never forget his grandfather, Brinks Madden. Brinks Madden was a kind, gentle, loving and caring gentleman. Forbes oftentimes wondered what kind of relationship he'd have with his grandfather and how his grandfather would have handled this modern day murder case, now put to rest amidst so much blood and fury. A truly fearless, loving and caring individual was his grandfather. It made Forbes feel proud from top to toe.

Forbes went back to his office, sat in his chair, and opened the leather bound diary of Lauren Madden once more. So many pages of detailed testimonial, he thought. A tribute to family history.

He thought back to his grandmother and for no reason at all, an old poem from someplace long ago crept into his exhausted psyche.

I sometimes think that never blows so red
The Rose as where some buried Caesar bled;
That every Hyacinth the Garden wears,
Dropt in its Lap from some once lovely Head.

The poem was by Omar Khayyám and resonated with his thoughts of his beautiful grandmother, herself a victim of love and circumstance. Ah, the past, Forbes thought…like water we come and like wind we go…

Forbes flipped through the pages lovingly. The last page was blank. Forbes studied it for a moment then picked up a pen.

Forbes wrote on the last page of the diary.

He looked at the final words and smiled wistfully.

He then spoke aloud what he had inscribed:

"The End."

Darkness cannot drive out **darkness;**
only **light** can do that.
Hate cannot drive out **hate;**
only **love** can do that...

–Dr. Martin Luther King, Jr.
Strength To Love, 1963

Made in the USA
Columbia, SC
07 February 2020